ADA AFAM

For His Muse Only

First edition

ISBN: 9798218547745

Editing by Claire Ashgrove
Cover art by Evgeniia Gurcheva
Typesetting by Crystal Ezeoke

This book was professionally typeset on Reedsy.
Find out more at reedsy.com

Contents

Content Warning

ACKNOWLEDGMENTS

I f it weren't for family and friends yelling—"Ugh, would you just publish it already? Damn!"— my story would stay in Google Docs Purgatory forever. And thanks, reader. Thank you for diving headfirst into this twisted tale of want and obsession. I hope it thrills and unsettles you.

PROLOGUE

Jesus, why won't he stop? My phone buzzes, along with my creeping anxiety.

Ping.

There she is. There's my girl.

I can no longer live each moment according to his guidelines. Something has to be done. The nightmares and stomach ulcers are all I have left—thanks to him.

Ping.

I need my muse in the worst way. Take that however you'd like.

But I don't want to anymore.

Sitting in my car, I tell myself to take a deep breath, but my lungs are constricted. The fluorescent lights of the police station flicker through the windows and cast an unsettling glow over the asphalt. He shouldn't have the privilege to map out my current life—little divots toward shameful pathways and landmarks that have my emotions in shambles.

Ping.

Don't do it. Don't sever us. It won't go in your favor.

Shit! Is he here?

I swipe the screen and grip my phone, feeling the cool plastic against my clammy skin. My heart plummets with panic flooding my veins. As I glance around the empty parking lot, every shadow quickly turns into a potential enemy.

Ping.

If you go inside, you're only doing one thing. Don't present a challenge for me because it's just an invitation to try.

"Leave me alone!" I screech to no one in particular.

Months of this have been a prison sentence. And I'm ready to be vindicated.

As I step out of the car, there's uncertainty, but alongside it is relief. I give one final look over my shoulder, then walk toward the entrance with heavy steps.

Enough.

I'm ready to fight back.

Ping.

Patience, as you've brought to my attention, hurt people tend to hurt people. Now, take that precisely as it sounds.

Of course, he would do this.

He knows deep down that's all it would take.

Because no one else deserves this level of torture but me.

I'm back in my car. I hit the gas and peel out of the parking lot. My adrenaline skyrockets as I drive away.

He calls, but I don't answer. Instead, I let it go to voicemail. Dammit, I must know what he plans to teach me next, or it'll drive me out of my mind.

So, I hit play.

"I fucking love you." His voice is biting. "And in the end, my muse knows she has responsibilities, right?"

I know it doesn't seem that way, but I really did try.

WHY ME, HARLAN?

I should have been paying attention. I should have felt him coming, sensed his pull before it was too late. But people like Harlan McCandles don't walk into your life—they seep in, unnoticed, until they're everywhere. He's not just someone you can push aside. He invades, demanding pieces of you that you didn't even know you could give. Like a parasite that digs deeper with every breath. I feel him even now, his presence lingering long after he's gone. His hooks are still in me, beneath my skin, so deep I can't pull them out without tearing myself apart. The message couldn't be any clearer as I lie awake in his bed. The door is always there, wide open, mocking me. And I wonder—will I ever have the strength to walk through it? Or will I keep waiting for the day he decides simply being his muse... isn't enough?

Mrs. O, Dominick is trying to kill the lizards for the third time today."

I raise my head from my desk and scope around my classroom.

A thin Hispanic boy with thick curly hair and beady gray eyes has climbed up on the shelf near the crested geckos. He reminds me of an acrobat, daringly taking his next leaping feat.

"I got it, Nadia. Thank you. You can see how Nyla is doing with her warm-up."

Nadia, my plucky mid-twenties paraprofessional, gives a thumbs up and abides.

"Dom, buddy—let's get down, okay?" I coax while approaching him. "We can talk about what's happening but can't hurt our friends."

"They're being jerks, Mrs. Okoye!" Dominick yells. He hangs from the middle shelf with ease. "I know they're secretly laughing at me because they think I'm stupid—because I don't know how to spell."

I sigh, my hands on my hips. "I don't think so."

"See? I knew you wouldn't believe me! They're gonna be so dead!"

"If lizards could talk, I'm sure they would think of more interesting things to discuss."

Dominick flares his nostrils, but his beady eyes follow mine. "Like what?"

"Roblox, what else?"

Dominick hops to the bottom shelf, and the tension finally leaves his face. "If I leave the lizards alone, could I play Roblox during our morning meeting tomorrow?"

"But, Dominick, the morning meeting is important for everybody. It's how we set our expectations to carry out through the rest of the day, so you can be your best self."

Dominick stomps his foot in anger. "But I'm only my best self when I play Roblox!"

I come over and run my fingers through his fluffy hair. "How about this: During our morning meeting—when we get to our show-and-tell part of the session—you can tell us how much you accomplished with your Roblox account. You know, teach a few beginners some things. Sometimes, Mrs. Okoye needs a break from teaching all the time and needs someone else to take over."

He finally smiles, revealing five silver fillings with pride. "Deal!"

Score! Always make them feel like they have input.

"Okay, let's go tackle your social studies warm-up."

After deescalating Dom, I walk around my classroom and observe my students for understanding of their classwork.

I call it the "calm before the storm" watch.

I have a caseload of three students in my behavioral needs classroom. How others perceive my class depends on which aspect of it they focus on.

Three students? That's a walk in the park. But behavioral

needs? Christ, good luck. For the longest time, no one was crazy enough to take my job. In fact, if I hadn't accepted the position three years ago, the class would've disbanded completely.

Knock. Knock.

"Come in!" I holler.

"Will you shut up?! I'm trying to work," Grayson, a hot-tempered third grader, scolds from his seat.

"I know you're trying to work, and I didn't mean to disrupt you, Grayson. But there is definitely a more appropriate way to communicate your frustration."

"Never mind, I'll go work in the freaking book nook corner." He grabs his things angrily and scrambles there.

Picking my battles comes with the job. We will have a breakthrough next time. Grayson's wanting to finish his work is nothing short of a miracle.

Ms. Bell comes through the doorway and smiles. "Hi, Mrs. Okoye! Here are their benchmark BOY scores." She beams.

I share students with Ms. Bell, a sweet resource teacher. She's in her late seventies but doesn't let most of her students wear her down. I see my class for the morning half of the school day, during their minor classes, like science and social studies. We also review their expectations and behavior goals, and then Ms. Bell sees them in the afternoon, solely for academics. I'm usually on standby next door in case a student needs to reassess after a meltdown in the resource classroom—which is daily.

"How'd we do?" I ask optimistically.

Ms. Bell has a pinched look. "I'm just thankful to retire next year."

"That bad?"

"Afraid so."

I walk over and flop into my office chair. "Remind me why you're retiring again?"

Ms. Bell rubs my hand lovingly. "You got this! You're a brilliant teacher, and you'll be fine!"

I smile, dreading the brunt of taking on these kids for an entire school day next year.

"Well, let me get out of your hair." Ms Bell's orange bob dances with each step. She winks before leaving. "Not like you have your hands full or anything."

"Thanks."

"Jeez, everybody cram it and stop talking!" Grayson yells from the book nook corner.

* * *

Students like second grader Dominick Rivera always get a bad rep because of his delusions and mild Tourette's. But after getting past all that, he's the sweetest kid.

Teachers aren't supposed to have favorites, but who are we kidding?

Then there's fifth grader Nyla Chambers, who doesn't have many outbursts, but her OCD affects how she socializes with others.

"If you don't check the lock three times every seven minutes, you increase the odds of a school shooter killing us all."

That's how she introduced herself to me.

Nyla looks much older than ten, which in the past, put me in the uncomfortable position of reaching out to her mom occasionally. She has a habit of coming to school with outfits two sizes too small. I almost lost it when Nyla's mother sent her wearing Daisy Duke shorts in below-freezing January. Despite that fact, Nyla is really bright, earning nominations for the Talented and Gifted program for two years in a row. But as you can imagine, she takes the screening test every year, which never goes according to plan.

And there's Grayson Morton, my new student with Oppositional Defiant Disorder. He's not much of a treat to have at seven-thirty in the morning. Grayson always has an opinion or tidbit to share. The cherry on my sundae was him telling the class I had a beard during our morning meeting last week. My cursed whiskers didn't stand a fleeting chance.

However, Grayson's fixation with NASA was the olive branch I needed to win him over. Whenever he calls me or my other support staff unpleasantries, asking him about Buzz Aldrin's feats calms him down. Grayson can go on for hours about him. Like yesterday, when he nearly bolted out of the classroom to avoid work.

"How dumb are you?" he'd say. "Everyone knows Buzz spent over twenty hours collecting moon rocks and photographs on the lunar surface. Duh."

I never said he's kind about it.

During our science lesson on the solar system, my excitement about teaching the wonders of space is up against constant disruptions from Grayson, who seems more interested in making paper airplanes than listening.

"Gray, can you please put that away and pay attention?" I ask, trying to keep my tone patient.

He rolls his eyes and reluctantly sets the paper airplane aside, but his attention quickly drifts to the window, where he taps on the glass. "This blows."

"As I was saying, did you guys know that billions of stars exist in our galaxy alone?" I address the class.

"Meteors can strike any time and kill us where we stand, if we aren't wearing tinfoil," Nyla says, chewing on her locks.

"Let's do our best to stay on topic and raise our hand rather than blurt. Yes, Dominick?"

"I wanna find new planets when I'm an astronaut!" Dominick inputs.

"Awesome, D! Imagine traveling through space and discovering new planets. Wouldn't that be amazing, Grayson?"

He shrugs, seemingly unimpressed.

So, I try a different approach.

"Okay, what if I told you that astronauts get to float around in zero gravity and explore the mysteries of the universe? Yes, Grayson?" I happily note he raises his hand.

"Hello? I know that already, but how?"

I hand out worksheets for the lesson. "Let's complete this *show what you know* activity about planets before we get there."

"I knew it. You don't care about space; you just want us to do your stupid work."

Grayson's hazel eyes light up in vexation, and he turns his worksheet face down. I've gotten ahead of myself.

Come on, NASA. Work your magic.

"Did you know NASA has sent missions to explore those same planets on your worksheet?"

Grayson shrugs nonchalantly, his chubby cheeks slightly blushed.

But I can tell he is listening.

"If you don't go to space school for exactly two-and-a-half years, your heart stops when you set foot in the spaceship,"

Nyla adds another tidbit.

"That's not true, and again, please raise your hand if you'd like to share next time."

Grayson replaces his excitement with a fresh scowl and forgets to raise his hand. "There's a lot more that happens in space, you know. We aren't babies," he grumbles, but his voice hints at fascination.

Hmm, I'll run with it.

"You're absolutely right, Grayson!" I cheer. "Did you want to share?"

This can either make or break our relationship. He could see it as a platform to share his knowledge or as an attempt to embarrass him publicly.

Instead, Grayson grunts in response. Don't force it, remember—power struggles help no one.

"Did anybody want to share?" I offer to the class.

Dominick spins around on the carpet, and Nyla plays with her locks.

A hiccup of teaching multiple grade levels is balancing multiple grade-level interests.

"What's the point? It's not like I'll ever go to space," Grayson mutters bitterly.

"Yeah," Nyla and Dominick join in.

"Well, let's bring space to you guys. Why don't we look up some cool stuff about NASA together and create a big class slideshow?" I suggest, hoping he'll take the bait. "I'll add ten extra minutes of Chromebook lab time each day until we finish!"

"Yes!" Dominick says. "Does Roblox count for Chromebook time?"

"No such luck, Dom."

Nyla smiles dreamily.

But Grayson is an unmovable statue. "I guess."

The bell rings, and we rush to pack up and transition to Ms. Bell's class. Grayson drags his feet while doing so, but then I also take it as a third time's a charm.

"Hey, Grayson, come here a sec."

Grayson turns and grudgingly walks over to my desk. "God, what did I do now?"

"Nothing, buddy. Listen," I start off, "I was wondering about your thoughts on today's lesson."

"What about it?"

"Well, NASA. Cool place. Right?"

"Duh. Next."

Encouraged by his response, I go all in. "I was thinking... Would you like to work on a NASA model project together? We could build a miniature rocket or create a model of the International Space Station."

Grayson's face warps into several expressions at once. Then, his face breaks into a troublesome smile. "You just want to do this with me because everyone else is too stupid to help you make the NASA model."

The ego of this kid is gargantuan.

"I figured we'd have a good time making one together. And let's give Nyla and Dominick a chance; they might surprise even you with unknown NASA facts."

"Whatever."

"So, you want to?"

"If I didn't say no, what does that tell you?" Grayson snides.

"A simple *yes* and *thank you* goes a long way, Gray."

* * *

Now that I'm home, my teacher persona fades, and my dutiful wife persona reigns. I'm almost finished making the coconut salmon rice, which took two hours to prepare—while I work on the side dishes. Pongers, our rottweiler, does her routine of sniffing for floor scraps, but I'm onto her. Pretty sneaky, sis.

"Girl, that already looks like too much salt." My best friend since elementary school, Neisa, warns me on a video call on my laptop.

"Nei, I got it."

"And your mama's side of the family's got hypertension. Boom. There's your mic drop for the day." Neisa adjusts her bust line. Her face reminds me of a sugar cookie. Sweet, round, and full. "Damn, tell me why I agreed to be the maid of honor at a wedding I have no business being at? I don't even like Tasha. It's not my fault she doesn't have any friends she can sucker into doing it."

"She's your cousin-in-law." I laugh at my almost sister as I fan away the smoke. "And it's the same reason you had no business moving to California to start a family without me. You're a mess."

"But I'm your mess, baby girl."

Pongers sniffs between my toes, like the eager pup she is. "Here you go, Pongy." I sprinkle bits of salmon on the floor for her enjoyment.

"You done yet?" Neisa nitpicks.

I take two eggs to create the egg wash coating for dinner rolls. "I'm manifesting my Gordon Ramsay-level cooking skills. Watch and learn." I crack them, and into the bowl they go.

"If Gordon Ramsay saw that crack, he'd manifest that ass.

The shell is still in there."

"Shit. Got it. Now it says *zest salad with lemon.* Do you even know what zesting is?"

"I mean, ain't it... enthusiastic squeezing?" Neisa says, squinting at her own screen.

"No. That's how I approach life, not lemons. I can just... shave the lemon with a sharp enough knife, right?"

"Sounds like a hack job."

"Whatever. I'm using a cheese grater. It'll work, trust me."

Neisa shushes some giggling bridesmaids in a corner angrily, then yells across the screen. "Nora, how many times I gotta tell you?! That faux ponytail ain't fooling anybody. It's too damn copper and shiny! Do you wanna look like a sorry-ass penny the whole night? Nah—save your tears for the bride, you hear me?!"

Laughter comes fast and swiftly, and I wouldn't have it any other way. My almost sister, who I've known since first grade, always amazes me. The idea of yin and yang doesn't even begin to describe us. If Debbie McAllister hadn't been absent that day, and if Neisa had played with her instead of me at recess, I can't help but wonder where I would be without her.

So—thanks for catching that ringworm, Debbie.

"Neisa, aren't you going for a successful bridal party? There'll be no bridesmaids left standing at this rate."

She gives her best babyface smirk, along with the peace sign. "Have fun with your citrus confetti! It's showtime for me. Gotta get these simple-minded bridesmaid hos together the only way I know how. Maid of honor perks, right? And Tasha has one more time to look at me sideways—I don't care if she's family—or she'll be wearing her wedding cake upside her head."

Knowing Neisa, she means every word. "Bye, sissy. Love you."

"You, too."

My bestie zips off the screen.

She's not here in the flesh, but she's here in spirit. And that helps.

I turn on the TV in the living room. Oh, goody! *The People Under the Stairs* is on—a Wes Craven classic. The mood turns into a spooky one as I gladly let it play in the background.

"Let's see... two dashes of paprika—"

I grab the spice near our laminated wedding picture tacked on the fridge.

Looking back, I still can't believe we went through with it. Who was that girl? The picture shows my face painted with such flair, and I'm wearing a dress that's a masterpiece of intricate embroidery and rich fabrics. It's a dazzling celebration of my Igbo heritage. And Obinna's style is twinning mine with a groom's touch.

I can still hear his mother, Agatha, gush happily about our union. *"My son is a lucky man. I know I should join the groom's suite, but I had to stop by and say I'm excited to have a daughter."*

Whereas my mom never failed at her stinging commentary. *"Patience, my lord, your backside in this dress keeps protruding! I wish you were more disciplined in slimming down for the big day!"*

This is the man I promised myself to—a silly college kid who won me over with his love for anime, Sci-Fi, and his Dave Chappelle impressions.

Obinna and I bonded over our constant reminders of bi-culturalism—how we were often told we could never truly be American, even though we were both born here. West

African influences kept us from most teen experiences, like house parties, hooking up, and sleepovers. But we rebelled from time to time. The many nights I would spend in his dorm room, avoiding visiting my borderline verbally abusive mother, are my favorite memories of us. We'd go through hours of *Cowboy Bebop* while pigging out on vending machine snacks.

Funny enough, it was the same anime we lost our virginity to.

Damn, I miss college.

The evening sun casts an orange glow through our living room window as I hear the familiar sound of the front door opening. Obinna steps inside tiredly, and Pongers paws over, drowning him in licks.

"Hey, Obi, how was work?" I greet him. Ugh, I try to ignore the fact he doesn't take off his shoes at the door, which gnaws at me.

Obinna sighs heavily as he shrugs off his coat. "Long day, as usual. Priya and I had a ton of cases to handle."

"What else is new?"

He pets Pongers, then eyes the TV with excitement. "Damn, I haven't seen this one in a minute. Did I miss the part where Fool runs into the cannibal kids?"

"No, they're still trying to break into the creepy racist couple's house and get to the treasure. How I missed the obvious jabs at gentrification the first time is beyond me." I take off my dirty apron and join him in the living room.

After finally peeling off his shoes, Obinna plops onto the couch while Pongers slobbers away, making a snack out of his toes. "Now that's a milestone. Might be the first time a Black kid took the lead in a horror flick. Honestly, I wouldn't mind curling up with this one tonight. I've been treating show poodles for conjunctivitis for an entire shift, and I'm spent."

I lean over and rest my head on his shoulder. "Maybe if you spent a little less time with poodles, you'd know your wife better than you know their tear ducts. At least you're home now. I'll dish out the rice at the table, okay?"

"Thanks. How was work for you?"

"Good, I think I actually reached a kiddo today. Grayson is such a—"

BEEP. BEEP.

"Actually, hang on. I gotta take this," he says.

Obinna goes to our bedroom and answers his phone. "Hello? Yeah. What are the symptoms? Good, sounds like it was caught early. I'll be there soon."

What?! I get back up and pace to the kitchen.

Then he pops back out. "On second thought, Patience, do you mind packing dinner to go?"

"Dude, you barely rested your feet for five minutes, and now you have to go again? Are you incapable of saying no to random animals?"

"For one, they aren't random animals any more than your students are random kids," Obinna clarifies. "I signed an oath as a doctor; they're my patients. Being a veterinary ophthalmologist means I can get called in at all hours of the day, which includes emergency cases. How does that still surprise you?"

"Sure, and where does that leave me? Stuck, I guess." I toss the serving spoon in the sink with a crash.

"Pat, come on. Don't act that way."

"But I can't remember the last time we did anything together that was actually fun."

"We went to my cousin's wedding a few days ago, remember? Charity? So many people from the Igbo community were there."

I shake my head and groan. "We owed that to her. She's family. I'm talking about the conventions we used to go to. We could have gone to the Scarborough Fair last weekend! What happened to your inner nerd?"

Obinna interlocks his fingers and pops them. "He's there all right but still has to work. At some point, that inner nerd has to grow up eventually, too."

But his veterinary eye practice has sucked him dry for months. The man who once aced a *Dr. Who* trivia night probably can't even quote *Game of Thrones* anymore.

And I know just who to thank. "I'm sure Priya will be there to assist?"

Obinna then pops his shoulder sockets and tries to ease the irksome wear on his face. He's quite a looker—smooth dark brown skin, muscular build, full lips, and a nose that's slender and proportionate to the rest of him.

As my mom would say, *Obinna is fine Nigerian stock, so don't give him grief. Especially when he could easily find a lesser, prettier hassle.*

Which is all the more reason Priya is bad news.

"Patience, I'd rather be here with you. But we have bills, and Priya is the only other ophthalmologist at the clinic who helps with back-to-back surgeries. I can't leave her hanging," Obinna explains. "Please, just please get it. Okay?"

I mope by the steaming rice. "She seems to know you a lot more than I do most days."

Obinna holds me close, emitting his Sauvage aftershave. "There's nothing but furry patients going on between us, I promise," he says, his words a soothing balm to my troubled mind.

"If you say so."

"I do."

Then Obinna picks me up and sets me on the island counter. He breathes into my neckline lasciviously, running his hands all over my curves. "Damn, if only you knew how badly I want to stay."

"Then why don't you?" I whisper daringly. I take off my shirt and help him pull off his scrubs. "Wouldn't hurt to be a few minutes late from taking care of your wife… on the kitchen counter."

"Patience, I can't."

"No problem, the bed or shower works, too." He's not getting away that easily. Spark, flames, fire begin.

I give him a steamy kiss and pull him on top of me. My legs lock him in as I gyrate my body on his. Obinna relents and releases all of that work tension onto me. "You drive a hard bargain."

"I know. You have your work cut out for you."

"Hey, I'm here now, aren't I?"

"Physically, hell yes. Mentally? Jury is still out," I say, poking him in the side.

"Good god… Patience…"

BEEP. BEEP.

Damn you, medical pager. We were so close to finishing! At least, I was.

"Sorry, it's best I don't ignore that one." Obinna climbs off me to rush putting his clothes back on. "We'll pick up where we left off. Promise."

Not him giving me a rain check. "I'll hold you to that."

He pinches my butt and gives me a lighthearted kiss. "Love you, Pat."

I nod as Obinna runs out the door for the umpteenth time.

I wonder, if it's for sure not Priya, then maybe it's what happened last year that's keeping him away from me. Despite expectations weighing on my shoulders, I know that, being surrounded by the ones I love, I am exactly where I'm meant to be.

Right?

* * *

Grading papers occupies me for a bit on a Wednesday morning until Grayson is escorted back into my classroom from P.E. Nadia holds him by his shoulders and pivots him in my direction.

"Tell Mrs. Okoye what you did in specials today."

"No!"

"Grayson, now."

"You're not even a real teacher, so get the hell off of me!"

"I think it's a good time to take a breath, everyone," I say, getting up from my seat. "Let's try it."

"So?! We breathe every freaking day!" Grayson yells. He runs to the cool down corner and buries his head in a pillow. "I hate everyone here!"

P.E. must've been a delight.

"So, what happened?" I ask Nadia, instead.

"He pushed Sarah Cox to the ground when she tagged him. Then he called her the c-word."

"Goodness!" I say. "He uses *freaking* religiously, but he goes as far as a see-you-next-Tuesday with Sarah?"

Nadia laughs and pulls up a seat. "That's ODD kid logic for you. He's scared you'll pull the NASA project out from under him. He kept asking about it on our walk over here."

Oh. So he does care.

"Thanks, Nadia. I think I know how to reel him back in."

"Need these graded?"

"Be my guest."

We switch off, and I head over to a distraught Grayson.

"Leave me alone."

"In a minute." I get comfy on the beanbag beside him. "It's my job to do check-ins when my kiddos are having a hard time."

"I'm not a kiddo, and I'm not your kiddo." Grayson lifts his head, and it's sweaty. "Just say we're not doing the project anymore already and go!"

Dominick tries to come over and join in on the fun. "Why is Grayson grouchy?"

"Your mom's grouchy, dickbreath!" Grayson yells back. "So, go away."

I handle Dominick's raw rejection with class. "He's having a moment, but he'll be okay. Thanks for caring about a friend, Dom. But go ahead and finish your work."

Dominick nods and ambles away. "It must suck to be angry all the time."

I gently rub Grayson's arm. "Okay, you have your privacy back. I'm only wondering what made you so mad to use such a hateful word against Sarah."

"I don't know."

"I'm not so sure about that."

"Then you're as dumb as Sarah."

"Grayson, that's not the way to address an adult."

"Oh my freaking god, fine already. So, I practiced to be the fastest at tag today, all weekend. I wanted to win the third grade TAG trophy in P.E. But then Stupid Sarah is taller—which means she ended up being faster than me."

I wait and cue a cross Grayson to keep going.

"All I know is that I was really mad, and in the beginning, I couldn't think of anything else to say to get her back and—and—"

"Slow down. And what?"

Grayson sits all the way up and wipes the perspiration off his face. "And I remember my dad called my mom that one time when they were yelling. It made her cry, like a lot. And I wanted Sarah to feel as bad as my mom did."

Jesus, help me—that's dark.

I scoot closer to Grayson, who now watches me like an owl, unsure of what to make of me.

"Grayson, I'm proud of you."

"Why? I didn't even do anything."

"Yes, you did. You were honest with your feelings. You found the source of your anger and explained the reason behind it in lots of detail. Few third graders can do that."

"Duh," he goads.

"But you owe Sarah an apology," I say, sitting cross-legged now. "Her feelings matter, too."

"I know, I know, I know! I will, okay? Now can we stop talking about this? Your voice is giving me a headache."

"Fine, go pack for Ms. Bell's class and remember to brainstorm some ideas for the NASA project next week."

Grayson rolls his eyes and gets ready to go to Ms. Bell's room next door. "By the way, last night, my mom asked me if I wanted to come back to this class next year."

My earlobes suddenly wiggle. "Oh? What did you tell her?"

Grayson walks to the doorway, then glances back. His face is suddenly brighter, accompanied with relaxed brows and raised cheeks. If I didn't know any better, I'd easily mistake it for a smile.

"I said, *Maybe.* Because... you're the least stupidest teacher in the whole school."

Then he leaves.

Chea! Okoye for the win.

* * *

It's a breezy September on a Friday, but no Seabrook Elementary for me today. I'm heading to our quarterly professional development training.

By the time I get here, parking is hella packed, and I end up parking at the rundown Family Dollar across the street.

I head inside and observe the following:

It's only eight-thirty AM, yet all the donuts are gone, and I want to leave already. The guest speaker, Ken Bishop—a squirrelly man with beady eyes, oval-framed glasses, and donning a wrinkled suit—keeps going on *about "Remember your 'why' during the highs and lows of education."* It's hard to take presenters, who only taught for two years and worked in administration for ten, seriously. By the fifth reference of the tagline, my ADHD kicks in, and I tune homeboy out.

I scan the room for any familiar faces in the sea of educators—nope. My senses fail to find me a partner in crime. Ugh. Dammit, Nadia. Girl had to settle for the paraprofessional development training instead, didn't she? Way to force me into anti-social status.

Wait a minute.

There is one teacher that catches my eye, but for a different reason altogether.

He is darkly dressed and broody, with messy, dirty blond hair that grows past his ears but hangs in hap-hazard directions. His stubble is even blonder, covering the bottom part of his angular jawline. The guy's a work of art. Tattoos encase both his arms with what looks like Sistine Chapel paintings from sleeve to sleeve.

What in the hell does he teach?

"…Now, let's partner up for the gallery walk activity, everyone!"

Huh? Crap, I must've zoned out a tad too far earlier.

What the hell is a gallery walk?

Everyone rises from their chairs, and some gladly flock to people they know. Others reluctantly trudge to unknown groups, anticipating acceptance or rejection. They are brave souls—can't say I'm one of them.

My eyes dart around, looking for a sign to combat my unrelenting awkwardness. Pairs and groups in the auditorium become more distinguished, leaving me feeling more alone. Lord, why am I like this? Just find a group and move your feet. Come on!

The tattooed individual meets my eyes for a split second, and my first instinct is to spin away. I'm so weird when I make things bigger than they need to be.

"All right, it seems like most of our groups have formed. If not, you'd better hop to it." Ken directly stares in my direction with a tight smile—dick.

"Hey, um—" Someone taps my right shoulder.

Tattoo Guy scratches his head and modestly extends a hand.

"I mean—if you're not partnered with anyone, did you want to?"

My brain short circuits from the intensity of his eyes. They are alien-looking, with flecks of blue and green jumbled up in sparkling clusters. Contact lenses could never be that creative.

"Patience Okoye!" a voice yells from a distance. We both turn to face a middle-aged teacher waddling over to us. Her denim dress swishes with each step. "Hi, doll! Remember me? You shadowed for my class four years ago at Saddlewood Elementary? I'm Mrs. Taggert."

I remember now, but her timing sucks ass.

"Yes, uh... hello, Mrs. Taggy—sorry. Taggert. How are you?"

Then Tattoo Guy clears his throat, grins, and starts walking away. "It's all good. Don't worry about it."

And he bolts.

Why do I feel bad? I don't even know him.

"Did you want to pair up? My gals would love to have you." She waves at a group of women roughly the same age as her, and they squeal and wave back.

I give a lukewarm smile and nod.

"We snagged a young, live one, ladies!" says Mrs. Taggert, dragging me along with her.

I wonder if relinquishing my teaching certification would be less painful.

* * *

The minutes creep along ever so slowly, and the hours pass at a snail's pace. The activity involves analyzing posters that break down effective classroom management strategies and jotting down our takeaways from them on sticky notes.

"So, you're married now? How exciting!" says Mrs. Taggert. She plops a peppermint in her mouth, and I silently thank the mint for ridding her of her rancid soup breath.

"For how long, and what does he do? Ooh, what's his name?"

"Obinna, married for three years. And he is pretty great." I become phony and play my cheerleader role for him, avoiding any conversation of genuine intent. "He's a veterinary ophthalmologist at Care for Paws Clinic. He's also taking on some emergency cases, too."

"You don't say?!" she replies a little louder than I'd like to hear. "My nephew, Simon, goes there for annual checkups for his tabby cat, Jasper. Small world! Bless his heart, working tirelessly to save the animal kingdom. I know most don't think so, but animal doctors are definitely real doctors, too. And don't let anyone let him or you think otherwise, okay?"

Well, I didn't. Until now.

"Anywho... any babies yet?" Mrs. Taggert's clumpy eyelashes flutter at me.

My stomach seizes. No one is ever ready for the question that can potentially ruin their whole day.

"Well, not yet," I say matter-of-factly.

"But soon? Please, let it be soon!"

Geez—cool it, lady. "Maybe."

"How old are you?"

"Twenty-nine. Thirty in November."

"Ha! Those pesky thirties sneak up on ya, don't they?!" Volume awareness seems to be a foreign concept for Mrs. Taggert altogether. "Better get on it. I'm sure your parents are itching to be grandparents, my dear."

"Well, that's up to science, not me," I snipe unintentionally.

Mrs. Taggert's face shifts from joyful to pity from my tone. No, no, no. Not what I wanted—fuck.

"Aww—my dear, it'll happen when the time is right. If it can happen to an old crow at forty-three like me, you have it in the bag."

People who give unsolicited, patronizing advice ought to be put down like Obinna's patients. Sorry, not sorry.

"Thanks," I say, disinterested.

Suddenly, Mrs. Taggert's phone blasts a nursery jingle, and she answers it. "Hello? Yes, Jean, what is it? What?! You found blisters where? Oh, for heaven's sake—I told you, he can't have pineapple, and of course, he'll tell you otherwise. Okay, okay. Never mind all that, stop crying. I'm on my way. I hope you've learned to heed my instructions carefully next time. Uh-huh, I've heard that before, so I won't put money on it. Goodbye."

I don't know who to feel worse for, Jean or whoever caught the blisters.

"Patience, I have to go. My poor excuse for a home care aid let my father get the best of her again. Sorry to leave you hanging, but I'm sure my colleagues wouldn't mind pairing up with you. They aren't as much fun as me, though! Ha!" She swats my arm playfully, but the brass llama rings on each finger aren't as friendly, stinging something fierce. "Take care, sweetheart."

With that, Mrs. Taggert takes off in a hurry, clanging the auditorium doors open in a huff.

As annoying as she was, I'm pissed because I'm alone again. To avoid entertaining anyone from the Golden Girls' inner circle, I plan to hack the rest of the activity on my own and hope no one sniffs me out. I make it a good ten minutes, aimlessly walking in between random posters and pretending to copy notes in my planner.

"You gotta be stealthier than that. Otherwise, you'll blow your cover." Tattoo Guy returns, snickering behind me from the conference panels.

My cheeks flush with both relief and embarrassment. "That bad?"

"Tragic. You didn't even try to pull out your phone and flip through apps to seem inconspicuous."

Good point.

"Who did you eventually end up with after I ditched you?" I ask.

"Some primary school folk. Couldn't be any further from having common ground. So, I bailed."

"Oh."

My tongue gets twisted when small talk fades, and my cheeks get hot again. I guess he picks up on that and holds out his hand.

"Harlan McCandles. Professor currently teaching Intro to Art at Colby Community College. You?"

I return his handshake; his palms are unnaturally soft. "Patience Okoye, Special Education at Seabrook Elementary."

Harlan taps on my wedding ring. "That's a helluva rock, Patience. Bet it could pay off a dozen tuitions at Colby."

Oh my, that's kinda forward. "Um, thank you. Wait? College teachers can attend this PD training, too?"

Harlan snorts and crosses his beautiful arms across his chest. "It's not an elite nightclub. If it's mandatory for a campus, then a requirement is a requirement. Enough said."

I immediately feel silly for asking. "How much classroom management do college professors need? I figured their students would have most of their stuff together."

"That's what you think," says Harlan. "That much responsibility for an eighteen-year-old can be maddening sometimes. In fact, six times out of ten, they absolutely do not have their shit together."

His thoughts come uncensored—already an improvement from Mrs. Taggert. "Ah. Gotcha."

"Got an evaluation from higher ups telling me I need more structure in my lectures and should provide clear guidelines in my rubric expectations or whatnot. So, they sent me here."

"Well, I would rather teach adults than kids most days."

Harlan raises a translucent eyebrow. "Is that so? Do tell."

Think of something witty. Think. Think. Damn, I've got nothing. I'm about as witty as a stale bran muffin. So, be straightforward.

"Well, if you must know, we raise kids now. Teaching academics went out the window after COVID."

"I believe about seventy-six percent of that is exaggerated."

"It's true!"

"Wee bit dramatic, aren't we?"

"Okay," I reply, assured. "You're welcome to come to my learning environment one of these days and do some damage control. Maybe wrestle a Chromebook out of a fifth grader's hands. A fifth grader who bites, spits, and throws other splendid bodily fluids. All while you're trying to teach a thirty-minute science lesson and being called a fucking moron."

The color drains from Harlan's face like clockwork. Ha!

Never fails.

"And if that doesn't scare you, I usually evacuate my classroom every other day."

"And the list goes on?!"

"...and we're seconds away from being out of compliance with student accommodations to boot."

"My god, you win."

I take a triumphant bow. "Why thank you, good sir."

"My students may not be throwing feces, but their artwork isn't far from it," he says. "Trying seems comparable to giving up your first-born son, if asked."

I laugh and circle back to the bizarre irony of my fertile predicament Mrs. Taggert pointed out. "Yeah right."

"Perhaps you could use some artistic guidance then, missy? Teach you a thing or two about capturing a moment."

"Now, see, that sounds suspiciously like after-school detention."

Harlan's nose crinkles at the thought. "Detention? More like an exclusive masterclass for the most discerning student. You look like you could use a color palette in your life."

The riffs keep on keeping on.

"Yeah, well, I could use a day without extinguishing little fires everywhere in my class. How's the world of abstract expressionism treating you? Trying to convince students that a blank canvas is a showpiece?"

"Precisely. It's a tough sell, but someone's gotta do it. I mean, have you ever considered the psychological impact of a perfect circle?"

Looks like I met my match. Who knew tall, dark, and sullen had a personality to him?

But there's a nagging feeling our conversation isn't supposed to be this enjoyable. "I've thought more about the psychological impact of a perfect tantrum. Much less an abstract. And now who's being dramatic?"

"Hmm." Harlan tiptoes in circles around me. "Figured it was my turn to be, with the way you'd rather walk through fire than to talk to anybody here."

"How long were you watching me for, anyway?" I ask, quite curious.

"It was that or watch the clock tick. And I guess you're mildly more interesting."

Nice save. "But I talked to you."

"Indeed, you did."

"And I survived," I say. "So, there."

Harlan huffs. "Whatever you say, Patience Okoye. What kind of name is that, anyway?"

"What kind of name is Harlan? Or McCandles?"

"I only meant—"

"It's African. Nigerian. Like me. And my noisy bangles." I wave my bracelets, waggishly.

"Ah, cool. I'm Irish."

I stand beside him, goggle-eyed. "Aren't you a little too blond and freckle free for a typical Irishman?"

Harlan has a toothy smile that makes me think of a modern day Dracula. "That's because I'm a rare breed."

"Thirty seconds until the gallery walk is complete!" Ken announces. "Then we come back as a group to discuss our findings."

"Well, in that case..." Harlan leans in slightly and takes my hand as my mind races, trying to figure him out. He places a card in it. "Maybe I'll catch you later. I only need four hours of this documented, so I'm heading out. Don't be a stranger.

Or do be one. Let's make it interesting."

Harlan winks and saunters away, leaving me astounded.

The business card in my hand has his Instagram handle with a message that reads, *Does my art suck? You be the judge. Muahahaha.*

I will, Harlan McCandles.

Another night of romance goes awry. Thanks to Punctual Priya.

"You promised," I say, heatedly. "Obi, you promised, and you're already going back on your word. How could you do this to me?"

"I won't be gone long, four or five hours tops." Obi quickly gets dressed in our closet. "I didn't plan on getting paged. Priya needs an extra set of hands and eyes for this procedure, baby. It's really delicate."

It would be nice, if the shoe were on the other foot for once, to have Obinna think it would be unheard of to leave this very second just for her.

I pause *JoJo's Bizarre Adventure* and look at my husband in disappointment. "Dammit, we were supposed to have DoorDash in bed. If I cancel now, they'll charge us a fee."

"I'm sorry. I'll cover it. Can't you find something else to do? Ooh, did you know there's a block party on our street going on outside? Now's a good time to make yourself known."

Way to pawn me off on strangers. "I already met our new neighbors."

Obinna glances up from pulling a fresh undershirt on and seems amazed. "Oh! How about that? What are their names?"

"Wouldn't you like to know? They've probably seen me more than you have this week."

Obinna squints as if my chatter is making him dumber by the minute. "Pat…"

"Well, what does it matter what I say? You already have your mind made up."

"It's not just any animal." Obi says, as he swoops on his scrubs. "I told you about Max, the Frisco police dog. Remember? The little guy has hundreds of successful drug searches under his belt. Now he's going blind, and we got to find out what that unknown mass is behind his optic nerve. His biopsy was supposed to be scheduled next week, but the mass is getting out of control quicker than we thought. Come on, Patience. He must be in a lot of pain. You're a dog mama, think about it—who's else is gonna lookout for him?"

Even so…

"Will it ever be just you and me again?"

Obinna plants a juicy kiss on my mouth, making it impossible to stay mad for long. "I'm working on it. I'll try my damn hardest, too. For you, Nami."

"Dirty pool, mister." Nicknames from freshman year are a surefire way to warm me up to him again. "Still pissed."

Our foreheads touch as his hands explore me. "It's the only way to play with you."

"Throw in a foot rub on our next date night, and we'd be getting somewhere."

"Deal. But if my pager goes off—"

"If that pager goes off, it'll be a permanent fixture in our rose garden." I trace his solid pecs with my fingers.

Obinna beams, with his charming, hundred-watt smile that still gets to me, even when he's being completely insufferable.

"So, do you accept my I.O.U?."

"I'll take it—with pizza. Because nothing says romance like carbs."

"Fine, I got you. You're the best, Pat."

"I know."

Then he leaves me to be by my lonesome.

Here's to another night at home alone, with Pongers sniffing about while I'm linked—ball and chain—to my phone.

At least I have a new pastime.

In the last three weeks, checking to see if Harlan messaged back has become a habit. Like it or not—he started a deconstruction of my life, and now I can't stop thinking. If I had stuck with my artistic hobbies, would I still be in special education? Where would I be today?

I scroll through our past conversation on Instagram; his name lights up my screen more than I thought it would. It's fine, though. Harlan McCandles is just... an interest in an oddity, like a gnome hobby I'm getting to know more and more about. Fascinating. Someone I can talk to about more than just current events. Someone who understands how a line in an abstract could shift an entire mood.

At first, I'd hesitate before hitting send, worried it might seem too much. Now, I don't think twice and want a chance to learn and get back at it. And it's only today, while absent-mindedly scrolling through my phone, I notice how Neisa's texts have become fewer and farther between.

@PatOkoye: Hey. I found your work

   @McCandlesRealismTM: and you found me

   @PatOkoye: that too

   @McCandlesRealismTM: thoughts?

@**PatOkoye:** of?

@**McCandlesRealismTM:** global warming. My work, what else?

@**PatOkoye:** oh lol, really ingenious dark imagery, neon splatters that captivate the jet black canvases radiantly, etc.

@**McCandlesRealismTM:** I'm not gonna find this review on chat gpt, am I?

@**PatOkoye:** I'm insulted

@**McCandlesRealismTM:** sorry I've been had before

@**PatOkoye:** meant every authentic word

@**McCandlesRealismTM:** thanks m'lady

@**PatOkoye:** just supporting the local arts. Meant to tell you before, I minored in art at UNT my first semester. Did some watercolor nature stuff, nothing big

@**McCandlesRealismTM:** what happened after the second semester, third, and so on?

@**PatOkoye:** I became my worst critic

@**McCandlesRealismTM:** Ooof. Happens to the best of us. How was the rest of Ken's PD?

@**PatOkoye:** I wouldn't know. I hid in the restroom the whole time after you left

@**McCandlesRealismTM:** seriously? That's a hell of an introvert tactic

@**PatOkoye:** I'm not a fan of people I don't know

@**McCandlesRealismTM:** but you teach kids to face their fears all the time

@**PatOkoye:** Okay, I'm a fraud. You don't have to rub it in

@**McCandlesRealismTM:** on some days, being a fraud is all we have left to go on.

@**PatOkoye:** facts

@**McCandlesRealismTM:** come see me teach this Thursday

and marvel at the fraudulent art my students turn in.

@PatOkoye: at Colby?

@McCandlesRealismTM: is that a yes?

@PatOkoye: potentially

@McCandlesRealismTM: see you then

* * *

Using a personal day from work, I step into Harlan's class-room, which is shaped like an inverted dome. The dim lighting of the room lends the space a mysterious quality, as though the art within holds untold secrets.

The room is spacious, with high ceilings and walls that adorn an array of various abstract paintings, sketches, and sculptures. The air smells strongly of paint and clay, and I'm immediately engulfed by the scenery that vibrates through the place.

If these are works of his students, he was ridiculously too hard on them.

A large abstract painting that dominates one wall catches my eye as I make my way deeper into the room. It features cubism—swirls of pastel colors dancing across the canvas, intertwining in a mesmerizing ballet.

"There she is!" Harlan remarks. He emerges from his office below and shows off by hopping over four steps to get to me. "Guess you're not all talk, after all."

"I wanted to see if Ken's tips on effective classroom man-agement paid off for you." My wit improves with each Harlan encounter.

"And which student is trashing your classroom in your absence today?"

"Since I'm here with you, not my circus, not my monkeys."

"Isn't calling kids furry little creatures frowned upon in your profession?"

"So is saying the art from your students isn't real art, you jerk!" I say, then slug him in the chest. "Everything looks great in here! Why did you say they can't paint to save their lives? The talent is impeccable."

He wipes his hands over his paint-splattered jeans and takes in his domain. "Yeah, it's fine, I suppose... like library or subway art. Passable. But none of it is original—all TikTok and AI inspired. I only hung it up because there's an unwritten rule that I gotta."

He must think I'm so basic for being amazed, while he's not giving a second thought to any of it.

"And?"

"And so it doesn't count!" he derides. "Whatever happened to embracing the macabre in works of self-expression? Creating a piece so unheard of... it's nearly inconceivable to the human eye? If I see another sketch of the thinking man currently trending on Reddit, I'll shoot myself."

"That's so messed up, and who cares? Artists draw inspiration from past artists for the common good."

"Then originality dies. When you're in the eye of a hurricane, that's where everything slows down. You can see clearly. In the chaos, life truly happens, and that's when we create great work. But a work of art that isn't based on feeling isn't art at all. Thank you, Paul Cézanne."

Ugh. He's being pretentious again.

"You should write fortune cookies," I say, shaking my head. "McCandles, you make it sound so simple."

"It *is* simple." His voice drops a notch. "We complicate it because we're scared of what happens when we stop pretending we know everything."

I lean against a table with my hands on my hips. "And you're never scared?"

"Of course I am, but it's all a part of the process. If you're not scared, you're not pushing yourself hard enough."

"So, you mean to tell me if I spat on paper, hung it up, and said it symbolizes the fear of retaliation that I have from rejecting oppression, my art would outweigh all the art that's strewn up here?"

Harlan flashes his vampire grin, loving the fact he continues to get me worked up.

"If it sparks an intellectual conversation that goes past aesthetics, then why not? Authenticity should always prevail."

Okay. Two can play that game. So, I do just that. I snatch a piece of paper from a nearby stack and cough up the biggest phlegm wad humankind has ever created. Spit soon follows, with a splat dab right in the middle. Then I ball up the paper as a finishing touch.

"You're asinine!" Harlan roars. His booming laugh echoes and rustles the hanging art. "Okay, I can roll along with it. Just know there's a method to my madness."

"Not like you have a choice, so practice what you preach. Let's hear what they have to say about it, and I'll bet you fifty bucks you won't get an intuitive response," I say in triumph.

"Professor Okoye, I can't wait to see how your thesis will outweigh the outcome. Students should arrive shortly."

* * *

I sit on the sidelines as a dozen freshmen and a few upperclassmen pour into Harlan's room by nine AM. He sits on his desk, like those teachers trying to be cool on a TV show, swinging his legs side to side and fingers drumming an incoherent rhythm. A handful of students place art projects in the middle of the floor as my interest piques even more.

"Professor McCandles, please be gentle. *The Veiled Lady* sculpture got squashed on the train ride over here," a red-headed girl whines over to him. "She didn't stand a chance and took a nosedive in front of the entire orchestra."

Harlan picks up the lopsided structure and inspects every inch with a thin-lipped wince. When he finishes, he plops it back into her hands. "Perhaps the veil came in handy after all."

"Professor?"

"She can still pull it off if you ask me, Kelsey." Harlan is clearly joking, but Kelsey is mortified. "It's very reminiscent of the *Man with the Broken Nose* by Auguste Rodin."

"No! That is absolutely out of the question! Please no, I cannot turn it in like this. If you could—"

"Let you turn it in next week, with no penalty? Stellar idea, Kelsey! Why didn't I think of that? Better get on it then."

Flustered, Kelsey nods and returns to her seat. Yikes. Being high-strung doesn't mix with Harlan's occasional humor very well.

"Okay, everyone, as you're coming in, please turn in your portfolios on the far right. We have our warm up analysis to get through."

The class adheres to him and faces the front. And as promised, my art is on display, spit gliding ever so gradually.

"Please tell me that's not it." Kelsey turns up her nose as she sits. "I know art is subjective, but you've gotta be kidding me."

Harlan narrows his eyes right past her. "Are there any artists or artworks that come to mind with this work?"

Silence rings throughout the auditorium.

"You're joking," says Kelsey from the front row. "Is it even—"

"Hold that thought, Kelsey. I'd like to invite a different perspective for now. Anyone else?"

"Um, what even is it?" a student asks from the third row. "Looks like it's from the trash."

"Nope, not from the trash, but appreciate your candor, Maurice, always a pleasure," Harlan replies. He tries his hardest not to laugh. "No, you see, it's a bona fide original."

A dreadful lull of whispers saturates the learning environment. Like I expected, no one knows what to make of the mess Professor McCandles zones in on.

"Still don't get it."

"Might be assemblage art."

"Couldn't be. Ready-made seems more fitting."

"It's obviously found art of some kind. With more than meets the eye," a mousey-faced girl chimes in.

"What's obvious about it, Susie?"

"That crumpled up paper could represent something off or disturbing. Maybe the stuff in the middle saturates it—to make it docile, limp, and not as scary. It loses its power. Like combating racism with Black Lives Matter."

Some students nod, while others are stuck on being confused, most likely by the term *obvious.*

"Okay, am I wildin' or is that not somebody's loogie on that junk?!" jeers a student from the fifth row. "Stop playing, Professor McCandles. How are you gonna sit there and let old girl call *Black Lives Matter* spit?"

The entire class erupts in fits of giggles, and I feel so bad for Harlan that I want to sink through the floor. Maybe we went a tad too far, but somehow, he's not rattled yet.

"Perspective has the potential to be limitless. But, hey? Don't just see it through my viewpoint. Question the artist herself. Mrs. Okoye?"

Son of a bitch. We had a deal! He's supposed to prove a point with my so-called art, not make me give a press conference. All heads turn in my direction, and I aim to kill Harlan with no shred of mercy.

"You did that?" asks Kelsey in disgust. "For what reason?"

If she doesn't shut up, I'll smash the rest of her art into the campus pavement.

"Yes, inquiring minds would like to know," Harlan adds.

"I... I..." I manage.

My throat seizes, and the confident banter I shared with Harlan earlier is nonexistent at the moment.

"Um, hello?" Kelsey relentlessly prods. "Anytime? Cat got your tongue? We know saliva clearly doesn't."

The class mockingly cackles, fueling my humiliation. Face it. There's no way I thought I could be this person who could run shit and claim it. It becomes quickly clear—Harlan didn't want to challenge me; he wanted to make a spectacle of me.

I rush out of his classroom and leave the entire class stunned, including Harlan.

"Perhaps we'll catch her viewpoint at another opportunity. Thanks to those of you voicing your input..."

Thud. Thud. Thud. Past the library, annex hall, and reference desk. I'm in the parking lot and make a beeline for my car. What am I even doing? Why was I even trying to impress a man I didn't know existed a month ago? Whatever. Doesn't matter, be done with it and leave. I open my car, slouch inside, and slam the door with conviction.

Before starting the engine, my phone lights up, and it's Harlan calling from Instagram. I let it ring until both the notification and my interest in Harlan McCandles fade wholly.

* * *

@McCandlesRealismTM: hey, you owe me 50 bucks. I'm here to collect

@PatOkoye: ...

@McCandlesRealismTM: you there?

@PatOkoye: what do you want, Harlan?

@McCandlesRealismTM: I just told you

@PatOkoye: still don't follow

@McCandlesRealismTM: Susie gave quite the intuitive response, didn't she?

@PatOkoye: I guess

@McCandlesRealismTM: so deals a deal. Like I said, original art can surpass the wildest expectations and interpretations from people

@PatOkoye: definitely worth it at my expense, huh?

@McCandlesRealismTM: now I'm not following

@PatOkoye: you embarrassed me in front of your own class to prove a stupid point only relevant to you

@McCandlesRealismTM: more like I gave you an opportunity to stand behind the statement you made before about "borrowing inspiration." Instead you chose to fuck off

@PatOkoye: I didn't fuck off

@McCandlesRealismTM: what do you call flying out of my

classroom like a bat out of hell then?

@PatOkoye: I was over it. And now over this conversation

@McCandlesRealismTM: not entirely unexpected though

@PatOkoye: come again?

@McCandlesRealismTM: when things get hard, you tend to check out. And when people force you to embrace the uncomfortable, you dig in your heels and attack.

@PatOkoye: you don't know me

@McCandlesRealismTM: I beg to differ

@PatOkoye: where do you get off making these generaliza-tions about me?

@McCandlesRealismTM: thought you were over this con-versation

@PatOkoye: first finish what you started and answer my question

@McCandlesRealismTM: it's endearing that you carry my opinion of you so highly.

@PatOkoye: fine. Fuck you

@McCandlesRealismTM: think your husband would con-done that offer?

@PatOkoye: that's really inappropriate

@McCandlesRealismTM: you offered

@PatOkoye: I don't feel comfortable speaking to you anymore

@McCandlesRealismTM: what a shame. I had such high hopes for you, Okoye

@PatOkoye: I don't care. You crossed the line

@McCandlesRealismTM: Here's the thing though. I want to be wrong about you. Please prove me wrong

@PatOkoye: what would that even look like?

@McCandlesRealismTM: a painting lesson with yours

truly

@PatOkoye: apologize first

@McCandlesRealismTM: I apologize for hurting and offending you. Wasn't my intention.

@PatOkoye: you didn't hurt me, it's the principle

@McCandlesRealismTM: if you say so

@PatOkoye: I do.

@McCandlesRealismTM: painting lesson tomorrow at 7? Or do you have to bake a tuna casserole for your better half or something?

@PatOkoye: I'll be there smartass

@McCandlesRealismTM: Smartass signing off.

* * *

I park at the place where just yesterday I swore to never return. The place where I was so embarrassed that I called for another absence at Seabrook the next day to recover from it. But the growing need to see what Harlan has in store for me supersedes any reasonable action.

Zzzz. Zzzz. Obinna's text reads, **Gonna be another long night. Show horse in Wylie may have a possible corneal tumor. Heading there now. Love you.**

And this is why he should've picked a lane and stayed in it. Saving every damn thing that squawks, barks, and moos isn't cutting it anymore.

So, I'm off, too.

After making three rights and a left down the evening–lit hallways, Harlan's classroom door comes into full view, left ajar for me.

"Anybody home?"

Further into the room, I spot two body-sized canvases with a tarp beside them. An incandescent lamp illuminates the area in a twilight nature, with Harlan's back turned from me and already at work. After lathering taupe paint on the mid-section of the canvas, he uses sandpaper to fine-grain the edges on the other.

His face when he paints is very meditative, maneuvering the art to how he sees fit. Then Harlan's brow furrows as he discovers a blank spot.

"You stuck?" I ask. "Maybe I can help."

"No, thanks, it's hopeless," he replies, irritated. "I've been at this shit for hours, and I've got to know when to call it."

"Like when to stop and let someone else take charge for a change?"

Harlan pulls his hair back into a bun with a quizzical look. "Or you can start on yours now, and I'll give my limbs a break. I suppose seeing your thought process could wipe the memory of art spitgate."

"Ha-ha."

I move toward an ethereal painting that resonates with me, featuring muted blues and greens. Some layers seem to absorb into one another. I look at it for a moment and allow my shoulders to relax.

"This one is the most prominent," I say under my breath.

Harlan steps up beside me. "Yeah? Why this one?"

I shrug and trace the lines of the painting with my prying touch. "You could just sink into the imaginary seafoam and disappear."

"You've got a thing for disappearing, don't you?" He lands too close to my truth. "Your canvas awaits, madame."

Harlan hands me a flat brush and snags a stool to sit beside me. I wait to see if he wants to add any tips or suggestions, but he merely gawks at my canvas.

So, I stand here with my thumbs in my pockets. "Where do I even start? I'm working with nothing."

Harlan smoothly twirls me a pencil. His fingers resemble a spider, long and spindly. "Create a simple pattern. It doesn't have to have any rhyme or reason to it. As long as it comes naturally to you. Then the acrylics come later."

"Do your tattoos have any rhyme or reason to them?" I ask as I draw.

Harlan brings his arms together and flexes. "What can I say? I've lived a colorful life. Traveled a lot before going to college—was homeless for a bit in my late teens, then back-packed across Europe for two years. Pretty damn fortunate. I met some cool people who took me in and showed me the ropes along the way. You could say my tattoos are in their honor."

The amount of envy that zips through my veins turns into a riptide. "How the hell did you afford to do all that?"

"Slept with dozens of well-established women."

I laugh with a biting pitch. "Good one."

Harlan doesn't blink. "Wasn't pulling your leg."

"Oh." Now I'm shamefaced. "I see."

"You're not getting judgy on me, are you?" he asks, then pulls his stool back a few feet. "It's not the greatest attribute to have as an artist."

"Not at all." I wonder if the number of women was exaggerated or downplayed. "To each their own."

"You asked. Besides, as you can imagine—sex sells."

"Harlan, wasn't this supposed to be a painting lesson?"

"Apologies. Please continue."

I loosen up and position my brush. "Okay, um, I think some maroon would be best for here, to, uh, bring out more earthy colors to the surface. Make it pop, but subtle."

Harlan pops his fingers and points at the color with his sharp chin. "You're the boss. There's the maroon for the taking, kid."

"On it."

I stroke and feel the smooth glide of the brush up and down, sensing Harlan's approval. The more I do, the more I lean toward his way of thinking about expressionism.

"How about emphasizing the maroon with tan?"

"Sure, Patience."

"Unless you think navy would be better? No, that might be a bit much. Peach could work, right?"

Harlan waves my words away and holds his finger to his lips. "Professor McCandles is calling it quits because of an artist's block, so I'm no help right now. Besides, I've done so many of these I've lost count, and I'm not interested in creating another one yet. This is your project, not mine. Do whatever the hell you want and get out of your head already. I'm sure it'll come out as an original Okoye piece. I'm not gonna hover over you and tell you how much you're pleasing me every five minutes." Then he winks and chuckles darkly, the sound reverberating through my belly. "I mean, I guess I could—but then that would get—"

"All right, all right." Why do I need his permission to try? "I'll go for it."

"That's more like it. But before you do, let's decompress, shall we?"

Harlan guides me by the shoulders and takes me back to my canvas. The prickles return, flushing through my skin from the firm hold of his hands. His torso behind me presses against my back, and I realize he's well over six feet.

Get it together, Patience. Do not even go there, or you can call the whole thing off.

But if I'm told not to think about something, what the shit else is gonna happen?

"Find your core color... here. It's what I like to call the tone of one's inner essence. What shades are your feelings and fervor right now?" Harlan delicately says in my right ear, resting his chin on me. He massages my temples with his thumbs. His stubble nicks at my sleeve, and the prickles travel down my spine, knowing full well I should've stopped everything thirty seconds ago.

"...Found it."

"Show me."

Turquoise jabs for his stubble that pokes through thoughts of wondering... if what we're doing is okay. Ultramarine slashes for the nerve synapses that buzz when our skin connects. Cyan wisps for his lips that graze my ear when he whispers and possesses me. And finally, ash gray clouds for the uncertainty all of it might lead.

Christ on a cracker. Intrusive thoughts helped no one.

"What do you think?" I ask eagerly.

Harlan beams at my work and claps with thunder. His faded Givenchy graphic tee billows with every movement. "That is my work taking a well-deserved *L* for once."

"Don't mess with me. Come on."

Harlan pats me on the back, then lifts my creation high. "Fuck that. Give me some credit. I wouldn't do that to you. Hasn't anyone commended you on your past art?"

I pinch at my elbows shyly. "Never really felt safe enough

to display mine before.”

"Well, I can be your safe space.”

There is an unspokeness between our words that continues to bubble to the surface. I battle with the thought of stopping it for good, almost saying, *"Thanks for the lesson, but it's best we end things here. I'm a married woman with a crush on you."* But the worst part of me wants to relish in every bit of what Harlan unleashes.

I just wish she wasn't so damn loud.

"Hold on, though. It needs a gloss finish. Otherwise, the primer binding it all together becomes useless. Could you pass that over from the top shelf?”

"Oh, wait, what?" Paying attention is not my strong suit.

"Hold on…"

Harlan steps over to the shelving unit in the tight aisle where I am and reaches for the gloss. I try to keep still, but it's hard when he's so close. So, I sort of trip against him, and the trunk of his body supports me back up.

Harlan notices, too. "Sorry—I thought you knew what I was reaching for. I thought it would be faster this way."

I fake a laugh and try brushing what just happened away. "You're not slick, McCandles. That's the oldest trick in the book.”

Harlan's eyes dilate. "What are you talking about? I barely touched you—you're the one who fell onto me."

Fast forward. Eject. Burn the footage to the ground. Great, Patience. Now things are weird.

"True, I'm just naturally clumsy. But man, it's late. I have to go, if that's cool.”

"Why wouldn't that be cool?”

"Right. Bye, Harlan, and thank you.”

Harlan takes a couple of steps back and dismantles the tarp. "Your work can chill here till it's dry. Then I can hold it for you. I don't mind dropping it off."

The consequences of that idea are up in the air but still not worth taking a chance on.

"That's okay. I'll come to you and grab it once it's ready."

"Cool. I'm proud of you, Patience." Harlan's kaleidoscopic eyes render me hopeless. "Frankly, it's the realest thing I've seen from you. So, don't disappear on me. Okay? Looking forward to more."

God help me; me, too.

"By the way"—Harlan stops me mid departure—"if I ever had an inkling to make a move on you, you'd goddamn well know it, no question."

"I'm sorry?"

"You heard me. Drive safe, Okoye."

* * *

I park in the garage, noting Obi's Porsche is back. I hope he's asleep because I'm not sure how to explain this impromptu night outing.

In our bedroom, I see Obi is in dreamland. So much so, he's passed out fully clothed in work gear. Ugh, germs. I try to strip off his dirty attire while minding any animal goop.

"Mmm, thanks, baby," Obinna mumbles. "Where'd you go?"

I should tell him about my revamped passion. Then he'll know and I'll finally clear my conscience. "To Kansas. To bury the rest of the bodies."

Yet, the worst of Patience Okoye beats me to the punch. I'm

truly wired differently than most.

But would he even care? It's hard to tell lately.

"Hmm, nice. Tell me more about it tomorrow." He's back to snoring.

And there's my answer.

My phone pings, and it's Harlan. I'm ashamed of how quickly my fingers zip across my smartphone to answer.

@McCandlesRealismTM: make it home safe?

@PatOkoye: yes, thanks for asking

@McCandlesRealismTM: so, question

@PatOkoye: uh, possibly answer?

@McCandlesRealismTM: free tomorrow, same time?

@PatOkoye: for another lesson?

@McCandlesRealismTM: nah, an art showing. I showed an art dealer your work, and he wants to feature it in his exhibit tomorrow. Inside the Taos lounge.

@PatOkoye: Harlan are you serious?

@McCandlesRealismTM: by now, you should know I wouldn't mess with you about stuff like this

@PatOkoye: still learning

@McCandlesRealismTM: here's the thing though

@PatOkoye: oh no

@McCandlesRealismTM: there's no catch, hold on. Promise not to be judgmental. Like for real.

@PatOkoye: okay

@McCandlesRealismTM: it's not like any old art show. There are some themes pretty out there to the average person

@PatOkoye: and you think I won't be able to handle it?

@McCandlesRealismTM: It's just I know you're an elementary school teacher and all, so...

@PatOkoye: Sounds pretty judgmental to me

@McCandlesRealismTM: I wholeheartedly surrender

@PatOkoye: I'll let you off the hook for now McCandles

@McCandlesRealismTM: so, you coming?

@PatOkoye: can I invite someone?

@McCandlesRealismTM: I'm no gatekeeper of your talent

@PatOkoye: I didn't know if it would be weird.

@McCandlesRealismTM: because?

@PatOkoye: forget it. I'll see you tomorrow

@McCandlesRealismTM: same, although, if you're bringing someone, it kinda takes the fun out of giving you a hard time. Meaning I have to be on my best behavior and stuff

@PatOkoye: You're right. That kind of stinks, doesn't it?

@McCandlesRealismTM: But it's up to you.

@PatOkoye: I'll come solo.

@McCandlesRealismTM: Wise choice, kid.

@PatOkoye: Night.

* * *

Damn, where is he? I feel overdressed and not brave enough to hack it inside alone.

"Miss, are you valet parking?" a man in a dusty uniform asks me.

"Oh, uh, no. Sorry."

"Then do you mind moving? You're standing in the middle of parallel parking."

Wow. You suck all around, Patience.

"Okay. My bad."

I'm in front of the Taos lounge, freezing my ass off in a

black split bodycon dress. I should've invited Obinna, like I was supposed to. Not like he would've said yes with his workaholic self.

And I asked if I could invite someone—not my husband. What was that about?

At least, I would feel less culpable about being bummed Harlan stood me up.

Frustrated, I quickly call him. People weave in and out of the bustling Saturday evening crowd, and I'm thinking twice about tonight.

"Damn, Okoye. You clean up nice."

"Huh, what?"

I turn around and see Harlan waving at me from the corner. He has on True Religion jeans and a black Milano crew neck. Plus, he's sporting a fresh undercut hairstyle. Gotta admit, he cleans up nice, too.

But not nice enough to make me forget. "You're late."

"Yeah, I know, sorry about that." Harlan moves out of some drunk passersby's way. "Parking is god-awful downtown, shoulda texted you. Ready to head in? Jayson is waiting."

"If it means getting circulation back in my frozen hands, then sure."

The minute we go inside, it's already a lot to deal with. The pulsating beat of the music reverberates through the chrome lit lounge. Strobe lights flash in rhythmic patterns and cast shadows on the walls and the bodies gyrating on the dance floor. Colors blend and merge, creating an electric climate. The DJ mixes sounds that weave a tapestry of melodies, enveloping the crowd.

"Jayson!" Harlan cups over his mouth and points at a bald man in the crowd. "Yo, man, we're here!"

The bald guy, or Jayson, motions for us to come through the crowd and enter the sliding doors in the back.

Taos is a sensory feast, where every movement, every sound, and every flash of light is also a product of art.

"Finally, some quiet," Harlan says, after shutting the sliding door behind us. "The shit out there kills my ears."

"Hey, guys, glad you're here! Happy to have you. I'm Jay," Jayson loudly introduces himself. He looks like a shorter Bruce Willis, with Versace threads. "And you must be the lovely artist of the *Shades of Okoye* abstract."

I shake his hand and greet him back. "Yup, I'm her. I'm not a professional or anything, but thanks for selecting my art to be part of your showing."

Jayson kisses my hand, and I get a bit ruffled. He then turns to Harlan. "Hmm. Exotic choice..."

I beg your pardon?

"...pretty and modest. Where did you find this one, McCandles? You strike gold each time, it seems like."

Oh, god, he thinks we're a couple.

"Nah, come on, it's not like that," Harlan says, luckily. "She's a colleague."

"Even better."

"And married," I add, while flashing my wedding ring. His slimy eyes skim over my body, and have me questioning my entire outfit.

"Serves me right for missing that meteor-sized bling." Jayson bows out. "No hard feelings. Please enjoy yourselves and let me know if you need anything. Harlan, I'll complete the payment by the end of the night."

Then Jayson walks back out to the Taos lounge through the sliding doors.

"Jayson's a colorful character," I say, hoping it'll be our first and last interaction.

"I mean, he's not wrong, though. That dress doesn't help you blend in with the crowd much."

My stomach breaks off into frantic shingles. "I'm sorry? What?"

Harlan sways in front of me. His jawline is more pronounced with the shave. "I'm trying to be respectful here. But look at what you're working with. Because how that dress hugs you doesn't leave much to the imagination. Not saying it's a bad thing in your case, either."

I must be mistaken. Is my so-called colleague checking me out, or what?

"I... um... I'm not sure... if—"

"Don't have a coronary. I'm only thinking out loud. I will be a gentleman the whole night, I promise."

False alarm. "Please do."

We make our rounds together and check out the rest of the art displays—more abstracts, some straightforward art, and others being simply found pieces. Like half a rusty bike covered in colored glass beads.

Nothing crazy or out there like Harlan warned me about beforehand.

As we keep going, he points toward a particularly oblique piece hanging on the far wall—a splash of reds, oranges, and black lines that seem to fight each other for room. "Hmm. My guess is that they were focusing on exploring the fluidity of identity, the way we shift and flow like water, which is never fully fixed. You?"

Don't tell me he expects me to solve artwork like Sudoku all night. "That's only a long-winded way of saying it's a total mess."

"But not despair? The human condition? Or maybe the artist just took a tumble with his paint and said, *Fuck it.* Hell, it's even still dripping as we speak."

A laugh falls from my mouth faster than I can catch it. "Oh, definitely despair. I can almost taste the existentialism."

"So cynical."

"You started it." Patience, stop having so much fun this instant.

"There's only one way to really find out, you know," Harlan adds.

"There is?"

"Yup. Just relate to the masterpiece."

He grabs a wet paintbrush from the display table, aims at me, and—

Splat!

Gobs of paint land squarely on my shoulder. "Nice—you're officially part of the showing now!"

What an Asshole! "Harlan! I can't believe you! Shit, how am I supposed to get this—"

"Shh..." he interrupts, lightly peeling the paint off my sleeve—no different from a banana peel. Then he plucks a splatter from my cheek, and the static from his touch blooms even stronger between us. "If you're not feeling the wardrobe color change, no problem. But hold off on the freakouts and read the pamphlets more closely next time. Our artist used a liquid plastic they tweaked just right for their work. See? No injured party here."

"Ha-freaking-ha."

"Would it kill you to not take yourself so seriously, Okoye?" The rest of Harlan's face remains relaxed, but his mouth—

one corner tugging higher than the other—hints at devious happenings about to unfold. "Live a little."

I accept the task with an open mind. "Fine. Where to next?"

"How about this one?"

There's a monstrosity in the center of the room. A pile of discarded electronics bathed in red light and accompanied by an industrial fan that sounds like a dying goat. I don't want to seem rude, but I put my hands over my ears, anyway. "This is what we're calling creative these days?"

Harlan puts a reflective finger under his upper lip. "What about provocative?"

I shake my head, but I can't help my amusement over his inscrutable delivery. "Provocative to induce vomiting, maybe."

"Touché. It's mine."

I dig my grave as we speak. "Harlan, I am so sorry."

He feigns offense. "They can't always be winners."

"Forget what I said, okay? What do I know about art, anyway?"

"Stop it. Your blunt delivery is refreshing in this sensory overload. It's not for everybody. No big deal."

"Thanks?"

Oh.

I'm acutely aware of the tickle of his arm hair on mine as we scope through the maze of artistic wonders.

"Ooh, let's go in here!" I express, pointing at the psychedelic door.

"After you."

There's no way this is in the same building.

I see tight-roping topless women, who wave at us several feet above. An Asian tattoo artist with green hair actively works on a few people who form a line by a translucent tent.

"Kenji, what's good?!" he shouts out.

The tattoo artist, Kenji, looks up and gives a peace sign.

"Kenji Sato's gonna be famous one day. His tats are pretty sick."

"Did he do a few of yours?"

"A good forty percent of them. Known him for about two years."

There are people freestyle dancing in cages to music that clearly only plays in their heads. The other art enthusiasts mingle with each other while servers pass out what looks like blunts and acid stamps.

Without a doubt, this display is totally out there.

What in the *Mad Max* is going on?

"Told ya," Harlan says, reading my mind.

"I'm fine. Don't babysit me."

How does this place function without getting shut down? Do people really have a solid trust system here?

"Enhancer?" a server dressed as a raver asks us.

I shake my head, whereas Harlan reaches for a blunt.

"Do you mind?" he asks, looking at me.

I shouldn't babysit him, either. It's only fair. "Please, indulge."

"Cool. And thanks, Roxy."

Roxy twinkles and curtsies. "Ooh, she's new. What brings you to Jayson's dive? Come on! Dish it out and tell!"

Wow. With how lit up she is, there's a chance she might have helped herself to the complimentary party favors she's offering. Her pixie cut matches her animated personality.

"Hi, I'm Patience. You can see my art right outside the entryway," I say. I'm not exactly matching her energy.

Roxy turns and examines past the see-through sliding doors. Her skull-print corset dress exaggerates her hourglass figure. "How dynamic! Jayson's lucky to have found you."

"Thanks."

"Hell yeah, he is," Harlan joins in. "Sure you don't wanna take your fifteen and hang with us? No one gets my humor quite like you do, Foxy Roxy."

Roxy pulls off a remarkable feat by blushing through her heavy makeup.

Harlan McCandles, forever the charmer.

"Sorry—still on the clock, but I'll catch you two later. Text me and we'll figure it out!"

"You got it, babe."

She's gone, and I'm elated she takes her high zest with her.

We find a couch by the gallery and sit, taking in the realm of Jayson's art sanctum.

"I never told you, by the way"—Harlan takes a generous drag from his blunt—"how much your work sold for."

"Oooh, a couple hundred bucks?"

"Try a couple thousand, hun."

"Harlan, that's unbelievable," I say. "There's no way I'm that much of a rockstar. I only started yesterday; I'm no expert."

"You might be on to something... think he's only buying for a chance to sleep with you?"

I could wipe him off the face of the Earth. "You're not funny."

Harlan bites his lower lip in a roguish way. "Come on, I'm a riot." After another blunt drag, he tilts his head back, and he's suddenly Puff the Magic Dragon. "You're too easy to mess with. And stop selling yourself short. Let your artwork speak for you—you might be surprised by what it says."

I try to seem as cool as he does, but the only thing that comes to mind is him seeing right through it. "So, my art talks to people now?"

"Maybe not to everyone, but it does to me." Harlan nearly sucks every ember out of his blunt in one drag. "I hear you when you speak, you know."

"Thanks."

"You're welcome. So from now on, walk around here like what you put out into the world... has some goddamn significance to it."

Whoa. He might've been a motivational speaker in a past life. "And you're considered far from a novice on the artistic journey?"

"I know my shit, Sherlock."

"Then tell me what the *Shades of Okoye* speaks about."

"That she's finally willing and able to stop hiding behind her self doubt. Because in the end, it turns out she has way more to fucking say than she thought she did."

It's only now I realize how close he is to me. His knee rests against mine on and off, sending those same zaps through my skin. Harlan doesn't cease his concentration, so he has me bewitched.

"Sound about right, Patience?"

"Um..."

"Evening, all!" An abrupt interruption happens when Jayson approaches the middle of the room with a mic, and the house music stops. "Thanks again for your attendance and contributions. Means plenty. Hope we're all enhancing the night away!"

"Almost there, bud!" Harlan calls out. He puffs on his

enhancer of choice some more. While I'm feeling further and further out of place.

Jayson puts on a game show host smile, and suddenly he's appraising us as though we're pieces up for auction. "Security, make sure this guy doesn't leave with his keys, would you? Cavity searches are encouraged."

Harlan shoots Jayson both middle fingers from the crowd and snickers. "Trust me, man, you couldn't pay them enough to try!"

"D'aww, it's all in good fun, all in good fun! Tonight's performance is a dive into the beautiful mess of—well, the near misses and close calls in life. But hey, why only take it from me? Without further ado, please welcome The Sabines!"

"Wanna check it out?" I ask him.

"Sure."

We join the others observing the gallery floor.

The lights turn a dark blue—quieting the crowd. Dancers dressed in nude-colored leotards emerge from the shadows. Each one's body falls in tandem with the other. The dancers glide onto the stage with sheer surrender in the way they move. They give a leap of emotion, a tumble of life without holding back, like Jayson predicted.

"They're amazing!" I exclaim.

"Yeah, they're all right." Harlan's seen it all, supposedly.

The music swells, and there's a moment where the dancers reach for each other, but just as their fingers are about to meet, they're thrown back—trapped in an endless loop, caught in a cycle of wanting and retreating. This openness, willingness to share, is what I've been searching for. And suddenly, I sense the utter absence of it from watching.

"Hey, you okay?" Harlan asks, with his brow bent in a

bother.

Dammit. When the hell did I start crying? Shake it off, idiot!

"Ugh... Sorry. I–I don't know w-what's wrong with me..."

"Patience..."

"I don't usually—I'm fine, really. This... it's all so stu—"

"Hey."

"Hmm?"

"Just sit with it. You're good when you're with me, any-time." Harlan gives my palm the gentlest brush with his fin-gertips before clasping my hand fully—my left hand wearing my wedding ring. He dares me to be seen with him this way. "A little waterworks never hurt anybody. I don't scare that easily, kid."

"Thank you."

"I'm your safe space, remember?"

My ring is searing hot now, and I swear it threatens to burn my finger clean off.

Why can't it be my Obi instead, telling me what I've been dying to hear for forever? I want him to accept all of me—flawed, restless—and never be in a rush to leave when things get strained. It gets to me more than I thought it would, with last year looming nothing but dark times. Overall, I'm still waiting for my husband to meet me halfway. When I tried to share anything real, it was only met with a calm, polite nod or a swift change of topic. I need to break free while I'm still able. There's too much at stake I'm not willing to lose in a freakish art dungeon.

"On second thought, it's getting late, and I should start heading back. Seeing in-laws early tomorrow morning for church, then brunch. And if I'm late, I'll never hear the end of it. So, I figure it best I don't get blitzed out of my mind for the night.”

“No need for your life story, I get it. I’ll hang back here for a little longer and enjoy the free show,” Harlan says, letting go of my hand first. He eventually becomes distracted by the dancers. “Bet you could easily give them a run for their money if you tried.”

Again with the blurred, unblurred lines.

“Later, Harlan.”

I go for the sliding door exit to the Uber that awaits me, acting as the embrace of normalcy.

'TRY AGAIN'

It's a new day, yet I still have a hard time shaking Harlan's finicky messages out of my ears—doesn't mean I won't keep trying, though.

Even after the gloomy drive from Walmart, I arrive at my classroom in a decent mood—despite the crappy weather. Lightning and thunder usually bother my students, but not me. I welcome the Halloween-ish theme, hands down. My supplies for Grayson's NASA project clatter when I zoom through the door.

"Morning, everybody!" I chirp. "Who's ready for the morning meeting?"

A guarded presence touches everyone in class. Nyla has her head down at her desk with her knees bouncing. Dominick's face is wet and runny from mucus tears.

What the hell's going on?

Then I eventually spot Nadia, who also looks just as traumatized. "Ms. O—I think you need to sit down."

"Why, what is it?"

"Grayson passed away on Friday."

The ground grows uneven under my feet, and I crash into my seat. Not our Grayson. What is this!? What twilight zone is occurring here?

"How... how do you know?" I ask.

"Ms. Bell told us when you were absent. She said you might have had difficulty getting through it. So, she felt it would be easier if she broke the news instead—since you and Grayson are close. Or were close. Wait, I'm sorry. I didn't mean it like—"

"Why didn't anyone call, text, or email me?!"

"She did—we did, but we didn't hear from you."

Damn. I remember now. After the fiasco in Harlan's classroom, plus guilt from my painting lesson and the art show, I kept my work text/email notifications on silent for almost two days.

"It's fine; it's fine." I hush Nadia in response. I motion for her to come to the side of the classroom, out of the student's listening proximity. "What did he pass away from?"

Nadia's voice turns grave. "He apparently had a rare heart condition he inherited from his dad. It just stopped beating in the middle of the night; that's all his mom told us."

I hold on to the supplies I bought from Walmart with the stupid thought we were actually going to have fun building this together.

As if life actually gives a toasted shit about what plans you had in mind.

I take the bag and toss it into the wastebasket.

"Mrs. Okoye, what about the morning meeting?" Nadia questions.

But I'm gone. I run down the first grade hall, passing the gymnasium. My face is boiling as I curse God under my breath each step of the way.

* * *

A reluctant Principal Vicci approves my request to leave.

I take half a day, and I feel bad about it—grappling with not being able to get out of my car. Obinna is home, but I already know he won't be for long. It's his lunch hour.

I go inside and meet him at the kitchen island as he plays Fortnite on his Nintendo Switch.

"Hey. Did your school have a conference day?" he asks, not looking up from his game.

"No, it was a student."

Obinna zaps away at enemies but doesn't fully commit to our conversation. "Yeah, I'm listening."

Typical.

"Obi, I'm trying to talk to you."

"I know, Pat. I can multitask."

"My student is dead. Can you multitask on that?"

Obinna officially stops the game with an agonized look and embraces me. "Damn, I'm so sorry. Today?"

"No, on Friday," I answer. "But I found out today."

"That's terrible. Are you doing all right?"

"I'll be okay. I just can't be alone right now. Could you call in, have Priya take over, and watch episodes of *Castlevania* on Netflix with me? I need a good anime binge I haven't had in a while."

"Pat..."

"Don't make me finish this one without you, like I did with *JoJo's Bizarre Adventure*. Find time to spend with your better half, why don't you?"

Obinna withdraws from me again. He picks back up the Switch and retreats to a lack of care. "Wish I could, but that's way too short notice."

My increasing resentment toward him ramps up. I snatch

the Switch from him and toss it in the sink.

"What the hell?!" Obinna yells, trying to fish it out of a soaking pot. "Be an adult."

"Sorry, that's way too short notice for me."

"I know you're going through it, but you still have to be reasonable. I can't take off work whenever on a whim. That is not how my practice runs."

I give him a choleric stare. "Nuh-uh. Your schedule was never like this before, so what really changed?! There are millions of doctors who have boundaries with their practice. They're able to even have hobbies! You could call off if you wanted, but you're choosing not to. Hello? Ever hear of family emergencies?"

"No one in our family died!"

"Really, Obinna?" I ask, in outrage. "No one?"

Obinna steps back, agog in his expression. "Come on. I meant today. Why does everything always go back to—"

"Because it'll be a year since it happened, and we never talk about it! You're not home long enough to even try!"

"Are you having night terrors again?" His voice rises as distress bleeds into it. "I thought we fixed that a long time ago."

"No. You don't even—Jesus, I'm not broken!"

"That never came from my mouth. So, calm down."

I'm so damn tired of him needing to be practical during every conflict. "Are you actually going to make me beg for your company? You're making me feel like such a chore."

Obinna shrinks from my honesty. "It's just—"

"What?!"

"If you're going to make me say it, then I guess I'll say it. Patience, you just want entirely too much."

A cement brick plops in my gut. If this is him trying his best, then we have bigger problems than I thought. "Run to the fucking clinic, Obinna. I don't care anymore."

Obi stares at me as though he's missed the boat on something. "Was that really necessary?"

"This conversation no longer is."

I grab my stuff and nope on out of there.

* * *

After Obinna leaves, I stowaway in the den and stay glued to my phone the whole evening.

Neisa looked so beautiful in her maxi dress while visiting the Cayman Islands last year. I flip through her Instagram and see what she's up to. California has robbed me of my lifeline.

Call her. What's the worst that could happen?

Boop.

"Patience! Sissy, come out with us in Los Angeles!" Neisa's FaceTiming me and dancing with some random girls in the background of a super bright club. It's so loud I can barely hear myself think, with cloud rap blaring from all angles.

"Hey, uh—I don't know if now's the best time to—"

"Now's the perfect time! Shit, fill my cup, bitch!" She's trashed and definitely no help, with an abundance of cleavage spilling out of her form-fitting top. Meanwhile, her lit entourage is screaming in the background.

Guess Malcolm's in charge of diaper duty at this hour. It's Mommy's night out.

"Nei, can you hear me?"

A woman with a blond buzz cut, snatches her phone.

"Neisa's gone, girl!"

Then hangs up.

It's true. Friends don't really hit the same after college, or marriage, with a boatload of kids. You just kind of socialize through text or the good old world wide web and make promises to get together that never happen.

Neisa checks all the boxes with her husband, newborn, and new beginnings. And I don't.

Which is another reason I pull away from my almost sister, despicably.

Sadly, she's not my first choice, anyway. I need paint. I need the therapeutic touch of a fresh canvas. Ugh. No—no I shouldn't. I'll only be a nuisance to him, too. A pest who doesn't know when to say when.

I wish I knew how to exist without overwhelming others with my problems.

Harlan's Instagram illuminates in my hands.

It's okay. Take a deep breath, stop putting off the inevitable, and just ask him.

* * *

@PatOkoye: hey

@McCandlesRealismTM: howdy

@PatOkoye: we're friends, right?

@McCandlesRealismTM: I believe we've reached up to that caliber, yes

@PatOkoye: ok

@McCandlesRealismTM: anything else?

@PatOkoye: I want to pick your brain about a problem.

@McCandlesRealismTM: that's a first

@PatOkoye: it's been a day

@McCandlesRealismTM: at ten past midnight? Someone is feeling nocturnal

@PatOkoye: Someone is tired of sitting around an empty house with no one to listen to her

@McCandlesRealismTM: ahh hubby ain't home? I'm getting the second choice jitters

@PatOkoye: don't take it to heart.

@McCandlesRealismTM: Coming from you that means plenty

@PatOkoye: I need to get some heavy stuff off my chest. Work was a lot.

@McCandlesRealismTM: maybe I can help. My dad was a psychiatrist

@PatOkoye: Woah

@McCandlesRealismTM: Don't sound so shocked

@PatOkoye: so he's no longer practicing?

@McCandlesRealismTM: He died when I was twelve. Car accident.

@PatOkoye: I'm sorry

@McCandlesRealismTM: it wasn't your fault

@PatOkoye: I never know what else to say with stories like that

@McCandlesRealismTM:I hear worse stories at my second job

@PatOkoye: oh yeah?

@McCandlesRealismTM: I bartend at the club Markos in downtown Dallas some nights. It's an okay place; can't text or make calls for shit though. Phone signal's never reliable once you're inside.

@PatOkoye: oh I didn't know that

@McCandlesRealismTM: now you do

@PatOkoye: lol Professor McCandles and Harlan the Bartender are one hell of a dynamic duo.

@McCandlesRealismTM: You can say the same thing about us, friend-o

@PatOkoye: thanks, friend-o

@McCandlesRealismTM: could a friend-o use a distraction if they're up for driving?

@PatOkoye: like to come to your place?

@McCandlesRealismTM: sure. Come on over to Casa McCandles. I'm working on a detailed marbling abstract and could use all hands on deck.

@PatOkoye: All hands on deck, huh?

@McCandlesRealismTM: mhmm

@PatOkoye: Share your address and I'll be on my way in 5

* * *

Go back, go back, go back.

I knock on Harlan's door, unsure of anything anymore. Obinna being emotionally stunted doesn't help in the least or make these feelings any less confusing. Facing McCandles is the only way out. Maybe he's got guilty feelings, too.

Yeah, okay, Patience. My logic for showing up here wilts over and over.

But then I think back to Grayson, and the waterworks are back on again.

The door creaks open a smidge, and Harlan is happy to see me. "Took you long enough. Any longer and the pizza I ordered would've been free, lady."

But after seeing my tear-smeared face, his jokes are obsolete.

"Woah, Patience. I'm sorry. You okay? Stupid, of course not. Come in."

I trudge inside his studio apartment. "Something happened at work," I sputter. "Something bad."

"Yeah, like what?" Harlan asks. He motions me over to the futon and signals to sit by him.

Rather than sitting right away, I check out his studio. I can't tell if we're in Texas or Manhattan, with his industrial appliances and concrete polished touches. It's impressive, to say the least, accompanied by his abstracts. There are also miniature art fixtures on his coffee table. They are sepia-clay figurines of misshapen bodies reaching above, dancing or shielding from an unknown threat.

"How long have you lived here?"

"Oh." Harlan shakes his head, and sighs. "Three or four years, give or take. Rip off, if you ask me—everyone hears your business left and right. Privacy is dogshit here. The location is why I stay since almost everything's a walk away. But uh—you good?"

My feet shift my weight from side to side, cowering with what I know.

I know when I go a day without seeing Harlan, I'm physically ill.

Harlan grows tired of the quiet and lets out an enormous yawn. I forget it's late and me being here must be inconveniencing him. He walks over to where I stand and brings me back to the looming present. He then towers over me in a protective stance. "No matter how bad it is, no situation is ever permanent."

I sniff. "That's what I'm afraid of."

"What are you wanting to avoid by being here?"

"My student died."

"Hell, that's awful."

"My student died, and my husband barely gave a shit."

Harlan doesn't even flinch. He waits for me, like always... Restoring the meaning to my name. So, I keep going.

"You got to me before, when you mentioned digging in my heels when I'm uncomfortable. I have a hard time relating to others sometimes, okay? Kids or students I can manage, but I don't get people. In most of my interactions with them, I'm just going through the motions, without substance. So, if I came off as stand-offish or whatever before, it wasn't intentional."

Harlan goes back to recline on the futon and dissects me, as the studio seems smaller now. "I hear you. So, come sit."

With me sitting beside him, we're as close as we were back at Taos lounge. That same knee of his, which touches mine, elicits a shameful admission—he's certainly more than a *friend-o.*

"But you're wrong."

"About what, Harlan?"

"Relating to people. I got you the first day we met."

I grow heavy and recline back on the futon with him. Sharing a bed for now is harmless.

"After the classroom visit, I thought you wouldn't like me anymore," I confess.

"May I?"

"Mhmm."

Harlan plays with my braids as they lay against his satin sheets. Normally, I'd be against it—hating to be on display— but he does it in a way that feels as natural as our hand-holding in Taos. "Well, damn, I need to work on my game then, because I've been dropping hints like nobody's business. What's not to like? You're an enigma, Okoye."

"I've been told that I... I want too much."

"Like want things? Or like—being too clingy?"

"Clingy."

"Ah."

I turn on my side and watch his lamp light hit the strands of his hair. It gives it a glassy texture. "What do you think?"

"I think..." Harlan lets out airily. "Wanting... makes you human. It's a hell of a shame we forget that too often."

I was fine until Harlan woke up whatever it is inside of me. Or maybe I wasn't—and instead, he was showing me what true fulfillment really looks like.

"Grayson's gone..." I say, quivering as tears continue to spill. "And even though my husband chose not to give a shit, now I feel like shit... because he wasn't the first person I wanted to tell to begin with."

"Really?"

"Now—after saying it out loud—I hear how ridiculous that sounds. I should go. Right?"

It's out now. The unsaid. There's no denying it anymore— no more word plays, scenarios, or hypotheticals.

I own the fact I look forward to his attention.

But now, he's back in his head.

"Harlan?" My insides are churning. Is he freaked? Turned off? "Don't hang me to dry. What is it?"

He says nothing for a while, and I squirm from his piercing gaze that seems to swallow me whole. "What would you like me to do... with what you just said?" he finally asks.

"I... well..."

"I see. So, we're no longer feeling amorous. Don't sweat it. You can say you were simply hurting or delirious from lack of sleep and take it back."

"Is that what you want me to do?" I ask, crestfallen.

"It's not up to me."

I want to die. As tone deaf as it is, I pray to be disintegrated from the face of the Earth, to forget this ever happened. And he couldn't care less.

But I can still redeem myself with—

"Um, where's the marbling abstract that you needed me for?"

Harlan stretches on the bed and doesn't answer, glancing at his bedside lamp. Great, he's fully over whatever this is now. I should leave. So—my feet make their way to his front door.

"Disappointing," he sneers. "You're not even gonna put up a fight?"

Is he being for real? "I don't know."

"For once—just go for it, girl. And if it's me... Well shit, I'm right here..." Harlan comes over, pulling me into his embrace, and I seep into him. "What happens next? I wonder, will you spend the next hour driving home or on another lesson on self-expression?"

I'm here, with another man who says he has all the answers but doesn't even know the first of my endless questions. But the magnitude of Harlan's presence, his tantalizing allure, is enough for me to stay put.

"But what about the abstract—"

"Jesus, there *is* no abstract, Patience. Focus. Focus and own your want. You want this."

"I want this?"

"You want me."

"I—no!" He cannot think that's all it's gonna take to turn me. "I don't want to want you, don't you get it?!"

"You're shaking. Has it really been that long since... you had him cling to your skin?"

"Harlan, please stop talking."

"Make me."

Harlan's whispers sit on my hesitant shoulders as he buries his face into my neck. Those same chills from before expel throughout me, strong and ceaseless.

"When you're holding back, it hurts pretty damn good. I was only waiting until you were ready—ready for what I have in store to teach you."

This is the part where I should get out.

I should.

I'm supposed to.

But... but not.

And he's noting it.

"I'm not your little abandoned housewife. I just came to paint." My hand is on the doorknob.

"Try again," he whispers, stubble scratching my cheek. "And stop lying to yourself. You're here, but it was never about finishing any artwork, and you know that."

"I don't know what I was thinking. I'm a good person." If I say it enough, it might come true. Mustn't forget to click my heels three times.

"Why settle for being a good person when you can be a person with depth? But I'm only going to say it one last time. Try again. I'm done making these types of choices for you."

His hands, god—his hands. They go over my hips and travel up my back. "I only wanted to forget about today."

Harlan smolders. "Not possible. I leave a lasting impression."

Harlan's lips press against mine with a tender touch at first, with my head cradled in his arms, tattoos meshing with my bare skin. His mouth is fresh—a geyser bringing life to dry terrain. "If you're going to use me, sweetness... at least let me know what for."

Sensations crash and ebb as I'm going insane from his caresses. "Teach me... teach me how to want... and how to feel again, Harlan."

"About goddamn time." Harlan lifts me up and holds me against the wall as I wrap my legs around his waist. "Did you mean all of what you said before?"

God, did I ever. But at what cost? "Of course."

"So, don't question what comes next. I wanna see you in my sheets. Now." Harlan smiles and brings me onto his bed, making his way back down my body again.

Tonguing down my neckline, he creeps along with his fingers... past my chest... past my belly button... past my... holy shit.

He locks me in his hold and flips me onto my stomach.

There, I'm denied to see what takes place next. Harlan hovers between my legs and teases under my skirt, breathing me in and out. Not like a paper bag, but gentle puffs that compare to inhaling ether. I bury my face in a pillow, gladly welcoming the igniting temperatures, then arch my back in response. My panties peel off. Harlan's tongue explores inside of me, encasing titillation with the warmth enhancing his mouth.

It's already too much.

"I'm gonna pass out... give me a second..."

I try to pull away, but he's undeniably stronger and grips me back in place with little effort, gulping me among his groans.

The ache only intensifies, and I lose my mind. A scream that sounds nothing like me follows, and then I collapse.

"Seems like you needed that. Still with me?"

"Mhmm."

He strips off the rest of my outfit, and I position myself on the bed. Soon comes the pressure of Harlan slipping himself inside me.

"Christ... you're well worth the wait, beautiful."

Harlan works his body over mine and sends convulsions throughout the both of us. He studies my shuddering breath and grips the headboard to stabilize himself as he mounts me wildly with clear gratification.

"You've sealed your fate, Patience."

"What?"

"I... inhabit you now..." he declares. "... and no one else."

"Uh..." My power weakens with each syllable, with each thrust.

"...Say it."

"...Say it?"

"Say. It." Harlan bites the tenderest part of my breast, and I almost go cross-eyed. "Say it, or I'll stop fucking you, and you'll never feel this alive again."

That scares me to no end. The valleys of euphoria that erupt become an overwhelming necessity. So much so, I relinquish everything.

"...Fine."

"Fine, what?"

"I'm yours."

We both climax and lay defeated on each other. Harlan turns

over, kisses the nape of my neck, and cuddles me from behind. I reach for his bedside light to—

"Leave it on." Harlan covers my hand over his and squeezes me in closer.

"Why?"

"I don't hide in the dark... and neither does my muse."

* * *

It's a new morning. Sun rays peep in, which makes everything look heavenly—even though what occurred yesterday was not. The fallout is what I want to avoid, but there is no excuse. I can't say who I became last night, shedding my skin and ridding myself of the woman I once was.

Meanwhile, the tattooed vampire artist basks in slumber.

I face Harlan in bed beside me, his solid chest rising and falling with each breath. His tattoos look more pronounced from the angle he lays across from me. Tousled hair falls across his forehead, and a faint smile tugs at the corners of his lips as I brush it aside.

Then, like a damn jack-in-the-box, Harlan's eyes pop right open. There's a look of confusion, quickly replaced by recognition, as he realizes I'm still here. Before I can say a word, Harlan's hand reaches out to cup my cheek and pulls me closer until our lips meet in a lingering kiss.

Save me.

"You stayed," he says as he props himself up. "Thought I might have spooked you off."

"Not yet."

"Well, then—good girl."

His studio is lovely to wake up to. Despite everything else.

Wooden grids dividing the glass on his windows break the sunlight into dozens of beams that stretch as the sun rises higher. Natural lighting hits each canvas differently. They reveal textures in the paint, brushstrokes patterns, and throwing the finer details into stark relief.

"Do the dozens of well-established women you've been with typically stay the night?" I ask.

"If they're gratified by my technique, I suppose."

Hmm, now he's just showboating.

"Was Roxy from Taos one, too?"

Harlan chuckles louder than expected. "A bold assumption. And an incorrect one, at that."

"Technically, I assumed nothing—only asked."

"She's cute, but there's not much there past cute." He scoops me back under him. "But would it bother you... if she shared sheets with me too?"

"Not sure if—forget about it. I ought to head out soon, before... Well, before he wakes up."

Pitiful. As if not saying Obinna's name out loud makes this easier to accept.

My brown body moves around in his sheets aimlessly as I attempt to leave his bed. But Harlan takes a proprietorial hold on my arm.

"Stay," he whispers. Tenacity laces in his voice. "I thought we could paint another abstract—call it a personal day and come up with more core colors." He licks and kisses my inner collarbone before he finishes. "Actually, I found a few last night."

"Did you?"

"Yes. Like Pinwheels of Cadmium, radiating the way you scream my name when you think no one's listening. I'm guessing he can't reach inside you the way I can—all the way to the pit of your ribcage, making you voice more of those long-buried illicit wants."

How does he come up with this stuff? "Come on, quit."

"But if you'd rather go back home to the man who dims your spirit, go right ahead," Harlan reprimands. "So, take your pick."

My feelings get hurt, and I wind away from his arms. "I'm married, and it's a commitment."

"Oh, really? No shit. So, tell me, what's it like to settle with someone who starves you daily of what I graciously gave you last night? And before you deny it, Patience, I felt every bit of that starvation in your cries, scratches, and bites. You're a woman who craves and craves hard. But I don't mind. I'll feed you at all hours of the day if I have to."

Harlan's words hit like a punch to the gut, reopening wounds I thought had long since healed. The memory of the big IT that happened, Obinna's distant silence in the aftermath—I can't switch them off... as our tryst plays on a loop in my head.

I cheated on my husband—my best friend since I was nineteen years old. I'm not someone this sort of thing happens to!

And for the likes of Harlan McCandles, no less.

"Look, I don't know if I'll—"

"So are you saying last night wasn't enough... that I wasn't enough?" he insists, pressing for an answer.

I've gotta make crucial amends.

"I have to go. I'm so sorry."

"Okay."

I get up, then get embarrassed when the sheets drop to the

floor to reveal me in the nude. I swear I see Harlan do a double take.

"He's a lucky son of a bitch," Harlan comments.

I grow increasingly uncomfortable. "Bye, Harlan."

"Bye, Mrs. Okoye."

* * *

By the time I got home to take a quick shower before heading to Seabrook, I found four bite marks. One on my neck, right breast, and both inner thighs. Seriously, Harlan?

I couldn't even wash him off. I stood under scalding water and scrubbed my skin until raw, but the marks he left—the faint red imprints of his teeth, like cursed gifts I couldn't return—stayed. My nails left scratches as they dragged over each bite, but the water wouldn't drown out his echoes, calling my name.

I thought work would distract me enough to get by, but not a chance. What made me offer myself up on a platter to him like that? Before Harlan, Obinna was the only guy I'd ever been with sexually. I was curious about certain experiences before but never enough to consider cheating.

I took what McCandles offered, and now it's the thing I can't put back. One choice, one night—Pandora's Box was unlocked, each bruise a reminder of what I unleashed—all impossible to wipe clean.

Dammit, who am I fooling?

The fault lies with Pandora.

Not with her box.

"Ms. O!"

No more dwelling. Back to work.

"Mrs. Okoye, can I have Grayson's old desk?" asks Dominick, with an Oreo smushed in his mouth. "Since he's not coming back and stuff?"

And here's another situation I can't even deal with. "Your seat is perfectly fine, Dominick. I suggest you find it before we start our morning meeting. Now."

"Ugh, no fair. It's not like he needs it anymore!"

Is everyone trying to test me today?

"Here's an option. Walk away before I take a privilege away."

"Fine, geez."

"Ms. O, you ready?" Nadia asks from the kidney table.

"Sure, coming, Ms. Gomez."

My walk to the front of the room is long, due to not wanting to state the sad fact Grayson is no more. Once it's said, there's no longer room for denial.

"Morning, everyone," I say in a neutral voice. "Today's meeting is going to be a little different."

"How come you're saying *morning* instead of *good morning* like you usually do?" Nyla questions, scratching her ankles on her desk.

"Feet down. Today's meeting is going to have more of a serious tone to it, that's why. So, let's talk and reflect for a second. Grayson passed away. We all know that now, right?"

"Right."

"Uh-huh."

"So, we're going to use today to reflect on how we feel about that respectfully. He wasn't in our class for very long, but he deserves to be addressed. Questions?"

Dominick tucks his elbows into his shirt. "Does it hurt to die?"

"That's more of a parent question than a teacher question," I safely avoid. "I mean, questions about Grayson specifically? Like maybe how we're feeling now that he's gone?"

Nyla picks her nose and wipes it on her two sizes too small T-shirt. "Kinda sad. We didn't talk that much, but I really liked his pictures. He almost finished drawing all the main Marvel characters. Grayson hadn't drawn Wolverine yet, and now he won't get to."

I admire Nyla's feedback and walk to her desk, caringly squeezing her shoulder. "Thank you for sharing such a sweet memory. I'm sure Grayson would appreciate it."

"No, he wouldn't." Dominick rebuffs. "I'm sorry, Mrs. Okoye, but Grayson was a jerk."

I was afraid this would happen. "Dom, you seemed pretty sad when you found out about it."

"I changed my mind."

"You can't say that. He isn't alive anymore!" screams Nyla.

"Just because someone is dead, it doesn't make them any less of a jerk. He was never nice to me or anybody else. He was even mean to you, Ms. O!"

"Dominick, I understand you feel strongly about Grayson. But let's chalk it up to you two getting off on the wrong foot. It doesn't mean he was a bad person. It only means trying to see things from his point of view."

"I liked Josh more. He was cool and played with me more than stupid Grayson did. Why did he have to go to another school, anyway? I mean, he only had one bad day here. I miss him."

"He hit Ms. O so hard... she fell over," Nyla looks up from her fidget toy with a sorrowful gaze. "That's why he had to leave. I was there."

The subject of Josh Brinks wears me down way more than anything Harlan could ever accomplish. Josh, a scrawny kid with square-framed glasses and ash-blond hair, had Intermittent Explosive Disorder. He was a student who I thought made huge progress with us... until the day he didn't.

"Hello?" Nyla jolts me back. "Ms. O?"

I pause and search their faces, trying to see if any of them can see the truth lurking beneath my demeanor. My hands instinctively move to my stomach, but I stop myself and force them back into my lap. "Josh had some big feelings that were too much for him to handle, and he needed a different kind of support. But we're getting off topic."

"Well, I don't care, and this morning meeting is dumb." Dominick runs off to climb the bookshelves again.

What a shitty start to our morning. "Nadia, sorry—Ms. Gomez—if you don't mind—"

"Way ahead of you!" She flies over to Dominick and takes him under her wing to calm him down.

My back pocket rings, and I quickly check my phone to see that Obinna has called twice. I gotta get back to him. This morning meeting is going nowhere, anyway.

"All right, friends, we're going to put a pin in this for now and pick up where we left off tomorrow. In the meantime, let's begin our independent warm-up for social studies. Nadia, I'll be right back. I'm just going to go to the teachers' lounge for coffee."

"No problem. I got it handled, Ms. O," Nadia says, reading to a de-escalated Dominick at the book nook corner.

Handled, she does.

Rather than make a beeline to the teacher's lounge, I go to the school parking lot to sit in my car and call Obinna. Okay, come on with it. Please pick up so I can get Harlan off my mind. His invisible hooks bury deeper with each unanswered ring.

"Hey, Pat. Everything okay?" Obi sounds out of breath when he answers.

"Yeah, I'm good. I was just returning your call." Harlan's bites singe through my lies.

He's everywhere.

"Right. Where were you this morning? I got back around five, and you weren't home."

"I was grading work on campus. I told you I can't concentrate the same way if I grade papers at home."

"Does your campus building even open that early?" Obinna asks in an iffy tone. "And you only have two to three students—do they get that much of a workload to begin with?"

Curse him for being so observant. "I also hit up Planet Fitness before then. Feeling like I'm getting out of shape lately."

"I don't mind your shape."

Unexpected turn, but I'll take it. "Hmm, maybe I don't mind you telling me you don't mind my shape."

"When's your lunch break? I wanna see you, and your shape, in person." Something tells me he's not having this conversation with Priya nearby.

"Eleven AM," I answer. "Think that's enough time?"

"We'll get creative. I miss you, and I'm sorry about yesterday—really."

Dammit. He just had to choose to be loving now, huh? "Obi, I miss you, too."

I sure have a funny way of showing it.

"Baby, I gotta go." Obi's line resounds with barking dogs. "Downtime is over. Can't wait for eleven AM."

"Me, too. Love you."

"You, too."

It's decided. I have to end things with Harlan today. It's not a perfect fix, but I gotta start somewhere. My fingers scroll through Instagram and type away.

@PatOkoye: Harlan

@McCandlesRealismTM: Hey Beautiful

@PatOkoye: I can't see you anymore

@McCandlesRealismTM: is that so?

@PatOkoye: yes. It's not ethical "to belong to you" or whatever

@McCandlesRealismTM: you bought that? I was talking in the heat of the moment is all

@PatOkoye: still...what we did—what I did—was wrong, and it stops with me

@McCandlesRealismTM: okay. Heard you loud and clear

@PatOkoye: All it was supposed to be about was painting, nothing else. And now it's gone too far. In the beginning, it was easier to ignore because nothing happened. Yet.

@McCandlesRealismTM: you're really still working on that sales pitch aren't ya?

@PatOkoye: But now something happened and it can't be undone, no matter how you want to reword it.

@McCandlesRealismTM: remember, you came to me yesterday

@PatOkoye: I know. And I'll have to live with that decision for the rest of my life

@McCandlesRealismTM: Patience

@PatOkoye: what

@McCandlesRealismTM: stop explaining yourself and sign the fuck off. When you change your mind, you know where I live

@PatOkoye: I won't

@McCandlesRealismTM: time will tell

* * *

I wriggle on the faux leather couch and wait for my therapist, Angela, to start. She's pensive as she fiddles with her lime-green glasses and taps onto her notepad. We both know the last visit didn't end well... discussing the baby that could have been and the night terrors that came with it. Obinna thought it was a good idea to see her after the failed pregnancy, only to dip out himself. But it's a new day, and things have long changed.

"Welcome back, Patience!" she starts. "I'm excited for you to embark on your journey to healing."

"Yeah, okay."

Angela's wavy black hair frames her simple, oval face. "Let's start with a positive. Since we last spoke, what would you like to share?"

I actually have one to share. "I stopped having nightmares about... finding the—you know. Everywhere."

"That's good."

"It is. I didn't sleep for a week while having them." I suddenly find myself talking really fast. "Having dreams of accidentally stepping in it within the floorboards, finding it in my cereal, in my hair. Nowhere was safe."

Angela lets out a dull hum. "Can you say the actual word out loud, Patience? Or would you like me to?"

Hmm. I couldn't before. Suppose I can now. "The remains of my miscarriage."

"How does that feel?"

"Don't know yet. Um—can we not?"

"All right. Let's start with a simple check in. What's new?"

Circling back to the teacher conference, I could've even showed up late or pulled a flat tire excuse and made no beeline toward Harlan whatsoever, but stars align on their own schedule.

"So, um, I slept with someone who wasn't Obinna, and now he's all I think about. I need your help to get me to stop."

Angela's mouth scrunches to the side. "Yes, we can tackle that for sure. But we—you—are going to have moments where you'll delve into the prickly parts of why. And I'm here to help you analyze them."

My breath quickens at the thought of opening myself up like a cat's cradle, to rehash the moment I gave in to Harlan.

Angela turns to a blank page and clicks her pen from the side. "I see you have bright new bangles today," she says, mentioning my bracelets. "Quite stylish."

"Thanks. I got these from our trip to Mexico four years ago. They were missing for a while, but I found them in the attic yesterday and thought, why not?"

"True growth in these sessions is to reflect on the underlying meaning behind the bangles someday."

"Not today, Angela," I reply, hotly.

"Well then, anytime you're ready."

It's not too late to bounce and get a frosty from Wendy's.

"It's laughable when you think about it. My mom doesn't

fail to remind me, *'Patience, stay on your toes because Obinna could always do better if he wanted to.'* And look at what I end up doing on top of that."

"Sounds like your mother may have preconceived notions about who you are as a person."

I play with the fidget spinner on the coffee table. "Joy Abara always sees my dad in me. So, I never started off on a great playing field with her."

"Meaning?"

"She uses me to groan about all the wrongs she committed in her life by marrying him—not finishing school and settling on being an x-ray tech rather than an OB/GYN, having me too young, etc. It's like my mother talks at me instead of to me. Then my dad or Franklin, cheated on her, started a new family, and never looked back. Maybe she wasn't far off."

"It must be discouraging to feel dismissed by a parent."

"I'm used to it."

Angela hastily gets up to grab her tea from her desk. "Pardon me, I need my ginseng break, otherwise I won't make it through the day." She takes a sip and presses on. "What was your childhood like growing up with her?"

I chew on the inside of my lip. "Like dodging landmines. Landmines that scream in your face when you're already terrified of getting your period at twelve, because you smeared their brand new couch. Or landmines that threaten to send you back to Nigeria if the dishes aren't spotless."

"I'm so sorry that happened to you. What role did your father play when that would arise?"

"The same role as the Tooth Fairy or Santa. I haven't seen or heard from him since I was eight. Makes sense now that he has a family he actually wants. He went from being the guy who'd pour my orange juice every morning to not being there anymore."

Seeing how everything turned out when Dad left Mom, Dad won the sport of a true do-over in the end.

"He would make me laugh with shadow puppets when I was scared to go to sleep. He loved Eddie Murphy movies and let me watch them with him, even with the swear words. Our main thing was dancing. We'd put on Bunny Mack records and just spin around the living room. I loved it. I was free. If you let my mom tell it, Dad apparently spoiled me. Thanks to her, she finally drove him off. The reminders he never provided enough for us eventually broke him."

Angela nods at every anecdote, with tea slurps in between. "Both your father and the treasured thing you two shared— gone. Double whammy."

"It was. Dad left, and it was like someone ripped the music out of my life. I think he wanted nothing to mess up his fresh start, including me. I'm my mother's daughter, after all. It was easier to tell people he died—so they would stop asking where he was. You can't blame a dead dad for not being able to raise their kid, right?"

"Suppose so."

"The last thing he ever left me were some plastic rainbow bracelets that came with a McDonald's Happy Meal. I wore them everyday till they bent out of shape. Then... kept replacing them over the years." My current bangles clink sadly at the memory. "God, I'm such a cliche."

"Those bracelets may be the link to feel rather close to your father again. Even a simple rattle from them can be self soothing—a reason for your reliance on them, that is." Angela's words were a spotlight on the grimy reality of my days.

"I get how people could see it that way."

"Did you have any people to go to during those hurtful periods? Pardon the pun."

"Thanks, Angela." I snigger. "Needed a laugh to save me from being a Debbie Downer. Yeah, I had some friends who came and went. But who I really had was my best friend, Neisa, and, well, Obi."

"What presence does your husband have in your life currently?" Angela pushes her glasses up her nose for the fifth time. "For example, is it consistent, infrequent, or spontaneous?"

"Absent. Like... like we're roommates that pass by each other every other weekday. Except, this roommate constantly breaks promises. Yesterday—Obinna was supposed to come see me during his lunch break to make up for a fight we had the day before. Here I was thinking—my only worry was to explain Harlan's hickeys away. But I made my way to the house, only to have him text me ten minutes before we were supposed to meet that *something came up, so please don't hate me and let's reschedule.* What could I do? I was already home!" I see Angela's back to scribbling on her notepad. "God, something always comes up. I'm so sick of it."

"And forgive me for the next question possibly being an obvious one, but... have you tried to bring that to his attention?"

"Obi just buries himself in more patients. He says he's an emergency eye veterinarian, so he's gonna work long crazy hours. Telling myself that, I guess—it's my way of dealing. My question is: How much of it is really outside of his control, and how much of it is he willingly seeking?"

Angela rests her manicured fingernails on her lap. "You presume Obinna is intentionally avoiding you."

I look away from her, eyeing the water cooler. "What's hilarious is, if I would have suspected our marriage would have an issue with cheating, I thought he'd be the culprit before me."

Angela puts her notepad on the coffee table and places her hands together as if she's praying. "Why?"

"His co-worker and longtime best friend, Priya."

"So, could we see the closeness as possibly threatening?"

Well, not anymore.

"It's how long they knew each other. I can't stand that she knows another part of him I didn't experience. Like their time in STEM club together back in high school, and how they grew up as neighbors. Priya relates to him in ways I don't—like being a doctor. But whatever. I'm dealing with it my way."

Angela's head wrap unravels slightly with each movement, then she takes my hand and whispers, "But that's just it, Patience. You're not dealing with it. After sleeping with the other—"

"Harlan." I let go of her hand, knowing I can't unring that bell. "I met him at a professional development training event for work."

"So, you're coworkers?"

"Not exactly." Imagining Harlan flipping his shit in a classroom like mine, I doubt he'd be able to keep up with Nyla's OCD and Dominick's manic episodes. "But we both work in an educational setting at different campuses."

Angela nods, then writes frantically and leaves no room for error. She switches her face from ruminant to studious while she maps the chapters of my life. "So, why him?"

"Huh?"

"Why select Harlan as your outlet in order to illustrate your desires for more? Does he represent certain opportunities where Obinna may fall short?"

Hmm. There's no way to say it without being outright heartless to Obinna. So, I won't. "I don't know."

"Well, let's start at the top layer, shall we? You're attracted to him. Why is that?"

God, enough already.

"Harlan is attractive, but it's more than looks. It's what he teaches me with his artwork... and what I'm now doing with mine. I never knew I had it in me. He makes me look forward to stuff again."

I can almost make out a pretend lightbulb that switches on in Angela's head.

"That's more than enough of a beguiling reason."

"But it's not the point of why I'm here—why I came back to you," I say curtly. I'm not interested in why she wants to know the specifics of Harlan so badly. I don't share my last name with him, so what the hell? "Look, I want to erase it—the ongoing desire to do it again. I'm not the type of person who commits adultery and goes to sleep just fine. I'm a neurotic mess, and there's only so much I can take."

Angela hands me tissues. "I empathize with you, Patience. I really do, but it's like I said. We're going to face some un-comfortable questions about our actions and about ourselves. So, let's stop here and pick this up next session. Okay?"

If I can make it that long.

A NIGHT AT MARKOS

Upside: it's a full moon, and Obinna wants to go out tonight. Downside: Priya and a potential date are coming, too. I was initially happy my husband finally heard me and agreed to take me out. But that went straight down the toilet bowl when all Priya had to do was bat those eyelashes and he caved to a double date. When going out with them in the past, it's always been tricky when my partner's the life of the party, and I'm the tag along. For one, Obinna still freaking keeps in touch with his friends from sixth grade summer camp, whereas the number of contacts in my phone says plenty. They have their own cliques, but I don't. And I can't remember when that became a thing.

But Downtown Dallas, here we come.

Hey, it's a start.

Ding dong.

I answer the door, and both Priya and Darrian—Obinna's friend from high school—are waiting on the porch.

"Patience, you look gorgeous!" Priya gushes, though I'm not sure what to do with myself.

"Thanks, you, too," I say. "Please, come in."

But that's not true. I'm not gorgeous; Priya is. She's petite, with a heart-shaped face and pretty cinnamon skin... way out of Darrian's league.

"Hey, fam, what up? What up?" Obinna hugs both of his buds.

Darrian pats him on the back. "Sorry, man, we would've been here earlier, but P held us up looking for an outfit to wear. I told her this ain't the Met Gala but—"

"Hey, unlike some people, I don't have a closet overflowing with enough clubwear to clothe a small EDM festival," Priya says as she smiles at me.

"You pre-gaming, fam?" Darrian points at the wet bar.

"Depends on what we got left, sorry. Haven't restocked in a while," Obinna admits quietly.

"Where we heading to first?" asks Darrian, scrolling through his Android phone. "Lot of what's nearby looks dead."

"Avia's?" I ask. "It's a thirty-minute drive but usually has a decent turnout."

"You mean it *had* a good turnout." Darrian shows me pictures on his screen. "Burned down three weeks ago. Electrical fire."

"Well, damn," Obinna responds after taking a shot. "Guess that's out. Looks like I'm low on Jim Beam, too. Not off to a great start for the night."

"Stella Verde?" I toss in another option.

"Nah, it's a gay bar now," Darrian says.

"So?"

"Hard pass, *chica*."

"I concur." Obinna grins.

"Oooooh! Obinna, what about Markos?" Priya proposes. "The new spot downtown? My friends from spin class say it's worth going to. It's chill, you know? Not a club that tries too hard. And their drinks are actually pretty good."

Markos?! The universe does not want me to pull through. Like at all.

"Um, I don't know. It seems kinda gimmicky." I try to divert.

Change their minds at every turn.

"It does?" Priya asks with a scrunched up nose. "The pics on Google reviews look legit."

"Yo, I wanna try the Tiki Tipsy Punch Bowl. Who's down?" Darrian asks.

"Us!" Obinna and Priya raise their hands high.

"Sorry, baby, he had me at the Tiki Tipsy Punch Bowl," Obinna finalizes.

Mission aborted. Shit.

Perfect. Priya: 1, Patience: 0.

* * *

I haven't talked to him in forever. But I try DMing Harlan to warn him several times before we arrive, but none of the messages go through.

Oh, that's right.

He mentioned the place had shitty phone service.

So, I'm doomed.

The place is low-key giving a *Little Mermaid* vibe, with the LED lights glowing beach theme colors. Hmm, what abstract art can I make out of all the apparent gaudiness?

We push through Markos's crowd and music.

"Ugh, no. Not Pop Smoke. He is so tired. Not to mention— uh, dead," Priya complains as we walk in.

"It's the first song, girl," Darrian says. He puts up his ID once we're inside. "I'm sure they'll play a sitar slow jam at some point."

"Oh, get fucked!"

"Anytime, my spicy little mango."

"Stop flirting so we can find seats," Obinna directs. "Let's try over here."

As we make our way past the bar, I spot Harlan across the room. He locks eyes with me, and those invisible hooks of his intertwine within my body. I can see the want burning in his leer. But I also see a flash of intimidating jealousy as Obinna pulls me to the side and waves our group down.

"Hey, y'all! We're over here!" He flags them down. "Bring bottle service and let's get lit."

"Eww, that's not your typical vocab! Cut it out!" Priya laughs, following behind us.

Obinna slides into the booth, then scoots over to make room for me. "What's typical is your choice in purses, P. I don't know what's louder, you or your damn disco ball clutch."

"Shut up! What do you know about fashion?"

"Says the woman who once wore a tutu to a bar crawl."

"Okay, that was a dare from my sorority sister. Besides, it had pockets!"

I hate when they do this—when they make human interactions so light and natural.

Priya elbows me. "Patience, you gotta look out for the real Obinna and ditch this lame decoy."

Must she acknowledge me like a friend?

"I'll get on that," I say, mildly. "Um, I'm getting a drink. Does anybody want one?"

Priya tilts her head. "Still undecided."

Obinna taps my butt and hands me his Visa card. "Guinness,

my dear—if you don't mind."

"Got it."

Anything to lower my blood pressure.

My legs pace to the bar slowly, and I wonder if I'm making a huge mistake by addressing him here, out in the open.

Harlan finishes serving a lesbian couple, and as they leave, I nervously approach the bar.

He scratches his ear and grabs a portable card reader. "Pick your poison."

Not even so much as a brow twitch. Oh. So, that's what we're doing. Now I'm in a fluster, not sure what to do with myself again.

"Um, a vodka cranberry and a Guinness stout, please."

With little to no reaction, Harlan nods and grabs two glasses for my order. It's getting to me that I can't read what he's thinking. Is he pissed, hurt, confused, or all of the above?

He returns with the drinks. "Twenty even, beautiful."

Normally, his compliments would make me swoon. But the generic tone he uses sounds like he's only seeking for a tip.

I hand him Obinna's card, and he looks at it, then at me.

"Problem?" I ask.

"Why would there be a problem?" he says, tossing a bar towel on his shoulder.

He's playing with me again. Fine, I can do it, too.

"And we would like bottle service. My husband's table is over there. We'll take the premium package."

Harlan tumbles Obinna's Visa card between his fingers. His eyes center on my plunging neckline for a split second. "For seven-hundred?"

"I mean, yeah. What else is there?"

Harlan purses his lips and swipes the card. "They'll be right out. Don't forget to grab a buzzer. Hey, Jose, I'm taking a smoke break. Cover for me." He tosses the towel in the trash and pushes through the back door.

I for sure got to him—sweet.

"What's taking so long?" Priya says in a sing-songy voice. "We sober folk are in need of debauchery!"

"Service is ass tonight," I say, pulling up my top. "Another reminder why I hate damn clubs."

Priya puts on a terse smile and flips her hair. "Not your scene? I can tell. Obinna wasn't sure if you'd like it, either."

"Is that so?" I ask in irritation. Why are they having side conversations about me?

Priya picks up on my vibe. "Hey, don't put him in the doghouse, okay? Don't stress. He loves you. I'm sure he was only trying to consider your feelings."

Unlike me.

"Well, I snatched up bottle service on his behalf to make up for the booze wait. Let's go sit before we miss it."

"Oooh, let's!"

And away we go.

* * *

As Darrian and Priya slosh and gulp down high-quality alcohol, Obinna is upset because I got too ambitious regarding bottle service.

"Platinum, though?"

"Why not? You never said what kind of bottle service. So, I improvised."

"I'm not happy with you. At all."

And he's right to not be. Flexing financially on his account doesn't gain any cool points—no matter how you look at it.

"Patience, that's not okay." Obinna pulls me aside to the dance floor to chat. "You could've at least given me a heads up before you pulled a stunt like that. Last I checked, the card's in my name."

"What's yours is mine, right?"

"Not funny."

Harlan or no, there's no reason to add insult to injury. "I'm totally sorry. I wasn't thinking—got caught up in the moment and went for it. You know I don't get out much." I stroke his shoulders and give him a longing kiss. "Anything I can do in the meantime?"

Obinna is putty in my hands. "Well then, you can start going that-a-way. Let's dance, girlie."

My saving grace. Let's.

Despite my social anxiety, dancing is the one thing I've mastered, owned, and conquered, thanks to Dad. It makes perfect sense that it's my go-to. Rhythmic movements don't require a lot of talking or introduction. So, I'm game.

"Ladies first."

Wizkid plays, and I finally loosen up more than I thought I would, given the circumstances. The dance floor is a world unto itself as it cocoons us in a bubble of stolen glances. Our bodies move together, flowing in sync with the Afrobeats music. Obinna's fingertips trace the curve of my waist. God— almost forgot how he could make me tremble just by tracing the small of my back.

If only he kept up with this from day one, I wouldn't be fighting the pining guilt I have now.

"This takes me back to when we tried to salsa at that dive bar in Mexico," Obinna shouts over the music, a childish smirk splitting his face.

I laugh like a braying donkey. "Oh, please. How could I forget the many times you tried to amputate my poor ankles? Corona is not your friend, my little drunkard."

"Hey now, I am a natural, Pat. Nothing wrong with a little liquid courage."

Obinna transports me to when all we needed was each other—warm, salty air, the taste of tequila on my lips, and him, clumsy but endearing. We were young, reckless, and utterly in puppy love.

So, what the hell happened?

Obinna chuckles some more. His breath is hot against my ear. "For someone who was so scared to lose her ankles, you laughed your pretty ass off all night."

I can't help but smile. It's true. Fear and laughter were strange bedfellows in those early days of our relationship.

"I was laughing to hide my terror, Obi," I confess. "But you were the right amount of danger for me."

He dips me low and licks his lips. "Still am, babes. Still am. And it's high time I remind you of that."

Gah, he smells so freaking good. "I've missed you."

Obinna twirls me again. When he reels me back in, our chests press firmly together. "Me, too. It'll be different with us, okay?"

"Pssh, no pressure."

"I mean it, though. I'll do better."

I raise a freshly threaded eyebrow. "At dancing?"

"At being here." He squeezes my hand, then spins me out into the flashing lights.

With each sway and turn, I feel Obinna's pull, and it's kinetic. So much so, I nearly miss Harlan returning from his break.

Harlan watches from across the room and entices a silent confession of our shared sin, with his eyes drawing me deeper into the sultry web we've woven.

All of this and more—unleashed in the secrecy of our Markos night.

"I guess you sure showed me," Obinna continues. "I almost forgot—you actually know what the hell you're doing when you move."

I miss this version of us. It's almost bittersweet.

I give my pleased partner a seductive spin and start whining my hips onto him. "Girl's gotta do what a girl's gotta do."

CRASH!

The club halts as everyone's focus turns to the bar. Harlan is completely red-faced and drenched in what looks like alcohol.

"Fuck!" he yells. He then jabs a finger at an alarmed coworker. "Jose, why wasn't this mopped up?! I wasted a whole table's order!"

His voice rumbles the building, and I am significantly worried about Jose.

"Harlan, my bad—okay?" Jose pats him on the back. "I'll take care of the order while you go dry off. Maybe cool off, too."

Harlan's face warps furiously, and he pushes Jose into the ice machine. "You first."

Then he leaves the bar, sprinting to the restroom.

"What happened?" Priya asks. She and her lapdog, Darrian, join us on the dance floor. "Were noses broken?"

"Bartender just rage-quit, I bet," Obinna says. "Don't expect timely service for a while."

"I'll be back. I need to go to the restroom," my voice pipes up.

"Don't be gone long." Obinna kisses me as he picks an eyelash off my cheek. "You're gonna need to finish what you started."

I wave before jogging over to the restroom hall, passing a group of people with matching metallic outfits. As I search, it's established I'm asking for it and know better. I should *not* try to talk to Harlan when he's this mad—even if it's to find out if it's because of what Obinna and I were doing.

But his hooks in me are unabating.

I make it down the corridor and spot the gritty, unisex restroom doors. Good. Now, I'll wait and see when he comes back out, and we can actually talk about what the shit just happened—

A vigorous grab yanks me into a closet, and I'm pushed into a wall. A bright lightbulb dangles side to side, and a steaming Harlan towers above me.

"Harlan?" I sputter.

"So, that's him, huh?" He cocks his head back and clicks his tongue.

"Yeah."

"And you absolutely had to make sure I understood that."

"It wasn't—I tried to warn you they wanted to come here but—"

"Bullshit."

"It's true! Besides, you tried to play me, too!"

Harlan wipes his mouth and laughs. "That shit with him in front of me was to prove what, exactly? You're too good for me?"

Unmoved, I stand tall and take him on. "Maybe you're not the only one who calls the shots."

"Is that right?"

"Yeah, that's right."

"Then, call this."

Harlan swoops me into his arms, then puts me high against the wall. He pins me up with his body—tall and lean. His heart beats with might, and he keeps me there as if I weigh nothing. I didn't think this far ahead and now I'm mentally kicking myself.

"So, was I missed?"

"McCandles..."

"It's one thing to wake up in my bed, but it's another not to claim me."

Harlan's left hand travels up my shaking thighs, slipping into my panties. He rests his fingers within the inner lace lining but doesn't move an inch further.

"Nothing happens until you say it."

Resist him. Come on—be stronger than this.

But the want is too great—the worst of who I am is in its full-fledged form. "Keep... keep going."

"Anything for my muse."

He pushes them up inside me, his fingers taking over. Harlan buries his face into my cleavage, using his teeth.

"No, wait." I pause. "That'll leave a mark for days."

"What else sends a reminder only I consume you?"

"I don't belong to you."

"Do you want me to stop?"

Why ask if he already knows the answer?

"Be careful, okay?"

"That's a laugh..."

The friction between his hand and me releases endorphins that dismiss all rationality. I pull his face from my breasts to seek the sharp taste of his mouth.

Harlan has other ideas. "Tell me you want all of me, Patience."

No. In fact, I wish to have never met the man who further complicates my life with my husband mere steps away. Yet again—a husband who allowed me to feel uncared for... for so long... that someone like Harlan could easily contaminate us.

So, for now, give me anything and everything. "I want—I need all of you."

"There she is. There's my girl."

Harlan lifts me even higher with a sturdy hand as the other goes for his belt buckle and drops his pants.

"Breathe."

Once he's in, Harlan becomes more animalistic as he slams me into the wall repeatedly. He bites and claws at my body with each plunge, my braids balled up in his fist. He's a man no longer deprived. "Do you understand... the restraint... the goddamn restraint it took for me? To watch him paw at you... and just take it?"

Who is starving for who here?

As for me, I'm in imminent danger of giving us away because of my irrepressible screams.

But he's not finished with me yet.

"Now... let's hear my name... croak from your beautiful fucking mouth."

"H-Harlan..."

"Remember this night," he hushes, squeezing my calves intently. "The night you called out mine instead of his. That's enough of a reason."

"Huh?"

"I told you. I reach you in ways he could never touch."

Knock. Knock.

Oh, my Christ.

"Hey, I hear screaming. Is everything okay in there?"

Priya's voice is on the other side.

Bad. Bad. Bad!

"Hello? I'm sorry, but if you don't answer, I'm getting security."

And even still—Harlan doesn't put me down.

"Make her leave," he says. "She's ruining the fun for everyone, you know."

I cry, no longer feeling like a goddess. "Harlan, help."

"I thought you said you needed to want and feel again when with me."

"I do—I did, but..."

"Then, let's want and feel past our capacities... till we're both numb."

Is that even attainable? "The girl outside knows who I am; she doesn't know about us. Please."

Harlan licks my tears, then lightly kisses my eyelids. "Well, since you asked so nicely."

I'm finally let down, and I readjust my dress. Harlan puts his boxers and pants back on speedily, then he opens the door a smidge.

"You rang?" he sasses to Priya.

From where I stand, with the look on Priya's face, she isn't having it.

"Look, I clearly heard a woman in distress in here and you opening the door isn't a good sign. Ma'am, are you all right?"

She really is a sincere person.

"Hmm, I wouldn't say she was in distress—per se. Quite the opposite, actually."

Dammit, Harlan. Chill.

"Dude—I'm not leaving until I hear from her. Ma'am, please speak up so I can know if you're fine!" Priya persists.

Harlan has a "you gonna say anything?" look.

"I'm okay... really." I raise my voice in a higher pitch. "You can go. I'll be fine."

Priya tries to look over Harlan's shoulder to locate where the voice is coming from, but he doesn't budge.

"Hey, so the lady is cool with being bashful, but I'm not. She's good. She told you herself. So, take a walk."

Priya tries to size him up, but Harlan is far from sizable.

"I'm still letting security know."

"You go do that."

Priya's heels hit the hallway and then click out of earshot.

"That was close," I say.

"Your friend is kind of a—"

"She's not my friend. She works with Obinna. Priya."

Harlan lets out a huff of laughter at the thought of them. "Really? She's kinda cute, but she's no you. So your husband's the only one allowed to have special friends, huh?"

"They aren't—that way. It's not like us."

"Damn straight."

I pull out a compact and use my mirror underneath the dangling lightbulb. A woman with the remnants of mascara smudged beneath her eyes, looks back at me. "Who the hell am I anymore?"

"Patience—"

"No! He said he was gonna do better—said he was actually gonna try for me."

"Why the fuck should I care?"

"I'm married and turning thirty in two weeks! I don't have

time for this shit. What am I supposed to learn from this, exactly?"

"Well, as Picasso once said, *Sex and art are the same thing.*" Harlan isn't thrown. He gives a tight-lipped grin with a stillness that wasn't there before. "I'm twenty-eight, going on twenty-nine, and I'm thinking—maybe a field trip on Saturday can bring a few things to light. At the Edith Museum around noon. So I'll see you there?"

My coping mechanisms involving him are getting wilder by the minute. "I don't know what you're planning. But I'm not falling for your spur-of-the-moment surprises anymore."

"I know you're a person who has felt stifled for as long as she can remember and who's trying to find pieces of herself again, unapologetically. I know that much."

How long have we been in this closet?

"On that note," Harlan says, sharing similar thoughts, "I gotta go kiss my boss's ass so I can keep a chunk of my supplemental income. Let me leave first. Then you can do the same."

"Okay. Fine. Hurry and go before Priya actually comes with reinforcements." Then worry smacks me fast as I pat myself down. "Wait, have you seen my—"

"Sure have." Grinning, Harlan holds up my lacy red panties. "And I'm thinking I'll hang on to them. A token, if you will."

"Give it back!" I demand.

He just laughs, the sound echoing in the cramped space. "What, these?"

I lunge for them, but Harlan is one step ahead of each swerve. Ugh. The musty smell of mop buckets and cleaning supplies fill my nostrils. The faint outline of his body is against the sliver of light seeping through the crack in the closet door.

"You... you aren't getting away with this."

"Oh, really?" he replies, in a superior way. "I think I just might."

"No!"

"Yes."

"Don't even joke like that."

"But the simple thought... of you walking around with a breeze below that wasn't there before—because of me... damn. It'd make my shift go a hell of a lot faster."

Then he kisses them.

Harlan's taking it too far. Can't he see what it's doing to me?

"Hey!"

He walks away, then looks back smugly—only to hang my underwear on the doorknob.

Yes. Thank you.

"Give me the benefit of the doubt, sweetness. I had you going for a second there, huh? Always do. Still, it's nice to dream. Tell hubby I said hey."

Out he goes.

My head is swimming with so many things that could've gone wrong for us. That could've gone wrong for me. No, I cannot take a stupid chance like that again.

Relax, it's over. I can leave now.

I twist open the rusty doorknob and begrudgingly take the walk of shame back to Obinna.

"It... it was you?" a voice calls out from a corner.

I turn around to find an aghast Priya emerging from the restroom door.

"I wanted to wait... because I didn't buy what that asshole

was saying. So, I hung around just in case. Patience... what's going on?"

My world as I know it rests in the unpredictable hands of Priya Ramakrishnan.

The air turns thick and gags me, leaving me unable to speak. Priya doesn't break her disapprovingly long silence.

A group of drunk girls tumble into the hallway, laughing raucously, and they disturb the quiet that stalls us.

"Y'all in line?" one of them, with harsh makeup, asks.

"No!" Priya and I yell in unison.

"Well—shit, then."

The hot mess express piles into the restroom like sardines, and they close the door.

"Patience, you have to give me something," Priya starts. "Anything."

But how? How can I explain Obinna's lack of participation in our relationship drove me to seek my needs elsewhere? She won't get it. I've told him till I was blue in the face I wanted more of him, but it fell on deaf ears.

So, I fell for Harlan.

"I wish... I could," I say shakily, unsure where it'll take me. "So much, you have no idea."

"What do you mean—I saw you! In there with him! With Obinna right around the corner."

"Please. You can't tell him, Priya."

"Please?! Is that what I'm hearing?"

"It will—he'll never come back from this." I try to find an ounce of care from Priya—within the shared belief we both want the very best for Obi. "It'll kill him."

"Don't pass the buck, Patience." Priya reproaches. Her forehead wrinkles with the same amount of offense. "You're already going out sad."

Nothing is working. Here it goes, a cyanide pill of a statement, coming right up. "If you do, then—then you'll only end up proving the one thing I've had a hunch about since I met you. You only want him for yourself."

Priya lets out a belittling chortle. "You need it from that asshole so badly that you'd guilt me into letting you cheat on your husband? I have tried to be a good friend to you for my best friend since eighth grade, and that's what you think of me? If nothing ever happened between Obinna and me for almost two decades, it's sure as hell not going to happen now!"

My intent to hit an Uno reverse on Priya fails incredibly.

"You're safe tonight because, unlike some people, I'm not in a rush to ruin Obinna's life. But you better figure your shit out soon, or else."

"I'm trying to, but he shuts me out! You know full well he never gets into heavy shit with me, or with anyone. I needed someone to talk to—to get why the last year and a half has been unbearable for me!"

Priya, as tiny as she is, pushes me hard. I let her because I believe she's owed one. "From what I heard outside the door... unless you and that tatted fuckboy both speak tongues, then your story doesn't track. Admit it. You two... weren't looking to just talk."

"Priya, come on!"

She turns and walks away.

"Must be nice to have a one-up on me for once," I call out.

"Or maybe you're not a likable person, ever think about that?"

Oof. That cut a little more than I'd like to admit.

After we both take the excruciating walk back to the boys, Priya sticks to her word and doesn't tell Obinna but stays distant. My excuse about getting sick suddenly prompts the night to end earlier than planned.

"But you seemed fine when we were dancing; what changed?" Obinna ponders.

"It must be a stomach bug I caught from a student at work."

It scares me how I default to lying so easily.

"Okay, but damn. I'm out seven-hundred bucks to only go clubbing for two hours?"

Priya shoots daggers at Harlan, returning to the bar to finish his shift. Then she does the same to me. "I'm going to Uber home; it's all good. Shit happens. I'll see you at work, Obi."

Obinna's disappointment keeps grappling with my sympathy. "You, too, huh? Well, okay, I guess I'll throw in the towel. But, Priya, stop playing, fam. You're riding with us; I'll take you home. No need to piss away more money for the hell of it."

"No, that's okay."

"Come on, stop being weird."

"Obinna, I'm good, really."

Drop it. Drop it now. He doesn't always need to be so chivalrous.

"Priya, your stubborn nature will never land you a husband," he jokes.

"Noted. Goodnight."

She then submerges into the crowd of Markos inhabitants and disappears.

"What's up with her?" asks my clueless husband.

"Sexual frustration?" says Darrian, securing his cufflinks. "Nah, that can't be right—she left without me."

THE MUSEUM TRIP

Obinna Okoye was starting out to be a man of his word. Was.

This morning, we did it in the shower, and he stayed awake to completion, surprisingly. Afterward, I made us breakfast in bed. When he finished eating, he said he would stay home the remaining Saturday so we could watch Sci-Fi body horror classics together. And that we could even build a 3D puzzle of Planet Planta from *Space Dandy*. Yes. Yes! It was all I ever wanted. My husband to myself. My Obi. It could've been the perfect happy ending, free of tattoos and infidelity. My hypocritical heart was soaring high.

The sun was out, TV was on, and we stayed cuddled up with Pongers sleeping at the foot of our bed.

Obinna squeezed me and squirmed while we watched *The Fly*. "When this movie is over, never question my dedication to science again."

"Okay, and if I'm ever impregnated with larva, you have permission to blow my brains out," I commented.

"I'd rather you not paint that image in my head, thanks. I'm already bracing myself for the fingernail scene, baby."

"Yeesh, sorry. I'm only saying even Jeff Goldblum can't convince me to go along with it—even with his weirdly kooky, twitchy charm."

"Hey, don't sleep on Geena Davis! She was a baddie—in fact, still is. I mean, she's got nothing on you, of course." Obinna rubbed my belly with his broad hands and let out a relaxed chortle. He honestly seemed happy to be with me. "Actually, your skin was flawless when you were in your first trimester with Miracle, and so were you."

"Oh?" It meant so much to hear about her from him. "Thanks, Obi."

"Pregnancy looks really... um—looked really good on you."

Tearfully, I looked up at him and smiled. I fell in love with him all over again when he noted the joy I had in carrying our baby—for however long I did—as he nuzzled my neck. This was big! Huge, in fact—

BEEP. BEEP.

What the shit, Priya?!

Obi passed me a nervous glance, knowing what was to come next.

"Pat... I'll... I'll make it up to you. This corneal abrasion is a big one—"

"Just go." As much as it hurt not to, I didn't let a single tear loose.

That was thirty minutes ago.

There's a chance it won't get any better than what it is. And I have to ask myself if I can accept his crumbs of care—every once in a blue moon.

Obi swore this time to be present, and I can tell he believes it—or rather believes in himself. That should be enough for me, and I want it to be.

But it's not. Not with his constant promises that never seem to materialize into anything real. I'm afraid to get my hopes up.

Too much has taken place since then.

Ping.

A text from Harlan appears. **On your way yet?**

So, I take a reflecting cruise in my Corolla.

Even though Harlan's upper-hand over me puts my marriage on the line—I use my change of plans as a scope to see what lesson he's bringing to light. I don't know how he does it; each encounter generates more questions—about us and about myself. It whittles away at me like sandpaper. My word continues to amount to nothing when I keep going back on my promise to never see him again.

I know what it seems like—the toggling back and forth. Maybe it's not so much about Obinna or Harlan. It's more about not wanting to be left alone to deal with my thoughts. Hell, I did everything right. I kept my nose clean, went to school, and found what others would say—the quintessential partner. Why can't I settle with just me, myself, and I?

Ugh, gotta put a pin in it—already here.

After nabbing a parking spot, I get out of my car and see Harlan, waiting with a radiant smile.

"Afternoon, beautiful." He greets me sweetly by the entrance with a peck on the cheek. "What's new?"

"I almost didn't come."

"Glad to see that wasn't the case. But why?"

Let him have it.

"Conflicted with not being a likable person. Priya knows—and my hourglass is nearly spent on when she decides to tell Obinna."

Harlan's mouth eases to a mild drawback. "Well, I like you, and you're *my* favorite person."

"Thanks." I beam, gradually coming around.

"But we can't have that happen again."

"What are you talking about?"

"Playing games with me. I can't promise I'll be as well-behaved next time, all right?" Harlan warns, straightening his v-neck.

Does he really think I enjoy having this internal conflict, being with him? I wait, wondering if he's testing me now—watching to see if I'll react wrong or show a crack he can pry open to get to more of me.

"Harlan, I don't even know what to say to that."

"Ta-da!" He pulls another move on the spot. "And the rest is history—I got you something."

"What for?" I ask, taking the small pink gift bag from him.

"Maybe it's an early birthday present. Sneak a peek."

I do and gasp. "Are you whacked? You can't buy me sexy underwear. It's too suspicious!"

"Trust me. Remember, there's a method to my madness. What's the harm in wearing special undergarments during a special outing?" Harlan puts his arm around me and guides us through the corridors. "So, go slip them on in the restroom before we start."

I still don't get the relevance here. "Why?"

"With everything else we've done, why not?"

Point made.

It's as if I'm in an obscure sitcom where a couple tries to spruce things up in their relationship. Still, a huge billboard sign in my brain screams: just because two mistakes were made doesn't mean I'm obligated to make a third one.

All the same... Is it too old-fashioned to say the devil made me do it? Then again, picturing Harlan as the devil makes my hair stand on end.

I'm in search of the women's restroom and find it on the third right I make. I rush inside, seeing an available stall among the commotion of museum goers.

Here it is. Hmm. Instead of Victoria's Secret, I realize the secret is... what's the appeal here? The material is much thicker than what I'm used to—some kind of latex or leather. They aren't hideous, but I would have rather picked out something more stylish.

Maybe it's a lesson on not judging a book by its cover.

With him, you never know—until you know.

As we step into the Edith Pryor Art Museum, the space and the history of the artwork immediately claim me. The soft murmurs of other visitors mingle with the echo of footsteps and create a symphony of sounds that add to the immersive experience. I'm eager to explore each exhibit as Harlan leads the way. As we walk side by side, I can't help how weird it feels to consider if this is a date. We've had sex twice, but I'm too nervous to ask or even signal for a hint.

There aren't enough words to express how preposterous that is for me.

"Harlan, what is this painting about?" I ask, halting.

Harlan takes a brochure from the bottom of the portrait and flips through it. "*The Lovers* by Rene Magritte. 1928. Oil painting. Kudos to them for getting some during the influenza epidemic."

I laugh at the sheer morbidity. "What else was there to do back then?"

Harlan looks over the painting closer, and his expression changes to a contemplative one. "The shrouds covering their faces gotta represent something. Not being able to taste, hold, or even touch the one you wanted. What core colors would that even look like?"

"I know." I'm not sure if he is talking to me or thinking out loud. "It's sad."

Not as many are crowding around as before, leaving Harlan and me to fawn over *The Lovers* by ourselves. But even though I already want to see other works, Rene Magritte's depiction still transfixes him.

"Can we go see other art now?" I pull at his arm. "This is nice and all, but there's so much more we're missing."

"In a minute," Harlan says. He doesn't break eye contact with the portrait after a grueling four minutes, and I get annoyed.

"Hey, what's going on—"

"Shh!" he hushes crisply. "You're an artist now, so act like one. I'm kind of processing here, and your whining doesn't help."

"I didn't mean to overstep..." I stand back and respect his space. "Thought you were off the clock today and were done thinking about work is all."

Instead, Harlan and *The Lovers* are having their own special moment. "Celadon peaks for the obstacles they might have gone through, only to be denied their human nature. Chartreuse stippling for the substantial cravings they have, but can't satisfy."

Oh! He's thinking about his next project, of course. And why not here, of all places? I feel stupid for not realizing there's not an off switch for that kind of thought process.

"Any more colors come to mind?" I hope to belong in his exalting experience.

"You tell me. I think it's time for another painting lesson."

"Now?"

Harlan spins me back around to address the portrait again.

"We can use this foundation to work on our next abstract art together, with a touch of Fauvism. Don't you agree? Really focus on the textures, the positioning of their faces through the shrouds, their body language. What are they searching for beneath the surface? What colors derive from it?"

I'm never sure what to say when Harlan gets into an introspective mindset. As much as he encourages me to respond, nine times out of ten I think I'll get the answer wrong and look dumb.

"I got nothing, Harlan. Let's go see some other stuff."

"Hmm, how about now?" he asks, pulling out a remote from his front pocket. He then presses it, and—

"What the fuck?!" I screech and topple onto him.

A mother and her two children gasp, and she ushers them away from the nasty lady with the potty mouth.

"Everything okay over here?" a heavyset security officer investigates.

"Perfectly fine, Officer; my girlfriend has a fear of spiders. The galleries could surely use some dusting. Sheesh. These cobwebs are insane."

The guard gives him a reluctant thumbs up, and then he's back on patrol.

Harlan turns back to me and toys with the buttons on the remote. "You like? Had them customized and made to be undetectable. Are we ready to take it seriously now?"

"You tricked me into wearing vibrating panties?!" I sort of whisper-yell at him. Not an easy task. "I'm going back to the restroom to take these off, and I'm coming back out to kick your ass."

"One, I did not trick you when I suggested you should wear special undergarments for our special outing. How you receive that is your win or downfall. Two, you're not taking those off, so there's no point threatening me."

"Why the hell wouldn't I?"

"Because,"—Harlan's voice goes steelish—"if you walk, then you're not the woman I thought you were, the woman who'd risk it all for the sake of self-expression."

"What are you—"

"It's just an elevation to tap into some new shades of colors. Take a chance on my lesson and see what you discover within yourself. You're a magnificent force to be reckoned with— your work is so damn untouchable. I know that... only wish you did, too. Suppress that fiery want all you like; it'll only come out in ways you never intended."

My worries swim to my brainstem, reminding me how I shouldn't be here. In a perfect world, I should be with Obinna, shopping for linens and preparing fufu for his mom and the rest of my in-laws. I know none of this is right, but I can't help but think back to...

"...and you'll never feel this alive again."

He knew what he was doing from the beginning. Harlan sunk his vampire fangs into me, and now I couldn't blow him off if I tried. The desire to be with him is beyond crippling, so the worst part of me is victorious yet again. "It'll be the wildest shit, I've ever done."

"I doubt that. Push through, Okoye," Harlan goes on. "It's just us, and no one else will know."

But I'll know. Doesn't that count for something? "Do you hear what you're actually asking me to do? Like out loud?"

Harlan's hair is more straw-colored than usual. He flips it

out of his brow line as he tightens his lips. "I promise we'll be discreet."

But it doesn't sit well with me in the slightest. And he spots that in an instant.

"Just play a role."

"How?"

"If it helps—leave wife Patience at home. But vixen or badass Patience can hang anytime."

It's this or back to the humdrum way things were before he introduced me to his irresistible ascendency. I can't believe I'm asking this, but...

"Just—how does the lesson work?"

Harlan smirks and resumes his questionable role as a professor.

"If you weren't able to reach that climax you're so desperately striving for, then how could you cope—what colors come to mind when thinking of such a concept?"

I control my breathing when Harlan tests me on the lesson. The vibration in my underwear is crazy rapid, but it helps paint another abstract picture in my head.

His presence—it's there before I even hear him—appears, standing so close behind me that his breath brushes the back of my neck, warm and soft. There's just the quiet thrum of his heartbeat in sync with mine. His voice, smooth like pouring milk, murmurs against my ear, "I'm right here..."

I see rakes of my crimson rage at not being able to resist him the way someone else's wife would.

I see puffs of carmine tie together the overwhelming surges of exhilaration that obliterate my lower half.

I see jagged strips of vermilion fear. Fear that I'm no longer myself, or this might be who I've always been.

"Well?"

"I'm... uh, searching... I mean, the lovers are searching for simplicity... mmm, of bliss within one another. Even if it's mostly... nuh, agony during their lifetime to, mmm, get there."

"And?"

"Their colors are orchid... coral... ahhhh... and cherry blossom..."

He doesn't have the right to my new personal core colors yet. It's okay to still keep some things sweetly to myself.

Harlan warms to me again and turns off the panties. I almost faint from the endurance of lasting that long.

I'm now in his colorful arms, as though we're the only ones in the museum. "I knew you could do it. Patience, you're incredible!" Then he gives me a warm, wet kiss.

But I part from him soon after.

"Tell me," I say, unsure. "I'm not the only one you've done this with, am I?"

"Would it make what we did less meaningful if that were true?" Harlan's tall frame dwarfs only slightly to a towering Renaissance painting behind him.

"Only you would answer my question with a question..."

"Ask me no questions, and I'll tell you no lies. I will say... you're the first married one I've done this with. That's a record."

Awesome. He's keeping score.

"I don't want to be a joke."

"Trust me, the joke's on those who underestimate the shit outta you. Happy to say... I'm not one of them. So, don't—" Harlan stops mid-sentence and traces my neckline, his face growing more serious.

"Don't what?"

"Compartmentalize yourself for him ever again. I'll take every bit of you without a second thought. Got it?"

When you worry that your want, crave, or need is an ugly thing—a bottomless pit, constantly needing to be tamed— that's when you want to hide.

"...Museum closing in ten minutes," the intercom buzzes.

"Man, I wish my car had tinted windows." Harlan steps back and rubs my upper arms clemently. "I don't think I can make it another five minutes without—"

"...Mine are."

But I'm not hiding this time around.

A storm approaches with darkened clouds and plopping rain. Overcome with the thrill, we barely make it inside my car before we have unbridled sex in the parking lot. Harlan drinks me in when he thinks no one's watching... and in that moment, I am everything and nothing at once.

Cars leave one by one, yet we're the only ones that stay among the destructive weather.

Nowhere near as destructive as we've become.

* * *

The storm quiets around six-thirty, which means we were at it for almost two hours. I catch my breath while slowly putting my clothes back on in the passenger seat.

"Wanna come back to mine?" Harlan asks, childishly drawing on the foggy windows. "The night's still moderately young, and so are we."

Before I can answer, a gleam comes from something wedged in the car seat. Once I pluck it out, I see it's a missing charm from my keychain Obinna gave me on our first date—a miniature Nami from *One Piece* brings me back to the real world.

No. I can't keep being this deluded. I'm not his badass; I'm not his vixen. No more. It has to stop.

I speed up getting dressed, but Harlan isn't in much of a hurry. He studies me again, sitting in his boxers and wears a debonair grin. "Where are you in a rush to?"

"To the life I'm supposed to be living... which means I never want to see you again."

"Oh?"

I glance at Harlan. His eyes are partly pleading, a hope for more clings to his chiseled face. His hand rests on my knee, but beneath the physical closeness, a chasm yawns. He emits vulnerability I've rarely seen from him before. The windshield fogs up with my breath as I make it known that we're through. "I don't like who I am right now, and it's because of you."

"Patience," Harlan speaks in a low rumble, and it cuts through the silence. "You could have it all... if you'd let me give it to you."

"You gave it to me three times. I think I got an idea of what you have to offer."

"Not what I meant."

I'm covered in tire tracks of contrition, treaded on by what we have, taking over me. "Harlan, I don't want to be another notch on your belt. So, I'm done."

The coldness of the leather seat contrasts with the heat beaming from my treachery. "So, you choose mediocrity?"

"I choose Obinna."

"What's the difference?"

"Oh, my—just get the fuck out of my car!"

"Wow. Jesus. Fuck you, too."

Harlan shoves his clothes back on, infuriated. Now I'm swimming with remorse.

"I... let me drive you to yours so you're not out in the rain."

"I'll manage. Thanks."

"I'm driving, okay?"

I make my way to the front seat and hop over, but then Harlan grabs hold of me and places me on his lap.

I'm immediately taken aback. "Hey! What are you—"

His tongue, instead, drives me to places I know I shouldn't go. I don't fight him because—just as expected—the undisciplined part of me wants to see where it goes.

Will it... will it ever end?

For now, it does—because Harlan pulls away and cups my cheek. "A little something to remember me by. Let's see how long you'll hold out this time."

Then he's out the door and dashing down the street like a madman in the pouring rain.

He's gone. I'm free.

I take a deep breath with the cold air hitting my lungs and try to keep myself from chasing him down to take back my words.

Angela... help.

* * *

This week, therapy better do an overhaul of work on myself.

Angela has on tangerine-colored glasses today. Her tinted lenses are that color, too, with pineapples etched on the side.

"So, last time, we left off on you contemplating the decision to keep a relationship with Harlan. How's that been shaping?"

I'm really outdoing myself—sex with my husband in the morning, then Harlan in the afternoon, all on the same day. Yeah, doesn't exactly scream *progress*, does it?

"I slipped up again."

"How so?"

"First, I went to a club with Obinna and his group of friends. Harlan was there—working. I ran into him at some point, alone. One thing led to another and—well, Priya caught us in the middle of it."

Angela coughs and clears her throat. "Patience, I understand it may have felt like things happened quickly, but we also have to recognize there are choices made in those moments—intentional ones."

Leave it to Angela to put me in my place. "Well, you'll be happy to know Priya told me how much of a shitty person she thinks I am, too."

"I didn't intend to make you feel inferior. Please understand that."

"Understood." I pick at my eyelashes. "Thankfully, she came through and hasn't told him yet. I want it to come from me. And I'm kind of relying on her friendship with Obinna to reflect not hurting his feelings. In a way, it'll work out after he understands why I did what I did. I needed more, and he fell short. Wow—after saying that out loud—I sound like a complete bitch. Angela, I get how it looks like I don't give a shit about Obinna. But I do! I love him so much, but lately, he gives me nothing. And Harlan, he offered attentiveness. I'm human, too, you know."

She gives a look of sudden condolence. "Is the loneliness that bad?"

It must be painfully visible if she has to ask. "You have no earthly idea."

"You're right. You're human. We all are." Angela adjusts her hair tie. "And you're expressing what you need from Obinna as a partner."

The museum trip looms in my head. But since I'm holding myself to a standard—sort of—I'll volunteer that as tribute.

"So, another thing... Harlan and I went to a museum last Saturday."

"Oh." Angela perks up from the update. "So, it was your first outing in public together, so to speak. After the sexual encounters."

The cringe factor in the term *sexual encounters* is at its highest peak.

"Do you have to say it like that?"

"Like what?"

"Nothing."

Angela looks as if she swallowed a block of ice. "If I misspoke in any way—"

"No, it's okay, let me finish," I say, fully committed. I absolutely hate starting and stopping and wish she would quit making it a total drag. "We went to the museum on Saturday and saw some of the art displays there. I learned a lot about the artists, too."

"And?" Even Angela calls bullshit and knows there's more to the story.

"Well, it was... unexpected, to say the least. Harlan's always full of surprises. My task was to figure out three colors for our next abstract art project together. Our inspiration was a painting called *The Lovers*. They were two people with cloth strips over their faces, attempting to kiss each other. The cloth denied them intimacy. He wanted me to experience what they felt."

Angela's cheekbones droop afterward. "So, how did he pull that off?"

I gulp my words at first, then exhale to try again. "He suggested I wear vibrating underwear while I analyzed the art in the museum."

Angela blinks twice, picks up her notebook, and jots down notes for an awfully long period—not good.

"Did you consent to this, Patience?" she asks.

I'm not touching that hot button issue. So, I stay on mute and attempt to tune her out.

"I'm not sure what's causing your silence, but for the sake of therapy... it's essential to understand consent is never ambiguous, and you need to be sure of that."

"Okay."

"It's important to establish clear boundaries and consent in any situation." Angela knows me all too well, that I tiptoe around that idea often. "How did you feel about it?"

"Honestly, I wasn't crazy about it at first," I admit. "But I didn't want to mess things up."

Angela resumes back to pen clicking. "Does Harlan seem accustomed to getting his way often?"

"I wouldn't put it like that."

"Okay. What would happen if you were to entertain the word *no* with him someday?"

"I already did. I ended it with him right after we left the museum."

Angela continues steering the dialogue. "How did Harlan respond?"

"Almost like he didn't believe me." I say, as I pick at a

hangnail. "Like he was looking forward to seeing me again soon."

"Remember, you matter, and it's okay to assert yourself."

Say anything to make her stop stating what's plain to see. "Yeah, you're right."

Angela smiles sweetly and finally relinquishes her notepad. "Good. And Patience, I think it might be beneficial for us to re-evaluate the focus of our therapy sessions. It seems like there are some deeper issues we need to address."

Nah, I'm good. Not in the headspace for that type of dialogue.

"Respectfully, lay off. I consented. I remember now. Done." Why didn't I give Harlan this much pushback at the museum?

Angela's hands are tied, and she knows it. "As long as you're sure."

"I am. Like I said, I told Harlan I never want to see him again, and I plan to come clean with Obinna tonight. Our love will survive this."

"Keep in mind, there were times you and Harlan— "

"It has to."

The townhouse is chillier than usual this evening as I hurry inside.

"Oh!"

Obi is surprisingly home, with Pongers curled up by his feet. He has his legs crossed on the ottoman, head down, and flips through his iPhone while stone-faced. It's early. Since when does he take it easy?

"Hey," I say, breathlessly. "You're home."

"Yup." He appears blasé, scratching Pongers behind her ear. "Priya's running things this evening. I needed the night to myself. Just like you wanted."

"I picked up some Thai food from that place on Fawn Street. You know, the one that opened up last Thursday." I set down the food on the island table and get bowls from the nearby shelf. "Did you want to eat from the container, or no?"

After a drawn-out sigh, Obinna gets up and turns around. "Thai food, huh? That's what kept you away from me this time?"

"Pull up a chair."

Obinna stays put. "I'm not hungry."

There's a flatness to his words.

"Obinna, what is it?" I ask as I head over to him.

He backs away and blinks like he's trying to rid the sight of me.

"Is it work? Is your family okay?"

"This family isn't," he says, still stone-like. Pongers leaves Obinna and licks my feet. I wonder if she's preparing me for the blow.

"Why?"

"Patience, you weren't telling the truth about your night terrors."

I freeze. My fingers curl against the console table. "Why would you say that?"

"They're back." Obinna continues. His pitch is even, but there's a soreness beneath it—a laceration barely hidden. "From what I can remember, Angela said stress usually sets them off."

"Look, if I woke you up, it wasn't on purpose. Work has been asking a lot of me lately, too. Same as you. So, let's sit, eat, and forget about it."

He refuses to deflate. His wide hands are in his pockets, and his eyes seem to look past my excuse. "You woke me up with the first one last night. Which was fine. You calmed yourself down and went back to sleep. Whatever, it happens."

Okay? And?

"But then, right before I had to go take a leak, I heard you again, and you didn't even notice me there." Obinna speaks with a quiet tremor. "Clear as day, no mistake. Do you remember what you said before screaming yourself awake?"

I suddenly lost my appetite along with him. "Um..."

"I'll lose everything..."

No.

"Priya knows..."

Please.

"Harlan... wait..."

No!

My husband's brow hardens at the very thought. "That name—when you kept on saying it... The way you were sweating and panting... It did a number on you. There's no way he's a figment of your imagination."

Dear god. The ability to speak escapes me.

"So... I guess all I need from you now is—what does Priya know, and who the fuck is Harlan?"

I try to remember the blurry edges of last night's sleep. But I can't. The overwhelming pressure to bottle Harlan within leaks out in spurts when I attempt to make room for anything else. "Please don't."

The set of Obinna's mouth looks a little too deliberate, as if he's practiced this confrontation in his head over and over. "So, you're really going to make me finish this out on my own? Fine. It clicked why Priya hadn't been the same since Markos. So, I asked her about it today, and she told me everything. You said you felt sick, so we left and came straight home. She swore she saw you with someone that wasn't me before then. I didn't want to believe her, but with the way your ass looks guilty right now—you no longer have the grounds to point the finger at us again."

Of course, Priya would be loyal to him. She never owed me anything to begin with. And I was kidding myself for ever thinking differently.

"Patience, talk!"

But I know whatever I say won't change what I've done. What I've tried my hardest to hide has already uncovered itself through my half-conscious whispers and careless words.

"Let's just take a beat. Give me a minute to collect my thoughts, okay?"

"Why?!" Obinna shouts, with his hands on his head in disbelief. "So I can give you a head start to lie?"

Kind of difficult to do when my heart cartwheels in my chest.

"Even when we had sex days ago... how did I not see it?" Concern is etched on Obi's smooth, umber face. "How you moved differently, like you were turning yourself inside out, working to jump out of your own skin and get whoever else it was out of you."

"I swear... I was going to tell you today, after seeing Angela."

"Tell me what?"

"I... I've been struggling. With us, with myself... with everything." No matter how it's delivered, I am the bad guy in every scenario. "Remember, I tried talking to you first, but you never seem to hear me. There's only so much rejection a person can take. I've been seeing someone else, but we're through. It's not about him. It's about us. About my reason for why."

Obinna leans in closer and his eyes search mine for empathy. "No. You're not running the conversation, I am. It's the least you could do. So, how long?"

"For a while now. Two months." I walk over to him and place my hand on his shoulder. "But let's be honest. You and I aren't on the same page at all, and it shows."

"Oh, please. You could've talked to me at any time, but you chose not to."

"Like, when?!" I scream. "You never come home. You're at the clinic or some other bullshit with Priya. Speaking of, she needs to mind her own damn business—"

"Don't you dare shift the blame with your role in this!" Obi gets in my face—a linebacker ready to tackle. "She didn't even want to tell me in the beginning. She actually had faith in you, that you would come to your senses and come clean. But after over a week went by and you said nothing, Priya felt weird working with me and keeping that knowledge inside. She did what you couldn't, which was to tell the truth."

"I'm sure she did!"

"Well, you sure as shit didn't, Patience!"

During the ordeal, watching Obinna put himself through the ringer over me is not conducive to my intent. So... out with it. "It hasn't been the same since we lost her."

Obi nods. "I mean, you're not wrong. But to use it as grounds to sleep with someone else is crazy. How does that even track?"

I say nothing, because I've got nothing.

"So, did you talk to this fool at the club about our unborn kid while he was dry humping you in the broom closet?! The bartender, of all people?"

Fucking Priya.

"I'm sorry for the way I've been slipping away, a little at a time, without even realizing it."

"Oh, I'm sure of it. So, how does our setup run? I bury myself with work to support you—support our family—as you smash every jerkoff that gives you an ounce of attention?"

It's all unraveling so fast. "Let's be real. You avoid me at home like the plague, Obinna. Baby, I—"

"You lost the right to call me that the moment you chose him over me," he says icily. "Such an embarrassment; what the hell am I going to tell my relatives?"

"Go ahead and tell them they were right about me—that I'm everything they warned about. I go against the grain of what I was taught about being a good wife. But what else am I supposed to do when my husband is never home?"

"Not that again."

"Yes, that again!"

Obi angrily throws his phone at the glass cabinets diagonal to us. The crescendo of the crash shatters deafeningly.

"I'm here now!" he protests. "So, say something worth saying!"

But what if it undoes everything that makes us, us?

"Okay... I've been taking art lessons. Making paintings people wanted and admired, if you can believe it. I had exposure to artworks that illustrate what it's like to actually try to contribute to the world again."

Obinna appears as though he wants to split my head open. His skin turns a boiling purple. "What does any of this have to do with seeing another man behind my back? Get to the point of it, and fast."

"Before, I was in a place that was unreachable. And he—Harlan—found me. I kept learning things from him, besides art. He made me believe I can do anything I set my mind to... like you used to."

"You did not just compare the both of us in front of me!?"

I can't cry. I won't. My strength needs to be prominent for what I have to say next.

"Obinna, you took the back seat to our marriage first, because you blame me for our baby dying."

"My god... are you serious?"

"I know you do. You wanted me to quit Seabrook Elementary during my first trimester, but I wouldn't—because I'm good at my job. Yeah, it can be a lot, but what job isn't? I thought, at least, you of all people, would get it."

Obinna eyes me wearily, and I turn into a lizard pod person who shifts in front of him—a complete stranger.

He doesn't get it and probably never will. The amount of strength it took me to conceal from my class that Josh's outburst wasn't just another tantrum was unendurable. That after he slammed his head into my stomach, I spent the night curled up in the ER, tears soaking my hospital gown as I clutched my abdomen. Like I could somehow hold on to the life slipping away inside me.

"What would you do if it were you?" I ask, with my fingers twitching. "When I was head-butted—I owned up to that, okay? I made the call to pick my battles, and when he didn't want to pick up his crayons, I should've left it alone. But no, the way he got to me—I couldn't let it go. And when he was escalating—it set it all in motion."

Obinna fans me away at once. "I know, I know. I read the damn incident report; you don't have to rehash every—"

"The day after it happened, I bled in my underwear. The day after it happened was the beginning of the end for us. And you can't stomach it, can you? We've been sleepwalking around the topic for far too long, and I want to wake up and face it!"

"You're not the only one who lost a chance at having a child. You wanna know how I dealt with it? I cried myself to sleep in secret every night because I didn't want to make you feel any worse than you already did. So what if I didn't scream *my baby died, poor me* on a damn mountaintop? You can go to hell, Patience."

"I'm already there. So, should I leave?"

Silence.

"Obi? Is there hope for us?"

More silence.

"Okay."

Palpitations ricochet through me as I go to our bedroom and pack a few things. I spot Obinna's shadow in the entryway—motionless.

It needed to be said, now the ball is in his court.

As I walk to the door, I catch Obinna with a shot of Grey Goose. Patience, say something. "Try not to um... to uh, overdo it, okay?"

"Ah, so you suddenly care if I have liver failure now?"

"Of course I care!"

"Are you going back to him? Now?"

Truth? I don't have a plan. Only an exit. "I think it's best to figure things out... while not being here. To spare you any more pain."

"Ha! *To spare me any more pain*, she says. Well... if you expect me to wait for you, please... *do* hold your breath."

More tears well in my eyes. "I wouldn't hold it against you if you didn't."

"Are you... even sorry?" Obinna whines.

After the confrontation, his words become an epiphany for me.

I park my suitcase by the door and walk toward his over-flowing pain.

"I just wanted to be loved richly by you."

"What does that even mean?"

"I'm not blaming you for what I did—I only wish you'd taken my pleas for more of you seriously. I regret the way I dealt with things and should've come clean earlier. But there's more to life than work and empty promises to be present."

Obi screams and throws his shot glass at one of our framed

family photos. The frame cracks as easily as his mental state. "How could you do what you did and feel justified for it?!"

"*I wasn't justified, I was drowning!*" Holding it in serves no purpose anymore. "I ran out of ways to tell you I was unhappy. It was killing me. Killing me! To wake up and even breathe, okay? Maybe if you cried with me over what happened last year, rather than in private, things would be different. Because then I would've known that you cared and I mattered, Obinna."

"With the level of backstabbing you've done? Patience, man... There's no saving you from yourself. So, cheers," he says, raising the Grey Goose bottle.

Well deserved. "Bye, Obi." Then I close the door to our former townhome.

There's a whole new plethora of aspirations that I'm tired of passing up.

* * *

I'm sitting in my car in a Kroger parking lot as the nippy night air chills me further. Why did I believe I could somehow have them both? I trapped myself in a labyrinth by telling myself it's a balance—the predictability of one pushing against the monotony of the other.

Now I have no one and no place to stay.

That's a lie. There's always Mom.

I should call her, let her know what's going on before she hears it from someone else.

But is it worth the trouble to hear her go on and on about how much of a disappointment I am?

Even at my wedding, she couldn't help herself from spewing

rage while I was in tears dressed in my traditional attire. *"Don't speak of your father on your union day, Patience. What's wrong with you? He made his choice when he left us to go back home with a woman twenty years his junior. What? Were you going to invite your bastard siblings to the wedding, too?"*

Shit.

I know where to go, at least where I'd like to be... just don't know if I should. Especially when it makes me look so untrustworthy.

Damn him.

A sob escapes my lips as I dial Harlan's number. It rings once, twice. Then his voice, deep and insouciant, fills my ear.

"Quicker than I thought. What gives?"

"I—I was... wrong."

There's a long pause on the other end. "Okay."

"I was at the end of my rope and thought it was something I was supposed to do. Like it was expected of me," I manage. "I didn't mean to throw you away like that."

"Now what, Patience?"

"I want to have it all, Harlan. You said I could, and I'm ready. If you don't already hate me... I want to make it right."

"Don't make it a habit."

"I won't."

"Then you know where I live, kid. I'm waiting."

Click.

* * *

I show up at Harlan's, flushed with the adrenaline of Obi knowing.

Please, with so much hurt down the line... Please make

telling the truth worth it.

"My little night ninja, how are you?" Harlan answers, his voice raspy. He's wearing Hugo Boss, with splashes of paint covering him from top to bottom.

"I told him... about you," I say.

Harlan gets serious and moves aside to let me in. "How'd that go?" He closes the door behind me, the soft *click* of the lock feeling like some kind of final decision.

"Well, it came and went, I guess."

"He's not gonna come over to try kicking my ass, is he?"

I'd pay good money to see that. "Don't think so. Obinna is too busy downing Grey Goose to numb himself."

"Sounds like a smarter choice."

I walk in and see he's having a field day in his studio, with five canvases of squirted paint streaks on each one.

"Working? At this hour?"

"Oh, honey. It's the best hour. Midnight is when imagination takes an acid trip. Have you ever seen any works from Sam Ebohon?"

"Who?"

Harlan does a patronizing head turn. "Shame on you; he's Nigerian."

"Whoops, guess I gotta get fined from the African Diaspora Committee," I snip back. "I feel like shit enough."

"Sorry."

"You were saying?"

"Right, well, Sam uses criss-cross linear strokes, which abstract his paintings. I kind of want to analogize that technique with a couple of my own to see what follows through."

Wait a damn minute. "You know this totally falls into my

artists borrowing inspiration from other artists argument we had earlier, right?"

Harlan bites his lip and hangs his head low, self-consciously—bested by little, old me. "To err is human. Anyway, wanna help?"

But the room is spinning. The burden of this decision, of leaving Obi, presses down on me. My breaths come faster, shallower. "Harlan," I gasp and hold my sides. "I can't breathe."

He loses the pompous look off his face and runs over to ease my panic attack. "Follow my voice," he soothes. "Slow down with me. Inhale, slow and deep."

"I can't do this."

Harlan's arms wrap around me like a warm blanket. "Hey, hey, it's okay." He leads me to his worn but comfortable sofa, his touch a steady presence. "You're here. We're here. So, just deal."

"I blew up my whole life an hour ago. How do I deal with that?"

Harlan sits beside me, yet he isn't crowding my space. "You did a big thing today, leaving him. It's okay to freak out."

He takes my hand in his. His fingers are long and strong as he gently strokes his thumb across my knuckles. Slowly, my breaths start to even out. The city noise outside fades into a low hum.

Then Harlan takes off my shoes to rub my tired feet. "Let's get you comfortable. Looks like your panic attack is over. But did you still want to talk about it?"

"I'm probably going to need a sedative instead," I say as I slouch further onto the sofa. "Anything to help me forget the look on Obinna's face once he knew I was coming here."

Harlan laughs evilly, as the crinkles on the side of his mouth dance. "I'm all ears."

I'm not in the same position to take it as a joke. "There are times I can't tell whether you're a psychopath or sociopath. Which is it?"

"Shit, really? And yet... you still came over."

Now I feel brainless. "They say psychopaths make the best artists. But surely there's more to you than that."

"Choose."

"Why?"

"It's your turn to indulge me. Because whatever you pick, that's the one you'll bathe with tonight." Harlan rests my toes on his lips and watches for my reaction.

"That's not really fair," I say, laughing nervously. "I don't think I know enough to make that judgment."

"Then choose the one you'd fear the most and make things exciting." My toes are being kissed and kneaded as Harlan speaks—his volume drops to a whisper, but loud enough to still carry weight.

He's most likely joking, but I have to put it out there.

"I've wondered if you'd ever hurt me. Deliberately or not... So, I would say you could be both... Ow!"

"And now?" McCandles asks after giving my big toe a motiveless bite.

"Asshole!"

"And you're indecisive. There's gonna come a time where you'll find out which one on your own. Someday."

What an odd thing to say. "So?"

"So, sharing a tub with me would make you a masochist." Harlan's fingers find the midsection of my bralette top and unhooks away.

"I chose," I let out in a hushed tone. "What happens now?"

Harlan gets up and steps forward as the wiry golden hair on his arms stands up. "Now," he says, "we'll see just exactly what you've gotten yourself into. Go. There's a good girl."

I head inside and see an old-fashioned claw-foot tub. I start the bath and see Harlan is quite the herbalist—bath balms and bath salts galore.

"It all looks so nice..."

"Nice is for a Pottery Barn. Did we forget how this works?" Harlan says shadily from the door. "Pretty sure clothes are forbidden."

He's clearly playing a role, and you know what? I can, too. Be light, better yet—malleable. Easy. It's the only way to pull through from losing... everything. Save punishing myself for another day.

So, I'll turn it off.

"Could you provide a little assistance?" I ask suggestively and pull down both bralette straps.

"From a psychopath or sociopath?"

"Surprise me. I wouldn't expect anything less."

Harlan walks toward me, his leer at its full intensity. I don't back away, but my chest cramps with every step he takes. There's a wild look on his face—a look as if I were standing on the edge of a cliff. And my toe still hurts.

"Harlan, you're staring."

"Apologies. Sometimes I don't realize how sidetracked I can get from eyeing my muse."

He keeps calling me that. How come? Yeah, it's a term of endearment, but it's an unusual one.

"It's okay. Obinna, he—"

"Did your husband ever stare at you the way I do?"

"You know the answer to that…" I let out in one breath.

"So, I don't want to hear about him anymore." We come together, intertwined with yearning tongues and lips. Then he pauses for a bit. "This socio—psychopath is no longer goddamn sharing you."

Turn it off and keep it off, Patience.

I experience continuous rhapsody with Harlan McCandles. As we sit and soak together, I lather myself with his body essentials. He sits in the tub and cradles my soapy back as I lean against his slender, yet athletic build. His lips and tongue find my bare skin, nuzzling almost every part of me.

"Don't you ever take these damn things off?" Harlan lifts up my wrists to pick apart my Naini Cuff bangles. "I can feel your separation anxiety from here, kid."

"They stay on," I say obstinately.

"Sounds like faulty manufacturing," he jests.

"They stay on, Harlan. They just do."

"Is it a cultural thing or—"

"Sure."

He finally leaves it alone, and I'm thankful white guilt prevails this time around.

"I can't believe I almost gave him a daughter," I voice for no reason whatsoever.

"Almost?"

"Miscarriage. A year ago. An old student got unruly on my watch, attacked me, and then I wasn't pregnant anymore." My throat forms a lump at the mention of it. So much for playing the role and keeping things light. "Had night terrors for a while, with stubborn insomnia. Sorry. I know you said you didn't want to talk about Obinna anymore but—"

"Don't apologize," Harlan instructs. "And never keep stuff

like that bottled up for too long. Internalizing is the worst."

He squeezes me and raises my face to his. His mouth is so soft and inviting; his eyes almost trap my thoughts in a mystic trance, but they're not distracting enough to stop my pity party.

"I have no place else to go. Yeah, there's the two-thousand dollars Jayson paid for the abstract, plus my savings here and there, but to put down first and last month's rent at a new place, student loan and car payments, not to talk about utilities—oh shit. I'm gonna need to afford a lawyer if our marriage is over—a real good one. I'll only get through the day by the skin of my teeth."

"So, then, stay here," Harlan problem solves. "I don't mind the company."

Could I? It's not like my days at UNT, where I'm camping out in my boyfriend's dorm. I'm legally married and acting like I have all the time in the world again. But what do I get out of being responsible? Ignored, cast aside, and discarded. I wasted my teens and twenties following arbitrary rules, and I refuse to let my thirties go out the same way.

"Are you seeing anyone else?"

"All I see is you."

"Okay. Only if you'll have me."

"Where's my Patience?" he asks, washing my hair. "Where could she be?"

"I'm here. I'm happy to be here with you."

"It's midnight, November 15th. Happy Birthday."

Oh my. He remembered. Hmm, come to think of it—he might lean toward a psychopath. If we were still playing that game, I mean.

But at any rate—

"I'm kinda freaking out."

"Why, beautiful?"

"Don't you think it's all happening too fast?"

"That's a lot of pressure to put on a guy."

"...A guy I might be falling for."

Harlan wraps his Sistine Chapel arms around me, and we both sit in the water to contemplate.

"Harlan's Patience. I like the sound of that." He seems pleased with himself.

"Me, too."

"It's a gamble, though," Harlan says as he lights up a blunt.

"What is?"

"To love me. I don't aspire to settle down like most women do."

"Oh," I reply, realizing I failed to see the big picture. "So, then, where do you see yourself in ten years?"

"Haha. Wow. This is a highly inappropriate job interview."

I splash him, smiling. "No, for real."

With the look on Harlan's face, I think I asked the wrong thing.

"I'm going to tell you this right now. I don't believe in ten-year plans. In fact, I reject them. Who's to say I won't keel over from a heart attack in two years? Then what was it all for? And, Patience, if that's what you're looking for with me, I think we should cut our losses now. Could you really say you wouldn't mind not being a suburban mom while with me?"

"I am a mom," I say adamantly.

"Right. Shit, of course," he retracts. "What I'm saying is, that's not for me, though."

"So, what about your immediate family?" I ask.

"What about them?"

"Do I have to spell it out for you? I know about you losing your dad, but what about your mom? Do you have any siblings? You never even bothered to ask me the same thing."

"Why the fuck would I if it's about stuff that drags me down?" Harlan says testily. "I brought myself up and relied on little to no one. And here I am now. Not everything needs a play-by-play. It's not my style. Besides, I'm more interested in this flawlessly sculpted woman sharing a tub with me... that I plan to devour as much as I please. Not the past. Let's just see where we end up from here."

On second thought, he's looking more like a sociopath to me.

Um, I don't want to play anymore.

Let's give it some careful thought a little longer.

I sit with the knowledge about Harlan. Usually, it's a deal breaker. But with a new beginning in store, let's try it. Let's live in the moment, not for the future.

A part of Harlan is better than no Harlan at all.

I think.

* * *

My mom left sixty-seven missed calls and completely maxed out my voicemail.

She knows. A little over two weeks after my birthday, Obinna finally spilled.

I drag myself out of bed and debate whether I should ruin both of our mornings.

Ugh. Rip off the Band-Aid and push through.

"Harlan? Are you here?"

No answer. Good.

I put Mom on speaker and hear the phone buzz on the other end. Maybe she won't answer because it's early. And she's most likely doing her walking exercise at the mall while doing intermittent fasting.

Beep. Wrong.

"Well, if it isn't the daughter who I no longer recognize," Mom snaps on the other end. "Patience, do you understand the gravity of what you've done to our family?"

"Mom, first off... what was told to you, specifically? I can't address anything until I know."

"Who is this white boy you are out gallivanting with—having no shame?! As if I would raise such a child in my household? Answer me!" The hatred in her voice voids any maternal aspects of her aura.

"I'll answer if you stop screaming," I try to rationalize. "I really hope you're not outside. The neighbors, you know."

"Shut your loose mouth!" Mom shouts. "Why do my neighbors concern you? Patience, concern yourself with your husband! Concern yourself with that instead of some shaggy-haired riff raff!"

"Mom, I'm not having this conversation with you then."

"It's because we stopped going to church, isn't it?!" she goes on with vengeance. "Our Igbo morals are dwindling! Jesus, give me strength."

When Mom gets like this, it's total word vomit for her. She has to get it all out before she even tries to hear from anybody else.

"You know... you truly are your father's daughter. An adulterous swine."

There she is! Step right up, Mother of the Year, everyone—passing on generational trauma for the next sucker!

I've accepted she isn't an easy woman to love a long time ago.

"Hello? Are you there?! I am talking to you!"

"Am I, Mother? An adulterous swine?"

"Patience, do not insult me by calling me your mother. I am clearly not that! No child of mine would drag our names through the mud." Her logic defies so much and so little at the same time.

"All right, if there's nothing else..."

"As a matter of fact, there is!" Mom says in a shrill voice. "You aren't worth the twenty-two hours of labor I almost died from."

A faint *tick* encases my eardrum. I believe it is my last damn nerve.

"Well, if it makes you feel better, there's a good chance I'm infertile."

"Ha! And you're proud of this?"

"If it means discontinuing our evidently cursed bloodline, then I guess so."

"Stay away from my funeral, you wicked girl."

Click.

Bye, Mom.

"Um, you want to tell me what that was about?" Harlan appears from the back patio, squinting as he adjusts to the morning rays.

I waltz up to him and place my fingers on his mouth. "I... do not, not in the slightest."

"Well, the lady wants what the lady wants."

Harlan picks me up easily. "Think we could squeeze in five minutes?"

"Yeah, uh—no." I come back down. "I have work in a few."

"Skip. Do it."

"Didn't we skip last Monday? You're a professor, right? Aren't you required to do actual research, publish papers, or go to staff meetings?"

"I'm what you'd call—in your universe—a long-term sub, darlin'." Harlan puts on a silly twang in his speech. "Or an adjunct professor. The PD training where we first met was a one and done deal. A limited-term contract means only having to do one-third of the work and with a loosey-goosey schedule."

I shake my head and grab my stuff for Seabrook, anyway. "It's been fun, but the real world calls."

Harlan stops me at the door, buries his face in my stomach, and pouts. "But I want to do something fun today."

My ears perk up. "I'm listening."

Harlan flashes a wink and takes out a bag with pills in it. Immediately, my ears go ice cold. "Harlan, what the hell? Drugs? At seven-thirty in the morning?"

"Molly has never let me down, and I'm hoping you don't, either." He places one on his tongue and swallows. My throat goes dry as I watch. "Well?"

I grow itchy at the thought.

"I—won't—let—anything—happen—to—you," Harlan says with a kiss between each word. "It's not like the nineties or early two thousands, when PSAs actually had grounds to scare people away from drugs. Usually, people take it at late-night parties, with crowds and shit. But I use it for my artistic process from time to time, and hey, it might help yours, too. Your talent has been there all along; it just needs a little more foreplay to come out of its shell more often. You know what I mean?"

I do. That's what has me very perturbed. I'm already out of sick days, so they might dock my pay for today. But to skip work to take Molly? Way too out of bounds for me.

"Harlan, I don't know. That's kind of a big deal. I never even smoked a cigarette in high school."

"You're joking. You mean you bypassed freshman, sophomore, junior, and senior year of both high school and college completely clean?" His eyes share his astonishment.

"Yes, sir."

"For some inexplicable reason, that's incredibly hot."

"Immigrant parents have a knack of throwing a wrench into those sorts of plans." I examine the bag. "So, this is a game changer."

"I know, right?" he says in a kittenish way. "The possibilities alone would make your toes curl. I'll take it easy on you. Take half and see how that goes." He tickles my thigh and, of course, wins me over.

First and last time, promise.

I swallow... and pray this pill doesn't end me.

* * *

After taking Molly, the phone call from Mom becomes a distant memory. While higher than a kite, Harlan and I commit to a hedonistic awakening with each other and pass out.

I wake up smeared in paint and in front of an easel, totally wiped.

Wait, did I create this work?

There's an abstract painting, fresh, too. The wet slick of the paint is still visible. The border core colors are periwinkle,

Prussian Blue, and sapphire with thin lines of gold as a nice touch.

But what wins me over are the eyes.

Harlan's eyes stand out in the abstract background and are accentuated by emerald rings. It's so jaw dropping. How can I not remember painting such a thing?

"So, that's what you were doing in here?" Harlan sneaks in to comment. "Way to take it easy on my new acrylic paints. Geez."

"Harlan, it's you." I pull him to the abstract. "Look! It's you! I must've done it when I was rolling."

Harlan continues to look at the art, but doesn't seem to share the same excitement.

"You… don't like it?" I ask, my smile faltering.

Noticing his lack of enthusiasm, Harlan simply stretches. "I mean—it's definitely something. The core colors mainly steal the show. It's only—you didn't check with me first, so you would've known I never put personal elements of myself in my work or allow it in anyone else's. If I can help it."

"Oh," I say. "But why?"

"It's only a preference. That's all."

I frown as I sense his insincerity from here. "But I was inspired and did it for you."

Harlan comes over and bearhugs me. He nestles his face in my hair, covering my scalp in light kisses. "I know you meant well. And I can see it means a lot to you."

So, why not the other way around?

Then his whole energy shifts into a different gear. "So, you know—whatever. I'm going to smoke for a few. Are you coming?"

I look back at the work I was initially ecstatic about and

wonder what it is about him that doesn't want to be captured.

Well, either way, it's not going to waste. I'll secretly apply for the Colby Arts Grant with the abstract to find out if I have something to offer the world, not just Jayson. Then he'll see there's a method to *my* madness.

But for now—

"Yeah, okay. I'll be there in a second."

* * *

The comedown from last night is kicking my ass at nine in the morning as I'm moping at my desk—feverish. My heart pounds, and I perspire like I swam five-thousand miles in the Mississippi River.

I am not in tip-top shape, but with my students, they're none the wiser.

And I hope it stays that way.

"Hey, Dominick—use quiet hands, please."

"I'm trying!" He's fidgeting with his pencil and tapping it on his desk. Dominick's always been restless, but he seems more amped up today. He kicks the legs of his chair and whistles to an ever-so changing tune. "Can I do a cartwheel? It'll help me calm down, like climbing bookshelves does. Please? I've been practicing, and I really want to show you!"

"Now's not the best time. We don't want to distract other friends who are trying to work." I try to pull myself together and make sure I don't sound like I'm on the verge of barfing when I speak. "Let's go over your science packet. Could you bring it to the kidney table?"

Dominick heads to my small group area. As he gets closer, he turns his nose up at me. "Geez, Ms. O, you're really sweaty.

Did you run up here or something?"

I panic and grab my compact from my purse. Using the small mirror, I see a sweat mustache and sideburns that pour and pour.

Talk about unflattering. "It's a little hot in our classroom, that's all."

"But December just started, and we're all wearing jackets in here."

"Let's focus on habitats rather than Ms. O. Here you go, number one. Double check your answer for me, okay?"

Nadia leaves her small group with Nyla and joins us, too. "Sorry to say it but, D is right, Mrs. Okoye. You've looked better. Are you sick?"

Yes! Let's roll with that. "Not sure. It sorta came on all of a sudden. But I might need to go see the nurse."

Nadia lends a supportive hand pat and a kind smile. "I can hold down the fort until you get back, so go rest. We need our Ms. O back in one piece."

Nadia rocks like no other. "Thanks."

I grab my stuff and walk to the door in a rush with damp hands.

Nyla jumps out of her seat in alarm. "Ms. O, look out!"

Dominick cartwheels straight toward the door in a burst of speed. I barely have time to react before he crashes into me. My purse flies out of my hands, spilling its contents onto the floor. My lipstick, pens, phone, old receipts, and wallet—all out for everyone to see.

"Sorry, I—I thought I could do one real quick before you noticed," Dominick says, regretfully.

I managed to get up and rub my sore hip. "Well, now we know. I'm sure you're going to be outstanding in the Olympics someday, but not today. See you later, Dom. Your science packet looks lonely."

"Okay."

"No need to fear, Nadia's here!" Nadia says. She shows off her pretend Street Fighter skills, then crouches and begins shoving things inside my bag at once. "We'll get your purse situated in no time."

But I don't joke with her. Because seeing the baggy of Molly in her hands almost sends me into cardiac arrest.

Why the hell didn't I switch purses before leaving for work?!

"Oh, um, thanks." I reach for it, which is my first mistake.

Nadia soon gets a better look at the baggie, and her full face quivers warily. "Uh, yeah, sure, Mrs. O, it's all yours."

She knows. She knows. Of course, she knows; she's younger than me and more likely familiar with the scene of people who do it often. What was I thinking? I have to cover my tracks and double down immediately. "Geez, I shouldn't flaunt my birth control so casually next time, am I right?"

Birth control?! That's the best I could come up with on the fly?

Nadia steps backward slowly, as if I'm infected with a flesh eating virus. "I gotta go check on Nyla. Go ahead and visit the nurse—like I said, get better soon."

She leaves me in the dust.

Figures. It's always something.

* * *

I put what happened yesterday with Nadia on a rain check because now I have Obinna on my tail. After responding to his lawyer through email, I involuntarily head to the court building for the separation meeting the following day.

The conference room is bare and drafty, providing no warmth.

Obinna and his lawyer sit across from me, in the middle of a hushed, fervent discussion. I sit with mine, the only one a public school teacher could afford, and I already have an idea this won't work out for me.

Obinna's lawyer speaks first. "At this time, my client is prepared to proceed with the trial separation as initially discussed—accompanied by the following stipulations. We will revisit the matter on the agreed-upon date to determine whether he wishes to formally pursue divorce proceedings."

Obinna looks off into space with disillusionment, and I imagine he's questioning our entire relationship. Tim, my prepubescent lawyer with braces, looks up at me for pushback.

I shake my head. "Whatever makes it as painless as possible."

"Don't lose your sense of humor," Obinna says, with his cheekbones raised and pupils reddened.

It's nettlesome that this is what I've turned him into.

"My client agrees," Tim supports. "Let's move on to assets."

Obinna whispers to his no nonsense lawyer.

She nods and turns back to us. "My client demands all stocks and bonds made under his name, his contributions to checking and savings within shared accounts, and removal of spouse from health insurance and beneficiary titles. He will offer a grace period of sixty days before these requests take place."

The more the list goes on—the more final everything sounds. Does being with Harlan equate to this much loss?

I nod. "That's fair."

Tim nods as well, while I'm unsure what role he serves in these delegations.

"In reference to IVF payments that were made a year prior—my client is requesting reimbursement for the last two cycles."

For god's sake. I know I have no right to make a scene, but that's nonsensical.

"Obi, please. That has no ties with what I've done to you."

Obi doesn't look at me—the tangential vapor that I've become to him. Instead, he allows Tim the courtesy of eye contact. "Tell your client she wanted to take a break from our marriage, and I'm simply honoring that. Those IVF cycles were meant to grow a family with my wife. Since she currently doesn't want that title, why should I keep paying for them? It's not like we got a kid out of th—"

"Watch it." My voice dips with an edge. "I get you're hurting, but when it comes to that—I'm not the fucking one."

"Does your client typically use such derogatory language?" Obinna's lawyer swipes her thin bangs out of her smudged eyeliner. "I mean, really? I thought she was an elementary educator."

"What business is that of yours?!"

"Enough!" an astoundingly forward Tim speaks up. "Let's bring the focus back to the delegations, please."

Everyone gives a slight bob of their heads to acknowledge him.

"My client and I will deliberate the request of the IVF payments and come to an offer that meets mutual needs at a future date. Is that fair to be agreed upon?"

Obinna and his lawyer whisper further.

She nods. "My client says that will do for now—"

"Are we even, Obi? You won. I'm disgusted with myself—just like you wanted!" I shout across from him. "Look at me! What am I not deserving of that anymore? None of it was supposed to happen—the affair, the lies—but it did. I needed you, and you weren't there!"

"Patience, get what I'm about to say through your skull. Nothing—absolutely nothing—can clear you from your actions. It's who you are. You're not an honest person. Not with me and not with yourself. Clara, I'm done. There's nothing left to discuss."

Obi rises out of his spinning seat, and his lawyer—Clara—works to chase after him.

"Well, it could've gone much worse."

Shut up, Tim.

I make my way out the door and pass the waiting room aisle by the courtroom.

Oh no.

Obinna didn't come alone. His parents are with him, hugging their son in solidarity. His dad, Godswill, whose head resembles a pumpkin, shoots me a dirty look before returning his attention back to Obi. Glad to see things haven't changed.

I am dirt to them. I failed to aspire toward his mother and father's matrimony fulfillment of thirty years plus. But what isn't clear is... is their marriage out of devotion or traditional duty?

Because that alone is a pronounced difference.

Agatha spots me off to the side. I want to run, but her glower sticks me in place. It's odd. In all my years of knowing her, Agatha was never scary. If anything, she is the complete opposite of my mom—soft-spoken and mild-mannered, never raising her voice, and was usually cordial in social gatherings.

But now, I broke her son's heart.

And shit, she's coming over.

"Aunty, I wish I knew what to say," I start. I'm taken aback by her beauty at sixty years of age. She has café au lait skin and is absent of wrinkles, wearing a cream Ann-Taylor suit. "I never meant for any of it to happen."

Agatha nods dejectedly, and in a twist, grabs my hand, giving it a gentle hold. "It was nice having a daughter while it lasted. Please bear in mind, the ones that only meet misery are the ones that brag to God about their future plans. How foolish of them to think it's within their control. So, I hope you find whatever it is you are searching for."

My principles shrivel up inside as she leaves me with those words. She does what my mother couldn't even do.

Demonstrating placidity and disappointment in me, hand in hand.

"Mom, let's go. There's nothing left for us here," Obinna calls out to Agatha as he looks at me, disengaged.

I guess not.

CAMP ARNICA

When I get back to Harlan's, the beat-down I took from Obi and his mother puts me in a deep funk. He loved me as his soulmate. She loved me as her own. Thinking of the caring words Agatha spoke before we walked down the aisle together takes me to a loving place.

"Wish me luck, Aunty?"

"No luck needed. Patience, you are meant to be Obinna's in this life and the next."

And I said fuck all to both.

I'm somewhat thankful that it's the weekend marking the start of winter break at Seabrook. My motivation is null—I have little to no drive to do anything, including work. I lean towards wanting to take a leave of absence upon my return, but I choose not to. I don't get to take the easy way out after completely blindsiding Obinna. Plus, my kiddos need me, especially after losing Grayson. I just need to figure out how to balance it all.

Harlan spots me sniffling as I bury myself in sheets, trying to escape the verdict.

I'm a trash human being.

He gets into bed with me and wraps me in his hold. "He's gonna be pissy about it, so it should be what you expected, right?"

"I don't know."

"Patience, come on—don't be so hard on yourself. He'll be okay."

But will I be?

"Hey, beautiful?"

"What?"

"It's time to go to Colorado."

Huh? Come on, now's not the time to mess with my head. "Sure thing, snag me some first-class tickets, why don't you? Better yet, a private jet."

Harlan takes the covers off of my head like a frustrated parent. "Hey, could you stop being emo for a second and listen? I usually go around this time of year, anyway. Plus, I know Camp Arnica will be good for you. And by the way—it's an honorary road trip."

That's already putting my mood toward higher skies. "What kind of camp?"

"The kind that makes you become one with the earth and try things beyond the devil's lettuce and nose candy. When I can't think of shit to create, it's the best go-to for a mind refresher. There's this art exhibition—at the Concord Gallery—that's two months away, and my inspo needs to be in tiptop shape for my work to stand out. I'm talking big time art collectors, like Corbin Reyes, will pop by."

"Who?"

"Google him or look up *Apollo Magazine* issues within a year. I'm sure he's in there... not to mention being loaded as hell."

I pull up his net worth, and my jaw unhinges. "Can we retire the term *starving artist* now?"

He laughs, then drags me by my foot to the edge of the bed.

Harlan suddenly has the energy of a breakdancer, leaping up and skipping to the closet. "And I'm over talking about it. We clearly need a reset, so quit stalling, girl! Move that nice derriere of yours and help me pack."

Harlan doesn't think about things like work, routine, and adulting. He's fueled by spontaneity. "Like now?"

"Like yesterday. I'll load the Jeep, and we can head out in a couple of hours."

Why deny it? I need a boatload of happiness and he's offering to supply. "Yes, let's do it!"

Can't wait for what our adventure on wheels entails.

* * *

Harlan and I hit the open road a little after dawn, with the sun barely awake and the sky painted in soft pinks and oranges. He drives, his one hand loosely gripping the wheel, the other draped out the window. His hair is tossed about, like he's just rolled out of bed, and I guess, in a way, he did.

On our way, we blast "Don't Fear the Reaper" by Blue Oyster Cult.

"What's going on in that wistful head of yours, kid?" Harlan asks. His voice breaks through the hum of the engine and the crackle of the old station he insists on.

I grin, modeling his vampiric smirk. "Nothing."

"Then get over here."

I lean into his shoulder and escape into his freeing way of living. Harlan grips firmly, as if I were in danger of shooting through the roof of his worn-down Jeep if he let go. "Ever been to Colorado before?"

"Nope. Never left Texas much, actually," I admit. There's a

ladybug in the rear-view mirror I watch crawl about. Obinna and I never really traveled, except to Mexico, for our honeymoon. Too busy with work, with saving, with planning for a future that never quite arose the way we'd imagined.

"You're in for a treat, then. It's like nothing you've ever seen. The mountains, the air... It reminds a guy to simply live and stay off social media for one measly second. Fresh, you know? Clean. I'm so goddamn jealous of you, experiencing this place for the first time. Mabel, the owner of Camp Arnica, is cool. She gave us a hell of a discount... um—most likely because we had, uh, history."

"But I've seen pics of her on the cabin website... isn't she almost fifty?!"

"She's a beautiful woman who takes great care of herself. Don't fault me for it. I was in a shitty place and she saw that. She took me in, and I'll always be grateful."

"When was this?"

"I was twenty-three. She was forty-four."

"Hold up—"

"Besides, she's married now, not with kids but like—fifty dogs, cats, and ferrets. Okay, maybe not fifty. What, you thought you were the only older woman I've courted?"

"I'm older than you by a year and a couple months, tops! Forget it. Just... just drive." I increasingly get car sick and ponder if this trip is a bright idea.

The endless stretch of highway seems to symbolize the possibilities before me. I left my old life behind—Obinna, my supposed soulmate of commonalities. The neat little house, the daily structure. Now, I'm here with Harlan, taking in the Colorado air. Go figure.

"You okay?" Harlan asks. He must have sensed my unease.

He's excellent at picking up on the things I don't say. "What's pressing you now?"

"Think I'll finally figure out what I want to do with my life?" I say, half-joking. "I hurt a lot more people than I thought with my past choices."

Harlan grits his teeth and doesn't take his eyes off the road. "When you get there, it'll all come together for you. I'll make sure of it."

"What if it doesn't?"

"Shit, wrong turn." Harlan swings a reverse that jolts his lax body posture forward. "If you ask me, I think you already know what you want. Just gotta give yourself permission to take it."

I'm caught between the life I left and the one I'm hurtling toward faster than I can stop.

We reach patches of light snow, letting us know we're getting closer. According to Harlan, we lucked out visiting this time of year and having the destination be in the southeastern region of Colorado. It's somewhat chilly but not unendurable. We stop at a diner, ditch our Texas threads, and change into slightly thicker layers.

After two more hours, Harlan and I pull into the cabin's gravel driveway. The sound of tires crunching on stone scratches an itch in my brain I didn't even know I had. The air is crisp, the kind that slices right through you, and the sky is an endless blue. I roll down the window to breathe it in.

"We're here."

A wooden sign swings gently from a post: *Camp Arnica*. It's carved by hand, each letter worn smooth by time and weather. We head to the front door, ready to rest our tired bones from the drive. Mainly Harlan, though, since I stayed a passenger princess the entire journey.

The door of the cabin creaks open, and an older lady steps out.

"Hey, gorgeous. Remember me?" He greets her with a hug.

"Harlan McCandles, it's been forever and a day!"

Who I can only presume is Mabel, has brown hair with a few gray strands pulled into a neat bun, a thin but lively smile and a slim figure.

I study the hug further and determine it's harmless. Like between mother and son.

Good. One less thing to worry about.

"Welcome!" she calls out and waves us closer. "Come in, come in! Arnica awaits you!"

"Thank you. This place is beautiful."

"We're glad to have you both. Patience?"

"Yes, ma'am," I reply, feeling a bit like a schoolgirl again under her watchful eyes.

The cabin is cozy, filled with the scent of cinnamon. A fire crackles in the hearth, and the walls are lined with paintings and photographs of the surrounding landscape.

"I hope you'll find this place to your liking," Mabel says. She hands us mugs of steaming hot chocolate. "There's so much to do here—crafts, massages, swimming in the hot springs... Whatever your heart desires."

"It's perfect," Harlan says, as he sinks into an armchair by the fire. "Exactly what we need. Maybelline, you never cease to amaze me with how you keep up with this place."

Mabel blushes, revealing her youth significantly. "Thanks, sweetness."

Where have I heard that before?

The cabin doors slam open and shut behind us, which

signals a new entry.

"Kenji!" Harlan exclaims, rising out of his seat. "What the fuck? Get over here, man! What brings you? I thought you mentioned bailing this year."

Kenji smirks and pulls Harlan into a quick hug. "Perks of being a freelancer—you can make your own schedule. Can't let you have all the fun, right? Think I'd let you keep this to yourself?"

"So, uh, where's Vanessa? I thought she would've had a knack for this whole cabin thing."

Kenji sighs and shoves his hands into his jacket pockets. "Nah. Might've had a chance with her if I was roided up like her new dude."

"Ouch." Harlan mock-clutches his chest. "Her loss, Ken. On to the next one."

"Pssh, already checking DMs, you feel me?"

I wobble from side to side with rolling suitcases, with my social battery already depleted. "I think I'll turn in; it was a long drive. Mabel—sorry—where's our room located again?"

Harlan swats at my leg. "Funny how sitting on your keister for ten hours has you plumb tired. I'm the one with the charley horse here."

"Oops—silly me, let's have some of our staff help you out with that and your bags." Mabel nervously jogs down a hallway and makes a left. "Hang tight."

"You're not seriously thinking of turning in this early, are you, art show girl?" Kenji comments. "Shit goes down when the lights do."

Harlan takes my luggage from me and nods his head to the back door. "He's right. Leave sleep at home. Have a free for all at Arnica. What do you say, Patience?"

Dammit. I say I'm outnumbered. "Ugh. Fine." If I choose to be a stick in the mud, I'll never hear the end of it.

"Told you she's cool." Harlan gives me a soft peck, just as Mabel's staff comes to take our luggage. "So, what are we trying to get into first?"

* * *

"Hey," Harlan says.

"Um, hey."

"Do you have faith in me, Okoye?"

"Yes."

"Then... It'll be fine. When you're with me, it'll be nothing less."

We start with Ayahuasca. How Mabel has these connections is a mind curdling mystery to me.

The drug kicks in, and at first, we couldn't take three steps without laughing our heads off. I saw green rhinos, and Harlan, pink giraffes. Then he and Kenji took turns riding on each other's backs, pretending to be these miraculous animals—back and forth on the patio. I never released so many endorphins before—watching two grown men try to use their makeshift riding crops on each other.

Kenji swore up and down he was going to pet blue elephants by the lake. While trying to do so, he yelled a bee flew down his pants. He ran around like a chicken with its head cut off, ditched his clothes, and hopped into the freezing lake underneath the cabin. Harlan was the first one to take a jab at him.

"Kenji! Nice ass, baby!"

By that time, both Harlan and I were rolling on the floor in giggle fits.

Kenji... was not.

"My dick! It stung my dick! Fucking hell!"

"I'm sure you're fine. Bees wouldn't be out and about in this sweater weather," I reminded him, sitting up on the heated patio.

"Why fight life's minor improvements?" Harlan said. He offered a hand to pull Kenji out. "If you're really stung, a couple extra inches wouldn't hurt. Let alone hurt you."

"Shut up!" An unusually frazzled Kenji shivered, almost battling hypothermia while trying to maintain modesty in front of me and put his clothes back on.

Bless you, Camp Arnica.

Once it's around five PM, the effect wears off a bit, but not totally. Just enough for us to settle down and get artistic.

Now, I'm sitting on a sun-warmed rock, a paintbrush in my hand as the mountain breeze carries the scent of pine. Harlan's laughter echoes across the valley as he adds another splash of color to his canvas. The colors seem to dance on the fabric of reality and begin blurring the outer field of my sight. Jeez, his laughter is infectious—I have no choice but to join him.

"Boo!"

"Harlan!"

"Shall we dance, my dear?" Maybe it's the Ayahuasca, but I see that Harlan's ribbons of sun-kissed hair frame his eyes. Like the clear blue of a summer sky with floating green balloons. He circles around and around the patio— resembling a spinning top.

Yeah—he's for sure, gone. "Don't drop me, dork."

"I'm adorkable, thank you."

Kenji appears dried off with a change of clothes as his silhouette darkens against the burning sunset. He holds a bottle, smiling as he approaches us. "You two look like you're having fun."

"We are!" I reply, laughing as Harlan lifts me up over his shoulder and spins me around. His hands smear my waist with paint.

"Holy shit, I'm getting dizzy," he admits.

"You're getting a new tattoo, too!" The Ayahuasca makes me childish, and I smear paint all over his face.

"Oh, I'm gonna have tons of fun punishing you for that."

"Quit it! Okay, okay, uncle!"

Kenji sets down two glass cups and tries to stay out of the way during Harlan's wild spins.

Harlan then shakes his head. "No more Aya for me, Ken."

"Well, you're in luck. It's vodka."

"I'll have a swig!" I gleefully request and hop down from his shoulders.

Kenji comes right over with the bottle, held up in a pouring motion. "No reason to waste a whole cup for a swig." Then he winks. "Tilt your head back and open up—Kenji's coming down your throat."

"Woah!" Harlan nudges Kenji away from me, jokingly. At least, I think it is.

Kenji stumbles back pretty far, and for a split second, looks visibly pained. A splash of vodka spills onto the patio deck. "Damn, McCandles, wasting good quality shit here!"

"You nearly lost your dick. Don't lose your life."

"Hey, I had to at least try it once, right?"

"Not on her, man." Then Harlan's smile thins.

Sheesh. I'm tripping over way too much testosterone.

Change the topic. "There's a lot of history here in these mountains. Multiple energies."

Harlan exhales through his nose and plays with the belt hoops on my jeans. "Energy's always good."

Kenji nods, taking a sip from his glass. "Yeah, but not all energy is good energy. I ran into someone earlier. Thought you should know."

"Who?"

"Tori's here."

Harlan's face goes blank. He puts his brush down slowly, as if he's afraid of making any sudden moves. "Tori?" he repeats.

Kenji takes another drink. "Yeah. She's up at the main lodge. Came with some friends, I think."

I look at Harlan, lost. "Who's Tori?"

Harlan doesn't answer, his eyes fixed on the horizon. He's miles and miles away.

"Hey, she'll probably keep to her side of the cabin."

"Damn. For real, Kenji?"

"You had a bad trip when things went left with her. It's not likely to happen again." His green-haired friend tries his best to console him. "No one's holding that against you."

"She will. Fuck this and fuck her."

Without another word, he walks back toward the lodge, leaving me and Kenji to stand there, dawdling.

"Hey! Where are you going?"

Harlan strolls farther north, either too far to hear my calls or refusing to answer me. I don't get it. Weren't we just having fun?

"Kenji, you gotta come clean," I say, approaching him.

"Who is Tori to Harlan?"

"Nah, I can't do my boy like that." Kenji takes his bottle and follows after him. "It's his business to tell, not mine."

No, not when I just got a piece of hallucinogenic escape. The easy, carefree world Harlan and I were building will crack if I don't understand. And I'm worried when it comes crashing down I'll be the one left standing in the rubble. "Please? I don't want this girl bumming him out the whole trip. Then he'll be no fun for either of us."

Kenji seems swayed over by my argument. "The closest thing to an ex. Lost his shit over her when she ended it, actually around this time last year in the cabin."

No way.

"Yeah, it was pretty bad. Why she broke it off with Harlan when he was high is anybody's guess. He was fucked up on a lot of stuff. Alcohol, weed, and the special variety... Harlan had to be, anyway. That's about it. You heading back? I'll walk you."

"Yeah."

We begin the journey.

"You two met at Taos a few years back, right?" I question, picking at my sweater sleeve.

"Yeah, I was his old weed connect." Kenji blows into his empty vodka bottle, turning it into a musical jug. "Then, he found out I was looking into getting in the tat business, and he let me practice on his arms a few times."

"Nice work."

"Thanks. Um, you know I was just messing around with the *going down your throat* bit, right? Sometimes my jokes are hit-and-miss." Kenji—with hands behind his head—flares his tiny nostrils. "Sorry. I sorta have a serious condition of foot in mouth disease. Kind of feels like high school all over again. Don't really have the best first impression pull like Harlan does."

I snicker in slight relief. "Hey, who hasn't become the epitome of cringe at least once?" The irony is, I'm liking him more already. It was big of Kenji to clear the air. He doesn't come off as scummy as, say—Jayson. More like a kid brother who doesn't know when to shut up. He's just a shadow to his more memorable friend, and tonight was a humbling reminder. "I already forgot about it. We're cool."

"Cool."

The Colorado chill follows us on our walk.

"So, you were married?" Kenji asks, while trying to skip rocks on the lake by the side of us. "Before meeting him?"

Crap. Way to make a good impression on my end. "Depends. What did he tell you?"

He lets out a quick snicker as his tan skin contrasts with his mint colored hair. "Playing it safe—I feel you. Only said he wasn't sure how into it you were trying to be because you seemed conflicted about the marriage, which I see now— you're not anymore."

"How observant. We're separated."

"You're... uh..."

"Go on."

"You're not the typical chick he would go for."

"What's that supposed to mean?"

"Have patience, Patience. I'm getting there." Kenji tosses his last rock. "Mabel and Tori, they differ on the eyes, but they're both non-traditional females. They don't want the house in the subs, the husband, well at least Tori doesn't. Especially the two point five kids."

As he goes on, I think—how long can I hold Harlan's attention for? Or am I seen as a quest for him to conquer, then attribute to a bedmate? "Yeah, Kenji, I think I got it."

"Just hold your own with him and definitely around Tori Clausen."

I thought I was running away from my past. But Harlan's? His past hitched a ride here, and I'm not sure if we can outrun it.

* * *

At the main cabin, I learn Mabel has a tradition of hosting dinner at the dining table at seven-thirty. It's a little unorthodox that she expects every single guest to come, but according to Harlan and Kenji, she likes the family-style approach. It gives guests an opportunity to get to know each other and make memories.

But before I make myself known at dinner, I decide to check on Harlan in our cabin room.

I hear talking, so instead of walking straight in, I peek inside.

Harlan's lying down on the bed, and Mabel sits upright, running her fingers through his hair.

"It'll be all right. Enough time has passed to where it'll be all right."

"Mabel, I hate she has that over me and doesn't fucking care."

"Yes—Tori and her... Tori-isms can be a bit much here and there." Mabel leaves his hair alone and straightens up his collar. "However, she means well. It's okay to accept some people just aren't compatible with one another. We learn from it and move on so we can grow as people."

"Gee. Nice to see you taking her side, gorgeous."

"I—um...would hate to see you get carried away over her again..."

He doesn't reply, finding the popcorn ceiling more fascinating.

Mabel picks up Harlan's phone and flips through it. "Mind if I take a look?"

"Knock yourself out."

She has her hair down, making her look like a petite Julia Roberts. She stops scrolling and sees a picture that makes her blissful. "Not that you asked, but I like Patience for you. I think she'll calm you down some, sweetness."

Harlan smiles with genuine reflection at the mention of my name, which sits well with me. "Yeah, kind of like you used to."

"Yes, well... those days are long behind us."

"I'll get over it. Thanks for talking to me. I think I'll zone out on Spotify until dinner is ready."

And then my stomach flips a bit... as I watch Harlan give Mabel a lengthy kiss on her forehead, while tickling behind her ear.

Not like mother and son.

Mabel wears several emotions in ten seconds. Enraptured, then surprised, lastly—exhibiting restraint.

The shit was that about?

She gets up and turns beet red. "Dinner at seven-thirty sharp, mister."

The door creaks open.

"Hey, Patience! Enjoying yourself so far?"

"Yeah um... so far." I can't even string my freaking words

together. "I thought I'd catch a nap before dinner."

"Don't let me stop you. See you two shortly."

And Mabel is out the door.

Harlan has his AirPods on, blasting them to high heaven. He looks straight up with his hands behind his head.

I accompany him on the springy mattress and yank out an earbud. "Missed you, painting buddy."

"Kind of in the middle of self-regulating here."

"I can see that. Want to talk about it?"

"Clearly, we're not understanding the meaning of self-regulating."

"You're being mean. I'm only trying to help."

Harlan finally graces me with his attention and takes out the remaining AirPod. He turns on the side while his bejeweled eyes give me a once over, and then rubs my arm. "I didn't expect her to be here."

"I know," I say, still laying beside him. "Kenji told me a little about what happened between you two."

He seems mad, but it's not directed at me. "Tori's hot and cold. She's always been like that, and it drove me crazy when we were together. I don't know what she'll bring out of me if I see her at the table."

"I get that. But I'm here, too. Shutting down like this... it's not fair to me, either. I've also dealt with hot and cold with my husband, and I'm not doing that with you, too."

"You're right. I'm sorry, Patience. I suck. Let's enjoy it here and forget the bullshit."

Take that, Tori.

"Answer me this."

"Question away."

"You're officially over Maybelline, right?"

"Wow, seriously, kid?"

"It's only that—"

Harlan gets out of the bed, crouches in front of me, and rests his elbows on my knees. "When we met, she had just recovered from breast cancer. So, she needed me just as much as I needed her. And then it was over. And then she met the love of her life—Carl, which a hundred of me could never measure up to, and—all I'll say is... I had no choice but to accept it. She means a lot to me, but it'll never be what it was. Okay?"

"Okay." That's actually kind of sweet.

"Don't ask me to cut her out of my life to make you comfortable."

"I heard you, Harlan." I'll let it go for the time being, although—I brood over the possibility he'd choose her over me in a heartbeat. "We'll make it through dinner and then some." I say, though I'm not entirely sure if I believe it myself.

"Yeah." He squeezes back, but his grip feels loose, like he's holding on, but only just.

* * *

The dining room is warm and inviting, filled with other guests staying at Camp Arnica. Mabel and her staff have just laid out the dinner: Roast chicken, mashed potatoes, green beans, and a fragrant herb sauce.

The Arnica staff members—really just four recent high school graduates—truly outdid themselves.

"Help yourselves, everyone, and gather around!" Mabel instructs. "We also have vegan options, so dig in."

"What a missed opportunity. You're not wearing your *Kiss*

the Chef apron I love," Harlan says.

"Hey, buddy, you want to take this outside?" Carl, Mabel's big teddy bear of a husband, jokes.

If he knows the history between these two, then this is a bold way for Harlan to toe the line.

We're seated at the long wooden dining table. A low hum of conversation buzzes around the room, with the clatter of silverware against ceramic plates. Harlan sits beside me. His hand rests casually on my thigh under the table. Kenji is across from us—dark eyes twinkling mischievously as he teases Harlan about how he never saw him as a "mountain retreat" type of guy when they first met.

"I have a bit of a Nordic bloodline. Why wouldn't I be?"

"Fuck outta here. He's full of shit, isn't he, Patience?"

I smile, quite buzzed, and take a sip of the crisp white wine the staff pours generously throughout the meal. "Maybe a little."

Guests at the table uproar in chuckles.

Harlan squeezes my bouncing leg. "Don't listen to him. I've always had a soft spot for nature and for women who know what they want."

"If that's another shooting your shot at my wife, I'm serving you up for dinner next, Wise Guy. Roasting on a spit, with all the fixin'." Carl adds in a pinch of sass salt for good humor.

The chortles and snickers echo around the table until we hear the cabin front door open. Mabel rushes there, and then exclaims with joy.

"Tori! Where've you been? I was getting worried. Thought I was gonna have to set out a search party."

I didn't notice her at first—was too wrapped up in a conversation about a possible hike—but the second Harlan's hand tenses on me, I look up. She's striking, with thick, wavy auburn hair that spills over her shoulders. Her lips are painted a deep, bold red, and her green eyes move through the room, owning everything they touch. She's dressed in a sleek black sweater and dark jeans, effortlessly stylish in a way that makes her stand out against the more rustic setting of the cabin.

Kenji's green hair fades from the sight of her sucking the light-heartedness out of the room. "Why—the prodigal daughter returns."

"I wasn't planning to. I'm only here for tonight," she says, far from fazed. "Life... has other proposals for me. Hi, everybody!"

Guests and Arnica staff return her grand welcome.

Except for Harlan and me.

"Harlan... didn't think you'd be here. Hey."

"Hey, yourself." He doesn't stand. He doesn't even greet her properly. Instead, he leans back in his chair, arms crossed. His pink lips are a little parted, as if he's thinking of something he won't stick his neck out to say. "I don't stay where I'm not wanted. But of course, you follow the beat of your own drum."

She hasn't even been here all of five minutes, and Harlan's kicking ass and taking names.

"Wow, that's... a lot to unpack." Kenji pulls up a chair beside him. "Care to join us?"

"If she must." Harlan's hand crawls up my thigh, and he places it under my skirt.

Um... okay.

Thank goodness the mood hasn't turned, and everyone else

carries on with the evening. Appetites are being fulfilled, wine is poured infinitely, and weed is smoked by almost everyone here. Mabel and Carl for sure earned the cool parents title.

"Is this quinoa?" Kenji pokes at his plate with mild disgust. "Shit, I thought we were in Colorado, not California."

Carl thunks him on the shoulder with his big meaty fists. "You'll survive, Kenji. One quinoa salad won't kill you. Maybe it'll put some hair on your chest."

"Why not? It already looks like a pile of pubes..."

"Patience, honey, what is it you do for work?" Mabel asks from across the table.

"I've been a Special Education Behavioral Needs teacher for almost four years now. It's been a treat to do... until field trips are involved. The last one was at a police station, and it set off their sensory issues."

"Ditch the tons of weed, she's a narc!" Tori fans smoke away dramatically. "Shit, if anyone asks—we bought ours by the ounce, legally."

"Cool it, Tori." Mabel chooses to not share any laughs with her.

"I'm joking—Jesus, the name *Patience* really suits you. I hate kids. Don't see how I can deal with them like... ever. Getting my tubes tied is the best thing I've ever done."

"That, ladies and gentlemen, is what we call an overshare." Kenji pops open his second bottle of wine.

"Hate is a strong word," Mabel adds.

Tori gestures for Kenji to pass her the wine. "You don't have any, Mabes. You get it."

"Not by choice."

The table gets quiet from Mabel's solemn admission.

Could her life be mine one day?

"Besides, a strong word—*hate* could be seen as ignorant. So, read the room, why don't you?" Each time Harlan tries to get the last sting, his fingers climb higher and higher toward a bashful place. What is he trying to do? And why here and now?

Meanwhile, it's Tori's world, and we're just living in it. "I can take a hint. On to other news; we start our tour next month. I'm really excited about it. Got to keep my lungs extra strong till then. We just got back from performing in Cali, and we're heading up to Florida and New York next."

Well, here's me giving her another try. "What are your socials—Facebook, Instagram, TikTok?"

"Damn, Facebook? Talk about using the Wayback Machine. How old are you, again?" Tori asks.

Her comments remain unsolicited as Carl sets down a plate of pastries. "Patience is a teacher. People who are in an educational or corporate setting are going to be more likely to have a Facebook."

Harlan raises his hand. "I have one."

Tori blows a raspberry. "I guess that checks out."

The more she talks, the more I slightly see how she irks others. Just needing to have everyone know what she's about at every interval becomes grating.

"Hey, don't let her get to you, okay? Compared to you, she's classless," Harlan says to me, under his breath.

But what I don't get is why his fingers are now teasing to get inside of me with everyone else so close-knit. The museum was one thing. This is self-serving on his part.

Am I being tested again? Is that it? It's subtle, so subtle no one would notice, but I do. The softness of his touch tingles through my skin and makes me aware of every inch of him.

I shift in my chair, batting away certain thoughts. Harlan's jawline is even sharper in the candlelight. He catches my eye and gives me that small, knowing smile. The one that promises more later, when the night deepens and we're alone. I shiver, but not from the cold.

Kenji makes more suggestions. "Y'all wanna swing by the ski slopes tomorrow?"

Harlan sniffs, looking directly at tonight's chatterbox. "Depends who's all going."

"Blowing with the wind I see, and why am I not surprised?" Tori flips her movie star hair in retort.

Harlan's digits move again, this time tracing small circles on the front of my panties. My stomach tightens, but I keep my face composed and nod like I'm still part of the conversation while instinctively pulling his hand away from my crotch.

"The slopes are definitely a peaceful choice." My voice sounds strange, even to me.

Kenji's eyes dart between me and Harlan, and I wonder if he notices anything. If he can sense the unspoken thing that's happening, he doesn't show it, just surveys the table and sips his wine.

"Be careful of the critters out there, though," Carl warns, while clearing his plate. "Bobcats mainly. Little bastards."

"Ooh—little bastards! Damn, that should've been the name of us!" Tori yells.

I smooth my skirt back down. "What is your band's real name?"

"The Sirens. Speaking of—Harlan, remember the guy you called a bastard just for wanting my autograph? Ha! Bro, what was that about?"

"Yeah, I'm not your bro."

Tori flips the middle finger, daintily. "Stop showing off in front of everyone and get to it."

"You and I both know... he wanted a little more than your autograph," Harlan says.

"Was it enough to nearly smash his face in, though?"

"Listen..." Harlan's pitch drops. "He flooded your fan page every hour. The asshole sent you flowers daily, then invited you to his penthouse for the weekend and left the rest of the band out. You're good, but you're not that good."

"Ruh-Roh. Harley, you're not turning green again, are you?" Tori quips. "Mabel—Mabel, I hope your insurance for this place is reliable. God knows we don't need another Hulk Smash repeat from McCandles. You had to replace three vases and an ottoman for chrissake."

"Tori, Jesus. Move on," Harlan says.

"Take your own advice, and I will, Slugger."

"Come now, you two." Mabel picks up after guests as they slowly clear the table. "You promised."

Tori glares at Harlan and completely disregards Mabel. "Someone has to keep his feet on the ground."

"He's so far into the ground, he's six feet under," I snap. "We get it. Can we change the subject, please?"

Hold your own. Like Kenji said.

Tori rolls her eyes. "Patience, right?"

"Right."

"How are you liking Camp Arnica so far? It could be a little overwhelming sometimes with the out-of-body experiences. Ask Harlan."

He chokes on his water, "You're pushing it—"

"And I could be wrong, but maybe... you seem a little out

of step with it—a watcher, not a doer. No need to be shy, babe—come on over to the deep end! The water's great!" Tori guffaws like she told the joke of the century.

She's such a suppository pill to swallow. "Actually, I'm having a fun time here, Tori."

"Ah, I'm sure you are. Harlan has a way of sweeping women off their feet. Just be mindful if you have an active fan club."

Harlan's fist clenches, but I place it under the table before he can respond.

And right back under my skirt.

She'll think twice about coming for us.

"Oh, Harlan didn't sweep me anywhere," I answer. "I walked into this with my eyes wide open. I'm good—I don't need anyone to carry me. As for that out-of-place feeling you might pick up on... It's called tact. Just silently taking it all in and not feeling the need to blurt constantly."

Mabel and Carl are beaming. Kenji applauds.

"Well put." Harlan's fingers are back in their natural habitat as I sit back with ease this time, with a newly inherited predominance toward him and the conversation.

This little bitch doesn't know me like she thinks she does.

Tori's eyes narrow slightly, but she keeps her smile in place. "Good for you. It's always such entertainment to see how the new fish out of water try to keep up. Posing one day, back to the real world in another."

"And it's always fascinating watching how the old ones struggle to let go, only to sink to the bottom. Oof. Kinda like what I'm seeing here with your last couple views on The Sirens TikTok page?" I openly brandish my phone.

Kenji snorts in his wine, clearly enjoying the show.

But it's getting harder to contain what's happening under

the table.

Tori takes out her vape and addresses the room. "I'm not worried. I'm bored and dying to sit by a fire pit. Anyone else wanna come with?"

A few of the guests agree to join her, and together, they thankfully push in their chairs.

I cover my mouth and do my best not to make a sound—as the ache expands. However, rocking back and forth onto Harlan's hand makes it difficult. He kisses my ear and doesn't make it any easier with his distinct leering at my flusteredness.

"Are you feeling all right, Patience?"

"I'm feeling fantastic. Not really ready to go yet."

"M'kay. Let me know when you're close."

Kenji pauses before leaving. "You guys tagging along for the pit, or no? What do you say, Patience?"

"She's coming," Harlan says. "We'll be there soon."

Son of a...

I grip the hell out of his knee and then sink into my chair with my eyes squeezed shut.

"How about now, beautiful?" he whispers.

"Mmm... mhmm."

"Cool, quick question."

"What?"

"Would you be terribly disappointed if we didn't go?"

"Uh..."

Which role will I play now?

Does she even have a name?

Decisions. Decisions.

* * *

I'm sure the firepit was overhyped, anyway.

It's midnight, and after making my little power move at dinner, I'm dying of thirst. Harlan's snores rumble like a trash compactor, so I'm not going to get any sleep, anyway. I slip on a long shirt of his and go to the kitchen.

The air feels cool against my skin as I walk barefoot. Polished floorboards creak under me. The main cabin is blanketed in a quiet that settles after a day full of talking, meditating, and whatever else they call "healing."

The kitchen's light peers out into the hallway. I see someone's already there.

Yuck. Tori.

Her frame leans against the counter while she stares down at a cup of tea. Then she looks up the moment I step in and offers me a stringy smile. "Missed you at the pit."

"Yeah, we had other plans."

"That's a given. Reminds me of the change of plans we had when Harlan swiped some guy's stash at Coachella. His sticky fingers actually came through for once. We were high off of mushrooms for days."

"Hmm."

"Let's not pretend... you weren't on the end of those same fingers at the table, though."

Deny. Deny. Deny. "Not sure I know what you mean."

"It's cool. Not to make you feel any less special, but I sat where you sat, too, if you catch my drift," Tori says, voice neutral, but there's a razor-like tone underneath it.

"Do you mind?" I motion for her to move out of the way for access to the sink... and also hinting at other things.

"Sorry, sure."

Her loose bun bounces with each step, the light hitting the

auburn in her hair.

We're two women who have had Harlan McCandles at his weakest. What stories were there to tell? Who owned his heart the most? Rather than answering these questions, it's more fun to be catty. Tori welcomes it too much.

"You and Harlan... You guys seem happy."

"We are."

She takes a sip of her tea and shrugs. "That's good. He's, uh, intense though, huh?"

I feel the hairs on the back of my neck prickle. "What do you mean?"

"I mean... When Harlan is in a good mood, everybody's in a good mood, right? But when he's not... Everyone including their great grandmother is gonna know. It comes with being his inspiration or muse, as he likes to call it. Being in tune with him."

She's trying to get in my head. Just like the whole fish out of water, not belonging thing. "Sounds like to me, that's a *you* problem. Believe it or not, no one enjoys being provoked. I know. Shocker."

Tori's smile widens, but there's no warmth in it. "Is that what he told you about what went down last year? That I provoked him? This freaking guy—"

"Don't worry about what he told me. So why be here? Why stick around Harlan if you hate him so much?"

"I'm only here because Mabel's been more of a mom to me than my own, and I wasn't gonna let him shit on that. Look, I know what I am. I don't mince words, and all my friends are pretty much dudes."

Don't tell me she's not like most girls.

Tori proceeds. "Harlan was cool with it at first. Liked how

I was independent and had virtue or whatever. But then one day, he woke up and thought I had a bit too much of it. And I wasn't dealing with his ass anymore. So, yeah, at the table, that was my own misdirected way of giving you a heads up."

I hate how she's talking like she knows him better than I do. Like—I get how she thinks she does—but we're two different people, meaning we would most likely have two different experiences with him. For example, I couldn't imagine being aggravated by someone like Tori while having a bad tripping experience. So, of course, we wouldn't get the same Harlan. She's annoying as shit! If she was more chill with her approach in the beginning, I'd be more willing to hear her. But that isn't where we stand.

I set my glass down a little too hard. "You're both creatives. Harlan's passionate about art like you are about your music. And it still didn't work out. What does that tell you?"

"It tells me I got off easy." Tori puts her cup down as if it helps her focus more on lecturing me. "He's an artist, yeah— so what? He feels things more deeply than most people, and that's not always... I'm only saying, that I've been where you are."

"Well, I'm not you, Tori. I can handle it."

She studies me for a long moment. "I thought the same thing once."

"Goodnight."

"Ask Harlan about Marsha."

"What?"

"Just ask about her. Then decide if what I'm telling you amounts to nothing." Tori walks off, leaving me in the dark.

But who is she... to *him*?

UNDER HIS INFLUENCE

rnica was heavensent for the rest of the weekend. Even more so after Tori left. But upon returning to Texas, I've been nothing but discouraged. Now, I can't evade it. I'm someone who discarded her vows for a future that's speculative. Which is why, despite Tori's suggesting I ask Harlan about *Marsha*, I can't bring myself to do it. If it means losing more than what I already have, Marsha can wait.

I return to mulling it over in bed, as a glum pig in a blanket.

Harlan climbs over me in his sheets and switches on his lamp. "Not this again. Quit with the lights off already, I told you about that. My studio isn't some bat cave. Plus, I'm all out of surprise trips to give, hun."

"I know. I'm sorry."

"Hey."

"Yeah?"

He sticks his tongue out and reveals a partly melted pill. "Roll with me, would ya? Let's go to Taos and get gone. Just you and me."

The idea of escape sounds extramundane. "Okay."

Nights at Taos are the closest I ever feel to nirvana. Besides Molly and the weed I partake in to shed my old self, Harlan has a connection through Taos, too, to score Ayahuasca.

And it pulls me further from being tethered to the world.

Once the music starts, and the Ayahuasca hits, seconds grow into years. I have visions of colors, never seen by the human eye before, come forward and render me motionless.

Motionless, but thankfully, not devoid of sensory input.

We sink into the same couch we were on our last visit before I was corrupted. With my head in his lap, I'm no longer connected to myself, doubting my state of consciousness. "Harlan, am I still alive?"

"I don't know. Ask me again later. My kneecaps keep sliding off, and my nostrils are melting."

Our essence floats above ourselves—teetering between Earth and the afterlife. It's poignant I'm only recently seeing what this drug offers.

I can't fathom a world where these experiences don't exist.

"Nothing I touch feels like I'm touching it. Like I'm touching through someone else in another multiverse. What if they know I know that I'm onto them?"

Harlan tickles my outer hip with his fingers. "Well, then, can she feel this?"

I'm a full body sneeze, navigating myself to tap into the pleasure I receive from his uncalloused hands.

"She can."

"Happy rolling, guys." Good old Kenji approaches us with his kit. "Want a freebie?"

I try to ask if it'll hurt, but I'm in hysterics, laughing in his face. Looks like Ayahuasca rids me of manners, too.

Harlan gets embarrassed for me. "Maybe later, Kenji. Thanks for the offer."

Kenji shrugs and totes his kit elsewhere. "No love lost, just up for any opportunity to practice. You know where my office is, if you reconsider."

As he leaves, Harlan lifts my chin up amorously and peers down at me. He leans in and lands a kiss on my forehead. The gesture is as simple and fitting as a cozy sweater. "What am I going to do with you?"

The ever so enlightening drug converts me to its will. "If I could bottle... what I'm experiencing with you and have it forever... I'll stay yours."

Harlan's eyes crinkle at the corners, and he reaches out to tuck a stray braid behind my ear. "Be careful. I might take you up on that."

The Ayahuasca might work a little too well, because Roxy appears out of thin air and emits green smoke behind her. She slinks over to us, mirroring a Cheshire cat.

"She's baaaaack," she purrs, crawling over to me on her hands and knees—with my head still in Harlan's lap. "So, Patience, what realm are you off to right now?"

"I—um—sorry, it's not you—it's me..." My laughter doesn't take a back seat for me to fully answer.

Harlan leans over and pets Roxy on the head, then strokes her chin. "Roxy, our Patience has left the building."

It keeps happening so much that I'm sure my abs will be sore tomorrow.

Roxy sits up and peers into my face. "Let's have a seance and bring her back."

She kisses me with spark, and the reaction I have is not what I bargained for. Her lips are much softer than Harlan's— rapturous clouds I want to be immersed in. So, I wrap my arms around Roxy and "get gone."

"Hey, giggles, knock it off. Before I give you something to

really chuckle about," Harlan apprises.

"Yeah, like what?" I audaciously say—parting from Roxy, who's now smitten. "Whatcha got under your sleeve, then?"

As always, Harlan has to take it a step farther. He delivers a seductive look to her. "You gonna stick around this time?"

Roxy winks jazzily. "I get off in five minutes. What do you think?"

"Then... wanna get out of here in a bit, ladies?"

I say nothing, but Roxy puts her arms around us both. "Like you wouldn't believe."

Truth? I lied. I'm kinda winding down—ready to turn in and was simply talking a big game, earlier. But it seems like Roxy is joining either way. Meh, sure. Continued bar hopping doesn't sound too bad. Play the role. Be easy.

I'm all in. "Let's go."

Harlan clouds over us like an omen as the rest of the night siphons into a dream.

* * *

I wake up to the soft rustle of sheets, the faint smell of paint in the air, and the sound of a brush softly scraping against canvas. The sun hits, and Harlan is at work all lit up. He turns into some kind of tortured artist from an indie film. He's completely absorbed, moving his brush in swift strokes. Fresh streaks splatter his sleeveless shirt. I turn to my left side, away from the morning's brightness, looking for more sleep.

"Ugh, where the hell are my pants?" a female voice whispers.

My eyes flutter open, and I'm immediately thunderstruck.

Awake, a topless Roxy gets up, shoves herself into a pair of jeans, and reaches for a nearby wrinkled up shirt next to me. "Harley, got any toothpaste?"

"Sure, check the bottom cabinet in the restroom."

"K." She trots her way there.

Okay, my limit is waking up to a strange girl in our bed. The hell?!

"What's going on?" I ask, curled up in the comforter.

Harlan doesn't answer. His focus is on the canvas—agile hands moving in quick, deliberate strokes that create wonders I can't yet make out.

"Oh, Sleeping Beauty is awake. Good morning!" Roxy walks across the studio with a casual grace, completely unconcerned. Her pixie haircut is now wavy and wet.

She's also wearing my shirt.

"You don't mind, do you?" Roxy asks me, tucking the shirt tag in. "Spilled wine on mine last night."

"I... how..."

"She doesn't mind," Harlan speaks for me.

I want to understand how I got here so badly. But my vocabulary is shot straight to hell from the shock.

"...should get going, but hey—you were fun. It was a nice night," Roxy adds. She gathers her things from the floor— jewelry, a pair of heels, a phone.

My brain grinds to a halt. "Huh?"

She flashes one of her famous dazzling grins and walks over to Harlan. Then she leans in and kisses his cheek like it's the most natural thing to come by. "Bye, Harlan,"

"Bye. Drive safe." He barely acknowledges her with his eyes fixed on the canvas.

Slack-jawed, I watch as she saunters out of the studio. A

solid minute of silence passes where I just sit there and stare at the door, trying to piece it all together. Dammit. I somehow always end up at this junction. Being problematic-free and high one minute, then dealing with a shitshow the next, sober. How do I catch it before it happens?

"Fill me in, Harlan. Is there a reason Roxy left here at eight in the morning?"

He pauses, looking up from his painting and finally noticing I'm in the same room as him. "Hmm?" He wipes his brush on a rag and tilts his head at me. "Oh, Roxy? Yeah... she's great, isn't she? You were right about her vibe. I'm glad we took a chance on her."

"We?" Not what I am saying in the slightest. "Why was she in our bed?"

"She was in *my* bed because I needed to rid myself of my artist's block." He sets the brush down and steps back from the canvas, inspecting his work with a satisfied nod. "You two helped."

"You needed both of us for that!?" I say, still struggling to make sense of it. I don't remember... any of what went down after we left Taos, and I'm going to hurl all over his sheets. "I go to sleep, and the following day, wake up to some coked-up rave chick—thanking me for a nice night? What the fuck?!"

"It's not a big deal, Patience. You were relaxed, and we were all having a good time. You and Roxy hit it off."

"I'm scared to ask how."

Harlan faces his canvas toward us and walks over to the bed. His hand reaches for mine, but I pull back before he can touch me. "We were drinking, talking, and laughing. It kind of... went from there. Quite the lionesses you were—ripping each other's clothes off down to a blur of limbs, lips, and tongues. The chef's kiss. Then we fell asleep. That's it. No drama."

"Holy shit."

"Ease up. You took turns making each other whimper. So what?"

"Are you telling me... I slept with her?"

"More like... we did."

My stomach drops. I sit up straight and pull the covers tighter. "It was supposed to stop at kissing! And I was cool with going to a couple of bars before coming home. That's all! You didn't even think to ask if I was okay with whatever happened?"

"You seemed okay last night. I thought we could enjoy the experience and add it to your list of firsts. And look"—he gestures toward the canvas—"I finally have a piece for the art show at Concord that might be up Corbin Reyes' alley. You broke my dry spell. I've created a piece from it, thanks to my muse."

Muse? Tori strikes again.

It's an abstract, of course, with swirls of soft colors blending into one another—reds, golds, and deep purples. I can vaguely see the shape of three figures entwined, but it's more about the emotion than the clarity. It's easy on the eyes, sure. But it's pyrrhic and unfulfilling to me after the fact.

Harlan decided on the threesome for us, and now he's standing there, acting like this is some grand artistic break-through. "Who cares?! Using me is an unacceptable source of inspiration."

"God, sometimes I forget how sheltered you are."

"Ow! What the—"

I feel a sharp pain coming from my stomach and pull up my

shirt. There's taped gauze on the right side of my belly button, with dried dots of blood and inflammation. I immediately hop out of bed, run to the bathroom mirror, and peel off the patch.

What the actual shit is this?!

A tattoo of a prism that shoots a rainbow from its tip cascades across my belly. The rainbow is in the shape of an infinity sign.

Toss salt in the wound, why don't you... no more surprises. Please, no more.

"Came out pretty good. Kenji's skills are legit." Harlan enters the bathroom to wash his hands. "He should look into charging more now."

No way. I don't recall any of that either. "You... let him... do that to me, too..."

My sudden interjections no longer derail Harlan.

"Well, when a grown woman says, '*Ooh, ooh, let's get matching ones, please?*' I tend to not question it, since I'm an ink connoisseur myself. We met up with him before coming back to the studio. I went all in right after you."

He flaunts a new tat on his ribcage.

"Relax. You'll get used to it, and soon, you'll forget it's even there."

But relaxing is out of the question. The memory gaps nip that in the bud. The tattoo may be done and final, but to prevent further unexpected body modifications and *menage a trois* occurrences, I think it's time Ayahuasca and I go our separate ways.

"Ayahuasca and I are on hiatus, effective immediately. Got it, Harlan?"

"Fine by me. Molly's more my speed, anyway."

"And shit with Roxy—there won't be another round of it."

I push his body aside and get in front of the mirror, chiding him to his face. "If we're doing this... an actual relationship, then I'm not sharing you with her!"

"Beautiful, chill. I hear you. I'm not going anywhere. It was only for my art, okay?" Harlan stretches languidly and becomes a bobcat before opening his eyes—his posture uncertain. "I was... trying to find encouragement, through the feels, the colors. It wasn't really about the sex, though. It was about what was flowing through all of us. That's what made me pick up the brush. It was electric. I thought you felt it, too."

With how quickly he reacted to anger when Kenji joked about pouring vodka in my mouth, I'm curious how he would deal if I looked for that same flow through him.

"No more, okay?"

"Gah, your jealous side wins me over each time."

"Don't be condescending."

"For real, Okoye. You're cute when you're pissed. But I care. No more sleepovers with Roxy. Got it." Harlan stops by the doorway. "Wanna help me finish the abstract? It could use your special touch."

There's still a main issue at hand. "But..."

"Yeah?"

"I—I don't... I still can't remember sleeping with Roxy, or you—or anything else before that. I'm totally blanking out here. Is that normal?"

"You were there, trust me."

Do I take his word for it? Or imagine the worst? "It's just—"

Harlan pushes back from the sink—all hasty-like, and he's no longer tolerant when talking to me. "Don't make this into something it isn't. Own up to the fact—you didn't have control over your high. Your high had control over you. It happens. Then move on already, damn. It's a helluva drug, and you're just having buyer's remorse... so, be bigger than that."

This, I have to believe because the latter of other possibilities freak me out too much. Or maybe I should allow myself to be angry and let it be clear to him. It's the smart thing to do. But I'm too perplexed. Was sex with Roxy and Harlan a part of a ritual? Picking up girls in hopes for new creations or... Hell, was this how he met Tori's Marsha?

Slow down. One at a time. Focus on what's now, what's current. "I don't know... maybe we rushed into—into what we are."

"So, you're afraid of this."

Afraid? Yes. Afraid of the way Harlan can pull me in and shut me out in equal measure. Afraid of the way his leer seems to hold me hostage every time, almost crushing me with a single look. Yet when I tap into trying to let myself accept it, I seek to figure out if this is really *us*. Or if I'm getting lost in his world again. Where nothing is coherent, except the art.

"Just don't make me regret ever knocking on your door, Harlan."

With his unrelenting honesty, he seals the promise by binding me in a tatted hug. "We'll be fine... because I don't regret answering."

* * *

My first Christmas and New Year's without Obinna and his extended family were tough. Usually, as memory serves, the scent of jollof rice and sizzling suya permeates the air. My mother, a whirlwind of jabbing comebacks and Ankara prints, directs the chaos in the kitchen with Agatha, who balances her out with diplomacy. My cousins scatter around aunts and uncles, serving a cacophony of greetings that's almost musical. Christmas carols, a comical mashup of American classics and Nigerian gospel, bloom from ancient speakers. Throughout the busy festivities, Obinna—already buzzed— would lay a wet fat one on my lips and say, "*Next year will be ours, Pat. Watch.*"

This year had different plans. Instead, Harlan and I stayed in with pizza and watched *It's a Wonderful Life*, pretty stoned. I stupidly didn't realize leaving Obinna would mean leaving a huge chunk of cultural traditions behind.

At the studio, I tried small things to get over homesickness, but Harlan's set ways would often clash with those efforts. One day, I made rice and red stew just because. The minute he came home from a long day teaching at Colby; it became another added aggravation.

"Jesus, Patience, I hope the smell gets out of my clothes by tomorrow, and don't get me started on my canvases..." he hissed, rubbing his nose raw while he played Call of Duty. "Was gonna paint some more tonight, but I can't even think with this stench—"

"Stench?! Okay, okay enough. It's Nigerian stew, not a chemical spill." I sealed the lid to everything—including Harlan's protests—and shoved the food in the fridge. "We've been eating out every day this week, and I only wanted to give you a taste of where I'm from. Sorry for the inconvenience."

"Fine. Cook whatever you want. Just light some candles or whatever next time... problem solved. I have a sensitive nose and palette, okay? No one's trying to take away your identity and stuff—goddammit, they spotted me!" Suddenly, a flurry of insults were aimed at a Ghost-acekilla87 online.

The irony wasn't lost on me, though. There weren't complaints when his studio reeked of turpentine and stale weed. Or the floor being sticky with paint splatters and energy drink spills. But my cooking somehow didn't stand a fighting chance. So, my stew remained untouched in the fridge, ultimately ending up in the trash.

In turn, being exiled because of my affair left me in a spiraling depression.

So, without fail, Harlan would find a way to lean toward that "one last time" with Molly for us. The high and lows couldn't be anymore opposite. Highs entangle more superlative art creations that surpass our wildest dreams. Then our skin would be on insatiable fire from the number of times we had sex under the influence.

When we get into these dives with each other, it almost, for a millisecond, makes up for what I shamelessly threw away. Not just with my marriage, but with old family friends, too. Neisa's text messages soon became fragmented—left on read, with updates about happenings with her and check-ins with me.

Sissy, Obinna told me. Stop playing and call me back before I whoop your ass.

I love her... but she can't keep up with me anymore. Or maybe I can't face her rejecting the new Patience.

Yesterday, though, it almost took a drastic turn.

We were at Taos as usual, with Travis Scott hitting the sound waves. The air was humid with body heat and spilled drinks. It was a heady mix that made me feel a little queasy, but not enough to end the night. We both were rolling out of our gourds but kept our wits about ourselves, while making out.

"Harlan!" Jayson made his way toward us. He had his usual slickness about him—expensive clothes, polished look, always with an air of someone who knew more than they let on.

"Well, well…" He met us mid-crowd, and his fat lips quirked to the side. "Didn't expect to see you two out together tonight. Again."

But before I could say anything, Harlan nudged Jayson and gave him a fist bump. "You know me, man."

"Still just a colleague, eh?"

"Fuck you." Harlan snickered. "Whaddya want from me?"

"Your life, you beautiful bastard."

"I try. Look, but don't touch."

It was all getting to be a bit much.

"Well done." Jayson laughed and held out his hand for a high-five, and Harlan slapped it without thinking, like it was some inside joke between them, some casual exchange. "You're right, she really does have legs for days—"

"What did you say?!" I demanded.

"I said… next time he'll have to teach me his ways. Just wanted to stop by and say hi. Harlan, again—congrats. And Patience, looking lovely as always. Take good care of him, will you? Oh, what am I saying? Of course you will."

What a complete dickhole.

I suddenly felt as though my clothes were see-through. This wasn't what I signed up for. I didn't leave my entire life behind to become some sort of punchline in their misogynistic private joke. Jayson left through the expanding crowd and Harlan attempted to pull me along, but I tugged his wrist back.

"You all right?" he asked, leaning in closer.

"You couldn't even help yourself."

"Do what?"

"The high-fives and gloating. It was insulting. Like you've been running your mouth about me to him. Or you two had some bet going about us."

Harlan's brow bent sharply, his arm slipping from around my shoulders. "Jayson's just Jayson, appreciating natural beauty like the next person. He's not suicidal, though. He won't try anything on you. I won't let him."

Bullshit. Harlan loved every minute of it. He didn't mind Jayson complimenting my body. Because it indirectly complimented him, too, with me on his arm. I was no better than a trophy Harlan won or some other extension of him.

"I don't care!" I projected even louder. "You acted one way with him and one way with me, and it's not cool."

"Oh, my muse is displeased."

"Stop, don't call me that shit right now."

"Okay, okay." Our lips touched, but barely. I didn't want to make it simple for him. "Let's get you a drink as a peace offering?"

"Whatever."

"So, that wasn't a no?"

I rolled my eyes, and he let me lead. We moved with the crowd. I excused myself and passed through, weaving through the throng as the bass hit on cue. There were glowing floating orbs that danced, and it wowed me. I wasn't angry anymore and became delightfully entertained by them— Molly in full effect.

Then a hand clamped roughly on my shoulder.

"Hey-hey, you got a dude or somethin'?" a slurred voice filled my ear. A man built like a tank, reeking of cheap beer, loomed to the side of me. He appeared energized, likely on a Molly kick, too, like most people here. Before I could react, his hand slid down my ass, and he gripped me tight.

Panic, cold and sharp, pierced me. "Get the hell away from me! Harlan, help!"

But he was nowhere to be seen.

What happened? He was behind me a second ago, then sucked into the ominous crowd. The creepy partygoer smiled at my terror. "Baby, I can keep you company."

That same hand clamped on to my wrist painfully.

"Hey!" I twisted around, trying to turn him loose. "Let go!"

He laughed, a wet, ugly sound. "Not until I get a closer look, Black Barbie."

"Get the fuck off of her!"

Suddenly, Harlan swam through the hectic circle—his face red, lips thinned, and chin pushed out. He shoved the man, sending him stumbling.

The drunkard straightened up with bubbling resentment. He was bigger than Harlan, but the raw power steaming off Harlan told me he had it handled.

"Or what?" the man spat. He took a step forward.

Just as quickly, Harlan's fist connected with the partygoer's jaw. The crack of bone echoed over the music.

People cheered and watched the slimeball tumble back from the force that flew to his face. When the guy hit the floor with a heavy thud, Harlan wasted no time. He landed hard kicks into his wide torso.

He kept on going and became a furious freight train with no brakes.

After a few more brutal strikes, he leaned over and spat on

the man's crumpled body. "That's what, bitch. Now go choke on your goddamn teeth. Patience, let's go."

"Harlan, what did you just do?!"

"Forget about it. It's practically dead in here, anyway."

We got as far as the lounge before Kenji stepped away from finishing a raver's tattoo and hopped down the stage to come over to us. "Y'all good?"

Harlan tried to sidestep him.

Kenji refused to budge, frowning. "Talk to me, guys. What happened?"

I took the initiative, filling him in. "We're fine. I lost Harlan in the crowd and some jerk got touchy."

"Ah." Kenji rested his hand on my shoulder.

Things tanked when Harlan bristled.

I felt him stiffen beside me while Kenji kept talking. "Wish I'd been there. Woulda looked out for you in his absence."

"Thanks," I said.

"It's what I do. I inked you for life, so why not?"

See, I thought things were fine. The dragon was slayed and such.

Yet his blowout didn't blow over as expected.

"We're leaving. Move," Harlan addressed his friend with finality.

"Come on, you don't gotta drag her outta here. Jayson's cool—he'll talk to the cops if they show."

However, Harlan was already wound too tight. "I'm not waiting for the cops, Kenji. So, step."

Kenji blinked, clearly bothered by Harlan's assertiveness. His eyes darted to me again, silently asking if I was okay with all this, but I didn't know what to say—caught in the middle of a thing I couldn't comprehend.

"She's good. What the hell are you double checking with her for?"

"Bro—relax. Just explain."

"I don't have to explain shit to you or anyone else, for that matter."

"Yo, McCandles, it's me. You ain't gotta do all that."

"*Are you deaf, motherfucker? Move!*"

Kenji avoided the smoke and backed away from his words. "Bet... It's all you."

Harlan grabbed my arm, and we surfed through the club before the bouncers could arrive to question him about the punch. From far away, I mouthed a muted "sorry" to Kenji and was gone.

As we pushed through the doors and stepped into the cool night air, I contemplated his actions. Maybe he had his reasons to pounce. But the stung look on Kenji's face tells another side to it. I was worried the bond they had between them just broke, due to whatever Harlan *thought* he saw between Kenji and me.

"Harlan... Harlan, woah—stop and breathe for a minute! I think we're in the clear."

Once we were outside by his car, Harlan turned to me, and his eyes slowly regained their usual glimmer. "Are you okay?" he asked, voice hoarse.

I threw myself at him and buried my face in his chest. "Yes, thank you. But where'd you go? You disappeared out of nowhere."

"Shit, sorry. I don't know what happened, but I'm glad I got to you before that fucker went further. I didn't mean to scare you."

"I was scared," I confessed. "Um... maybe next time let the

bouncers handle it?"

He laughed and seemed abashed. "Maybe you're right. I just couldn't stand seeing him touch my favorite parts of you. It was an instinct to give him hell."

"You probably owe Kenji an apology, though. I know we were trying to dodge extra trouble, but I don't think he deserved to get yelled at."

Harlan quickly soured again. "Sato will be all right. Tomorrow, he'll forget all about it. We were just giving each other shit, that's all." He propped my neck up to look up at him, his favorite thing to do. "I'm not worried about him, and you shouldn't be either. Now, let's go home."

When we got back to his place, I thanked him some more. The sweat from our bodies glowed in the midnight light that peered through his windows.

"See this... this is my weakness. Right here." Harlan twiddled my hair to the side. "My soft underbelly."

"Aww. Too bad I'm thinking of losing the braids soon." I took a massive scrunchie and tied it up in a chunky ponytail. "We're heading into March. It'll be getting hotter again, and I was thinking of going for something shorter. Less heavy."

"No way."

"Yes way."

"But it's one of your best features—among others." Harlan then shook his head. "Request denied."

I released a laugh clumsily, and waited for a, *Well, you do you.*

Never happened.

"Just saying." He goes back to the preoccupation of my braids.

His comments sat with me. I couldn't gauge if it was his

own way of suggesting to keep them... or if he was *telling* me to keep them?

But his battle wounds were more pressing matters.

"Oh, my god, look at your hand." I daintily kissed Harlan's pink knuckles. "You need ice on this. Bad."

"Jesus... don't do that to me just yet."

"Do what?"

"Make me watch you with those come-hither lips on my skin. I don't think I have it in me for another round."

Streetlights bounced off his hair, and it hit me all over again—how devastating he was. "You could have gotten arrested."

"Totally worth it. In case it wasn't clear, I don't want anyone else touching you." A naked Harlan took one last puff from his blunt before putting it on his bedside table. "And I'd do it again."

"But Roxy did."

"Which I permitted... under my watch."

Permitted?

Though we were both quiet, only Harlan looked as if he had a million and one things on his mind while he stared at me. So, I borrowed his catchphrase to see what was up. "Where are you right now?"

"Had a thought. I don't know if I should say it. Not really considered socially acceptable and stuff."

"So, then, let's play a game," I said. My head rested on his bare chest. "Let's share the craziest idea that pops up this very second. As usual, no judgment. I'll go first. We quit our jobs, buy a camper van, and road trip across the country, stopping at every national park. We make a living as watercolor landscape artists. What do you say?"

Harlan's voice was steady, but he visibly shed discomfort. "I say your idea is milk toast compared to mine."

"I'm waiting."

"First, let me see you."

"I'm right here."

"You know what I mean." He gave a crooked smile, ogling as he pulled the covers to my feet. "Well, I've had days when I'd look at you and think—yep, she breaks the mold. You're true perfection. A masterpiece."

"That's really sweet."

"Not done. Sometimes, I wish I could wrap you up in a specially crafted box or display case. Then—take you out and put you back when I've had my fill. Others could look at you... as much as they want. Hell, I'd encourage it—I love showing you off. But no one would touch the beauty that's in my bed. No one. Only then will my muse be truly mine. Maybe I'd lose my cool less often."

There was a tiny prickle of pins and needles within me, with the mood turned a bit off-kilter. Was he still rolling? No way—he seemed too sane and composed. Why else would he say such a thing? Maybe I read too much into it. Maybe it was just his strange version of kink.

I also promised no judgment.

"Uh, I'm flattered?" I lied. "In a see-through box, huh? What next, parts sold separately?"

"You're making me sound like that shitheel from Taos."

"Never. But you've always said what's on your mind with me so far. Why stop now?"

Harlan flipped me onto my back before answering. The way he hovered made his tattooed arms resemble two totem poles. "I didn't want it going to your head—the power you have in driving me up the wall."

"I got it like that?"

"Modesty can only get you so far."

"I admire the admiration... only—don't take it to a place you're not able to come back from."

Harlan's smile shrank as he returned to his side of the bed. "I'll try, Okoye. But if anyone comes for you, they'll be in for it. So, I wish them good fucking luck."

"Down, boy," I said, peering at his bedside lamp. "And could we have one night sleeping with the lights off?"

"Let's not and say we did, anyway?"

"Wow, I didn't see that answer coming."

"You should've."

While in his embrace, the fear from that night slowly went away. However, the image of his cutthroat defense of me remained.

Sleep found him first, then found me last. But it wasn't till fifteen minutes past three in the morning, I wake up to—

"Patience! *Patience!*" Harlan bolts upright.

The sheets are now damp with sweat, wrapped and fixed around his leg. Blinking, I try to adjust to the dark as he sits up.

"Nuh... huh?"

"My lamp—why is the light off?!" Harlan feels around his bedside table in a panic and ballistically uses his fist to smash the switch on. "Damn, where's the—you had no right. None!"

Oh, shit. Well, I saw an opportunity when he started snoring first and took it. I don't get why the lights are so crucial for him. It was only going to be for one night and having them on all the time gives me migraines. It's kind of hard to relax with lamps burning holes throughout the studio.

"Sorry, I thought we could have one night without them."

"No!" Harlan stops, then whips around the room like he's searching for something, or maybe someone. "Teal chair... beige couch... egg-white ceiling... okay... okay, I'm okay..."

I gawk at him as he mutters in a state of compulsion.

Harlan gawks back, defensively. "Patience, I have my reasons for why things are the way they are. Get over it!"

"What's going on with you?"

"Just respect my goddamn wishes, okay?!"

"Are you serious?!" I sit up fully now, with the comforter around my shoulders. "Why? Why is it so important? You never explain it! We should be able to tell each other anything, right?"

The room feels colder now.

"That true?"

"Yes, it is."

"Then tell me about your stupid bracelets."

"They're not stupid! They're an essential part of me, me and a reminder of someone I lost."

Harlan flicks at them, while up in arms about it. "You don't take them off, like ever! You're wearing them in bed for Christ's sake!"

"I–I misplaced them before, and I don't..."

Out of nowhere, Neisa comes to mind—like when she beat up Jessica Browder in 7th grade for swiping my golden bangle cuffs. "*Lie through your snaggletooth again and see what happens! Turn 'em loose!*" Even she knew how much they meant to me and didn't think twice about scrapping for them.

Letting out a breath, I try to figure out what exactly to share and what to do with these atypical pieces of us.

I look at Harlan, wondering if he can picture it. This little girl with plastic rings dangling down her arm that her daddy gifted her, a wild mess of a child who didn't yet understand—what her father leaving the very next day—would mean. "It started with wearing them for good luck after my dad left, like somehow—if I wore them long enough, he could come back someday. Dumb, but as a kid, what else would you be?"

Harlan's mood cools down further, and he nods for me to go on.

"They used to be all kinds of colors and sizes, but they were always there for the same reason. Needing that coolness against my wrists, the little clinking sound just to get through stuff, you know? Like college. And panic attacks. Then they weren't a security blanket anymore, but a crutch. One day, I couldn't find them, and I was running late for work. I thought, *Whatever, I'll go without them.* Then my student, Josh, rammed his head into me, and I lost the baby I was carrying—on the one day I forgot my bracelets."

My silver wooden bands have grown into armor rather than mere decoration now. With how caught up I am on my students' diagnoses, it's come to my attention that I could have one, too. I know people rarely have attachments like mine, but... it's in me, regardless.

Harlan reaches out and runs his fingers over each thin bracelet, trying to learn their story through touch alone. He has the same look Angela gives me when she's probably thinking, *Oh, you poor thing.*

"Come on, kid. You can't possibly believe—"

"Don't you think I already know how it sounds?! Shit, I'm not crazy!"

"No one's saying you're crazy, Patience."

"I—I just can't have another bad thing happen while I'm not wearing them. I don't need something else to be my... my fault t-too." Cue tears. "Anyway, wasn't this fight supposed to be about you and your stupid lights?"

Harlan turns to me, his eyes wide and glossy. "Well, here's the short version coming from me. Maybe we should just let your shit be your shit, and my shit be my shit."

His is more than about being afraid of the dark and needing his lamp, though. Similar to my bracelets being more than a critical fashion statement. We both aren't ready to part from them. So, there.

I scooch into his technicolor arms and peer up at him. "Do you want me to go?"

Harlan hisses and lays back in bed to catch his breath. He could pass for someone who has the flu, with how out of it he looks. "I was obviously taken by surprise and only being an asshole, so get over here. No need to be dramatic. Just don't do it again."

I curl up in his sweaty hold and try to get comfortable. But I can't deny that this part of tonight will stay with me, too.

* * *

"Urm..."

Gaining four more hours of sleep doesn't make me feel any better, but at least it's a sunnier morning. Yet, the energy I'm expected to have in order to address students with behavioral issues is such an overburden right now. Harlan's still asleep, snoring throughout the studio. I don't get it. I usually ingest half a pill and him—a full one. We take Molly around the same time together, and he's still hunky dory—able to function, get a good night's rest, and work two jobs. I loathe his stamina. Whereas, I'm holding myself together with tape over here.

I won't glorify Molly, a chemical kiss with its siren song of fleeting bliss.

So, if we're going to talk about highs, I should get into the lows, too.

The lows are a bitch to go through. Number one downside of Molly is the havoc on my serotonin levels. The more I take, the more I have to push myself overtime to eat, sleep, and basically function. My moods go from sluggish to screaming in pillows because I feel like absolute death from the comedown. And what makes me get better? More. Which is typically tapered off with weed and benzodiazepine. I guess that's why they call it the never-ending cycle.

Zonking out becomes the norm. Sleeping and eating are on the back burner.

My feet trot over to the bathroom. Then I grab some stale toothpaste and start brushing. Ouch! Another side effect of the stuff—constant jaw clenching and teeth grinding. Everything looks okay, but I should probably see a dentist soon. Don't think it's typical for teeth to hurt every other minute.

But after brushing for a bit, a headache strikes in full force.

"Ow! make it stop," I say, with my hands over my ears. But it doesn't help, and I'm wailing—curled up in a ball.

"What's going on over there?" Harlan then yells from bed. "Patience, are you all right?"

No. I'm not all right. It feels like my brain is being stabbed with an ice pick, thanks to my withdrawal symptoms.

"Hang on, I'm coming, okay?"

Harlan runs to me and scoops me up from the floor. His blond strands create a halo from the way they rest on his head.

"Take it easy. You're probably just really dehydrated from rolling last night."

"It hurts, and I can't believe you made me do it with you in the first place!"

Harlan's nurturing touch turns into an upset one as he lets go at once. "Will you relax? I'm trying to help, but if you're going to be a total brat—"

"Ah—now my stomach hurts! I can't move! I can't breathe! There's something really wrong!"

I have trouble seeing, and I'm suddenly sensitive to light. My freakouts are so bad, I almost don't notice that Harlan leaves, until he comes back with a fresh blunt. "Smoke it. Seriously, it'll help."

"Are you crazy?! You think more drugs will help?"

"Will you shut it and hold on?!" Harlan lights the blunt angrily. "Stop fighting me on this and take a puff. Worst-case scenario, you probably got a hold of some bad shit and need to get it out of your system to relax your nerves. Or you can still freak out, but I'll tell you what—you won't be doing that under the same roof as me. So pick."

"Shouldn't I go to a hospital?"

"Ever hear of making a mountain out of a molehill? Smoke. Do it."

His tone isn't one to be messed with. I puff a careful drag from his blunt, and soon after, my panic attack ceases. My lungs can fill again. I release happy tears rather than sad ones.

Harlan smoothes my hair out of my face and pinches my nose. "Damn, okay—okay. I have a soft spot for you, kid. Glad you met my special stash with a blend of magnesium.

Told you it was safe."

"Sorry again for turning the lamp off on you." I'm acting silly, burrowing into him like a rabbit.

"Forget about it. If you're good, I'm good."

BEEP. My phone gets an Outlook calendar message that reads, *Urgent Check In meeting with Admin today at three.* Doesn't seem like winning news.

"On second thought, Harlan... I'll take another puff."

* * *

I'm sitting in the cracked leather chair outside Principal Vicci's office, my nails digging straight into my palms. The waiting area is too quiet, the kind of quiet that amplifies everything else. My heels have been tapping against the cold linoleum floor for ages.

"Mrs. Okoye, she's ready to see you now."

Feet don't fail me now.

I head inside her office and meet a slender woman in her late thirties, scowling at me.

"Morning. Please have a seat."

I do, reaching for my laptop.

"That won't be necessary," Principal Vicci declares. "What I have to say will need your full, undivided attention. You'll get notes on the employee portal after the meeting concludes."

Not so reassuring.

"Okay."

"Mrs. Okoye, let me start by saying I'm in a tough spot here. You've been an exemplary teacher for the past three years at Seabrook. Special Programs Teacher of the Year Recipient last school year."

So far, so good. Keep going.

"But I've noticed some concerning trends in your performance lately. You submit lesson plans infrequently, and there have been complaints from parents about lack of communication."

"Yes, Principal Vicci, but if you let me explain—"

"In a moment," she says, maintaining a calm tone, but with a hint of firmness. "Within the past three weeks, your absences have alarmingly increased. And when you are present, your attentiveness is open to question. Paraprofessionals have had to take on extra tasks initially considered your responsibility."

It sucks to hear Nadia's take on things. However, I'm thankful she didn't mention the baggie she found.

But she wasn't off-base in the slightest.

I've been MIA.

"I'm at a loss on what to do. This isn't like you, so I would like to give you a chance to provide some disclosure if need be."

As much as I want to tell her about the separation from Obinna, I don't. New Patience mustn't cross Old Patience's work life. The two need to stay apart in order to not get bogged down with the self-reproach that keeps biting at me.

"Principal Vicci, I sincerely apologize for my recent performance stats and will ensure I do better in the future." I give my best political answer. "I've had some personal matters to address, but from here on out, they will no longer take a toll on my work ethic."

"Good."

Phew. Crisis averted.

"There's only one matter left—witness signing a performance review form."

No. Not the teacher's kiss of death. Anything but that.

"We will revisit in a month to see if these expectations are met." Principal Vicci hands me the form with a limp hand.

I take it from her, begrudgingly. "Do I have to sign it, even if I don't agree with it?"

Principal Vicci sucks in her breath sharply and points to my laptop. "You are welcome to share your concerns with HR—if you feel you have grounds to do so, that is."

Not worth the hassle. I already have a huge target on my back as it is.

"Nevermind, I'll sign."

I hand the paper back, grab my stuff, and go for the door.

"Are you sure everything is okay, Patience?" Principal Vicci pries. "We used to have such constructive rapport during our meetings. I would like to think we still do."

Look how far we have fallen. "What's done is done, Principal Vicci. Much appreciated."

Then I leave her office—more lost now than ever.

* * *

I need a fix.

For paint fumes.

To get over my performance review blues, this evening, I'm wrapped up in a new abstract as I blast Kid Cudi from my AirPods. After teaching at Colby, Harlan is working a double shift tonight, and Fridays are usually his busiest nights at Markos, but I welcome the solitude.

"Needs more carnation acrylic. Crap, where are the extra paints?"

Ever since I got more into it, I've noticed Harlan getting more stingy with his art supplies. So, I promised to buy more of what I've finished. However, I don't know... I can't help but point out there might be more to his annoyance.

Or maybe it's because I'm making his thing my thing now.

I don't mean to piggyback on his hobby, but my new outlet of expression gets me carried away. And by the time I'm done, I have three fresh canvases splattered to the brim.

Knock. Knock.

Who could that be? And after eight PM no less?

I put up my paint and easel to the side and walk to the door. With the peephole in reach, there they are.

I seriously believe I'm God's little punchline.

My mother and her church group huddle together like busy hens in front of Harlan's apartment. Their matching African scarves adorn their bobbing heads as they wait for someone to answer the door.

The way a million and one things can go wrong sits on my chest. How in the hell did they find me? What do they even want?! I ought to ignore them and not even answer the door, but knowing my mother—the busybody that she is— she would never stop until her mission is accomplished. So, answering the door when Harlan isn't home is the best choice.

Ugh. "Hold on. Coming."

I open the door and watch them file in without an invitation, with my mother leading the charge. Behind her is her church squad. Their Sunday best clashes with the free rein style of Harlan's apartment.

"Whoa! Mom, what on Earth are you doing here?"

"Patience, what have you done with this life you are living? Have you forgotten who you are and where you have come from? If so, we and our prayers will kindly remind you." Her voice cuts with vitriol. Full cheeked and wide-hipped, my mother knows exactly who she is and dares anyone to question it.

They've come for me as an intervention—a rescue mission.

I swallow the crackle on the back of my tongue. "Mom, I'm fine. And I thought we weren't speaking."

"Fine?" she scoffs, scanning the apartment like a crime scene. "You've left your husband, a good, God-fearing man, for this... this!" She gestures vaguely around the room.

The church women nod in agreement, their hushed whispers are a chorus of hummingbirds.

"Where has your love for Obinna gone?! Where?!"

"It's not gone... It just doesn't fit where I am in my life as of now."

"No, this is not your life, little girl."

"It is. I'm happy."

Gasps echo through the room. My mother's jaw drops. "Happy? You're a married woman living with a degenerate. A man with no respect for our culture, our values."

The stew debacle comes in focus now, especially after my mom's comment about culture. To be fair, Harlan never told me to stop cooking my food—he just suggested lighting some candles. But somehow, I haven't been able to bring myself to try again. I don't even know why—it's just easier not to.

"First off, most degenerates wouldn't have a job as a college professor. As for him not having any respect for our culture and values—have you ever had a conversation with him?"

"My dear, there is no need. Trading security for—for bohemian antics? Are you mad?! I did not bring up my daughter to throw herself at a man who chooses to live in a blasted shoebox." My mother's superficial viewpoints were bound to pop up, eventually.

I try to smooth the wrinkles from my forehead as she threatens to create new ones. "It's called a studio apartment."

"Same bloody thing!" Mom walks in a zigzag line in the middle of the living space. "Obinna has a career—a future. You work through things. Patience, you don't run off the second it becomes difficult."

I half expect her to twist the knife in my stomach for one more jab—she's got a sixth sense for catching me when I'm about to breathe a sigh of relief. "How did you even find me?"

My mother's mouth shrivels up tighter than a raisin and she looks at everything as though it's covered in grime. "Obinna's cousin, Charity, spotted you two at a gas station. She took pictures and showed them to us. I nearly fainted at the sight of my daughter—half naked and kissing all over her colonizer! It was her duty as a loving cousin to follow, find out where you've been staying, and report your whereabouts. Lord knows I wouldn't get that from you!"

Damn it to hell, that bitch! I knew she was pissed that we got her a SMEG Williams-Sonoma toaster for her wedding!

I remember the recent trip to the gas station, though. The munchies were coming on strong that night. I didn't think our public display of affection was that bad, and excuse me for thinking I could get away with not wearing a bra.

"You have a responsibility to your family," Mom continues. "To your community!"

"I have a responsibility to heal myself. I don't owe you or anyone else anything. Especially if it means finding joy in the little things again," I say, as my inner strength soars high. "If that's what you're going to be preaching about, you can save the prayers and get out."

The conversation descends into a barrage of accusations and recriminations. I blank out most of it and focus on Harlan's mini sepia statues scattered across the coffee table.

"And what's this, a bed in the middle of the living room?!" one of my mom's church friends, Mrs. Adebayo yells. "Is this where you disgrace yourself with him? Without thinking of what it'll do to your husband and your mother?"

The hens cluck on, and my mother nods in agreement.

"Foolish girl!"

"God is watching, always."

"Our people come from royalty. Why roll around in the mud with swine?"

Click.

"Oh wow, this looks cozy. Thought I'd end work early, and instead, I walk right into a family reunion."

Oh, no! Why, now?!

With all of us so distracted, Harlan sneaks in the front door with a self-satisfied look. "Evening, ladies, what brings you to my place of residence?"

"So many tattoos!" Mrs. Adebayo says, horrified.

"Drug dealer. Of course!" a nameless church woman exclaims.

"My place would be a tad more upscale, if that were the case," Harlan says with savvy.

My mother runs right up to Harlan and points a fat finger in his face. "I am taking my daughter home. She is not staying with you."

Strike me with lightning or drop a meteor on me. For shit's sake, even a thousand comets! Just enough to put me out of my misery. The humiliation is too much to bear.

"Okay... that's up to Patience, not you. She's proven she has quite a mind of her own while being here... a force to be reckoned with. Am I right?" Harlan tries to work his charm on eight huffy Nigerian women in their fifties and sixties.

And he is tanking big time.

"Do not speak of her as if you know her!"

"Getting to know her has been a pleasure and pleasurable. From what makes her tick to what makes her—"

"Harlan, that's enough!" I step in, fearing how that sentence would end. "I'll handle it."

"Then handle it. I'm going to bed."

"This is her father's doing," another church member, Mrs. Akem, whispers loudly in Igbo as she scans Harlan from top to bottom. "Why else would she be involved with such a person?"

"Didn't anyone tell you whispering is rude in front of others?" Harlan chastises her.

"My friend, I beg your pardon?!"

"Just saying. And don't think I hadn't noticed those looks below the belt earlier. If, by chance—in your lovely language—we were wondering if I'm circumcised... Well, hun... I'd ask Patience."

The volume of howls and screeches comes close to peeling paint off every work of art inside.

Harlan continues to troll while plugging his fingers in his ears. "Tough crowd."

Kill me now. Anytime.

"Lord, our heavenly father," my mother randomly begins, "we will not allow this white devil to derail our plans."

"The fuck?!" Harlan exclaims.

"We ask you to deliver our daughter, Patience Neka Abara

Okoye, back on her righteous path. The path she was meant to stay on since the moment she was born—"

"You're such a disgusting hypocrite," I interrupt. There's no way I'm letting her get away with switching up on me.

"You say what?"

"You think he's the source of my unhappiness, but it's you, Mom. It was always you. Instead of giving me a hug after I lost my favorite bumblebee sweater, you called me a waste of space. After I told you cousin Emeka would try to cop a feel of my training bra, you said I was asking for it. God, when I was ten, you took me out of dance class, which I loved, because you thought it was making my thighs too muscular and I'd attract the wrong attention! I was ten! Why would something like that be at the top of anyone's worries?! Dad was done being your emotional punching bag, and so am I. If there's a Lord *you* worship and pray to, I want no part of it. But what I do want—is for you to get the fuck out, take them with you, and never come back! Now!"

Harlan takes a step closer to me with his hand in mine. "Are you sure about that, kid?" His voice is soft, but his eyes pierce through everyone else in the room.

I look at him, then at my mother and her friends. They stare at me, waiting for an answer.

"Yes, Harlan. I'm sure."

"You heard her. Get moving."

My mother's face falls. She shakes her head and turns to leave, followed by Mrs. Adebayo, Mrs. Akem, and the rest. As they walk out the door, I hear my mother's hurt. "I don't blame you for becoming such a failure. Rather, I blame myself."

"Blame yourself on the other side of the door, Mom."

The door closes on that chapter.

Harlan turns back to me with a clownish look. "I think she likes me."

He doesn't get it. It's all shits and giggles to him. "My life falling apart is quite the stand up material to you, isn't it? Damn it, Harlan... You weren't helping the situation at all!"

"Hey, if I'm gonna have a bunch of old bags invading my apartment, I'm having some fun till it gets stale."

My panic attack creeps inside, cold and insidious—the walls closing in like before. The floor rushes up to meet me.

"It's too much... it's always going to be too much..."

I sink into a darkness deeper than any canvas ever painted.

But Harlan catches me in the nick of time. "It's okay, you can fall apart now. They're gone."

I crumble into his arms, and I let myself cry.

"Seriously. Proud of you, Patience."

"Thanks." I push through a smile for him. "She did everything but spit on the doormat on her way out. By the way, you missed her *how dare you trade security for bohemian antics* speech."

"Bohemian antics," Harlan repeats, chuckling. "Catchy. Maybe I'll put that on my next syllabus."

"Just... thanks for not totally losing it on them. I know it was a lot."

"Don't thank me yet," Harlan gets up, moonwalks poorly to the coat closet, and unlocks it. He hides his hands behind his back, and his face drips with sneakiness. "You don't have the faintest clue what I've got up my sleeve, girl."

"What are you hiding?" I ask.

"Me? Hiding? Never." He drags it out, and there it is—a towering, pristine, glorious easel—before us. "I'm presenting this big ol' beaut' out in the open."

I blink, taking in a magnificent oak easel polished to a shine with ornate carvings along the edges, sturdy and adjustable with sleek brass fittings. It's not just an easel; it's a throne for art.

"For me?!"

"That was the idea."

I stay in awe on the floor and instantly forget how my legs work. "Are you insane?"

"Insanely in tune with your aesthetic needs, maybe," Harlan says. He sets up the easel by turning a few notches. "I'm here to class up your *bohemian antics*, one overpriced gift at a time."

He runs a hand along the polished wood while I have trouble expressing my overwhelming rush of gratitude.

"But really, do you know how many canvases I'll need to fill this thing?"

Harlan shrugs. "You think I didn't factor in a canvas budget? Patience, have some faith in my reckless decision-making." He grabs my hands, pulls me up, and wears a cunning expression. "Let's prove your mother right then. Leave responsible choices to the Obinnas of the world. We've got masterpieces to create or at least *attempt* to create. That part's up to you, sweetness."

"I don't know how I'll ever make it up to you."

"I can think of a few things. It'll involve you needing to be more flexible than usual, though."

"God—you're hopeless, Harlan."

"Only when it comes to you."

Maybe I am making a mistake. But I'll embrace it... if it's one that makes me feel less alone in this cosmos.

* * *

Tonight, we're going to a new club, Eden. After Harlan knocked out the creeper during our last visit at Taos, we didn't want to risk him getting sniffed out by bouncers, leading to the arrest we avoided last time.

So, to Eden we go.

Once inside, it's not much different from Taos, and the music vibrates through my sternum. It's another physical whirring that courses through my limbs. Everything's electric as usual—the strobing lights, the pounding house melody, even the club's dank sweat sticks to my skin. Harlan's hand is a distant memory on my hip, lost somewhere in the mass of bodies around us. The Molly, which we both popped an hour before arriving, kicks in—more so for me than him.

I grow a fluid response to the music and become a tangle of uninhibited joy. Harlan tries to hold me and have me dance onto him slowly, but I'm supercharged and seeking to be interactive. "Come on! Give me more!"

Harlan moves but stiffly, then lets out annoyed grunts here and there. His slumped shoulders give away his lack of care for the dance floor. I'm a little disappointed and recall how easily Obinna would compliment my moves when we would go to the club. But I'll make it work somehow.

"Here, try moving like this," I suggest, winding beside him.

"I'm doing fine on my own, thanks." Harlan immediately dismisses me. "Just wanna hang back for now."

"Aww, you're not even trying, though."

Harlan bobs along with a smile plastered on his face that doesn't quite reach his eyes. "Don't fuss over me. Go do your thing, and I'll do mine."

Ugh. His mind is made up. Fine by me.

With every twist and dip, the crowd celebrates. First, a few whistles, then a chorus of catcalls—pump me up even more. I launch myself into formation with my hips controlled by the rhythm. My body is weightless with every movement, and it becomes an extension of the music. The crowd goes wild as their energy charges my own, and I'm a supernova, radiating so intensely I might burst.

"Hey, sexy! Can we dance with you?" a tall woman with her much shorter partner asks as she tries to keep up with me. "You're killing it!"

My cheeks hurt gloriously from smiling so much. "Yeah! Of co—"

"Nah, we're good," Harlan answers for us, curtly.

"Don't be rude, Harlan."

"When will you learn? You don't always have to make nice to anybody that pops up. Not everyone has the best intentions."

Well, his intentions certainly don't appear to be so great either.

I sigh in resignation. "You're being ridiculous. Do whatever you want, but I'm dancing with them."

I miraculously pull off a front handspring and everyone continues to cheer. Wow, I haven't done that since high school gymnastics. I have a superpower!

"Nice panties!" a guy wearing ear gauges yells from the second floor. "Can we get an instant replay up here?"

Before I could though, Harlan totes me to the side by the bar for a one-on-one.

"Hey, Patience, dial it back." Every muscle in his face is pulled taut like the string of a bow about to fire. "You're doing a lot right now."

What's this? Harlan McCandles is not a fan of the spotlight?

"What happened to letting me do my thing?"

Rather than answer that, he face-palms. "Just cool it, damn."

But I continue to feel myself and so does everyone else around me. The DJ drops a new beat, and the tempo sky-rockets even more, putting my moves into overdrive.

If Harlan chooses to stay lame, he's staying lame by himself.

"Hey!" A girl in a black jumpsuit grabs my attention. "DJ Wally has his eye on you, look!"

A man with pink cornrows near the dj stage yells, "Get on up there, girl!" He points at the miniature stage on the left with a dancing pole. "Show us what you got!"

I'm being summoned!

The idea sparks a wild possibility. I glance at Harlan, searching for him to pep me up, but he's evidently pissed. It's weird seeing him so insecure—no better off than being picked last for kickball, for crying out loud. Screw it. I move forward before I can talk myself out of it and clamber onto the small platform to overlook the dance floor.

The crowd roars, and the rush of sound lifts me higher. "Stage!" they chant, over and over.

The thought starts a rebellion within me. I'm not dancing for him, not anymore. I'm dancing for myself and for unadulterated fun.

"Let's hear it for Tonight's Eden firecracker! Work that pole, baby!" DJ Wally comments.

And I do. Molly can either make you fearless or socially unaware, if you're lucky. I unleash my inner exotic dancer and gain applause—twirling for the long haul. Yes. The night is mine.

But Harlan is gone.

"Bring that fine ass over here and show some love to the people. Don't be shy, now!" The DJ says as he hands me the mic.

I grab the microphone while on stage, my voice barely audible over the techno beats. "What's up, Eden?! Lemme hear you, bitches!" I scream into it.

The people howl with approval. With a burst of encouragement, I launch myself off the stage and into the waiting arms of the ecstatic mass below.

I surf the human ripple, and a sea of sweaty bodies carries me on its shoulders. Arms reach out to touch me, many going for high fives.

Patience Okoye, a tangible force.

But then a hand grabs my wrist, yanking me down.

It's Harlan, on a mission to bring me back to planet Earth. "What the hell are you doing?!" he hisses and hauls me toward the exit.

Oh, so that's where he was—a snake waiting to strike.

"Aye, yo man, let baby girl go!" DJ Wally scolds.

The crowd follows his lead and boos Harlan, supporting his demand for my release.

"You're spoiling the night. Knock it off," I protest, but my voice sounds shrill, even to my own ears.

"Time to go now," Harlan growls. His grip tightens as he leads us out even farther. "You might not think so because of your current elevated sense of who you think you are, but you're making a fool of yourself."

"Were we at the same club?! They loved me! You saw it yourself!"

"God, can you really not tell when people are laughing at you versus laughing with you? You really are out of it then."

No. That can't be what happened. I was there. I saw! They enjoyed every bit of what I put out on stage. Or... maybe Molly made everything perfect and not as it seemed.

There's no way to ever truly know, is there? Harlan drags and drags me outside till we get to the car, at last. "Unbelievable. That can't happen ever again, got it? Or I won't be seen with you in public. Period."

"We're here. Let me go!" I scream, which he does. "And what can't happen again? What are you even talking about?"

"Acting like a low-class stripper on a Tuesday afternoon. Having your ass hanging out of your dress for half of the night. Embarrassing me in front of all those goddamn people. Should I go on?!" His volume extinguishes the last embers of my high. "I've never seen such obvious attention whoredom in my life. Get in the fucking car!"

Outside, the cool night air hits me like a slap. Streetlights cast a glow over the parking lot, a stark contrast to the electric dream I just left.

"Drive yourself home," I say, contrary to his command. "I'm not riding in a car with you talking to me that way."

Downtown Dallas feels vast and undefined. But it's looking a lot better than Harlan's passenger seat as a choice.

"Where are you going?!"

"Somewhere you're not!" I retort. After slamming the passenger door shut, I storm off into the night.

* * *

I barely make it ten minutes on my own after Harlan leaves,

then I catch an Uber to... my old townhome I used to share with Obinna, in order to clear my head. It's so off-putting being on the other side of my old life, but I couldn't stay away. Not sure what answers I expect to find, being here. What would the old me think of the new me now? Shouldn't I know?

I sit across from it on the bench by the greenery, safe from being spotted. It's one AM, and I know I look creepy, stalking my former husband—wondering if he has a woman up there, or if he's doing things with her he refused to do with me. His car is home, so it's possible.

Or maybe I'm only hoping he does, so it can ease the fact I cheated on Obinna first.

PING.

Harlan calls. As prickly as I am with him, it's mean to leave him crawling with worry about where I am, so I answer.

"Hello."

"Thank god, you answered. Where are you?"

"Why do you care?"

"Don't be like that. Come home to me."

"Is it a good idea to be in company with an attention whore?" I ask, tensely.

"I'm really sorry. All those eyes on you... drove me batshit crazy. I was only looking out for you—didn't want a Taos repeat with some drunk asshole trying anything sketchy," he coaxes.

"I can take care of myself."

"But not the way I can, Patience. So, again, come home and let me take care of you."

I shake my head, disappointed. "Respect me, Harlan. That's all I ask."

"Well... you have to be here in order for me to get cracking on that, beautiful.”

“Seems like you have it all figured out.”

“I just miss having you quake on my tongue.”

While mine just sits inside of my cheek from what he uttered.

“You’re smiling. I can tell.”

“You suck.”

There he goes again. Okay, Harlan’s been run ragged long enough. “You’re lucky we got away before the crowd tried to beat your ass.”

“You’ve always been a showstopper, though. But... is it a huge ask to dance like that only for me?”

“I’ve had bigger.”

“Um. Not ideal for a man to hear.”

I giggle immaturely.

“Your laugh just made my whole night. Now... make my whole week and show up.”

“I’ll be there soon.”

“Sure my muse doesn’t need a ride?”

Ooh. The last thing Harlan needs to know is where I choose to reminisce these days.

“No, I’ll Uber back. I’m a big girl.”

“Hurry. I’m owed a private dance from you. Pronto.”

Harlan hangs up, and I resume my daydreams of *what if* with Obi. Face it, I chose what I chose. So did he. And we owe it to ourselves to stick to it to see what entails.

“I gotta let him go. It’s only fair,” I say to myself, eyes shining. Plus, the later it gets, the more unforeseeable the streets are for a woman out alone.

Uber to the rescue.

THE FEASTS OF WANT VERSUS ASUNDER

The day of the Art Exhibition at the Concord Gallery snuck up faster than we thought, but here we are—pursuing the drive in Harlan's beat-up Jeep through the congested streets of Bishop Arts District Downtown. It stretches ahead of us in all its upscale glory—gleaming glass and steel towers framed by lush greenery and graffiti.

Harlan's knee bounces up and down like a jackhammer. Every few seconds, his hands move to his forehead, wiping imaginary sweat as he fights like hell to sit still.

The nervousness is a sight to pity.

"Harlan…"

"Don't."

"It's just an exhibition," I try my best to soothe the growing tension during the drive there. "You've sold your works before like you've done it in your sleep. Concord shouldn't have you second guessing yourself."

"What do you think it's all been about?" Harlan snaps. "This is *the* exhibition, Patience. If my stuff doesn't sell there tonight, then what? Back to the drawing board?"

"Yes! Is that so bad?"

"You may accept a teacher's salary, but I don't. You think collectors like Corbin Reyes show up to anyone's gallery? This guy just came back from a showing in Spain less than twenty-four hours ago!"

"Are you stalking Corbin on his socials?" That's so unlike him.

"He awards not just seasoned but upcoming artists, too. He purchases their shit on a whim and drops a crap-load of cash on their art." It looks like he's holding in the urge to spit. "You don't get it—I'm sick of being passed over every year. It has to be me tonight. It has to."

I bite back a sigh. I know better than to downplay things when Harlan's in one of his moods. But I also know if I let his self doubt get the best of him, it'll be a disaster before we even park the car. He doesn't mean to be mean. I see why he pushes harder than most and why it drives him to these lengths.

My hand reaches over and rests on his leg to steady it. "Hey, let's simmer down. You've worked hard for this. Your art is incredible, and someone's going to see that tonight."

Harlan looks at me for the first time since the drive, and his bejeweled eyes soften. But they still have that wild, anxious energy. "Yeah, well... let's hope someone with money sees it, too."

We pull up to the upscale gallery. The bright lights from inside the glass building spill out onto the sidewalk, and a small crowd is already gathering, milling around with their champagne flutes and practiced smiles.

"Ready, champ?" I ask.

"Stay by my side," Harlan states, kissing my sticky, glossed lips. "Could you?"

"Where else would I be?"

Once inside, the white walls, stark and clean, make the art

pop. The chattering of the crowd in the packed gallery echoes off the high tray ceilings. People cluster around various pieces and nod appreciatively. But no sign of anyone buying yet.

Harlan's painting of the night—*The Feasts of Want*—hangs prominently in the center of the room. It's the one of him, Roxy, and me. Thankfully, that notion is only clear-cut to me.

Does this seem right to you, Patience?

Wait, what's happening?

Think it's fair Harlan should gain a profit from a moment you don't even remember?

Stop. So what? Taking Ayahuasca with them was a trippy experience—one I can say I've had once—

Twice.

Whatever. Twice... and I'm happy to move on from that.

Then why is your stomach hurting?

From bad champagne, what else?

More like from the idea of him serving you up to be sampled however he wants, without you having a say.

Leave me alone. Now's not the time to hear voices in my freaking head!

Quiet.

Thank you, God.

Now, back to the showing.

I can see Harlan trying to hold it together as he stands near his work, but he makes hand movements like he's wringing out a towel. Oh boy. He scans the crowd to spot out who could crown him the next genius of the art world. And me—I've been here, by his side, no better off than a piece of furniture, sipping white wine, and smiling at strangers as they browse. But it's okay, I owe him. He's shown me time and time again how art can unlock many possibilities. I'm truly thankful, and I find myself saying that often—almost like a reassurance.

"Holy shit. There he is." Harlan nearly bursts a blood vessel. "Corbin just showed up."

He's nothing like I imagined.

Corbin Reyes is of average height, maybe shorter. His brown hair is thinning at the top. He has a pale face, almost sickly, with deep-set eyes framed by round glasses. Corbin's clothes seem out of place—with wrinkled khaki slacks and a loose button-up shirt I bet hasn't seen dry cleaning in years. No sharp suit or commanding presence like I'd pictured. If anything, Reyes resembles a tired accountant than an art world heavyweight.

"Why don't you introduce yourself?"

"Yeah, this isn't a mixer, hun," Harlan says, scathingly. "You gotta be subtle with these things."

"Trying to help here."

"He looks bored already. Great."

"Well, standing around here isn't helping your odds either," I reply, pulling up my strapless dress.

"Hate to say it, but you're right." Corbin stays fixed in Harlan's line of sight.

"Go mingle. Talk to people."

"You sure?"

"Yeah. I'll be fine."

"You know... I couldn't do this without you, kid."

I smile brightly, happy he sees how I anchor him. But I can tell he's still weary as he drifts into the crowd.

I stay back, close to his painting that stands alone on the far wall. Well-heeled patrons mill about, their conversations blending into a low hum of wealth and sophistication. The space smells faintly of wood polish and the subtle perfume of fresh flowers set in tall vases around the room.

Harlan's already chatting with a group of art dealers a few feet away—arms sweeping through the air as he passionately explains his latest abstract piece. He's totally in his element with his CELINE shirt half untucked, in such a way only he can pull off. People are captivated, hanging on his every word and clearly dazzled. I can't help but smile—those nerves are long gone. He's not only selling his art; he's selling himself.

"Yours?"

"Huh?"

A lady with a bulky Burberry mini-dress appears. She barely smirks and keeps her toothpick-like fingers on her champagne glass. "Sorry, I didn't mean to scare you. I was asking, is this yours? I'm Camilla Morton."

Her name doesn't ring a bell, but with her pricey getup, I'm sure it's supposed to. "Oh, no, but the one beside it is my... my partner's. Harlan McCandles. I'm Patience Okoye."

"Pleasure." Camilla's birdface centers on Harlan's *The Feasts of Want*. "Hmm... Well, it's certainly appetitive."

I'm detecting a *but*. "Is that all?"

"I'm familiar with his work."

"Harlan's a master at making the darkness contrast with the vibrancy of everything else. What do you think?"

Camilla sneezes. "Um... I'm familiar with his work."

Ouch. "I didn't expect him to, but he taught me so much and has helped my process."

"Oh? Do you have any work on display here?"

"Um..." I do. Mine is on the Featured Wall with the dis-claimer *accepting commissions* in parentheses. Called *Asunder*, it's a quiet scene—mist rising from a field at dawn. However, as it's an abstract piece, it's not quite made clear. Simple, nothing like the stormy works that scream from the rest of the room. Harlan's idea of a friendly gesture was to include me last minute. After all, it's his night. Not mine. He's wanted it for longer and prides himself on that. "Yes, in fact. Right over here."

We get there, and Camilla's serious expression melts, as if she's falling in love for the very first time. "This one. It's quite simplistic and earnest. What's the story behind it?"

"There's no story. Just felt at peace creating it, really."

"And how much?"

"Oh, that one's not for sale," I say. Harlan insisted it would make the exhibit feel fuller—a backdrop to grander works of art. I expected no one to notice it. Especially not someone like Camilla.

"No?"

"Sorry."

"Won't you humor a gal for a bit? I don't yet have a painting that borders between natural abstract and landscape art. It's a rarity," she says, trying to twist my arm on the topic. "How about ten thousand?"

Well, Gatdamn! I could use the money, but there'll be other galleries. This one isn't meant for me. "Camilla, you're very kind... but it's my boyfriend's night. I would love for it to stay that way."

"Is it?"

"Yes." The words sound weak, even to my own ears. "And I'm here to support him."

"Supporting him by hiding behind his work?" Camilla gestures to my painting. "Your piece is one of the very few here that speaks plenty of promising aptitude, and it shouldn't simply be on some looky-loo wall."

"Camilla—"

"It has comprehensibility. Which Harlan's... doesn't easily come across." She steps closer, and her pitch drops drastically. "Don't let someone else's ego eclipse your talent. Or let obligations dull your inner shine, only to allow others to shine brighter. In short, I will purchase *The Feasts of Want* along with *Asunder.* Deal?"

I glance back at the painting. My painting. The one daring to go up against Harlan's. For a second, I let myself imagine what it would feel like to say, "Yes, it is for sale." To step out to the forefront and claim an accomplishment for myself. But—

"Hey, Patience, can I talk to you?" Harlan takes me by the hand while waving to Camilla. "Hello, Ms. Morton—my apologies. I'll bring her back shortly."

"No apologies necessary. Patience, it was nice speaking with you, and here's my card."

I take it from her and am relieved to part from our meddlesome conversation. "Thank you. Take care."

We power walk past the attendees at the exhibition, and then make a right in the u-shaped hallway. "Tom's Diner" by DNA and Suzanne Vega plays over the art gallery speakers, then grows fainter with every step.

"Hey, where are we going? Is everything okay?" I ask him, noticing we're no longer in range of the event whatsoever.

"Hang on... hang on..." Harlan mumbles. "Need some privacy. Over here—"

"But, wha—"

"Please," he insists. He's already guiding me toward a small door in the back of the gallery, marked *Supply Room.*

He slips inside and pulls me in after him. The room is full of clutter, including boxes of extra brochures and half-empty crates of wine. Noise from the gallery ceases as the door shuts behind us. Harlan turns to me and rakes through his hair nervously.

I'm not able to take the suspense any longer. "Look, don't be mad about Camilla. We were only talking and—"

"Beautiful, I'm fucked," Harlan exclaims, while he sits in a foldable chair. "I mean, the event is halfway over and most of the important people have already left, including Corbin. Turns out that asshole was only slumming for contemporary art this year."

He rocks in his chair, then locks his hands together on the back of his neck, applying an insane amount of pressure that turns him a fruit punch red. "I thought... I thought this was going to be it, you know? The big payoff. But it's not."

He's overthinking it; the night isn't done, and for all he knows, people like Camilla could save the day. The only thing he needs to do is sit tight and cool down. And if nothing else, being realistic should be front and center of Harlan's line of thinking. Not trying to be harsh here, but he knew his odds. Corbin Reyes shuffles through thousands of new artists, so he shouldn't be riding this so hard. It could have gone any direction.

A light bulb flickers, and suddenly, Harlan leaps out of his chair. "Jesus, what was that?!"

He pauses, eyes wide, pupils dilated as the light sputters above us. The flashing seems to set off a charge in him. His hands shoot up to his face again, and he stumbles, gasping for air.

"It's just... it's only a faulty light bulb. Are you feeling all right?"

Now Harlan has the pallor of someone who's had bad shellfish. "Anyway, no one's even giving *The Feasts of Want* a second look." He's fixated on this worry for weeks now. His art isn't selling fast enough, and it's eating away at him.

I try to take his hand and give him reassurance, but he barely responds to it.

"Just fake ass smiles and talks of having somewhere else to be."

"Look, you've got eyes on your work—I've seen it myself," I say, keeping my vocal inflections even. "That's a good thing. Give it more of a wait for yourself."

Harlan shakes his head and gets up. "Nuh-uh. They don't get it. I can see it in their goddamn faces. No, they think it's too derivative, too..." His volume drops, and he glances around before whispering, "Fucking trendy."

BOOM! An innocent box gets kicked into the air. Then a couple more.

I have to stop this before it derails into a bigger eruption. "Hey, hey! You are blowing everything out of context! Did anyone even say this stuff to you, Harlan?!"

"They don't need to! I can feel it! Fuck!" Harlan's now smacking his forehead and comes close to ripping his hair out. "All of them looking at me—like, I'm an imposter here... like I'm complete shit or—"

"Stop!" I throw myself into his arms and put an end to his self-hating tirade. "I don't wanna hear anymore."

There's shaking as we hug. Man, he's really torn up about how everything's going. What comes next are hot tears that land on my forehead and drip into my mouth. I can literally taste how much this means to Harlan.

Anchor him again, Patience. Now that you have him listening. He's been a shoulder to cry on for me plenty of times, so it's time to return the favor. "You're noteworthy, and this is just one event. One out of a million to come."

Harlan's sniffing stops, and he drops to his knees. "I don't know what I'd do without you. You're the only thing keeping me sane."

"Same here. Focus on the finish line, not just the first lap in the race. Can you see clearly now?"

"Yup, the rain is gone."

"Glad you feel better enough for jokes."

I thought we were done. I thought we were finished. Until Harlan lifts up my dress and buries his head under it, and I'm automatically reminded of our first night together. Fingers travel as he inhales and exhales in a way that has me riveted. His tongue is far from a stranger of what's underneath.

"Harlan, the gallery's still going."

"Shh... Just let me have some."

The ache grows slightly, but not as strong as before... because tonight isn't like the rest. I could be discovered, taken seriously as an artist by a legit collector. This isn't the time nor the place. Actually... Markos, The Edith Museum, and the dining table at Camp Arnica—those weren't the time and place, either.

"Shouldn't we go back now?"

"I had a bad day... Just a taste longer... There's a good girl..." Harlan nibbles teasingly as his hold on my waist compresses. "Jesus, you're intoxicating."

"Seriously, anybody could come in."

"Let them watch... We'll put on a show... I don't care..."

"Well, I do!" I push him out from under me. "So quit!"

Harlan hits the floor, taken for a spin from me bucking up to him.

"Patience, whoa... I—"

"Didn't you hear me say no?"

"I don't know. Did you?"

Didn't I?

I toss my shawl at him. "I'll be in the car. Don't forget to wipe your mouth before coming back out."

Now supply closets will forever rub me the wrong way.

* * *

"Sweetness, wake up. I have news."

"Nuh... hmm?"

When Harlan finally climbs into the Jeep, his face is glowing. He slides into the driver's seat and turns to me—with his bright canine teeth in full view. "Someone bought my piece! Someone bought *The Feasts of Want,* anonymously! For seventy-five hundred dollars! Yeah, it's not the big Corbin bucks, but it means people are talking and there's more where that came from and—shit, could you believe it?!"

"I'm happy for you," I say, contrived.

Harlan dissipates from my response. "You're the first person I wanted to tell. Lighten up, would you?"

"Harlan, we need to have a serious talk."

"Really? Now?"

"Yes." I unbuckle my seatbelt to face him. "Because what you tried in the supply room made me very uncomfortable."

He glares at me for a moment, then shakes his head and mutters a few words I can't quite hear.

"What was that again?"

"I said, '*It was all in good fun and you never minded before.*' Why get heavy on me now about it? I was bugging, and I thought you were trying to make me feel better."

"So, when in doubt—go down on Patience?! In a public place?!"

"I dunno about you, but I'd wear that slogan on a T-shirt, any day."

"Oh, please. Kiss...my...ass..."

"Hey! I tried going for your ass, but you pumped the brakes too soon in the supply room, remember?"

No. I'm done going along with Harlan's racy public displays of affection. He tries to pass it off as liberating, and initially, it was easy to pretend it wasn't me doing them. Instead, it was someone who could match this mysterious artistic guru's sexual prowess. Then it grew to be needing to prove an undeclared thing for reasons I'm not even sure of anymore. Why do I have to bend? Why can't he bend for me? When it's just us in bed, it's great—pretty much bliss. But being used as a tool for risqué pleasure—with others there to possibly witness—might be someone else's cup of tea, not mine. And I'm allowed to change my mind.

"Harlan McCandles... lose the fetishy bullshit or lose me. No more close calls with people walking in on us. Got it?"

The quiet rings louder than ever. Harlan's eyes adjust to my sudden demand. "Just like that?"

"Exactly like that."

"All right then." Harlan starts the Jeep. "Guess we gotta head home because we got some making up to do."

I buckle my seatbelt. "Making up?"

Harlan leans in and looks me over. I can tell he wants to

kiss me but doesn't—maybe thinking I would respect him more in a way. "Look, I won't do it again. I'll do anything to keep having you... till there's nothing left. We're going home to celebrate. I picked out an outfit for you and everything."

He hands me a congratulatory sash. I snort, barely enlivened.

"I suppose you'd like for me to wear this with it."

"I'd like you to be wearing... just this."

"Oh."

"For my muse only."

"We still have a long way to go."

"I meant it when I told you the first time. I hear you when you speak, Okoye. It'll be only us and no one else in range of us. Because, by the time I'm done with you, questioning what you mean to me will be out of the question. Am I forgiven?"

"I wanna see how tonight goes, then we'll talk." I pinch his ear and sit, pleased with myself at how it all came together. Harlan doesn't know the full story, but I don't need him to. This is his moment, and I'm content with it.

As he pulls out of the parking lot, I glance back at the gallery and experience both loss and satisfaction. My *Asunder* painting is gone, while ten grand processes in my bank account, thanks to Camilla's purchase. All I can do is hold Harlan to his word that he'll no longer attempt to involve me in his iffy sex quirks... and not secretly plotting to find more personal margins of mine to cross as we speak.

THE SUN AND HER ICARUS

I walk into a catastrophe happening in my classroom Monday afternoon as things go disastrously under my paraprofessional's watch. Nadia is trying to calm down Nyla, who starts frantically jumping from table to table.

"Nyla, stop it, or your sticker chart is going to the red zone!" Nadia tries to redirect.

"I hate fractions, and you can't make me learn them!" she screams.

Nadia and I shield ourselves as Nyla sends huge workbooks flying.

Nadia's methods seem ineffective, so I step in.

"Nyla, woah! Use your words, hun. It'll be okay."

"I've got it under control, Ms. O," Nadia retorts gravely, with pink cheeks. "Her behavior has escalated like this for a while now. So much so I'm seeing a trend."

That long?

"Go away! I hate this school, and I hate you!" Nyla's aim at my head takes the cake, and my brow bleeds profusely.

"Fuck!" I scream unintentionally. Remaining students visiting from Ms. Bell's class jump out of their chairs in total stagger.

"Ms. O said a bad word!" shouts Dominick, who jumps up

and down.

Ms. Bell's students share their input, too. "Oooooh!"

"This class scares me."

"Fuck-fuckity-fuck-fuck!"

Nadia gives me a *you gotta be kidding me* glance.

"Everyone..." I say in my deepest authoritative voice. "Clear the room now! Ms. O is serious."

Kids scatter out of the room, which leaves Nadia and me with an irate Nyla.

"CPI Hold, Nadia."

"But I'm not—"

"Do it!" I direct. "Besides, I'll be here to guide you—on the count of three."

Nadia timidly nods and takes her stance.

After three, we get on either side of Nyla, take hold of her arms, and push the back of her head forward.

"You're hurting me, you stupid bitches!" she yells like she's possessed.

Nadia looks visibly heartbroken.

"Well, it'll hurt a lot less if you calm down," I tell her, as I rub Nyla's back. "For your safety and ours."

"I—I'm so mad."

"Why, baby?"

"Because the cafeteria ran out of peaches today, and I was picked last for hockey at PE, and my shoes are too tight— "

"And fractions were the last straw, huh?"

Nyla falls into my arms and cries to the point she's inconsolable. "I wanna go home, Ms. O. Please?"

"Well, let's start with putting our room back together, and we'll see what we can do, okay?"

We spend fifteen minutes cleaning without saying a word. In mid cleanup, I head to the nurse to clean my brow wound. By the time we're fully done, specials class for Nyla is in five minutes.

"Can I go to art class, since we're done cleaning?" she asks.

"Yes, only because you took ownership of your feelings and helped clean."

Nadia viciously snorts. "She hit you with a book. You could've needed stitches."

"No harm, no foul," I say with a smile. "We all have rough patches every once in a while."

"I love you, Ms. O. And I'm sorry," Nyla says, squeezing me. "Can I give Ms. Gomez a hug, too?"

I turn to Nadia and gather the decision... she's not a fan of that idea.

"Maybe later. Now go, don't be late."

"Bye!"

As if thirty minutes earlier never happened, Nyla skips out the door.

"Mrs. Okoye, I know it's your planning period, but could we meet briefly?" Nadia asks.

Her shift in energy takes me by surprise.

"It's just us, Nadia. You know you can call me Patience. And don't take what Nyla or any other kid of ours says to heart when they're flipping their lid, okay?"

Nadia frequently blinks as long overdue tears follow. "You're never around when we need you, and now you expect me to trust your judgment?"

"What?!"

"It's true! Why do you think Nyla decided to freak out now? Half the time, her teacher is nowhere to be found. You know about her abandonment issues. And when I try to step up to the plate, I'm seen as the bad guy because I'm not you. Ms. O, none of it is effective if you're not here enough. We will always be on square one, if that's the case."

Her words stab, so I get defensive. "I have other responsibilities, Nadia. But it doesn't mean I'm not dedicated to my job."

"So, then hire another certified teacher, not a para!" Nadia exclaims. "I'm a twenty-four-year-old grad student who makes eighteen bucks an hour. I didn't ask for the extra load."

"I thought I was offering you an opportunity to gain experience if you ever wanted to get into Special Education," I say despondently.

"It sounds like you took advantage of me as your para for you to keep running errands. More than personal errands, might I add."

Zing! All of my credibility goes out the window.

I thought I could balance it all—play all the roles I wanted and then come back as good old reliable Ms. O. But I suck as an educator, unknowingly shoveling it all onto her plate.

"Thanks for not telling Vicci, by the way," I segway. "About the pills."

Nadia looks everywhere else except at me. "Does it help deal with what happened to Grayson? You don't even talk about him anymore. It's none of my business—I get it—but what the hell are you doing with that stuff? You're a married, successful woman. It's beneath your caliber. As stupid as this sounds, I sort of looked up to you, Patience."

"I apologize. Okay, Nadia?" I walk over to her and take her quaking hands. "There's no excuse—personal stuff or not."

"Thank you." Nadia sniffs. "But as a heads up, I might take

a personal day tomorrow."

* * *

The personal day Nadia asked for yesterday is a direct correlation with another urgent check-in meeting with Principal Vicci this afternoon. I'm sweating badly while sitting in the waiting room, and I haven't even taken any Molly yet. Damn. It's too bad I'm all out of benzos to level me out.

It hasn't even been a damn month.

The peeled *hanging in there* cat poster is an accurate depiction of my current state.

"Mrs. Okoye, she'll see you now," Jordana, the receptionist, says.

I take my green mile walk to her office.

Knocking first, I go in.

"Hello?"

Principal Vicci is not alone. A man—about late forties, with a toilet seat receding hairline—sits across from her. I get a sinking feeling he is not for me, but against me.

"Please come in, Mrs. Okoye. This is Daniel Farber from HR. I thought it would be best he attend, too."

I slouch in a pinchy leather seat and gawk at them both.

"Right, so let's start with today's agenda, shall we?"

"Actually, I'm curious Principal Vicci—" I take the lead. "Why is this meeting taking place if it hasn't been a full month? That was the term I agreed to regarding my performance review."

Principal Vicci exchanges a look with the HR rep and blinks swiftly. "Yes, that was the initial plan. But after certain recent events, I—rather, we—need to discuss a few things."

"Like?"

"Like yesterday's incident with your student, Nyla Chambers. Nadia—Ms. Gomez—left a very detailed report about what took place, and we're taken aback by what we read."

So, Nadia finally did me in, huh? "Please, what does it say?"

"For instance, when Nyla struck you with a book, why wasn't she reported to the discipline committee? That way, a proper MDR meeting could've determined whether the act was a manifestation of her disability. Also, let's not forget the vulgar language you used, which was even verified by other students. We frown upon that here at Seabrook."

The hole Nadia dug for me is a cesspool, and this is her comeuppance.

"Also, Ms.Gomez stated she was pressured to do CPI hold on a student, even though she isn't certified to do so. Policy states that if students need to be restrained, only certified professionals in Crisis Prevention Intervention can assist. In the state of an emergency, you should have sent her out to get another certified professional or administration immediately."

Great—drugs have officially rid me of my common sense. Because how else could I have overlooked all of this SPED 101 spiel?

"During the moment of escalation, I had to act quickly and didn't have time to process the rest," I plead my case. "I know it wasn't my finest hour, but with the service I've given to this campus, I would hope that you would reconsider—"

Principal Vicci draws in a rushing breath, then shakes her head. "It's because we remember what you've done for this campus that we're letting you finish out the school year. However, we will not be renewing your contract for next year."

Everything stops in slow motion. My eyes glaze over, and my hearing becomes distorted. The one thing that kept me a respected figure is gone. So, why not cut ties now?

"Mrs. Okoye, where are you going?"

"Somewhere where none of it makes a difference anymore."

Both administrators look up at me, bemused.

"I lost my only pregnancy because of my decision to teach. I'm through with defining myself by my career."

I walk out and never look back.

* * *

"Don't worry about money. I'll take care of you as long as you take care of me."

In the first couple of days after quitting my job, the idea of being Harlan's kept woman wore at me. There were days we would paint for hours—nothing but dusky and overcast abstracts coming straight from my jaded view of the world.

Then there were days I would gladly rot in bed, with Harlan nearby to fool around with, cynically.

As for some new developments, my night terrors are back, but not like before.

They fuck with me the most. The substances I'm taking to escape my increasingly disorderly life are amplifying my paranoia.

My dreams of the uncanny valley take place in Harlan's artwork.

They vary—in one, I'm trapped in his glass box with my

palms against the walls. It's smooth, cold, and opaque, with smears blurring the glass. Suddenly, a vat of sludgy ink pours in, filling it to the brim.

Harlan appears.

I see the back of him standing from a distance, and I screech at the top of my lungs for help.

He turns around.

And has no face.

Only smooth, featureless skin where his eyes, nose, and mouth should be. He raises his head and watches, quiescent, as I panic inside his transparent cage.

The ink penetrates every pore and open space until I gasp for air. My arms flail, stirring as viscous sludge echoes back at me. Skin blisters beneath it and peels back, layer by layer. Faceless, Harlan watches on, pressing himself against the glass, and it's not clear whether he moans in ecstasy or pain. Ink finds a way into my muscles, then threads through my pliable body. My skin sloughs off, revealing open flesh, and beneath it, bare bone, pure and white in the dark—slathers red with my blood. The sludge claims my soul from the inside out, finally puddling me to my death.

In another dream, I stand in darkness with neon tentacles swirling around me. They're alive—slithering, tense like a coiled spring, and crawl into my mouth. I scream, but the sound gets lost in the dark hues. Artwork demons with rubbery, slate-colored skin and rotting baby teeth find where I am. They hide within the borders and don't want me to leave, wanting me to become one of them. And the worst part? Sometimes, when I look into those swirling black depths, when I hear their whispers calling my name, I'm tempted to answer.

I told Harlan about it last night, and he made light of it. "My paintings... They're not just art. They're mirrors. They'll show you what you refuse to see. Also, take it easy on my stash, will you?"

Hmm. Maybe he doesn't fully understand it, or maybe he does, and he's secretly drawn to it, like me to him. The duskiness in his art isn't just creative genius—it comes alive when I sleep. Every brushstroke, every color, every neon flash against the black, it's all part of something bigger. Something ancient and hungry.

And I'm the offering.

Morning welcomes a turn around from past disappointments. There's a letter addressed to me. It's from Colby Community College, and I read it aloud with butterflies in my stomach.

"Congratulations, Patience Okoye! You are the recipient of the Colby Arts Grant for the 2021-2022 school year. We look forward to your future contributions. Thank you for considering us."

I swell up with so much gladness that I squeal and hop around Harlan's confined living space.

"Yes! Yes! I got it!"

Harlan comes from the bathroom and rubs sleep from his eyes. "That better be a winning lottery ticket. Because nothing else warrants that much screaming."

"Harlan, I got the grant! See? From the kaleidoscope abstract I made." I rush the letter in his hands.

For a second, I see Harlan's face crease—deadpan. "So, you're messing with me, right?"

"Huh?"

"Do you have selective hearing or what? I told you about

my process and told you several times. I don't like putting my personal elements in artwork. The hell, Patience? This isn't news to you."

How can he hate what we—more or less—made together?

"Why is it okay for your *The Feasts of Want* to feature Roxy and me in a threesome with you? That's a personal element I wasn't too crazy about," I say, miffed.

Harlan scratches his unshaven jawline crisply. "Those were unidentifiable bodies of flesh that could be anyone. You're not special. Nobody has eyes like mine."

It's like he takes pride in being conceited.

"I'm really proud of my piece. Let me have this."

"Irrelevant."

"Harlan—"

"No, you listen!" he barks. "Those are my eyes. I'm the one who decides if they should be captured and displayed for the world to see. And you think I'm supposed to be proud of you? It's the most unoriginal thing you've done."

"I thought it would bring us closer together."

"I think you say shit for the sake of just saying shit. So what if you won a measly three thousand dollar grant? I wipe my ass with that money."

"It's not about the money. It's about proving myself, improving my skills, and being around other people who appreciate my artwork, too. Besides, you're a community college professor and a bartender," I say. "The last thing you should do is wipe your ass with that money."

"Easy talk for someone who's no longer employed." He looks me up and down like I'm compost.

"Why are you ruining it for me?"

"Because it's not always about you!"

Harlan pushes me out of the way and grabs his wallet and keys. "I'm getting some air. I'll be back when I'm back."

* * *

Harlan doesn't come home for two days, and I am near molting my skin with worry. He doesn't call or send texts to help me settle down. From Harlan's stash, I continually feed my paranoia with weed and Molly.

He chose a real fine time to put me on a timeout.

I play on my phone while navigating my high when I receive a text.

Patience, I'm worried. I just want to know if my almost sister is okay. Call me.

Neisa doesn't need me like she believes she does. I'll only let her down like the rest. Sadly, she's reduced to playing a cameo role in my life, so I switch off my smartphone to protect us both.

My body's splayed out on the futon as I look up at the ceiling. It's funny how his apartment is my morning, noon, and night now. The walls start melting and galaxies form, shooting meteors inches away from my head.

But then I see the frozen bodies of astronauts reaching for me.

This isn't fun anymore.

Get up and take off. Simple. Except it isn't. My legs might as well be attached to the bedpost. They aren't budging.

What in the world is that?

The rotting bodies hover over me, jeering and laughing. Their flesh is slimy and plops onto me, as I'm not able to move out of the way. Ice cold sticky mess covers me all over.

A tall, blueish, zombified astronaut grabs me and throws me off the bed onto the ground.

I hit below with a malady of a *thud*.

"Patience, can you hear me?" the Astro Zombie asks. "Your eyes are open, but you're not blinking. Fuck, how much did you take?"

"Who are you?" I ask. But it comes out like "*Cloo bar chew?*"

The astronaut zombie tries to take off my clothes, and I am officially losing my shit. "Hang on. I'm going to have you take a cold bath to snap you out of it. It's okay."

I still can't move anything, but my lungs work just fine. And I'm going to let Astro Zombie know that, too. I scream bloody murder directly into his ear to let me go. Or to, *"Get be show."*

"Stop, I'm trying to help!" The Astro Zombie screams and forgoes stripping me. Instead, he tosses me in the tub, still partially clothed, and I jump up awake with a chill-bursting splash.

"Go away! No! No! No more!"

"Hey! Hold on to me, you're perfectly fine."

Huh?

The zombies are gone, and so are the galaxies. I'm in Harlan's home, in Harlan's tub.

And in a flash, I'm here with Harlan.

"So, I take more Markos shifts after teaching for a couple days, and you party here all by yourself?" he jokes, rubbing my forehead. "You have peculiar priorities."

"Did I overdose?" I ask, sleepily.

"Not necessarily, but I would hate to see how close you came to that if I weren't here. What were you thinking? Don't go all out on this stuff without a second pair of eyes to look out for you. You're a newbie."

"You take it, too. You take even more than me and make it work. How?"

Harlan uses a damp washcloth to pat my eyebrows. "Well, it took a while to find a good balance and timing for my tolerance levels. I work out, drink plenty of water, watch what I eat, and I don't fuck around with taking mdma back to back, which is where weed and benzos come in handy. M can do irreversible damage to your brain if you're not careful. That's why you should only do it with me."

I work on keeping my head above water. "I can't do Molly anymore."

"I think that might be for the best, too."

"You do?"

"You weren't just doing it only for me, were you?" he asks, nonplussed.

I'm not ready to admit that yet.

"Patience, I could take it or leave it. It's not a big deal. Just stick to smoking weed."

I wipe my nose. It seems all I ever do is weep lately. "I thought you were still mad at me."

Harlan takes a pitcher of water and carefully pours it onto my head. "I found a way to get over it. Let's get you out to dry."

After rehydrating and drinking one of Harlan's protein shakes, I'm feeling loads better. Midnight arrives, and we sit by the window to create a new abstract. His ring lamp shoots across the worn canvas, dappling it in a mosaic of light and shadow. Harlan comes up with sandstone, marigold, and bronze, claiming to be inspired by the story of Icarus.

"I kinda remember that one," I say as I get comfortable. "His dad created wings using wax and gifted him a pair, right?”

"Yep, the same one. Kid disobeyed his father. Flew too high, sun melted the wax, and whoosh—down he went." Harlan swirls another shade of orange from his palette, the rich color a stark contrast to his pale skin tone—a man of meticulous strokes. "And he plummeted into the sea to await his death."

I dip my brush back into my palette and let his words stick. "A depressing story of teenage rebellion."

"It is," Harlan agrees, his gaze drifting back to the abstract. "But it's a reminder. A fiery drive can be a double-edged sword."

"Meh, sounds more like crappy parenting to me."

"You know, one could also see the sun as a treacherous lover."

"This oughta be good." I'm snorting at the idea of Harlan's personification in the tale. "Don't you think you're reaching a bit?"

Harlan lets out a frustrated sigh, sets down his palette with a clatter. "It gets kinda old repeating there's a method to my—"

"Madness. Yeah, I got it."

"So, then, do me a favor."

"Name it."

"Never burn me, Patience."

"Huh?"

"I said, never burn me," Harlan says, his voice deepening. "How's hubby? You took a visit to your old place, I see—on the night of our fight at Eden. Google street view still shows the Okoye Residence banner on your doorstep, for Christ's sake."

Oh god. But how did he...? "Harlan, were you looking

through my phone and Uber app?"

Then again, Patience, how hard is it to put on a screen lock?

"Did you fuck him?"

"Did I what?!"

"Let's hope I don't run into his ass soon. Picturing you and him together makes me want to break his—"

"You did not just ask me that!"

"Yet here I am, waiting for an answer." A sinister look takes over Harlan's face. He stays focused on the abstract—not me. "They say you lose them how you get them. A lesson as old as time."

I stop what I'm doing to question him. "Are you saying I'm the sun? Where is this coming from?"

"I'm saying I've been fucked with before... and... I couldn't take that coming from..." Harlan talks shakily—with his pupils glazed over, and I wait before consoling him. Then he throws a palette knife across the room with a loud *clang*. "Goddammit!"

"Harlan, talk to me."

"Forget I mentioned anything."

"No, out with it. Please."

"Once they get to know me... They always leave."

They? Is he being metaphorical? Or is there... more? I lean toward wanting to scoff, to call it a bad case of artistic angst. But... the fresh self hatred in his words makes it difficult to dismiss.

Harlan wipes his nose frequently and stares straight ahead. "It keeps me up at night that you're here—because for the life of me, I can't figure out why. There, I said it."

I step between Harlan and the canvas. "I need your eyes."

"You got 'em."

"Now ask."

"Where are you right now?"

"With you. And burning you is the furthest thing from my mind. Yes, I went to my old house, but only for a second. I needed to sort through some old shit in my head, and that's all. I didn't even go inside to see him."

"I want to believe that so damn much," Harlan says as he twists my braids around one another, thoughtfully. "But when was my muse ever going to tell me?"

I lower his hands. "When I had a chance to. And looking through my things—it makes me think you have ulterior motives."

"That's reasonable."

"I hope so."

"Now that's cleared up, I gave you my eyes... Now give me your lips..."

My lips find his, and we get lost in each other. Not for a second worrying about being found. Maybe Harlan has finally overcome his doubt and skepticism.

But there's one thing I need to rectify.

"Don't... don't threaten to hurt Obinna anymore, okay?"

"Don't give me a reason, and I won't."

We turn back to our canvas with a commitment to a new masterpiece and a new desire for each other that burns bright, without consuming.

* * *

Sunlight hits the blinds, this time painting the place in a luminescence. I stretch, yawning, as Harlan lets out grizzly bear snores. I pick pillow lint from his hair—at odds with

262

what I'm thinking. After we made up last night, I might end up erasing just that by going to Colby to see about my grant today. Needing the fresh air, I'd rather head to campus than check online for myself. I could lie about going, but he'd find out anyway since he's employed there.

Who knows? Maybe Harlan will change his mind and be happy for me. Maybe he'll even give me a ride on his way to work.

Or maybe he'll blow a gasket.

"Hmm... morning." He's up.

"Morning."

"Up and at 'em, already?" Harlan's fingers let me know he's more than awake himself.

Hate to burst his bubble, but... "Um, yeah. Sorry if I woke you. I was about to head out."

Harlan takes a while to adjust to the morning rays, then fidgets. "Head out where?"

"I'm going to the Colby enrollment department for an update on my grant—and figure out if I can start signing up for classes now if they're covered." I reply, getting dressed and trying to keep my voice light. "Remember? The one I told you about?"

"Yeah.... kinda hard to forget. I'm involuntarily a part of it."

"I know you said what you said about it... but I'm going to accept the grant for the semester."

The covers yank back. "It's cool."

Harlan says it through his teeth, which makes me think *cool* isn't the case. I try to caress his shoulder, but he shrinks away from me and walks to the closet.

"Are you sure?" Hurt, I follow him there, though he refuses

to connect with me. "I don't know; it seems like you're mad."

"Could you keep your shit on your side of the closet? I'm having a hard time finding mine through the mess." Harlan pulls off several of my tops from hangers and tosses them to the floor.

"Hey, take it easy!" I don't like him when he's like this—spiteful. "I'm talking to you about something important."

"And just like you, I can do whatever the hell I want and find more important things to do with my time."

"Oh really? Such as?"

"Maybe go to an ex-girlfriend's house and shrug it off as shit happens."

"How many times do I have to say it? There's nothing to tell!"

"You expect me to believe you?!" Harlan snaps off the bar holding our clothes in the closet and stomps it in half. "Don't forget—with the right persuasion, I know what you're capable of doing." Then he lewdly grabs himself.

I knew it. He's not letting the visit to Obinna's go. Not by a long shot. "We're throwing low blows now? Our situation is going to be complex. He's my husband—was my husband—and I was his wife!"

"The same wife I had squealing in the back at the same club her husband tipped me seventy bucks at. Classy."

The slut-shaming barrage comes in hot. "Fine. Stay an asshole. So, then what does that say about you?! I thought we resolved this!"

Harlan—with a down-turned mouth and beet-red face—punches the door knob clean off of his closet, and I scream in surprise. "How's that for resolved?"

"What is wrong with you?!"

"I need a minute. I can't even look at your damn face. Go."

"Harlan, I—"

"Don't make me smash anything else. Who knows if it'll be repairable this time... "

What in the world does that mean? Forget it. I run out of the studio, head to my car, and start the drive to Colby.

* * *

I'm just glad the drive to Colby can have my mind wander elsewhere in the meantime.

Space is a great reset for the both of us, because I'm worried Harlan's temper is getting worse. Not only that, but it takes a lot longer than usual to calm him back down.

I'm light-years away from the person I once was, and Harlan's proclivity for me squelches down Tori's warnings of stripped independence with him. So, like I said—I'm really banking on that reset.

Focus on the positive, rather than the disaster it clearly is. After being awarded the grant, I'm happy to receive it and become a student again. Even though I'm no spring chicken, it's invigorating to learn a new concept despite what Harlan thinks.

Maybe I'll be just fine.

My phone goes off, and it's from a number I don't recognize, but I answer anyway.

"Hello?"

"Hi, this Patience?"

"Oh, Jayson." I can recognize his smarmy voice anywhere. "How can I help you?"

"Ah, running a business ain't a breeze, but thanks for asking. Say, do you have any more works I could take a gander at? I'm having another showing next week and would love another piece of you. Ahem, excuse me—from you."

Saved that plane from a nose dive, didn't he? The guy is as slimy as a sewer lid, but he has a good eye for art. I'll give him that.

"Sure, I may have some works worth looking at."

"Another six-thousand can cover it, right? If it's to my liking?"

"Yeah, no prob—"

No, that's not right. "I'm sorry, Jayson, how much?"

"Oh, I said six-thousand. Like I paid last time to Harlan so he could handle invoicing. Never liked keeping up with that stuff. Is that cool?"

No, it's not. Because Harlan only paid me two-thousand. Where's the rest of my money?

He wouldn't; he couldn't. But all signs point to...

"Hey, Jayson, I'm kind of tied up here and gotta go. I'll get back to you, okay?"

"No worries, even though you were hard to get a hold of. Freaking McCandles wasn't much help. Till then!"

Click.

There has to be some sort of explanation for this because none of it literally adds up.

I make it to the Colby registration center and try my best to push the idea of Harlan stiffing me of my abstract sale out of my head. But the notion locks on and rids me of giving him the benefit of the doubt.

Later, Patience. We're here now, so deal with it later.

"Good morning, I'm here to enroll in a few classes for the

upcoming semester. I'm also a new recipient of the Colby Arts Grant."

The receptionist—a black-haired goth girl who seemed a tad lethargic—tilts her desktop screen.

"Name?"

"Patience Okoye."

"Degree or program of choice?"

"Associates of Arts."

"One moment, please." She types what feels like forever, clicking and clacking on and off.

"Um, there's apparently a hold on your grant—and on your enrollment application."

What is she talking about? How? "I don't understand."

"Hold on, let me get someone who's more seasoned in this department than I am. I'll be back." Goth girl leaves me at the edge of my seat.

Two minutes later, she returns with an older woman who's barely four feet and addresses me rigidly.

"Hi, Patience. We actually sent you an email this morning pertaining to your grant. You're currently under investigation for plagiarism."

Please. Anything but this.

"Plagiarism?!" I say it like it's a foul word. "By what grounds? My work is, and has always been, original."

"A fellow staff member here accused you of publishing someone else's work under your name. While awaiting supporting evidence to document this, the investigation started effective immediately. Now, please keep in mind, no formal decision has been made, but if you would like to compile evidence on your behalf to dismiss these claims, now would be the time to do so."

It's official. Harlan is actively trying to sabotage me. How could he?! I can't believe it—after all the shit it took to get to this point.

I'm going to be sick.

WHOOPS, SEE WHAT YOU MADE ME DO?

I barrel into Harlan's apartment and ask myself how he could flip on me as if our time together never took place? Before, we had frisky back and forths and days we would collaborate ideas for our next project. Those times, I could simply look into his kaleidoscope eyes he's blessed with and swim in them. Now the days feel so long ago—like another lifetime.

"Harlan, get out here! Now!"

His place isn't massive, but the echo that travels through the studio adds to the illusion.

"Hello? What, you want to accuse me of plagiarism, but now you want to hide?"

Still nothing.

I pace around his living area to not miss anything or spot clues, maybe. No wallet, no keys—ugh. No luck.

Unmistakably, the vents let out steam from his restroom. Sound of flowing, splashing water, too.

Then I hear it.

"Right there... please..."

A woman's voice?

My legs wobble over to the door and push it open at once.

"Wha—"

My heart seizes from the sight of them. It's her red hair that strikes a memory. But I won't run out of here because of her attempt to embarrass me again, like she did in his classroom. They give a sick spin on the term Teacher's Pet.

Kelsey and Harlan are upright and in the shower, having sex. Kelsey's fiery hair enchants like a succubus. She doesn't see me at first, her face glossed over from the heat and the rushing impulses.

Yes, I know about those all too well.

"Don't stop..." she says as Harlan licks almost every part of her upper body. "Don't stop what you're doing."

Harlan finally catches me staring and has the most wicked, egregious vampire smile ever. "As long as you're a good girl, I won't."

I take a soap dish from the sink and throw it as hard as possible at the mirror.

CRASH!

Both of them are startled.

"Oh—my—god! It's you!" Kelsey screams and pushes Harlan off of her. "Get out, you psycho!" She struggles to step out of the shower and keep her balance.

She had better stop and stop soon. She has no idea what I'm capable of with the ignition of malice I have simmering inside.

"Did you hear what I said, you crazy bitch?!" Kelsey tries to toughen up, but her hands are shaking while trying to wrap a towel around herself. "Leave!"

Harlan looks on at us both and shrugs with no intention of adding any commentary. His blank stare confounds me— clueless to the fact he's the center of the chaos. But I'm happy to remind him.

"She's practically a child, Harlan! How could you?"

"Don't talk to him! I'm the one who—"

Kelsey stops at once, gasping for her life.

And it's because I slapped her.

"Hmm. Interesting response to her being practically a child," Harlan says, holding in laughter.

I jolt back to my senses and step aside to let her pass by.

"Help me! Help!"

Kelsey screams hysterically and pushes past me to run out the door and grab her clothes.

SLAM!

Harlan sucks in his teeth. "Damn, she took my good towel."

Now there are two.

Shocked from assaulting Kelsey, I lean against the sink. Harlan quietly gets out of the shower, grabs a secondary towel, and has the audacity to walk right by me.

Well, what do you know? I'm full of energy again.

"Are you going to act like that didn't just happen?! That any of it didn't happen?!"

I follow Harlan to the kitchen and see that he's making a protein shake. Then it hits me.

"You timed it to where I'd have no choice but to see you two."

Harlan snides across from me. "It just sort of happened. I didn't plan on it. She came over; we talked about finals and did some Molly, and shit—you caught a snippet of the rest. Maybe if you would've joined us, you would've enjoyed yourself. Threesomes aren't your first rodeo, Okoye."

"You asshole, you promised! You promised it would only be us and the art!" I slowly grow weak-headed.

"If we're being technical, I promised no more Foxy Roxy."

He's actually joking about it. "Kelsey's a moron, anyway, and it meant nothing."

"*Of course it did!*"

"Are you done?" He speaks sardonically. "Are the theatrics ceasing soon, because if not, you know where the door is. Then again, maybe if you knocked—"

"Ten years, Harlan."

"What?"

"Ten," I repeat. "For ten years, I was with Obinna. Yeah, I said his name! Obinna Isaac Okoye. Things were fine before. Not perfect, but peaceful... but then after losing the... I started checking out and put the brunt of the blame on myself."

Stop. What the hell am I doing? He doesn't deserve that story. He doesn't merit the measure of anguish it had on me.

But here we are.

"Just so we're clear... I wasn't dying for you to leave him for me." Harlan refreshes my memory. "You showed up with a suitcase, a tear-streaked face and those pouty lips. In your head, it was a done deal, and I was a sure thing."

"You never stopped me, either. You had me believing that you were a safe space... and now..."

I stop to cry and cry hard. Gut wrenching sobs that prod into my ribcage prevent me from finishing.

Harlan walks over to try to console me. "Patience, look... you're hyperventilating. Let's—"

"*Don't touch me! You will never touch me again! Ever!*"

Harlan jumps back and recoils as if I were doused in gasoline.

"I gave up an honorable man for... this?!"

I take one of his miniature statues and aim it at him, striking him in the leg with a massive thunk.

Harlan tenses but does nothing. "I'd advise you not to do that again."

So, I get back on my soapbox.

"Who cares if I had to tell him more than once I was depressed? If I had waited till he was ready and able, we would've figured it out."

"Guess we'll never know now, huh?"

"He was a good person! A better one than I'll ever be. What a hell of a mess I made of everything! Today, I no longer recognize myself, and Harlan, you are single-handedly the most vile fucking human being in the world, and I fucking hate you!"

"Anything else?"

"I wish you were dead."

"Cool stuff. But now it's my turn... if I may?"

Harlan puts on a shirt and sweatpants and plops onto the futon. His socio-psychopathic tendencies are at play.

"Your kaleidoscope abstract is a very remarkable piece. I meant what I said when I stated you found the right hues and tints, without a doubt. But, Patience, just because I taught you everything you know doesn't mean I taught you everything I know."

The hell is he trying to say without really saying it?

"You're not making sense. Hurry up with—"

"Nope. My turn. Do you know what sectoral heterochromia is? It's why my eyes look the way they do. I was born with it, and the trauma behind them changed my entire brain chemistry. That fraction of my life is mine. Mine and mine alone. Who the fuck do you think you are to publish my life and my hurt under your name? Jesus, you're more fraudulent than I thought. So much for burning me being the furthest thing from your mind."

He thinks I betrayed him. After everything we've accomplished together artistically, that's his conclusion to decide to take me apart. The pettiness is so palpable nothing can help me get past it.

Harlan's stoic demeanor breaks a little as he waits for me to retort.

"Your jealousy is so ugly, Harlan."

"Jealousy?!"

"What else do you call never handing over all the funds for the abstract art Jayson bought from me? Did you think I would never find out? He called, asking for more art, and listed his quote from the last purchase, dumbass!"

"Ever hear of a finder's fee?" Harlan's eyes dart to the left when he says it, just for a split second, but it's enough—a tell, that he's lying. He opens his mouth, then closes it, his jaw working to find the right spin. "It's common with art sale transactions."

I'm pretty sure skimming seventy percent off the top of an art sale isn't what most people mean by a *finder's fee*. "You're so full of—"

"Besides I'm owed, aren't I? I helped you learn how to speak through your work."

"I know how to speak, so hear me loud and clear! To think—it's because of me Camilla Morton bought your stupid painting when no one else would!"

"What are you smoking, hun?" Harlan laughs so hard, he buckles over in exaggerated fits. "No, really, because I said it was bought anonymously."

"Yeah... wake up. Camilla did that as a courtesy for me, and I can prove it with receipts!"

It's high time he knows she only wanted my work and nothing to do with him. Point-blank, period. I was trying to protect his feelings, but that can go straight to hell, too.

Harlan places his hands over his head and his eyebrows waggle. "You think you're hot shit, don't you? Get one thing straight—I don't need your lucked-into-it-with-painting money from Jayson or anyone else."

Unbelievable. He is really going to sit here and try to save face, no matter what.

"You're lying." I get ready to catapult more ammo. "Don't take it out on me because I took what you started and made it even better! I don't need you to express myself anymore. So, you want it back? *Take it!*"

I grab another haphazardly built sculpture and fling it at his muntin windows. Now he is fuming.

"Oh, hell no! Over here, now!" Harlan tempestuously snatches me by the wrists and holds them above my head against the brick wall. I'm unable to move, and in my mind, I scream to gain back control.

"Ow! Harlan, you're hurting me!"

"How unfortunate. Mind your fucking attitude."

Those last words hang in front of me and become a welcome sign to his breaking point. His eyes narrowed, with his teeth grit so hard they seem close to a shatter. A vein joins in, too, pulsing busily in his temple. "Now, I'm going to let go of your hands. Then you are going to get yourself together, quickly. All right?"

He's trying to pacify my anger, but it does nothing of the sort. "Put me down! You're not my father."

"If I gotta straighten you out, I'd prefer to be called *Daddy*."

"Shut up!"

Harlan finally releases my hands. "Maybe if he was around more, you'd know how to regulate your emotions."

"You're one to talk!" I channel my inner Tasmanian Devil and do just about anything to pummel Harlan's figurines to dust.

"Stop! Hey, quit it!" He tackles me to the ground.

Harlan is frustrating to kick at, as I miss each opportune hit. He dodges, bobs, and weaves, but I'm out for more blood. Eventually, I tire him a bit.

"I'm warning you! Enough!"

"Then give me my life back!" I demand. "Now!"

"Don't put—Patience, I swear to God, if you don't—"

Bingo. I pull at Harlan's hair so hard that golden strands rip apart in my hands and he gets off of me. "Talk your shit now!"

"Shut the fuck up!" Harlan grabs me by my braids and shoves me turbulently into the coffee table—where I find more ugly figurines. "What, you gonna cry now? Break another one, and you'll be sorry."

I walk up to Harlan antagonistically, push him back, shoot the middle finger, and snap the head clean off. "Whoops." *BOOM!*

"Whoops! See what you made me do?!"

Plunging darkness takes me before I hit the ground.

* * *

"Urm..." I'm in the bathtub filled with warm water and suds. Towels and soaps come into full view as my eyesight sharpens. What gets me is that my head feels wooden, and I have trouble moving my neck and back.

Why am I naked in his bathroom, unable to move?

I find a bit of consolation in that he didn't strip away my bracelets.

With them, I'm not fully exposed to him.

"Hey, you're up." Harlan appears in the doorway with a steaming face towel. His face—worn down and tired, but somehow softer. "Try to avoid moving so much—that's a pretty serious back sprain you got. I thought a hot bath would help before painkillers... or weed, if that works."

I only have the strength to look up at the man who, over time, unstitched and unraveled significant parts of what made me, me. What he's done, he's done in small bits, almost insignificant in the grand scheme of things to notice.

"Ow."

"Baby... don't talk, I got you. Rest." Harlan begins washing me, minding my sore spots, further confusing the abysmal situation.

He's never called me that before.

"It hurts."

Harlan stops to come over to my side. "I wish you'd believed me when I told you it was a gamble to love me." He strokes my hair and gently wipes my face. "The moment it happened, I wished I could take it back."

His vulnerability delays me from asserting myself, but I try to, anyway.

"Harlan, I want to... ugh... I want to leave."

With a great sigh, he gets up and turns away from me. His knuckles are deeply raw, and after I spot the freshly dented trash can, I see why.

"Your attack on my things woke up a sleeping beast in me. A beast I thought was dormant for a while."

"Please... I wanna go home..."

But where's that?

Harlan keeps going, anyway.

"When I was fifteen, my stepfather beat me so badly I was in a coma for about two weeks. We're talking brain contusions, staples in my head, the works. Then, when I woke up, I couldn't see for a week after. To describe the dread and trepidation a teen faces with the threat of permanent blindness... you can't imagine it... *Shit!*"

Then, Harlan cries with restraint and sinks to the floor like a child. It's extremely odd to see his face so contorted from a few feet away from me. He rocks back and forth and screams, hitting his elbows against the brick wall, and all I can do is watch it unfold.

Until it comes together for me. "The lights. That's why... why... you need them on when you... sleep."

"Light causes a quick neural reaction in most blind people, even when they're not able to see. It helps me improve how I adjust my vision in a way that waking up with the lamp off doesn't. It's like stretching the muscles in my retinas twenty-four seven. I don't want to lose it again. Being in the dark too long, it disorients me."

"Ever since?"

"You're the first person I've ever told. It's not something I enjoy talking about. So... there you go. Constant visual stimuli..." Harlan puts his arms together into the letter x and quivers his bottom lip. "The real rhyme... or reason for my tats."

The fear of his sight abandoning him again turns him into the teen he once was.

Harlan cries even harder, and his heaves make speaking

difficult. "Whatever faith I had left in God, I used to help me get through each taxing day. And just like that, it came back, and I could see again. The way I yelled, '*I take it back, I don't want to die anymore!,*' you would've thought I was inches away from death. But I wasn't far from turning it down, either. Those figurines you threw—I made them a month after regaining my sight. I put in all my effort to show I wouldn't take seeing for granted again. So, you see, usually when anybody triggers memories of my traumatic injury... It's only a matter of when, not if, but when, I would make them pay severely for that."

I grow anxious and try to sit up in the tub, but the pain is too great. I should *not* be here.

"Are... you going to hurt me again?"

Harlan jolts up and crawls over to me. I see that he's committed to a full beard these days, giving him a slightly unstable look.

"Patience... hate to be that guy, but I didn't start it. You did. So, who's blaming who here? I was only trying to get you to stop, so it was no contest. Like bringing a lamb to a slaughter. Yet you've grown on me. For that reason alone, we're not finished yet."

I sink deeper within the soapy water after his declaration. I threw the statues and tried to trash his studio, yes. However, was it enough to bring out such a diabolical side of him? He could've paralyzed me, or worse. He has no plans to let me go. I'm in some alternate reality, where days are no longer my own. Where life happens to me cataclysmically, as opposed to me simply living it.

He's still talking, and I notice I've been tuning him out.

"I'm an artist. What you did with my creations that landed

you in this mess was blatantly disrespectful to my craft. I think an apology would be a great start, don't you?"

Choose. My pride or my well-being. "Sorry."

"Was that so hard?" Harlan grabs a large towel and drapes it around me with his detailed arms. "Time to get out. Let me help you. Here—grab on to me."

"No!" I scream as I splash him while pushing him away from me. Ultimately, my pride shines through his trap. "You can't force me to stay here if I don't want to. Otherwise... Otherwise, that's considered holding me hostage. Harlan, are you holding me hostage in your apartment? Yes or no?"

I put it out there as plain as day, so there's no room for any hidden intentions or loopholes. He must know that I see right through him because he flings the towel at my face.

"Fine, fuck it. I won't stop you."

Harlan does just that and plods out of the bathroom, huffing and puffing. In turn, he grants me privacy to get out of the tub, get dressed, and the right to never relive this nightmare again. As I put my shirt back on, my prism tattoo from Taos is a solemn reminder of his imprint on me.

It doesn't stop there. I see a quarter sized purplish bruise at the nape of my neck where he ripped out my hair.

Harlan used the braids he treasured so much against me. I see five of them sticking out of the trash can. They must've come loose from him grabbing a handful and throwing me into the table earlier—no longer my crowning glory.

I cannot be subjected to any more of it.

Fully clothed, I pack what I can and make a mental note to send for the rest later. Harlan watches me—with his eyebrows descended and eyelids droopy, maybe hoping I would reconsider.

"Can we at least—"

"No. I'm going. We're done."

I limp to the door, unsure whether to support my back or my stiff neck. Catching myself in the mirror, I discover, to my horror, the person I've become.

I have aged ten years in the last six months. My once full cheeks are now sunken in from stress and weight loss. Skin that was once light brown is now closer to pale and chalky.

Feeling sorry for myself gets stale, fast. Time to go.

But I can't move. Here I am, ordering my feet to walk, but they don't. Take off, already!

"You don't have anywhere else to go, do you?" Harlan brings to light. He comes out from the doorway and walks over to me. His statement isn't harsh, but an observation meant to cushion the inevitable blow. "Do you?"

He's right. Obinna, family, loved ones—even work—they never stood a chance against our mayhem. There are so many burned bridges to account for, and I wouldn't want them to be a part of it now, either. I'm too altered.

Harlan's arms are now around my waist, and as tall and angular as he is, he smells my hair with infatuation. His pointy chin pins onto the top of my head and centers me.

Like a hex, I'm completely immobile from his touches.

"I still hate you."

"Stop it. You could never."

"Your face—when you were with her, and everything else that came after... I mean, my god—"

"She's not... I thought of you the whole time." Harlan kisses the bruise where he nearly scalped me. "As for the rest of it, I didn't mean to. I guess it was your turn to get me going."

"It's so much more than that. Harlan, this is bad. Really

bad."

"I know."

"You let it happen…" I croak. "Only for me to be knocked down a peg and left with nothing? It's unforgivable."

He shudders so much his heartbeat thuds against my back like a hammer against a thin tent. I absorb his blows as he intertwines mine—creating a monosyllabic cognizance between us.

"Maybe, if so… it's because I'm incredibly weak for you. We're an incorrigible pair. The fact I'd do anything to keep my muse by my side… says so much. You're in everything that I do."

"That's so fucked up, though…"

"Never mind what I said before. Stay… and I swear, I'll make it up to you. I will never throw you against the wall like that again. Hell, I won't harm you again, period. I'll cut my eyes out before doing that. So, will you have me back?"

Before I can reply, there's a loud knock at the door—a sharp, authoritative rap.

"Perfect timing," Harlan groans.

I back away and keep my distance as he goes over to check it out. A knock at the door right after a fight never bodes well.

So, we shall see.

When he opens it, two young officers are standing with clipboards.

Harlan answers with a half-assed smile. "Evening, is there a problem?"

One is a tall Black man with a small, square face who steps forward. "Hello, I'm Officer Johnson, and this is Officer Pike. We received a call about a disturbance. Someone said they heard shouting coming from this apartment—people screaming profanity, then a loud thump."

Harlan chuckles, then runs a hand through his hair like there's some big misunderstanding.

"Oh, that. Please, come in."

He steps aside and allows the officers to check out the studio. "Sorry, I was in the zone and forgot how thin the walls are in this complex. I had on music and was working on a painting. Guess I should've stuck with AirPods, huh?"

"What were you playing?" asks the chipmunk-faced officer, Pike.

"The *House of 1000 Corpses* soundtrack—"Everybody Scream" by Rob Zombie, heard of it?"

"Just a second," she writes busily, then stops to look at me. "Are you going somewhere?" She points out my packed bags.

"We were just heading out," Harlan says.

"I believe Officer Pike was asking her." Officer Johnson walks toward me and frowns. "Ma'am, are you all right?"

I want to say so much. The words rise in my throat, but Harlan cuts access to me and the officers without even trying. His sectoral heterochromia sends a glaring warning behind them.

"Um..."

"I can step out for a sec," Harlan says.

Johnson nods, easing the tension in his cheeks. "Might be best."

"Sure. We were on our way to visit her mother. On Thornridge Drive, right, babe?"

My pulse thunders in my ears. That's my mother's address—a part of it, but a crucial part. But I never told him where she lives. What's he trying to do? What type of performance is he putting on—while not breaking character?

I want to think he wouldn't bring Mom harm, despite our strained relationship. However, knowing about the threats he made against Obinna, beating up that guy in Taos, and almost doing the same to Kenji, Harlan could cause harm to anything or anyone if he sees a reason for it. Even if they were to take him now and release him in a few days, he still knows where she lives, and it's his word against mine.

"Ma'am, is that right?"

Keep Mom safe and worry about the rest later. "Yeah. That's right."

"I'll take your statement out here, sir," Pike escorts Harlan out the door. "Officer Johnson will finish with her shortly."

"Okay."

They both leave the studio and me in Officer Johnson's hands.

"What's your name? And what's your relationship with the occupant on the lease?"

"Patience Okoye. He's my boyfriend."

"You two ever get into any arguments?"

"No... um, not many."

"I'd like to hear this next part directly from you rather than him. Why the packed bags?"

"Visiting my mom's for the weekend."

He looks up from his clipboard suspiciously. "Mind explaining why someone called us then? Before either of you could leave?"

Inhale, exhale. I can do this. Explain it away to make him cozy enough to leave. "We were wrapping up to go. His music was blasting, and I knocked over one of his heaviest easels, which explains the thud. It's a cramped space; you can see it for yourself, so we kind of work on top of each other."

Officer Johnson writes, then squints at my posture. "Are you in any pain? That's the third time you reached for your back just now."

Aw, hell. I quickly pat my braids down and hide the bruise Harlan left on my neck.

"Not pain, just discomfort. I've been working on an abstract for hours, hunched over. It's a—a little stiff."

"Help me... help you. Are you in trouble, ma'am?"

He reminds me of Obinna. But I can't go there. Most likely, never again. "I'm not in trouble, but thank you for checking in. I'm fine."

"If that changes, reach us anytime." Johnson closes his metal clipboard, just as Pike and Harlan come through the front door, done with questioning.

They hang around for a little longer, and then she addresses us first. "All right, it looks like things are copacetic here. Remember to keep it down and be mindful of your neighbors."

Harlan leans against the door frame, all casual. His charm oozes through and through. "In the future, we'll keep the music down and keep the mosh pits to a minimum. Promise."

Officer Pike takes in the studio's ambiance, wearing an impressed smile. "In the meantime, keep up the good work with your art, guys."

Harlan hands her a business card to sweeten the deal. "Hey, thanks a lot. If you could, support us on Instagram?"

She takes the card, blowing my mind even further.

As Pike and Harlan talk, Johnson and I exchange a glance. Then, I swear, we connect, sharing a depressing belief—a recognition of the unexpressed. Whether he fully believes me, he knows how people like Harlan wield their privilege and how he continues evading lasting consequences—only to most likely re-offend. But with how Officer Pike hangs on Harlan's every word, making her look less like a cop and more of a fan, I watch Officer Johnson sigh. He's seen this before, and there's no other way but to play along until it might be too late.

"Well, Patience—like I said, you know when to call us." He speaks to me directly, which I'm sure Harlan is not a fan of. The longer they're here, the tighter the noose is on my mother's neck.

"Yeah, all right. I will."

Harlan thanks both of the cops and closes the door behind them. He uses the peephole and waits until they are out of sight.

"Great job being cool about this." He comes over to where I am and resumes clinging to me. "The last thing we need is those pigs sticking their noses in our business. We can work it out ourselves, don't you think?"

"Don't go after my mother, or I will call them right back."

Harlan doesn't change his facial gestures. "Huh? Do you wanna run that by me again? Seems like you've been lacking a good night's sleep and just saying any old thing now."

I open my mouth to argue, but the exhaustion is too much. He keeps doing these things—shaping occurrences until I question myself.

Beside us, I catch sight of his tall buffet lamp with its skinny body propped up. A wild thought rushes through me, fueled by the hateful things Harlan's done.

I break from his hold.

I don't need the police to bring retribution. He doesn't get to do this and walk away unscathed.

"Okoye, wha—"

BAM!

I bring the heavy base across his cheek that crashes with a clinking *thud.*

"Christ!" Harlan screams while he grabs his face—now worse for wear. Blood oozes out of his light brow, freely. His look of outrage disappears, and instead, what replaces it is disgruntlement.

Harlan lunges at me, and in one swipe, snatches the lamp out of my hands. He grabs me by my upper arm so hard I'm terrified it's within moments of snapping. "That's all you get. Do you hear me?!"

After hurling the lamp into a corner and breaking it into several pieces, he lets go.

He continues to aggrandize more and more out of me to detestable proportions.

Tori's heads up to leave him revisits me, to no avail. It's easier said than done. Harlan's ingrained in my system.

He's right.

In order to leave, I would need somewhere else to go. With his *I will go to the ends of the Earth for you* speech—to involve anyone else in the craziness that's myself and McCandles—is highly irresponsible.

I set my bags to the side. My back is on fire, so I curl up in a fetal position on the floor and resume crying.

"Good girl. Once we get you to bed, we can forget all about today's bullshit," Harlan says. He's not even stalled by the blood going past his shoulder.

He scoops me up and walks me there, while I flop in his arms without making an effort to stop him.

Because frankly, what's out there for someone like me now?

"Let's admit we both behaved badly here, okay?"

It's his go to anytime I try to discuss it.

My unreliable narrator.

Another April morning tumbles in. Staring at the chipped blue paint on the window ledge, the city blurs into a hazy abstract outside. Sleep clings stubbornly to the corners of my vision but never stays put. I don't know how long I've stayed since after the fight, but the days congeal together more often than before. My mornings, afternoons, and evenings take place on the futon, with the covers wrapped around me in mock comfort. At first, I stayed because I wanted to keep Mom protected, remembering his veiled threat. But even that takes its toll as it festers like a sore crusting over and permanently fusing me to his bed.

Thanks, clinical depression.

I'm picking at the broken nail on my thumb, a relic of the altercation. It was a doozy, the kind that leaves me with existential thoughts and the taste of bile in my throat. The day after the attack, Harlan was at my beck and call; so remorseful, every fiber of his being pleaded for forgiveness. Each morning before work, he would rub heated oil on my back, then dress each sore spot with a hot towel, more apologies and self-deprecation, sobbing into my lap, distraught.

"I'm such a piece of shit…"

"Don't go, please…"

"Things just got out of hand…"

"You can only imagine what this does to me, too."

I'd weakly nod and send him on his way. Only to repeat another day of contradictions… with Harlan saying he's not worthy of me, yet not wanting me to leave him.

Then came the flashbacks. Reminders that his outbursts weren't limited to shouting anymore. Gone past the harsh punctuation marks to the string of insults we hurled.

Sex grew quieter, gentle—more careful with plentiful kisses to spare—in order to rewrite history. It became one thing I didn't think Harlan could ever be, which was predictable. Each time it was over, he would say the same thing. "Jesus, I missed making you feel good."

In my thirty years, I've been through hell and back. Why is my fight with him the one thing that fastens me to the ground?

The answer hangs suspended in the falsehood of Harlan's dedicated care for me. My spirit is at its absolute lowest, and I know why. He had to have known what quitting Molly cold turkey would do to me. I can't cope without outside help. Withdrawals hit hard, and that's when he swoops in like a hero. As Harlan comes home from work and dedicates every bit of his time to my needs, like bathing, feeding, and dressing me, I get by somehow. It took a while to get used to—with him having a hand in my absence of agency—but it's been bad enough to where I would be borderline comatose with no other way around it. The exertion of starting my life over doesn't surpass the release of caring anymore.

Sometimes, I try not to stare at the window ledge for too long. My thoughts go to some very heinous places in order to fly away from here. It's confusing. I see how much of my life he's picked apart, bones and all. Yet the buzzing warmth he gives when he's providing for me makes him my personal brand of Harlan Heroin, replacing my past Molly binges. I can never get enough to tide me over, and my serotonin is officially fried.

The woman who wants more for herself... She visits, but sparingly. When Harlan's gone, she has moments when she gets ready, even managing to pack her things. But as she's almost out the door, that voice pierces her resolve to reinvent herself.

'The fact I'd do anything to keep my muse by my side says so much. You're in everything I do.'

There's no end to the number of doors he'd knock down, leaving no stone unturned. And then she becomes his muse again, restoring peace and balance to the world.

Guess he doesn't need to create a specially crafted box for me... because here I shall remain.

I haven't painted in so long, and I miss it, whereas Harlan's trademark dark borders and neon splatters with canvases of night continue to populate the studio. My eyes drift to the new easel he uses by the far wall.

It was supposed to be mine, a surprise gift that encouraged me to create even after my mother picked my life choices apart. From my understanding, it's as if he's squeezed me out of my own present, which I technically bought for myself, due to his controversial invoice practices.

So now, here it is, his—just like everything else I try to hold on to. Harlan's brushstrokes have no room for anything else.

While lying in bed, I watch him paint and offer to help, unsure when I last left his sheets.

Or what day it was.

"Can I join you? Maybe split a section? I wanna feel useful and try out the easel, too."

But Harlan always appears reluctant with the idea of me even holding a paintbrush.

"Your presence inspires enough, baby. Now that you're here more often, my artwork has a reason to... Well, to be. Just rest," he says. "I'm breaking it in for you."

As extremely nervous as he makes me these days, I want him to see my curious nature poke through. Lately, I've been trying to distract Harlan, acting like I'm more interested in what motivates his choices. Anything to keep him from stirring up a tornado and whisking me away, never to be seen again. "What's it like, going blind and then getting your sight back?"

Harlan pinches his brow as though to stop a stabbing headache. He leaves the easel and comes to bed. Sunspots that weren't there before have sprouted on the bridge of his nose. "When I couldn't see, there were only shadows—fuzzy outlines and shapes if I was lucky—but nothing that stood out as something I could identify clearly enough. I was stuck in a vacuum of no perception and nothing to compare it to, without distinct colors either. It's a total myth that you see complete darkness when you're blind, by the way. But at least when the lights were on in my hospital room, I could practice making out stuff if I tried hard enough. When there wasn't any light, I couldn't practice. Even now that I can see, being in the dark is just a fickle bitch to deal with."

"Is that why your abstracts have jet black backgrounds with

bright colors in them?"

"Partly," Harlan admits. "But mostly because I need to see it all while I can. As bold as I can. I need to memorize every color, every shade. In case... you know... it all goes wrong again."

There's a sharp pang of worry I notice coming from him. "Do you think it will?"

He shrugs, looking back at his canvas. "I don't know. There's always that chance. But thanks to you, my days are brighter when you're here."

Harlan brings me against his chest with his hand stroking my back, then my tattoo. The tease of a smirk plays on his lips. "You'll most likely be the end of me someday, and I don't even mind."

"Uh—"

"May I... have you this evening?"

Sadly, when I'm under him, I feel safest. "Okay."

For the rest of the night, we forget all about his abstract, and of course, we sleep with the lights on.

I don't want to come close to stepping on his toes with art again, which is why I forgo taking a semester at Colby or selling my art to Jayson.

The bleakest, darkest truth of why I stay: admitting to being very wrong about Harlan will shred my remaining pieces of eminence.

How I'm still prideful in this position is a quandary.

But I sense today will be different.

"Patience?" Harlan says, freshly dressed. His voice is lighter now, edging into the bed.

I turn my head slightly, and there he is, carrying a tray with eggs, toast, and coffee, all balanced with a sort of careful precision. Although, the cute little heart he made in the coffee foam doesn't mimic the state of mine.

"Good morning. Here's breakfast, beautiful."

"Thanks." I sit up slowly. The pain still shoots through but dully—not like the agony I felt the first day. I try not to let it show, proving to myself that his past cruelty doesn't define me.

Whereas, the hit from the lamp I gave him doesn't even leave a scar, impacting absolutely nothing for him.

"How's my muse this morning?"

"I'm okay."

"Let's get you better than okay."

Harlan adjusts the pillow behind my back. I've become a porcelain doll on the verge of cracking. I observe how tender he's being and how he tries to make this okay with a blandly presented tray of eggs.

"I'm no chef, but I think I pulled it off. Here, I got you covered." He cuts up the omelet and feeds me.

I hate this part, but I don't have the heart to tell him, even after nursing a bruised spine.

"There. What's the consensus?"

"Um, pretty good."

Negative. Harlan can't season food for shit. He looks relieved, though, like my acceptance is all he needed to make everything all right.

But ick, he keeps on spoon feeding me and looks so sorry for his existence because of what he did. On the outside looking in, you wouldn't think much of us—a doting boyfriend looking after his better half.

"I'm getting full."

"A couple more bites oughta do it. For me?"

I force another smile, but inside, I'm weirded out. Maybe some couples don't mind being fed this way, but he's infantilizing me. I watch him arrange the silverware, trying to make it into some grand gesture.

Does he think this makes it all better?

When I'm finished, Harlan leans down and presses his lips to my forehead. "I always start my day off right taking care of you." His sandy hair curls around his ears. "Don't I?"

Those eyes. Dammit, they see past every lie I've told myself, every excuse I've made. They petrify me. And I think, deep down, that's why I'm here.

"Y-yeah."

Harlan takes my tray to the kitchen.

"I'm going to campus." He grabs his keys from the coffee table. "Then Markos for extra bartending shifts. I'll be back, whenever. Try to get a little sun for me today."

"Okay," I manage, staring at his brick wall. It'll be another long stretch of boredom, buried under the blankets.

Harlan stops mid step and flies back to me, sitting halfway onto the bed.

My lips barely curve upward. I try to be a good sport, but it's hard.

"Where are you right now?" he asks as he fondles my hip.

"I'm here."

"Good girl."

None of it should be normal. But now, it's my normal.

He kisses me affectionately.

"Hey."

"Yes?" I ask.

"I love you."

This is new. We're talking fresh off the presses. I'm drawn

to Harlan in a nonsensical way, for sure—just not sure if those feelings involve that in particular. With recent happenings, we aren't there yet. Well, I'm not.

And I'm using *yet* pretty generously.

"I—it's um..."

"Only say it when you're ready," Harlan cautions. "Okay?"

"Uh, I think I need more time."

I haven't forgotten what he's done to me. It's my silent, shielded way of rebelling.

"Take all the time you need. I can't wait to come back home to you." He springs back up again, on his way out the door.

When Harlan's not home, everything feels like a total comedown, and now I'm missing Pongers terribly. Whenever I had blah days like this—or even a serious case of PMS—Pongy would pick up on it right away. She'd come over, guard my feet with all her fur and those loving licks, and then growl at Obinna if he dared to steal cuddles from me. I hope she's sneaking all the treats there are to sneak. The world is her oyster.

The toll of boredom strikes, so I do one thing I haven't done in forever and stalk people on social media.

On mine, I get a memories notification on Facebook. They're from the Dallas Fan Expo album pictures that Obinna and I took two years ago. I flip through and smile at every goofy picture he's in. The one he took with Phil Lamar, an established Black voice actor that played our favorite cartoon characters as kids, is where he looks the happiest. I, conversely, was battling food poisoning from the day before.

Those stupid deviled eggs from the school potluck had a vendetta against me.

But to see the sheer joy Obinna had from being there, and

with me by his side, it was next to nothing.

Shit. He's the real reason I couldn't answer Harlan. He'll always be. Love like that never fully goes away.

I hop onto Seabrook Elementary's Facebook page.

There are pictures of Nyla and Dominick with their home-room classes, taking part in field day. As it should be. For some silly reason, it gets to me they look so happy without Mrs. Okoye.

Wait—oh, nice! Dominick made Seabrook Student of the Month! Apparently from writing a poem about his favorite teacher. I didn't know he had it in him.

We're The Ones She Took
　　By Dominick Rivera, 2nd Grade
　　No one wanted me,
　　They said I was too loud,
　　Too wiggly, too wild,
　　I made them all frown.
　　But you saw me, Miss O,
　　With your kind eyes,
　　You didn't get mad
　　When I couldn't sit right.
　　You opened the door,
　　For all of us here,
　　You told us we're special,
　　And we learned not to fear.
　　You taught us with patience,
　　With hugs and a smile,
　　Even when I mess up,
　　You stay for a while.
　　I feel like I belong,

In your big, loving room,
Because you believed in us,
And we're growing like blooms.

Oh, Dom. Tears are spilling, and I'd give anything for him to cartwheel into me again. Both he and Nyla deserved more than a generic goodbye letter from me. I guess I can't expect a grand exit after my recent... let's call it *'episodes.'* But hey, even a hasty departure can't erase the memories of the students who made it all worthwhile.

My fingers scroll further.

Grayson?

His memorial page pops up.

So many pictures of the fragments of his life are tugging at me.

I can't, and I don't know if I'll ever be ready.

I swipe the impairing sadness away. I'm so sorry, Grayson.

My phone scrolls to Nadia's Instagram, which shows that she is transferring to Sherwood Elementary to take a job as a second-grade teacher. I warm up inside and am immensely happy for her. I wish I had the guts to tell her that.

But I'm me.

I scroll through others and land on Neisa's. She looks happy; not a shocker. She's wearing a pink satin dress with frills on the sleeve.

With a round belly to show off. Again?!

My eyes water at the memory of her saying, the minute she found out she was pregnant with her first child, we would pig out at Waffle House.

Who else is living their best life since I left theirs?

Obinna still has me blocked, so that's a no go. I wonder if

Priya will make a move on him now. Shush... too soon. Too soon.

Harlan's laptop lights up, and I'm suddenly feeling nosy.

A notification from his Facebook reveals a message icon. Beside it shows an open tab—a text from Marsha Roberts.

Marsha... Marsha... why does that—

"Oh! Marsha!"

Tori's smoking gun.

What could she be incriminating Harlan for?

Do not contact me or my family again.

What?

There's no previous message thread to reveal why Harlan contacted her, so I have little to go off. Why would she be relevant to him? He swore Kelsey meant nothing and Tori was past the point of no return. It's the pot calling the kettle black when I realize I have the nerve to wonder if my boyfriend is cheating on me.

Ping.

It's been thirteen years, Harlan. Will it ever stop?

Then Marsha signs off.

Shit. What exactly does she have on him? And could it potentially affect me? Cheating is no longer the worst of scenarios.

Social media stats on Marsha have me actually occupied for once. She's a real estate agent in Allen, Texas, and she's married with two kids.

I can't pass up reaching out to her. After finding her Instagram handle, I'll wait for the cards to fall. Here's hoping.

@PatOkoye: Hello Marsha. I'm Patience. You don't know me, but I know Harlan reached out to you. I'm in a weird predicament with him that needs some clarity. I was hoping you could tell me how you met?

@MarshaKKRealEstate: How did you find my handle?

@PatOkoye: I'm sorry, let me explain. I saw you responded to him on Facebook and I see that you have a history with Harlan. I was wondering if you could tell me what happened?

@MarshaKKRealEstate: What hasn't happened with the sibling from hell?

@PatOkoye: So, he's your brother.

@MarshaKKRealEstate: I've said too much. I don't think it's best I continue messaging you

@PatOkoye: Please. I'm really scared because of what I've allowed him to do with my life so far

@MarshaKKRealEstate: You have good reason to be. Are you in a relationship with him?

@PatOkoye: if you can even call it that

@MarshaKKRealEstate: how do I know this isn't him?

@PatOkoye: here's my zoom link. I'll leave his place and will be free to video call tonight if you can.

@MarshaKKRealEstate: I have kids and a husband to think about and if anything such as a thread connects to Harlan... that's something that absolutely cannot happen

@PatOkoye: I understand. But if he brought danger to you before, all I ask is that I get an idea of who I am dealing with at the moment.

@MarshaKKRealEstate: 7 PM.

@PatOkoye: Thank you.

* * *

I'm at a Starbucks in a cozy private corner, glued to my laptop.

299

My thoughts race, regarding what his sister could tell me about Harlan that I don't already know. Hmm...

Over the course of our relationship, it didn't even cross my mind to at least try picturing what he was like as a kid. Was he adventurous? Bookish? Maybe mysterious. But from what I can recall, when Harlan alluded to his stepfather, he was the lynchpin that made him the person he is today.

Harlan's yearning for visual arts and the sensitive nature of his sight go hand in hand. But the lengths he went to in order to make me understand that still leaves me maladjusted.

Ping.

A lady finally appears on the other end of the call and wanly smiles. "Hi, Patience. It's good to meet you."

She's a full-figured and round brunette, with brown eyes and peach skin. I couldn't see the resemblance between her and Harlan, but I guess it happens over generations.

"Hi. Same to you, too. You really don't owe me anything, but I appreciate it a lot."

"Sure." Marsha squirms in her seat, mouth pulled in tightly. "I'll do my best, but please bear with me. So much has happened since, and to hear he's back at it again makes me want to vomit."

"Back at what again? What did he do?"

Marsha sits back and lets out a ragged breath that takes over her whole body. "I'll come out with it. Harlan McCandles is not a good person."

My insides dip from her sentiment of her brother.

"Could you... Do you mind starting from the beginning?"

"Hold on a sec." She sips bourbon from a glass that comes in full view. "Sorry, you don't know me well enough to know this, but booze loosens my tongue. Unfortunately, repressed memories, too. I've got my kids tucked in, and I have hours of a hectic childhood to sift through, so buckle up."

"I'm buckled." I return her smile, and I'm grateful for her light nature in it so far. "And ready whenever you are."

"I'm from Wyoming, so the rugged landmarks of the land cradled me. My family lived life by the three smalls: small town, small school, small expectations. My mom was a librarian, and Dad was a truck driver, so you get it. When I was thirteen, my mom passed away from a brain aneurysm. It was tough, but Dad and I clung to each other. For a while, anyway. Then we moved to Texas and ended up in Denton."

"I'm sorry for your loss," I say, wondering where my mom is this very second.

Marsha loses her assurance, nods her head, and dabs her eyes with a tissue. "Thanks. At such a sucky part of my life, when I was coming into the world as a woman, too. Luck of the draw, I guess... Who knows? A year later, my dad remarried a woman named Sheila—an interior decorator he met during his stops. Not too long after, I had a stepmother and a stepbrother. Both strangers were thrust into my life like a kid tossing random toys in a cabinet. Harlan was always someone who would be tough to miss in a crowd. Height wise, look wise—you know. Girls had a thing for him from what I picked up."

Still do.

"But somehow, he still had issues at school and was a loner. Only ever participated in the local school art club, which was fitting—his work was good. Not sure if I would say great, but eye of the beholder or whatever. His mom, Sheila? Super gorgeous, too. She made my dad happy again, and I respected her for that. Sheila never made the mistake of assuming I'd automatically hate her for being with my dad. '*Give me a trial run, you'll see,*' she told me the first day we met. '*I'll grow on ya, kid.*'"

Trying to figure out Harlan in high school has me dangling over each of Marsha's words. I hope she gets back to that soon. For now, I'll be polite and let her delve into nostalgia because it seems she's been wanting to for a while.

"She sounds like a compassionate lady."

"She was," Marsha grimly corrects me. "But I'll get to that in a minute."

Uh-oh.

"See... it started out small at first—on our walks to school, he would show me his artwork. And he never said much, but just, '*What's up with you lately?*' He would hang on to my every word. And well, I'm naturally a chatty person, so I talked away, and he would reply with '*cool*' or '*you're right, sounds lame.*' The way he would look at a person when they were speaking, it was very Machiavellian. I don't know, but mostly, it was harmless. Ugh. I'm probably not making sense here."

What sets me on the balls of my feet is that she's making perfect sense. Harlan really does scrutinize people a lot. He scrutinized me the first minute we met at the conference and those who were centered in my life.

Now, with the way he makes me the highlight of his routine, I hardly hear of Kenji, Jayson, and Mabel these days.

"Patience, you there? Your screen is black."

"I'm here!" I wipe the smudge off my lens. Stupid leaky coffeehouse ceiling. "Go ahead."

"We were a happy, blended family. I hadn't seen my dad so happy in a long time and didn't want to crap on that. And then the other shoe dropped. I noticed the cracks in his facade.

Man, I never seem to have enough booze when I talk about the dark stuff…"

"Marsha?"

"I'm gonna send you an attachment, okay? I fought tooth and nail to get access to it."

"Okay."

Once the file pops up in the chat, I click away.

Date: [May 27, 2007]

Prepared by: Laura Flynn, Juvenile Case Manager

Subject: Harlan Marion McCandles (Age 15)

Incident Overview:

Harlan McCandles was admitted to the Collin County Juvenile Detention Center following a physical altercation with another minor. According to the police report and multiple witness accounts, the altercation occurred after the minor performed a skateboard trick for a group of peers, which included Harlan's younger stepsister. During this interaction and without prior provocation, Harlan struck the minor in the head with a skateboard. The minor did not sustain permanent injuries. Following the incident, Harlan allegedly stated, "Go find another freshman to finger. She's mine."

Background Assessment:

The observed possessive behavior, particularly involving his stepsister's social interactions, suggests a pattern of control that may warrant further investigation. Family interactions, as observed, and Harlan's response to this incident indicates emotional and behavioral concerns that may have previously been overlooked.

Psychological Evaluation:

During the intake evaluation, Harlan exhibited a lack of

remorse for the incident and expressed disconcerting views regarding his relationship with his stepsister. He has been resistant in counseling sessions, often deflecting responsibility and demonstrating manipulative tendencies. His apparent sense of entitlement leads to considerations of underlying psychological issues that may require in-depth intervention. A comprehensive psychological assessment is recommended to explore potential factors, such as trauma or attachment issues, contributing to these tendencies.

Recommendations:

- Immediate individual counseling focused on anger management and boundary setting within family structures.

- Continued observation of violent or inappropriate behavior, especially in group environments.

- Family therapy sessions to address potentially unhealthy relational patterns.

- Regular psychological evaluations to assess progress and adapt intervention strategies as needed.

Conclusion:

Harlan McCandles exhibits behaviors that may pose a risk for future incidents if unaddressed. His willingness to use violence serves as a need for ongoing monitoring. Given the severity of this incident, Harlan will remain in the facility for continued assessment until it is determined that he no longer presents a risk to others.

Signed,

Laura Flynn

Juvenile Case Manager

My god. Harlan was and continues to be a boundary pusher.

It's in his DNA to get off on making others un-comfortable. Especially women. But I sit reeling over what Marsha reveals and aim to point out an inconsistency between his retelling of the past and hers.

"So, Harlan's behavior started before the—"
Stop, Patience. Prepare her for the question first. Before she needs two bottles of bourbon on deck. But Marsha already catches my pause mid sentence.

"Before what? Were you going to say something?"
Better now than never.

"When and why did your—uhm—Harlan told me his step-dad or, your dad... beat him unconscious. And that he came close to losing his ability to see. Is that true?"

Marsha draws back in her chair and her nostrils flare toward the ceiling. Her round eyes squint at a menacing angle.

"Bastard. Of course he did. Harlan and his versions of past events are a dime a dozen. Supposedly, he had a massive turnaround at the juvenile center and they released him after a couple of months, which was complete horseshit. He even figured out how to win over psych professionals. It was the love my dad had for Sheila that allowed him back under the same roof as me. Jesus—right after she cried her eyes out for that jackhole."

"I figured," I say to console her. "So, what happened that day?"

"That night," Marsha whispers. "Harlan snuck into my room and tried to... The fact he tried it with such confidence says volumes. Picture waking up to find your step brother's hand over your mouth. He was so heavy, so unnaturally heavy, that alarm bells were ringing everywhere in my brain. I tried to fight him off, but would you call that a fair match? He was already six feet as a teen."

Marsha puts both hands to her face and lets out an audible yawp. "'*Just be a good girl, and I'll be fast, I promise.*' That's what he said to me after I begged my brother to not violate me in the worst way imaginable. That and some other dark shit he called me, which I can't quite—"

"His muse."

"Yes—yes, muse. That's right. Oh, I'm sorry, Patience. I didn't mean to upset you. It's okay. I've gotten through it in the end."

I spot several tears on the table. Have I become that detached from my emotions since being with him? Thinking now about when we've slept together—how he had to make it known I was no one else's. Him repeating phrases over and over until the message sunk in. "I'm fine. Please—don't worry yourself over me."

Marsha nods, then plucks another tissue to blow her nose. "Luckily, my dad had a canceled trucker's shift and came home early. When I heard the front door open, I bit Harlan's hand, making him let go—then called for help. That was when my father ran up to find Harlan on top of me and lost his ever-loving mind."

He should have put him to sleep for good.

"Serves him right. I know he put his hands on his wife's son, but a father has a right to protect his daughter."

"She didn't see it that way," spits Marsha. "She called me a whore. Blamed it on me because I was wearing floral low-cut dresses and enticing him. With the way she turned on me, I got whiplash from it all. My father told them both to get the hell out. Except Harlan wasn't moving. Sheila took almost thirty minutes to drag him all the way to the car, load him up, and take him to the hospital, without reporting the injuries made by my dad. That's my little tidbit on how she knew I was telling the truth."

"Maybe she could tell you herself someday," I say hopefully. "People can change or... some more than others."

"Doubt it. Oxy overdose a day before Harlan woke up from his coma. No funeral."

The dominos of the McCandles family continue to fall, catastrophically.

Marsha prattles on. "His odds of waking up were already unstable. She didn't have any hope that he would come out okay and pulled her card too soon. As much as I wished him dead, Harlan being alive means he will live the rest of his life realizing he tried shit with the wrong family."

True.

A lull passes over us, and it's a sign to wrap up for the night.

"Marsha, I can never repay you enough for tonight. I know it brought back some painful memories. But you helped me so much with having the strength to leave."

Marsha first simpers, then her scowl lights up my screen. "Be careful, Patience—okay?"

"You got it."

"No, hang on. The Harlan you know isn't the one I grew up with. He's smarter, older, skilled at committing deceit and ruin—masking his behavior. So, when he has someone in mind, it's over. You've already lost if you underestimate him because he studies this for sport. Do you realize how impulsive you act when you're around him? That's because he's perfected the technique to make you think it was your idea in the first place."

"Oh." A flurry of life events jostle in my head that highlight what Marsha references—quitting Seabrook, leaving Obinna, going no contact with everyone.

"You're not the first of Harlan's victims who's come to me. They were smart, like you. College-educated women who had it all, and he bulldozed right through each of them. Even tried to blow through some of their trust funds. One even attempted suicide because she couldn't deal with the damage he caused in her life. He can never know that you're on to him, okay? He's also a hell of a habitual liar."

My skin prickles with unease. "Did any of them press charges?"

Marsha's volume drops, and her eyes dart like a ping-pong ball. "Some of them tried—brave ones. But Harlan continued to set them up to knock them down—me included. One girl got her tires slashed every day for a week. Another found dead animals in her yard—cats and birds. He broke into my house, but the only thing he took was my peace of mind. We eventually all dropped the charges, hoping he'd stop. He did, and it gave us the illusion that we were safe. That was then, and this is now, until he decides to preoccupy himself with us again one day."

Harlan's limits are non-existent, which leads to a terrifying notion that, as much as a total prick he came to be, he's also an exceptional manipulator.

"The police did nothing?"

She shook her head almost immediately. "He made it look like a string of coincidences and kept playing the system. Nothing we could pin on him directly. So, please don't give him any reason to think you're about to make a move. Women who fought back too loudly were left with more problems than before. Be covert, okay?"

I'm now claustrophobic from her warnings. However, I'm still very thankful.

"I can never repay you for how brave you've been telling me about these, well, lack of a better word, shitty turn of events."

"Call me, don't text, and let me know the moment you've left him for good."

"I'll call, promise."

"Good luck, Patience. You'll need it."

Ping.

Fuck.

* * *

I'm able to return to the studio apartment—even after hearing the dismaying character analysis of fifteen-year-old Harlan McCandles. Now that I know what Harlan has done, the ugliness of it drips over and over like Chinese water torture.

Harlan tried to rape Marsha.

Him? The same person I left everything for?

Harlan tried to rape Marsha.

But there was so much sacrifice—a total metamorphosis in order to have him to myself. Now this?

And even still... Harlan tried to rape Marsha.

There's no way around it. None.

Welcome back, Patience. It's about time you came back to your senses.

I know, I almost lost them for good.

Remember me? The best part of you? The worst part has taken over long enough. It's time to stop ignoring the signs. Harlan's showing you his true colors, and it's not the core ones he raves about in his work. Wake up!

God, nothing he's done recently can cancel out, counteract, or neutralize his inexcusable actions toward his stepsister and numerous people. I refuse to be associated with his past and ongoing actions.

But I have no game strategy. I'm stuck, and that's exactly how he wanted it.

For now, I should play it cool. I won't make a move until I have an actual plan to get out and stay out.

I'm inside now and walk right into a home shopping catalog. There's no way. Harlan must've hired a professional interior decorator to make the place look so royal.

"What's this?" I ask, seeing a newly purchased, round, marble dining table in the middle of the room. There are several lit candles, giving the place a romantic touch. Two plates, each with seared salmon, roasted veggies, and a cup of red wine, are set on the table.

Whatever Harlan did, he went all out on a hefty dime.

"Hey, stranger," a low voice comes to the side of me. Harlan is wearing a white iconic Oxford shirt from Ralph Lauren, with matching pants and a clean shave. I face him, and he steals my lips with a suave kiss. "I missed you. Where'd ya run off to?"

"Oh, um, went on a coffee run," I reply. I'm unsure what to make of his getup.

Harlan appears skeptical. "For three hours?"

"I'm very picky about my java. But also, what's up with the formal dining theme?"

Harlan, by a lucky chance, forgoes future questioning and stretches his arms out toward the dining table. "Don't think I haven't noticed you've been a little down in the dumps lately. I wasn't sure if you wanted to go out for dinner, so I brought top tier cuisine to you. Or rather, Grubhub did."

Every time I think I'm getting closer to understanding him, he pulls a thing like this. And I'm back to square one. "Harlan, everything looks amazing. Um, thank you."

"Well, it's not here to just look pretty. *Bon appétit!*"

We sit and eat; the salmon bursting with savory flavor and the wine hitting the spot. But my mind is restless. A specific statement further distracts me from our dining conversation.

Harlan McCandles is not a good person.

None of what you're doing with him is okay. Did you already forget what Marsha told you she went through with him growing up?

I know.

So, why not leave and tell him to fuck himself?

I'm making sure I have a way out.

Patience. Stop it.

Seriously! I am!

The only reason you haven't left yet is because you don't want to admit how bad things really are.

It's not that easy to just up and leave like that.

You have a point. Let's ask Obinna.

Not cool. He kept so much from me. I was dying from loneliness.

So, being nearly penniless and directionless is a fair trade?

Like it or not, I'm riding it out.

"You're awfully quiet," Harlan cuts in and pauses the inner debate I'm having with myself. "Is the fish that dry or—?"

"Sorry. I'm only thinking." I pick at the salmon further to appease him.

"About? I'm trying for some dialogue here."

"Creating more art pieces to sell. I had something going,

didn't I? And should've never stopped."

From the candlelight, Harlan kind of resembles Peter Pan. Boyish, with a hint of mischief. He lifts up one corner of his mouth and pours more wine, not looking up. "I thought we agreed you were gonna take a break from painting?"

We, huh? Told you.

"Uh, I don't remember joining a pact or saying anything like that. I stopped for a while, yeah, but now I'm ready to get back at it."

"I hope you handle it better when things don't go according to plan again," Harlan adds.

I push my plate back, piqued by his reply. "It's safe to say it takes a while to adjust to being accused of plagiarism by someone you were sleeping with."

Checkmate.

Harlan kicks at the base of the table and leaves a ring of wine spilt from each glass. "For fuck's sake, I recanted that, didn't I?! Why bring it back up again?"

"Because it speaks to bigger issues with us." I get ready to leave the table.

"We've bumped heads on certain stuff before, that's all." Harlan has me appearing as if I'm blowing everything out of proportion while he twirls his wine glass between his fingers. "No need to drag it out."

"Is that what we're calling it? When you were angry with my choices, your end goal... was to cut me at my knees. You even made it into an actual project."

"Jesus, I didn't mean to hurt your feelings, okay?"

"No." I push the wine glass back and cross my arms. He's no longer going to skirt around the issue. "It was beyond saying mean things, and you know it. I carry the reminders in my neck down to my back daily! Knee-jerk reactions like that, stealing my money and taking showers with Kelsey are heartless, Harlan!"

Now we're talking.

"Not sure what you're aiming for tonight, but—" Harlan gets up from his seat to join where I am. He slips both of his hands under my shirt, and his spindly fingers seek to work me. "Shit... it gets me going when you yell my name like that. What are you trying to do to me, girl?"

"Stop. None of what I'm saying is easy to talk about," I say, pushing him off of me. "It's hard."

"Tell me about it. So am I."

"Give it a rest already!" I head to the restroom to shield from his advances.

Harlan grabs my left arm and constrains me from leaving. "Hey, let's at least talk about it. Be mature here."

"You first. Let go of me."

Okay. Now it should be done. Now it should be over.

But I'm still being held prisoner, and the look on his face is scaring me.

"So entitled and thankless, aren't you?" Harlan's voice chops into the air and becomes a machete. He finds pressure points in my arm that dig into me further. "Most women would be head over heels to get a treat like this and just enjoy a nice dinner at home. But here you are, doing what you do best, and nitpicking to death. Will anything make you happy?!"

I get in his face and merge my tone with his. "If you don't back up, we'll have a serious problem in a nanosecond. If you think you've seen me in my most unfavorable light, you're highly mistaken."

Yes, the fuming giant shrinks.

Then he lets go.

Harlan takes the plates and wine glasses, then crashes them into the sink. "That's the last time I ever try to be thoughtful."

"Let me know when the first time shows up, asshole!" I yell at him from the doorway.

Thank you!

No, thank *you.*

I lock myself in the bathroom and try to retrace my steps on how this led to such a clusterfuck. There are so many complications, messy expectations, and too much to fix with very little payoff in our relationship.

That magical, artistic flame that was once there between us is now in a state of being blown out.

I can't refute it anymore.

I miss things being easy.

I miss my old life with Obinna.

And I've made a huge mistake.

"Patience—come on, would you let me in?" Harlan calls from the other side of the door. "You're totally right. I'm an asshole, and I wasn't listening to you."

Oof. He sounds a lot more nasal pitched and nervy. I'm aware of the effect he has on me, but I never thought of the idea the other way around.

Click.

I open the door slowly, not sure what to expect from him now that the forecast is clear. "Your words feel empty. And if you ever grab me like that again—"

"I get it. I was only angry at—"

"I'm talking!" my voice turns into pop rocks and tries to make itself loud and known. "If I no longer think I'm protected with you, then we're done."

"It won't get to that point."

"I don't like who you're becoming."

"And who exactly am I becoming?"

"Someone I don't recognize or care to be around anymore."

Harlan corners me against the door and tongues me—'till I go powerless and limp. "Don't go to sleep hating me... I couldn't handle that..."

Shit, no. With my serotonin unreliable half the time—even after quitting Molly—he's the closest thing to it.

It's a malignancy that still draws me back for more. I know better now than to take what Harlan says seriously once he has me right where he wants me... There's no way I would've ever agreed to any of it if I had the intuition of what my world would be. But now I'm in too deep without a buoy in sight.

We both sink to the hardwood floors, my shirt gone and my bra barely hanging on by a thread. His touches and lips are desperate, not obtaining the power they once had before.

What we have isn't love. It's more of a primal dependency within. Harlan keeps going while I'm barricaded underneath his ripped physique—a dark, electric current that hurts to hold on to and hurts even more to let go of.

I say nothing, but my body ultimately responds. Harlan senses me quaking and holds my neck up to look at him. "There she is... There's my girl..."

Not sure if I drank too much wine, but the way he tries to connect like this makes me mad.

"Baby, look at me... won't you please?"

It seems incomprehensible to rediscover my sexuality through him, and yet he's now the entity I no longer trust because of it. So, I turn my head to the side straight away.

Then I close my eyes and change my scenery. Obinna—who

I've set my heart on since day one—is now with me. I sense his breath, touch, and body. My husband wants me again and life is good. I'm so close to—

"No. Up here." Harlan grabs my face back hard and locks it in place. He pinches my cheeks with his no longer gentle fingers. He doesn't like that. "I need to know you're here with me."

Absolutely not. Done.

My body, mind, and spirit reject him and his make-out session in one great big push. "I'm not in the mood anymore. Get away, Harlan!"

"Whoa, what did I do?!"

His inability to see how his need to dominate me continues to impede us is dangerous.

"I'm going to sleep in the tub. Don't follow me."

"But—"

"I have a right to speak on how I like to be treated." I yank my shirt back on. "And it's nothing like what you just pulled. So, leave me the hell alone."

It's good with him... until it isn't.

As I grab some pillows and a comforter, Harlan takes his shirt off, now slighted, and goes to bed. "Fine. I'm no neanderthal. Go for it."

Is spending the night here after what he did a smart choice? Should I pack everything I own and walk out the door—sleep in my car even? Money is too scarce to book a hotel room for an X amount of days elsewhere. The ten grand Camilla sent— more than half of it went to pay my lawyer for the separation prep, owed IVF treatments to Obinna, and late car payments. And no job equals no steady income. Relying on Harlan for essentially everything erased so many of the milestones I reached.

Enough. What's the real reason leaving right away isn't an option?

Okay. But that isn't the biggest hurdle.

I'm scared shitless.

There's no way to be handling my avoidance of Harlan without kid gloves. Like Marsha said, he mustn't know that I'm on to him.

I close the bathroom door and make a shallow pallette in the tub.

I'm a bit uncomfortable but glad I broke his spell. It sounds like a small victory to me.

* * *

When I open my eyes, I'm somewhere else.

Why does this continue to happen?

There's an atrocious landscape made of jagged shapes and sharp angles. A deep, unnatural purple sky, streaked with lines of yellow and orange similar to a bruised sunset, hangs above me. The cracked and uneven floor beneath my feet shifts under my weight.

My legs refuse to cooperate, and every step is a struggle. What the—

I sink into the jagged lines and spot him across the way.

Harlan?

He's standing in the distance and watches me. "Say it."

His voice is all scratch and no voice.

Harlan holds a paintbrush in his hand, and with every stroke he makes, a new creation is made. The cracks beneath me grow wider, the sky darkens, and the shapes grow into execrable forms.

Eyeballs with deformities of all kinds.

"Stop it! What are you doing?" I scream.

"Say it."

"Say what!? What the hell are you talking about?!"

The eyes. They're bloodshot, malformed, and weeping streaks of moldy matter. The eyeballs oscillate on stalks—plants from some hellish garden.

When they move, they don't blink. They just shift with an eerie glide from side to side, as if floating in a fog. Each sclera is an oily dead man's gray, reflecting light in a way that makes it look reanimated.

They seem to follow me, even when they're still. No matter where I stand or which way I turn.

Like someone else I used to know.

I try to run, but can't. Looking down, I see my legs aren't legs at all; instead, they've merged with the swirling landscape. White tendrils of sinew stretch tight as piano strings and prop me up against the border, where my elbows should be. And bone—jagged, splintered, and wet—protrudes through the mess I call my knees as I bleed ink.

"Help!"

I try to set myself free, but it's useless. The more I struggle, the faster the transformation happens—now my arms, then my chest. His swirls surround and wrap me in their asphyxiating embrace.

"Please! You're killing me!" I sob, but Harlan doesn't even look up. Only a swipe of his painting tool from him.

Oh! My mouth is gone. I have no mouth, and I must—

I try to scream again, but nothing comes out—speech stolen by his work, nearly complete. It all fades around me as I become only another stroke of Harlan's brush.

Finished. Stuck to the page, frozen forever and...

"Beautiful." Harlan kisses his work. "If you won't say it—then I will."

* * *

What began as a creative rebirth for me spirals into a fight for my sanity.

I wake up in the middle of the night and scream.

And back in Harlan's bed.

The bathroom door appears propped open, with the sheets I brought hanging in a disheveled state from the tub.

How much wine did I really drink?

When I try to move to collect them, I find out I can't. Harlan's tattooed arms entrap me to his body with snores galore.

It's hair-raisingly too tight of a grasp that I have to wake him up to see what his deal is.

"Harlan, what's going on? Why am I here?!"

"Hmm, what?" He eventually awakes from my voice. The fact he could sleep through my screams earlier makes me question so much more.

"I wanted space. Couldn't you at least give me that?" I snap.

"Oh." Harlan kisses my shoulder, totally unbothered. "I couldn't sleep and assumed whatever you were griping about before was old news. I needed my nightly dose of cuddles, and you being knocked out helped."

The narcissism that bears in his words is so telling.

"Have you always done whatever you wanted with me in

my sleep?"

"Don't give me any ideas, now."

"I'm serious. That's not okay."

I scoot away from him, feeling like I let myself, Marsha, and even Tori, down. Practicality keeps being thwarted by my involvement with Harlan, and I'm hoping Angela can help me tomorrow.

"What's with you, Okoye?"

"We've had more downs than ups lately," I say. "At what point do we say, *Well, we tried our best?*"

"I don't want to call it quits. I'm finally whole with you."

It's not my task to make a grown man feel complete.

Harlan returns to hold me tighter than usual, as if his subconscious is trying to prevent me from jumping ship. Since I threatened to leave, he's become such a sad sack.

He is not the same Harlan I first met. The quick-witted, full of himself Harlan has vanished, leaving this needy and unpoised one in its place.

Maybe it was all an act to begin with.

"Harlan... why do you even love me?" The words jump out before I can stop them.

He seems to sense my dissatisfaction. "Yikes. You're not one of those girls, are you? Why do you need a reason, anyway? I just do. I didn't plan to fucking love you. It's not fair. I was living my life before you barged into it."

Honestly, I don't know what it is I'm looking for. I listen to his words, but they don't penetrate the wall I've built around myself. So I lie here, tangled in sheets and doubt.

"Hmm."

"How about this? I love you... for waking up beside me every morning and no one else? Is that good enough? When you're here, my artist block is gone, and I can create without a hitch."

It all circulates back to him.

It's no longer a mystery. His recent behavior only proves Marsha's end of things.

"Besides," Harlan adds. "What does it matter… if I already know you better than you know yourself?"

"Um, debatable."

"Whatever you do… just don't go, Patience…" Harlan drifts off.

"Why shouldn't I?"

"It wouldn't be good for me."

I sigh, not sharing the same sentiments, and start planting the seeds so I can let him down gently. "I'm sure it'll feel that way, but like you said, no situation is permanent."

"You don't get to use people and put them back on a shelf of convenience—not after I've invested so much time in us. Don't I get a say in this?"

"It's possible to move on from what we had before, McCandles."

"And it's possible that hurt people… tend to hurt people."

"What did you say?"

He's fast asleep, and there's no waking him back up to repeat it.

Girl… girl, you're in deep shit.

I lay in bed, with those foretelling words of his, and wait for a new dawn. His figurines haunt me from the side table, and now it's my turn to have trouble sleeping. One of them is missing a head from the day I threw it at him ruthlessly.

Harlan opportunely turns over in his sleep and allows me a brief moment to explore. I go to the miniature statues and turn on the flashlight from my phone to take a closer gander at them. Yep. Still ugly—yet a symbol of his passion for art during his adolescence.

Ooh, hang on.

There's a blank sticker on the bottom of each of them, one losing its adhesive. The dangling sticker covers up some writing, so I peel it off.

"Artist Kelsey Kerishmeister. A liking to a Haniwa warrior," it reads.

Not again. I rip off the rest. Unbelievable. Kelsey's name printed on every single one.

Jesus. Lies coating lies... coating lies.

While he sleeps without a care in the world.

* * *

Another morning. Gotta get ready for my last session with Angela.

And my last day here.

His words continue to float in and out of my ear canal.

"It's possible that hurt people... tend to hurt people."

Nuh-uh. Harlan hasn't changed at all. He isn't even remorseful. I was foolish for thinking differently. If nothing else—even before that, the way he held my face with such a grip last night, such severity, his hands rough and insistent. I trace the phantom lines with my thumb, a paltry attempt to ground myself in truth. Imagine what kind of hell that would be for a fourteen-year-old.

Fearing the idea he could go after anyone in my family— isn't enough to keep me stuck here any longer. I'll check on Mom when I get my bearings, but I can't wake up to him another morning. So gotta put the getaway plan into motion

322

after my session. No more excuses—no more forcing the puzzle piece to fit where it clearly doesn't.

Exactly. Now we're getting somewhere.

Ow, all right already.

I peel off Harlan's compressing arms so I can get a second to breathe. I pray I don't wake him... because deep down, his shocking words last night kept me trembling.

During Harlan's snores, I pack and sneak things in my car as much as I can to make a smooth exit. He's off from both jobs today, so now's the only time to do it. One wrong move, one creak too loud, and it's over.

The echo of awareness hits... I had this coming for a while.

Almost done. Now I only need the last bit of things from the top drawer.

RING! RING!

"Ugh."

Shit. No.

His work alarm.

He forgot to turn it off.

"Where are you going?" Harlan wakes. His voice cracks and is sleep-laden but with a touch of menace.

I can't talk. Why can't I talk!?

"Uh, Patience?"

"My, um therapist. I—I'm going to see her." There we go.

Harlan gets out of bed and resumes towering over my stature. Before, it felt protective. Now, it only serves to place me in a shade of submission. "You never told me you were seeing a therapist. Since when?"

"For a couple months. I've had to... get used to a lot of huge changes. You get that."

"I thought I was all you needed to get your mind right."

"Harlan…"

"I'm joking."

But his overall mood tells another story, and I want to confront that one while I have him. "Um, so last night, you said something that sort of freaked me out."

Harlan snakes one arm behind my back as his brows slightly raise. "Let's hear it."

"It's possible that hurt people tend to hurt people. Were you serious or being lyrical?"

"I never said that."

No way. "Yes, you did."

"Didn't."

"Did!"

"Are you sure you're not still intoxicated?" Harlan undermines my accusation. He stretches passively and then rubs his kneecaps. "You drank half of that bottle of wine last night—which also explains why you weren't much fun to be around."

"No, and it wasn't half, thank you. I heard you loud and clear. There's no pretending this away like everything else. And another thing—with what you told the police… how did you find out where my mother live—"

"Look, hear whatever your little heart desires," he insists louder. "I'm not trying to hash out old shit with you."

This is getting nowhere. Marsha's warnings keep calling it. "You're never going to own up to any of it, are you?"

Harlan towers over even more, his blank stare unblinking while he touches my lips. "There's nothing to own up to saying. Except—you look exquisite in the morning light from here."

But his habitual lying stops with me.

"Whatever. Forget about it—gotta go. I'm already late." I take my things to load in the car. But there's a problem.

He's blocking the door. "Why all the extra clothes?"

"Laundry."

"That many loads? Did you raid your entire closet?"

Dude, let up! "Just trying to be proactive here and get ahead."

Harlan's lips stretch even thinner. Bad sign. "Why at the crack of dawn, though?"

"Is that okay with you?" I say sassily. "I'm really not a fan of explaining myself to anybody, by the way."

"You're under my roof—living here, all expenses paid. Excuse me for wondering what you have planned for the day." Harlan's eyes now have a glint of hostility in them. He holds the back of my head in his palm like a basketball. It's not affectionate, more of a reminder of who has leverage over who. "You're sorta acting snippy, hun. Not up to anything else, are you?"

"What reason would I have to lie?"

The same sinister shadow casts over him. "Call me crazy, but I had a dream..."

"Okay." I humor him.

"You were trapped in some wedding photo with *him*. Even after all we've been through and shared with one another, you still went back to your beloved Obinna. Weird, right? Because you already knew—if you tried to leave for good... without me knowing... there's no taking that lying down... There's no telling how far I would go to win you back. It's just your luck—I never felt this way with anyone else before. My muse, my paramour—my goose who lays the golden eggs known as her art. Shit, how does that story end again? Anyway... as for the dream... glad that's not the case."

"Uh..."

"I know you don't love me..." Harlan tightens his hold on the back of my head. "But you'll learn to."

You have to go now!

"I need to—"

"Yes, baby?"

"Harlan, I—I have to go."

"So, go."

My head is still stuck in his trickster grasp.

"Did you hear me? I said you could go."

"Hey, what are you—"

He laughs rabidly as he watches me try to fight free. "I thought you were leaving. Thought you were in a hurry."

"Hands off—I don't like this."

"Haha. Gotta do better than that. Can't keep her waiting."

"I don't understand!"

"Got to show your therapist you respect her time."

"Stop!"

His amusement at my reaction disgusts me. Please—make it out okay. Harlan spins around and jerks me along with him, hurting the base of my neck.

"How badly do you need to see your head doctor, huh? Pssh. Not bad enough!"

"You're being... What are you trying to prove?!"

"Guess." Harlan keeps laughing like it's the funniest thing known to man. He has me by an arm's length. We both circle around the studio, while he leads—on the verge of salivating from the fright in my voice.

"I'm—I'm not—I'm not playing."

"But I am, and I'm winning."

"No, you're a lunatic!"

Safe word unlocked.

Harlan lets go of my head, not before giving me a slight push backward. "I was fucking with you, god. What happened to being able to take a joke? Relax, you're fine."

He's wrong. I'm not fine. I stand in terror, remembering why I was in such a hurry to leave him. Who in the hell have I lived with all these months? Who?!

Obinna would never—

Of course not.

Harlan stares at me, shaken up for a good while, and the message apparently sinks in. "Hey, you okay? Come here. I'm sorry. You're too adorable, shaking like a leaf and everything."

Light switch McCandles. Night and day.

In a cryptic twist, Harlan locks onto me crushingly and pats my back. "I didn't realize it's too early for those types of pranks."

His idea of a prank is something I never want to entertain again. "Please... can I go now?"

Harlan puts on another mask and wanes his aggression. I look for the man he once was, the tactful intellectual I fell for. But his current dead eyes—they're hard as the concrete beneath my feet.

"Safe travels, beautiful." Then I'm released.

I gather as much stuff as my arms can carry and dash out from under him before he changes his mind. My legs hurry down the hallway, footsteps echoing in the quiet building.

Ah!

My bag strap gets caught on the doorknob of the mainte-nance closet and slows me a bit.

"Come on... easy does it."

Yes.

After freeing myself, I'm back in my stride.

There's the main garage door to the parking lot. Perfect.

But why do I hear—

"Oh, one more thing—did you ever finally decide?"

Harlan emerges from his apartment corridor and finds me. Pinched reddened face, frigid features, twisted mouth— revealing his true intentions for me after my betrayal.

None of them are good. "Urm... Decide?"

"Am I more of a psychopath or sociopath?"

"Maybe we shouldn't—"

"Allow me to help you with your decision. Risks. I like 'em but... don't confuse risks with being ill advised. Some people... will bungee jump without thinking about the fall. Others? They jump because they want to see how close they come to the impact."

He knows. Oh God. "This won't... won't change anything."

"Me personally... I love watching the bodies of people who try to dupe me have a mishap... and splat stylishly each time. Does that give you a better idea now?"

My phone. I need my phone.

It's buried deep in one of your bags. By the time you get to it, he could knock you out and drag you back inside.

Okay, second best option.

"I will scream if you try anything." I say, clutching my bags to myself. "So, I'm going."

"Aww, is this where we are with us now?" Harlan points at a neighbor's door. "Do you really want to involve an innocent person with your bullshit? Hmm, if we must. I say go for it—scream. Let's see who's gonna get to you faster. The cat lady with an artificial hip or me? Trust it won't go the way you think it will."

"There's gotta be cameras poking around somewhere in this building."

"I'm a lunatic, right? Why the fuck would I give a shit about cameras?"

He'll say anything to make me cave in. "Go away!"

"You weren't listening." Harlan snickers as if he remembered what Christmas mornings were like. "Leaving wouldn't be good for me. Or you. We can talk about it. But don't even think about walking out that door."

Fine.

I'll run instead... because time for talking is obsolete.

"Hey!"

So does he.

He's gaining momentum. Put a stop to it.

CLUNK!

I throw a less essential packed bag directly at his feet. Harlan hits the ground hard. "Dammit!"

I burst through the parking garage entryway and slam it behind me, then use the outdoor trash can to create a barricade. He's yelling through the closed door, but I don't stop. I run to my car with my hands unsteady as I fumble for the keys. My heart pounds in my ears while sweat begins to bead on my skin.

BOOM!

The parking garage door flings open, destroying the barricade.

And here comes Harlan, charging at me at full speed with skinned knees. "Get back here! Patience!"

I hear his footsteps, growing louder with each passing

second.

Get in and drive!

My keys finally give entry, and I'm inside my car with almost everything I own. I look in the rear-view mirror and peel out.

After losing Harlan on the third floor of the parking garage, I drive farther down to the first floor, calm down, and reach the automatic gate arm to the exit. Good. Have it scan whatever it needs to scan and vroom out of here. There's a strip mall about ten minutes away where I could park and wrap my head around what took place. It'll be okay. I'll be okay.

CLANG!

You gotta be shitting me.

"Open the car door, now."

A muffled Harlan is speaking to the right of my car. As he orders, he taps irately on the passenger window.

Where the hell did he come from!?

"Do you hear me talking to you!? Okoye, do it!"

Serves me right for celebrating too early.

THUNK! THUNK!

Harlan's body slams against my poor Corolla. The full throttle rocks me inside of it with each hard judder.

I'm not going to make it if I follow common driving courtesy.

Come on! Now!

Just in time, I see him slam against the back window, pounding furiously on my car. My foot slams the gas pedal, and I drive straight into the automatic gate arm, knocking it clean off. Tires screech as I fly onto the freeway.

"Fucking bitch!"

I glance in the mirror again, and he's still there but growing smaller, a lurking figure against the lowly lit parking garage.

The hatred in his gaze as he sees my escape sears into my eyelids. I grip the steering wheel tightly, my knuckles white.

Harlan's Patience is no more.

* * *

Angela's office has gone through a whole Zen makeover, too. Calming paintings in muted tones adorn the walls, and soft lighting casts a warm glow over the space. Plush armchairs sit beside small tables topped with magazines, though my mind is too preoccupied to focus on reading material.

"Thanks for seeing me again, Angela, and I apologize for how long it's been since we last spoke. I wanted to let you know this is my last session, since I won't be able to afford anymore. Obinna took me off his insurance, and I'm currently not employed. But I think I figured out what I want, anyway. Now that I'm clear-headed."

"Appreciate the sentiments, and I'm sorry to hear our time ends here," she comments and smiles. A gentle crease forms by her cat-like eyes. "What was the resolution?"

My legs uncross and get caught under Angela's shaggy rug.

"I left Obinna and Seabrook. Then I was sorta living with Harlan for a couple months. But a big thing happened that gave me the strength to leave him and never look back. He's the source of so much going wrong for me, including my new night terrors. Make this last session the one that counts, please?"

Angela stares at me a tad longer than usual, then gets up to pick a textbook from her bookshelf.

"Patience, have you heard of the term Borderline Personality Disorder?" Angela asks.

My mind draws a blank. "No, why?"

"I'm not a diagnostician, but based on my notes from your accounts of Harlan and the profile form you completed on him, I feel confident saying he displays many of the traits I've seen before. While it doesn't all fit, much of it does."

"Looks like I've learned something today."

Angela proceeds. "Borderline Personality Disorder pinpoints a mental health condition that affects the way people feel about themselves and others. It's hard for them to function in everyday life. Harlan seems to have a pattern of unstable, intense relationships, mood swings, as well as frequent impulsiveness."

I'm officially freaked out. I haven't even relayed what Marsha told me about him to Angela yet, and she's hit the diagnosis nail on the head.

"Yeah, it started out subtle. But Harlan has this way of making the craziest ideas sound completely casual—like doing drugs, getting unplanned tattoos, having threesomes while high, and other things I'd rather not get into."

Angela scratches the side of her pointy nose. "You know what I'm asking next, right?"

"Uh, possibly."

"Thinking back on those sexual experiences with Harlan and others involved, do you feel clear about what you could consent to, given that you were under the influence?"

"It only happened once."

"Hmm... not what I'm asking."

I focus hard on the sound of cars rushing by on the highway outside, wishing I could just zoom off—to drive far away from the question I've sought to avoid since my last night with

Ayahuasca.

Angela's chin tucks down further as she wears a dismayed look. "Patience, if we even have to think for this long... chances are—"

"Still going down the list here. We also got into a fight... and it got physical on both sides."

Angela's face looks as though she's just breathed in a mouthful of soot. "Are you okay? Do you think you're still in danger?"

Her response alone lets me know it was much bigger than how he made it out to be. "I'm fine. He seemed to be really sorry afterward. When I woke up in the hot bath he made, he looked after me."

"Whoa, hold on a second—woke up? Meaning, he undressed you without you being aware of it?"

Not to mention that he knocked me out. But there's no need to add that to the list; she seems troubled about it enough.

"Well... um, yes. I guess he thought... with the amount of times he's already seen me naked—it was like, whatever."

"I'm hearing there was more than simply on and off conflict between you two. Harlan continually erased the lines you kept drawing for yourself, especially when things were already tense or even physical. How are you feeling about what you've shared so far? This lack of consent and respect for your autonomy coming from him is deeply troubling to me, and I want to make sure you're feeling safe to explore it here." The more Angela stops and analyzes the situation, the more I shrink.

Harlan's temperament is that of a coiled viper—always prowling. That night—along with this morning—the venom spilled.

"I know it's a lot. I'm right there with you."

"But are we there with consent, yet?" she counterattacks.

"Yes. Like the museum, for starters."

"So, are we backtracking on stating that you consented before?"

"I guess, in a way, yeah. I didn't mention before that I found out they were vibrating panties only after he activated them."

Angela gives her sharpest disapprobation from the update. "There's a name for such an act, you know."

"Yeah, I do." However, I don't dare say it out loud.

Angela nods, and I realize this is the longest time she's gone without writing.

"How would you describe intimacy with Harlan?"

That question needs a mental health day, because where do I even begin?

"Exciting at first—a breath of fresh air, exhilarating. Then, on the verge of exploding... a ticking time bomb."

"That's quite a jump."

"He used to leave bite marks, like a message. But he doesn't need to anymore." I suddenly have heart arrythmia as I speak. "It's as if he wants me to know he's the one controlling the pleasure I feel—no one else. Maybe he's trying to convince himself of that. Since the fight... sex makes me feel like a passenger in my own, um..."

Angela lowers her volume. "Body?"

"It was supposed to keep him calm and not crazy. Then even that stopped working."

"I see. Evidence of strategic consent. Go ahead."

"Two women from his past tried to warn me, but by then it was already too late. I was bound to him."

Angela shows an unmistakable side eye. "That is a very

specific analysis, Patience."

I shrug.

"Does that bother you at all?"

I shrug again. Tears flow freer than usual, and Angela comes through with Kleenex.

"When I tried to leave this morning, he chased me down and called me a..."

"A what?"

"Nothing. I'm—I'm just tired."

"It's okay to be tired."

"I wish I was normal, that's all."

Angela nods. "What does normal look like to you?"

"Happy," I say. My tone sounds girlish, but I can't help it. "Content and secure. But I can never get there. I came close with Obinna when we dated in college. But right after getting married and, well, other stuff—we were on pause."

"That must be tragic to experience. You know you don't need either man to validate who you are as a person?"

"Yes, I see that."

Angela checks her watch, and now I'm apprehensive.

"Angela, you're killing me." I flail my arms. "Are we out of time?"

Angela smiles suggestively. "I won't tell if you won't. Five minutes."

I smile back. "I made art in his tribute, but he accused me of capturing aspects of himself that he didn't want exposed for personal gain. Then he got upset when I visited my old house, discovered he had stolen from my art sale, and caught him in the shower with one of his students. Who does that? His stepsister said he tried to force himself on her. At fifteen. And do you know what I did? I stayed."

Angela slams her notebook closed. "And you stayed, because?"

Time to purge.

"It was my way of repentance. Righting my wrongs. My wrongs against Obinna, my friends, and my family. Don't forget—I put my unborn baby in harm's way at work. It would've been easier to accept if I had a miscarriage of natural causes, but I didn't. So, I'll never forgive myself. I don't deserve a break or to ease my soul. I deserve Harlan McCandles."

"Okay, that's it. I would like to present an alternative." Angela sits up alert like a pelican and points to a Chaise lounge chair. "Have you ever tried hypnotherapy before?"

Sounds experimental. "No, what is it?"

"Hypnosis is a state of immersive relaxation and precise concentration. A collaborative effort between mind and body. I will provide verbal cues, repetition, and specific imagery. When you're under hypnosis, ordinary distractions aren't the focal point. You'll be more receptive to guided suggestions to make alterations to improve your mental health."

"Anything's got to be better than what I have going on now."

Before I know it, I'm lying on her special therapist chair with my eyes closed and body relaxed.

I sense her hands apply light pressure to my shoulders and then travel up to my brow bone. She smells of eucalyptus and citrus. Then I hear a chime ding from her therapeutic instrument.

"You will hear three of these."

Chime.

"And then you will let it all go. Is that okay?"

"Yes."

Chime.

"I'll be waiting right here when you get back."

"But what if I—"

—Chime.

My eyelids are heavier than I thought they'd be.

* * *

It's night, and I'm in bed, trying to sleep, but can't. Sleep paralysis has me frozen in bed, a useless heap, when thunder and lightning strike. God himself makes a declaration to the sky.

That's when I see him, and he's no longer human.

A demonic Harlan climbs over my frozen state. His vampire grin stretches past realism, his skin a pale, corpse-colored gray. He covers me with unwanted touches. "There you are. Did my muse think she was finally rid of me?"

But his eyes are a whole other vital force.

They're two round pools of black paint. The paint bleeds down from them, forming thick tendrils down his evil chin. Harlan's mouth is a gaping maw. No teeth, no irises, just an abyss that sucks the light from existence. He reaches for me with hands around my neck. His voice is a dry whisper that promises oblivion. "I could take the breath from your lungs, watch the light leave your eyes, and there's nothing you can do about it, baby."

I rattle with anything but intimidation in his hold. All of this and worse, while I'm unable to get away.

Please. Please stop here.

One hand leaves my neck and squelches into my mouth.

Harlan reaches down my throat, all the way to his elbow. The buildup of the pressure in the back of my head almost blinds me with stabbing discomfort. My jaw is on the verge of dislocating, as it feels like he's pulling my insides out.

"Don't fight it. That will only harm you and please me."

The voice I try so hard to forget drips with a sickly persuasiveness. Nuh. Harlan yanks his arm out of my mouth, and I almost choke.

"Not quite. Let's try here instead."

His hand sinks into my chest with preternatural ease. There's a torturous rip, a tearing sensation once he does, and a wet, pulsing mass emerges—a crimson heart—held aloft in his grip. My heart.

"It only beats because I allow it to—it's how I show I care."

Demonic Harlan taunts away as his eyes ink out thick paint that drips tears of night, spilling over his mouth and becoming a grotesque smile. His face is a deathly white—the way paper looks after being soaked in water. The scream I locked inside of me dies in my chest. It's a strangled sound, swallowed by the storm.

No one ever hears my cries for help. Maybe I'm not worth saving.

There's a horrible fascination in Harlan's torture of me, a predator savoring the hunt. Paint rushes out of his orifices and spills directly into my mouth, non-stop. It's forced open, and I can no longer breathe.

I'm drowning in Harlan, literally and figuratively. We're so entangled, I don't know where he ends and I begin.

"Patience! Wake up! You are all right!"

"Ahh! *Stop!*"

I'm now sprawled out on Angela's textured rug, all out of

sorts, as she fans me with an old magazine. "Hypnotherapy... shouldn't have this great of a reaction from you. I'm picking up on some serious PTSD. Talk to me."

"Angela..." I moan in subduction. "I forgot how to do this."

"How to do what?"

"Fight."

"You'll pick it back up in no time." Angela gently lifts me back up into a sitting position.

"What if it's too late?"

"No, Patience. You do not deserve the toxicity Harlan brings you. This guy is the worst—gaslighting tactics to the max. Ultimatums on top of ultimatums. Do you even remember the last time you made a decision that didn't revolve around his demands? For the past six months, I have watched him try to deplete you of who you once were. A woman you can still reunite with today. Who is caring, attentive, a brilliant teacher, and someone who is very in tune with her feelings. Reclaim her!"

I take more tissues and stay with her words for a second. Harlan robbed me of plenty, and I assisted him with that. What would my world look like today if he never arrived in it?

In any case, I have to end the self-loathing that binds me to him.

"You're right. I miss her... I miss me. I want to learn how to dig myself out from under him."

"Help... like a police report is a good start."

"Okay."

Angela claps. "The last thing I'll leave you with is to find your community. Whether it's *no one person is an island,* or *it takes a village to raise a child*—pick the one that resonates with you the most and run with it. It doesn't hurt to have a support system and for it to not be one sole person, either. It takes the pressure off. Plus, you're young! Have fun and discover new interests along with new people."

Social anxiety isn't a picnic, though, and Angela knows that. I knew how to mingle and stand out with Molly, but just as myself... I'm Clark Kent again. Aside from that—if I had a network of kindred spirits, instead of relying on Obinna and Neisa the entire time, Harlan wouldn't have become such an urgency before.

"I'll work on that, too. Baby steps, though."

"Cut yourself some slack. You've come far to your new path—so pave the damn way."

"With guns blazing?"

"With guns blazing."

PAITENCE OKOYE PART DEUX

Neisa's kitchen is a chef's dream, with state-of-the-art appliances and gleaming countertops. I can only imagine the delicious meals that are prepared here daily.

"Pancakes or waffles?" a homemaker Neisa asks, with flour dusted on her elbows.

"Waffles," I choose.

"Wa! Wa!" Hailey blabs. She chews on her teething ring elatedly.

"Okay, baby," she responds.

California—the state I hated so much for taking my best friend away—is now my salvation. Now, more than ever, has become the best time to take Neisa on her offer and use this visit to restart my life.

Easy to do, since I haven't heard from him in two weeks.

Unfortunately, the first week I arrived didn't feel like a complete escape to Cali.

I forgot to block him on one app. The last time Harlan reached out was through two WhatsApp phone calls that I simply sat on the other end to listen to.

Since I never said a word back while I listened, Harlan's monologues turned deranged.

"It's picturesque out here tonight, and I hope it is wherever you are, too. Just like you, beautiful—like the moon reflecting on still water. It's disappointing that life has to always disrupt it. A ripple, maybe. A splash... Let me hear your voice to get me through the night, please?"

Sometimes, he talks in riddles. Other times, he's frighteningly more direct.

"My sheets still smell like you... and yet, my muse isn't here. How am I supposed to just accept you're no longer mine? You couldn't even give me the courtesy to say it to my face. Is that your thing? To pretend you aren't a fucking whore, then worm your way into the naivety of men's lives? Understand one thing. You're my sun. I flew too close, and now I crave you beyond scorching me. They say curiosity killed the cat, Patience. But what about complacency? Doesn't that leave you wide open? A flower waiting to be picked? Baby, I'm in love with you. How did I become someone you could fold away so easily, never to think of again? Shit, I'm almost jealous of your ability to do so."

I don't know why I listen to these calls that obviously disturb my psyche. He could've just been blowing off steam, but even with Harlan gone, why is withstanding him never an option?

Sorry, Angela. My unfinished police report stayed just that—when I was in a deep dive of *what could go wrong if I hit submit* research. Maybe I should've called the police, but I wasn't ready to acknowledge it was real. A piece of paper stating he should stay a hundred yards away from me would only add fuel to the fire.

I've seen too many true crime documentaries go left right after it happens. No, thank you. If I lie low long enough,

Harlan will forget about me. I won't be like the brave ones who fought him too loudly... and lost.

But to top it all off, the night terrors came on even stronger. With what I had experienced with Harlan's volatile moods—both Tori and Marsha's recounting of things, sleep for me was next to none.

At first, they were just unsettling, strange—otherworldly painted figures slipping through my dreams. But they got worse. The ink demons pulling me under, the feel of being one with his abstracts.

"Patience..."

Arriving the first night, I swore he was right there in the guest room with me as my body broke into a cold sweat. I checked the locks on my doors and windows twice.

"Patience!" I spun around and there he was.

Harlan was happy as ever to see me, while exuding his natural darkness. "You'll always have a piece of me. Wanna see?"

I'll never forget the grisly snap...

CRUNCH!

...that came with ripping off half his face.

Violent colors erupted from that newly crumpled, sharp chin of his. His jaw—half-buried in the pinkish mush dripping onto the nylon carpeting. McCandles' left eye dangled from a ropy vein and stared blankly back, with his nose in a no better position, both swaying from his head. A freak show swing set.

Harlan's breathing became a loud, moist noise—like a large dog lapping up water as ligaments leak out from his oozing openings. "Here's that piece. Now... what will you give me in return, beautiful?"

Fuck. The fright I gave poor Neisa and her family, when I woke up wailing in hysterics, took over her entire house. Wetting the bed didn't help matters, either. The terrors were never as violent after that one. However, I was afraid of what the violent ones meant.

None of it went away, even after telling myself it was all in my head.

What if it wasn't and Harlan was out there, watching, waiting? What if he followed me all the way to California, and the dreams were signs?

What scared me most wasn't even the nightmares themselves. It's the way I started to see and hear them when I was awake.

Anytime I even saw a shadow, I believed McCandles was around the bend, somewhere. I felt him trying to keep tabs. He twisted something inside me, something I can't undo.

I'm not sure what's creepier—hallucinating from psychosis, or him arriving at LAX.

So, I confided in Neisa the day I landed—losing the baby, the affair, quitting work, family, and the hoops Harlan made me jump through in order to keep me under his thumb.

Him calling, though, I tucked away in secret; I wasn't in a rush to alarm my heavily pregnant friend yet.

"I can't believe you bottled all that in for so long. You know you could've told me, and I wouldn't have thought less of you."

Those words helped a lot then, and even more now, as she takes care of us both.

"You need help with dishes? That way you can change Hailey," I ask.

"That works. Come on, stinky butt," she pokes fun.

"Yeah, she's been needing a change for a while."

"Who said I was talking about Hailey?"

"Neisa, you're a total mess."

"But I'm your mess, so shut up."

We chow down the waffles and bask in the remainder of the late Sunday morning.

As Neisa leads me through the sprawling mansion, I can't help but marvel at the extravagance. We pass by a spacious living room with floor-to-ceiling windows that offer a panoramic view of the manicured gardens outside.

She's got it made.

Malcolm, her husband, works in cybersecurity. So, unlike Obinna, he's always home, working remotely. He stays out of the way, exchanging a "what are y'all up to" and "sounds great" while we marathon our favorite trash reality TV shows, laughing our asses off.

"Wanna rewatch season three of *Love and Hip Hop: Hollywood?*" Neisa suggests.

I shake my head and nestle in her cozy couch and blanket. "I'm okay, just soaking it in for now."

"Soaking what in?"

"It's just... I was here before the stretch marks and the late-night Amazon orders for nipple cream. Then Malcolm proposed, and his job relocated your family here two years ago. When the texts and calls started dropping off, I slowly felt less and less like your sis. I didn't fit in Neisa's bubble anymore."

Neisa leans back, folding her arms and sucking her teeth. "Uh, who ghosted who?! Nah, don't act brand new with me."

Uh-oh. I've gone and done it now. I tense up and brace for an unexpected verbal smackdown.

"Sis, I'm exhausted. Like, coffee-can't-fix-it, running-on-empty exhausted. My life isn't just mine anymore. It's diapers, spit-up, and making sure my lil' nugget stays good. And even with all that, I still reach out. Only for you to keep blowing me off for months."

Oh. So, we're playing emotional Russian roulette, and I didn't even realize I threw the first knife. "I—I'm really sorry. I thought I was trying to protect you. He might've—"

"Who?" Neisa demands.

"Nothing."

"Patience." Neisa massages my leg. Her voice is no longer jovial but distressed. "You're not alone. Girl, you have people—quit acting like you don't. Talk to me, now that you have me."

Oh, Nei. Here it comes. "It's like you, Malcolm, and Hailey are floating up on this parachute of success, right? And I wanna join you guys so badly, but my fuel keeps lagging on my balloon. Setbacks keep dragging me down. And I don't want to drag you down either."

"Don't even. You couldn't do that if you tried."

She's so wonderful, it's unreal. "That means a ton, Neisa."

Neisa sets her popcorn bowl on the coffee table with a *thud*. "Now, be completely one hundred with me. I know things weren't okay with Obinna for a while. But what was it about Harlan that made your ass step out on your marriage in the first place?"

I let out a brittle laugh, anything to peek through my cloud of misery. "Where do I even begin?"

"He must've been laying down some serious pipe because— "

"Neisa, really?!" The blatant nature of my bestie continues

to take me by surprise.

"Sorry, sorry. Well, who exactly is Harlan McCandles?"

"Smart, sentimental, and sometimes a visionary." I lay back on the couch and paint a mental image of someone who continues to mystify me. "Yet cold, calculating, egotistical, and explosive."

"Nah, I'm good on all that." Neisa clicks her tongue. "I like my men to be predictable, no offense."

"Believe it or not, when we initially met, Harlan helped me discover how to tap into unknown sides to myself. But as it turns out, I didn't want that from him. I wanted that from Obi the whole time."

"Shit, that's tough. Lesson learned, though, right?"

"How did I let it get this bad, Nei?" I snuffle. "I mean, ignoring all the signs of what Harlan was—is. God, he almost broke my back in two during one of his fits. Yeah, I kind of started it, but he knows he's so much stronger—how much more damage he could've done. But he didn't care."

"Did you press charges on that motherfucker?!" Neisa asks. "Did you tell your mom, shit—Obinna? Despite where y'all stand now, he would not be down with any man putting their hands on you."

I've honestly missed the security I had with Obinna more and more lately. But with what I've done, reaching out to him would be an insult.

"No, and I get what you're thinking—what's the holdup? Truthfully, I want Harlan to leave me alone and not retaliate. He's pulled this shit with women before, according to his estranged sister, by constantly playing the system. If I were to call the cops, it might drive him to the edge. In fact, I know it would. Over time, it'll all blow over, and he'll lose interest like he did with the rest."

"You're not… secretly *in love* with Harlan, are you?" Neisa scratches her bulbous head. "Maybe your feelings got all, uh—and you're sorta protecting him without meaning to. You'd tell me, right?"

I nearly feel the waffles I just ate coming back up in my throat. "In love?! Jesus, no! Look, what feeds Harlan's self-centeredness is acknowledgment. His muses are more appealing when they're fighting back, kicking and screaming. I'm not giving him the satisfaction of either."

"I got to take notes. The tea is too piping hot to track."

I question whether I should say this next part but do, anyway. "When I caught Harlan and another girl in the shower together… how he looked at me… It's like he got off on reducing me to a puddle of tears."

"You caught his ass in the shower with her?! Patience, I need you to go get tested."

"She was actually one of his students, some red-head named Kelsey. I reported him anonymously to his campus. I'm pretty sure she's not the only student he's done this with, so—better I do this discreetly than with a police report. Kelsey may hate me now, but she has no idea what she's escaped. I couldn't live with myself if I knew he was doing it to someone else without trying to stop him."

"Amen," Neisa preaches. "But I ain't worried about some little white girl. Keep guard and watch your surroundings. Be gangsta."

"I will."

Then Neisa cracks up. "Speaking of gangsta, like when your mom caught us with a switchblade we found during sixth grade gym class? And she thought I was a Crip for years because my favorite color was blue? Damn, I just wanted to show it to Jamal Turner, so he'd think I was cool. Ugh, he was so fine. Lord."

I laugh so hard I almost pee. "Nearly forgot about that. She was about to enroll me in a *Beyond Scared Straight* program because she thought you were initiating me into it, too."

"And she had the nerve to think I was no good because I was boy-crazy. Only to be blind to your little ho ass coming a mile away!" she says, sticking out her tongue.

"Neisa, I am on my knees here. Have mercy." I throw a decorative pillow at her swollen feet. "I know it's painful to be... but be nicer. You promised. No judgies."

"Damn. I did, huh? 'Kay, 'kay—no judgies. Maybe I'm still a little salty that you overlooked my check-ins for months. Did I miss the memo on your no-reply policy?"

"It won't happen again."

"I know. But your mama's still racist as hell."

"Prejudiced, not racist."

Neisa brings over more blankets. "Stay as long as you need to."

"Thanks."

"I'm just trying not to think of my sissy on the news. You're family, Patience, and if anything were to happen to you..."

"Neisa?"

Neisa's new mood is no laughing matter as a single teardrop falls down her cherub cheek, and her lips pucker. "Real talk, don't you ever believe you can't tell me anything again. Harlan McCandles ain't shit as far as I'm concerned, and Neisa Norwood has a license to carry."

We hold each other for a bit, bonding further. I try to understand how someone like her could slip through my fingers for all these months. After getting it all out, Neisa has helped me regain my right-mindedness. No more unraveling at the seams with day and night terrors. I'm happy to give her all of me again.

"Nei…"

"Just know… people like him… are only as powerful as *you* make them out to be."

I wipe my face and feel reborn. "Ready to marathon season three of *Love and Hip Hop: Hollywood*, if you are."

"Bitch, let's go!"

As Neisa fires up Hulu, Mom's name lights up on my phone. Flip a coin. Heads answer. Tails voicemail.

The flip reveals heads.

Sure. I didn't feel like enjoying the rest of my day, anyway.

Answer it. Considering all that's happened, she could be in trouble.

"Hang on, I gotta take this."

Neisa nods, and I rush to the guest room for privacy.

"Hello?"

"Yes, okay—hello."

"Mom, did you need something?"

"Well, now that you ask, I would like to know if my only child is still alive, that's all."

Amusing.

"I am."

Mom smacks her teeth on the other end slovenly. Ugh, sounds like she's chewing on stock fish like jerky again.

"Okay, so, when will you come visit? Months came and went, yet my daughter poofs like a ghost."

"You think I would come visit after that stunt you pulled with your church group?!"

"What is the harm in a brief prayer?"

"That wasn't a prayer. It was an ambush. Also, last I checked," I dully remind her, "I wasn't your daughter."

"Who said that?"

She has to be on crack, because there's no damn way.

"Mom, you did. On our last phone call, remember? And actually, I'm done with you saying hurtful things and pretending they never happened."

"Calm down."

"I am."

"What do you want from me, Patience? It makes me angry that the daughter I raised on my own ruined her family by cheating on her husband, knowing what your father put me through."

"But I'm not him!" I yell. "Dad and I are entirely different people! But since I was a kid, you've refused to see that, huh? Belittling me every chance you get, making me feel less than worthless. Your words really wounded me! So much so that I self sabotaged my life for someone else who was majorly abusive. Not too different from you."

Mom's breathing changes to hoarse. "The white boy, he used you? He harmed you?"

"A little of column A and a little of column B. Aren't you going to say I told you so?"

"Why didn't you tell me?"

"Because of the reasons I just listed twenty seconds ago, Mom. I can't talk to you."

She's quiet for a bit. Then she says, "My mother couldn't talk to me, either. Because she never raised me."

"Okay."

"She was a child herself. Fourteen years of age, married

off to a man whose age I'm ashamed to say. She pawned me and your uncle Simon onto numerous faceless relatives. Back then, I wished I had a mother to talk to... and to show me how to be worthy to talk to."

"I get that."

"I have lived a hard life. Therefore, I am a hard woman. I have more yesterdays than tomorrows, so I will do my best to make amends. You *are* my daughter."

I know this chick isn't making me sob and reflect during my vacation. "Wow. That's a big deal, Mom. Um... it's gonna take time for me to—"

"Yes, I imagine it will. But it's a start."

"Thank you."

"Ahem, since you have teaching experience, I've been meaning to ask you—the youth division of New Haven is hiring for a project manager for our upcoming children's programs. I thought of you and told my committee my daughter is more than capable of the job."

Hmm, that timing, though. "You weren't saying all that earlier to fill a quota for church, were you?"

There's an indisputable laugh on the other line. "My heavens, no. Call it a mother's intuition. God sent me a sign to reach out—that you needed guidance."

"I'm not a regular churchgoer, though."

"That's quite all right. Your love for children will shine, and the Lord will see this."

I pray and give thanks to the big guy upstairs for connecting the dots. "This doesn't make up for everything but—it helps. Like you have no idea."

"Good. Please, come see me soon."

"I will."

She sounds fine. In fact, she sounds great. I'm so glad that asshole didn't get to her and was only flexing her address before. He flexed a lot of things to keep me afraid and meek. But with stopping me from seeking better days for myself, he's a day late and a dollar short. "I love you, Mom."

"It may not seem so, but you are my whole heart."

Click.

Nei never fails... I *do* have people in my corner.

Which means that he doesn't get to take away the possibility of a new job opportunity and bonding with my mother again. She needs me, and I, refreshingly, need her. But I have to play it smart if I go back. After those WhatsApp calls, I'm not biting first. McCandles can't see me coming or predict my next move, so I'll have to forgo my digital footprint and social media for a while. There's a silver lining in all this: knowing him down to a science and how his mind games work gives me an advantage.

Christ. Is that what you truly think, or what you're hoping for?

Why not both?

Have you learned nothing?

I can learn to stay out of his way and live comfortably too. Look at Marsha—with a beautiful family and a blossoming career, regardless.

Yes, as Harlan continues to pop up like a growing weed in her life.

I'll deal with him, understand? But not full force. If I keep tightening the screws, he's only going to get worse.

You're just telling yourself anything at this point.

My point is... it's time to stop running. After week four of my stay, my vacay is donezo.

The next morning, suitcases line the grand entrance of Neisa's house, as I grow more and more sad I'm leaving. The marble floors gleam under the soft glow of chandeliers that hang from the high ceilings. We wait between the corridors lined with family portraits, each piece adding to the sense of opulence.

What is it like to have all of your dreams come true? Will I ever know?

After I give a heartfelt goodbye to Neisa and her family by the door, I order an Uber to the airport.

"L.A. is your second home. Remember that," Neisa sniffs, resembling her toddler, Hailey. "Visit again soon. Before this new bun in the oven goes to college, please."

"You know it!" I squeeze her tight. "I'll be a better auntie, promise."

But then she gets sassy real quick. "Promise me one more thing. The minute he starts showing his ass again, I don't care what bulletproof plan you think you've got cooked up. You go back to that police station and walk inside this time to file a report. Okay?"

Dang. There goes being stealthy. But who am I to break a promise to my almost sister? She saved me from utter hopelessness, so I'll willingly let her have this one. "Fine. Only if he tries anything else, as a last resort."

"Caring for family comes with the job. It'll happen for you, too, you know."

"What?"

"Motherhood. It has a funny way of happening when you least expect it."

Let's get my life back on track first before that becomes a thing.

* * *

"Excuse me, what aisle are your acrylic paints in?" I ask a teenage store employee.

"Hmm, try sixteen, ma'am."

"Thanks."

I push my cart down the lanes, searching for quality colors, and it feels so damn good to paint again. Since coming back, it's kept me good company. The outlet releases everything—joy, excitement, fear—way better than drugs ever did. Serotonin never seems to decide though, whether it wants to stay or go—but it's a work in progress. But healthy living and positive thinking sounds like the place to start. Night terrors hadn't been my reality in forever. The thought of him stalking me didn't hang around anymore, and that felt like a miracle.

I still can't help but ponder sometimes. Did my anonymous report to Colby's administration serve as Harlan's wake-up call? Maybe it was just enough to scare him, but not so much that it would make him screwy; he probably realized he had messed with one too many victims and needed to chill.

Who knows? Come to think of it—I'm better off stopping the rationalizing of his lunacy.

"Oh, found them!" I happily pick up shades of auburn and heliotrope. "Score."

"Yeah... I thought that was you."

"Sorry?"

I spin around, and a Priya with blond highlights stares back. Her eyes wander, searching for common ground, while her expression appears drained. "Guess it has been a while, hasn't it?"

This blows chunks. I am so not prepared. "Hey, Priya. Uh...

how are you?"

"You don't care about how I'm doing, Patience, and that's perfectly fine. I really did try before—to bond with you. But I got rebuffed each time. So, message received, okay?"

"I'm trying to keep things light…"

"Hmm."

But I can't keep things light with Priya because she reminds me of the bad things I became when Harlan was a factor. She was right. I wasn't a likable person then, and I'm not interested in moving backward.

"Please… How's Obinna?" I push my cart to the side and stand beside her. "How's he doing since… things changed? Pongers, too?"

Priya appears lost in thought, then pushes her cart to the side, too. "Nah, let's not brush it under the rug. You wronged my homie dirty, and to top it off, tried to drag me along for the ride."

"I know."

"Also, if I hadn't told him myself, I wasn't sure if you would ever get around to it. Because of Obi, I really tried to find a friend in you and see what he sees. Only to—whatever."

I reach for her sympathy with caution. "It was wrong to try that line on you, and I sincerely apologize and was only deflecting—hadn't dealt with some serious shit I went through."

Priya then does a slight tug on my jacket sleeve. "Please tell me the truth. You aren't still seeing that loser, are you?"

"No, it got pretty bad between us. He did a number on my mental and physical health. So, I left," I say guardedly.

It's unclear if she believes me.

"Good. Not that he—but that you got away."

"You don't hate me?"

"Well, I did for a bit, once I found out. You made it kind of easy to," Priya says, uncouthly, as if she just remembered who she's talking to. "But over time, I grew more unbiased. You both went through a terrible period and had trouble moving on from it. Obinna told me how abandoned you felt after the miscarriage, and yeah, it doesn't condone your actions with cheating, but people do off the wall shit when dealing with unresolved trauma. I wanted to see him happy—to see you guys finally win."

"Wow, Priya." I half-expected her to go on some holier-than-thou kick. "You're the sister Obinna never had."

Her chin pulls up, but her gaze is elsewhere—almost distressing. Unsure what else to say, I take it as an opportunity to leave on good terms. "Well, I hope you have a nice—"

"Speaking of which," Priya's voice wavers slightly. "My sister Dora had a stillborn three years ago. After that, she emptied both her and her husband's bank accounts on pyramid schemes behind his back. Even then, I couldn't judge her, and I wouldn't want anyone else to either. So, I get that there's more to it between you two."

Shit got heavier than intended.

"Thank you for sharing that with me. I'm sure it, um, wasn't easy." I fumble out of my mouth.

Priya nods and returns to her cart. "She's okay now and is raising twin boys. But I better get going. Um, Pongers is good—better than Obi lately. Not gonna lie, from what I've noticed at the clinic, it's clear he really misses you."

Ugh. That's the last thing I wanted for him. Poor Obi. "I appreciate you telling me... and should've appreciated you as a person much earlier."

I ended my marriage, and she had no hand in it. Period. Embracing the first step of growth feels good.

Priya flutters her full eyelashes at me with a forgiving smile. "I just have a feeling Obinna will be glad to hear you're doing okay, too."

We aren't friends, but we are in an understanding place.

I forget where I am and hug her as I try not to let the waterworks show.

Priya freezes. "Patience, wha—"

"If I didn't say it then, then I'll say it now." I wipe my face before she sees. "I'm glad Obinna has you in his corner. Tell him I wish him nothing but great things. Not good, but great."

Then I leave a floored Priya back to her shopping.

* * *

After I get home and put up my fresh paints, I call my coworkers on Snapchat to pick out an outfit for tonight. I've officially conquered my social anxiety! Sorta. Some days, I still find it hard to believe that there are people out there who simply like me... for me.

"What time did you two get home last night after karaoke?" I ask on video.

"Twelve, maybe. I had fun! So, glad you came out P!" Sophie, New Haven's bubbly youth pastor, replies. "Last night was a blur."

"Not too blurry for me," Miguel, a New Haven church tech crew member, answers. "Sophie flashing the middle finger made my New Haven's Snapchat reel! Pastor Johnson will see you in a new light!"

She moans, then facepalms. "Rude! But accurate. Ugh. My

hangover is killing me."

"So was your rendition of Taylor Swift's "Trouble," bae," Miguel jokes.

"I just can't have it all, can I?" Sophie whines.

Giggling at my friends over our karaoke hijinks, I grab a pair of earrings from my jewelry box. "I think we sounded great last night."

"Patience, I didn't know you could dance like that, though," Miguel goes on. "Like, professionally. Damn, you're the total package—diva legs matching diva lungs."

Blushing, I think back to yesterday. My new friends are far more laid-back than I anticipated, considering where we work. Miguel yanked me by my wrist, and Sophie followed suit onto the small karaoke dance floor. They flailed like no one's watching. It had been so long since I went all out the way I wanted to. In my head, I was ten again and no longer feeling self-conscious in dance class. Then, I shifted back to Eden and took charge of that night, with no one to police me or my body.

I couldn't believe I almost let dancing be stolen away from me. Connected to a force grander than myself, I turned into a collective energy that was grounding and grew a sense of invincibility. My cheeks were flushed, but not from anxiety anymore. From the thrill of being with my tribe and letting go of months of apathy. As Miguel launched into his hilariously butchered version of "Living on a Prayer," I couldn't help but laugh, a genuine, unrestrained laugh that felt strange, yet lively. Those... I'll hang on to for the longest.

I'm close to completing my outfit for tonight, then show off my footwear on the screen. "M'kay, having a shoe crisis over here. Flats or wedges?"

"Flats," they both blurt.

Sophie takes out her rollers. "Trust me, your feet will thank you, instead of barking for days later."

Miguel irons his shirt and head bobs. "What she said."

"All right, looks like I'm set, then. I'll see you guys tonight!"

"Bye!" Sophie peeps.

"Later, mamas," Miguel follows.

Snapchat goes black.

I would so get a gold star from Angela because I finally found my people! As May brings in the Spring Festival season, I'm breaking down barriers. New apartment, new job, and new me.

"Where are those costumes? The kids are going to need them for the second half of the Spring Showcase!" I rummage through my small apartment.

Managing the children's program at New Haven, kids will be kids anywhere. It's a sweet gig, and it's helped me gain a sense of ownership in the workplace. A nice bonus is giving them painting lessons after they choose their favorite biblical characters to illustrate. A lot of colorful David and Goliath interpretations come to fruition every once in a while. My favorite works from the kids were of Daniel in the Lion's Den. They made paintings of lions that looked more like nightmare fuel versions of Pongers, which sure pushed the meaning of interpretation.

I stop for a second and stand in the middle of my new apartment, taking it all in. The blinds ooze the light of the setting sun over the hardwood floors. There's a pang of happiness as I look around at the carefully arranged furniture and the little touches that make it feel like home. My new abstract art, that I painted sober and far from under the influence, frames every wall in my residence.

It's the first time I've ever had a place of my own, and I can't help but tap into a sense of accomplishment. It's not much, but it's mine, and that's enough for now.

But I gotta hurry.

New Haven church has an ETA of thirty minutes, and there's only so much time to get the second grade girls into their costumes and makeup before the final showcase rehearsal. Hustle. Hustle.

I can see Mom now, running around like a madwoman, screaming for somebody to find her "biscuit-headed daughter."

A daughter who sees everything she's done to change for herself.

I pack the costumes I finished sewing after pulling them from the coat closet.

"Woah!" Almost tripped over my stupid extension cord in the living room, but not today, Satan. Today is the first day in forever that I'm winning.

My feet skip to the bedside table to take my car keys.

BOOM!

A loud thud echoes through the unit, and my paranoia lurches into overdrive.

I'm still in my bedroom.

Panic surges through me as I strain my ears, listening to the unknown that surrounds me.

Swoosh!

It sounds like my faulty pipe finally burst. Wish I had invested in a decent mop. Damn, the maintenance staff had one job—guess I ought to report this to the leasing office.

I walk to the source of the disturbance and get ready to determine how high the damage is.

And boy, do I find it.

Please. No.

"Hey, Patience. How's Marsha?" Harlan comes around the breakfast nook with a glass of water. His face reads a dubious look as the streetlights that filter through the curtains cast eerie shadows across my small apartment.

My mouth hangs open with unfortunately no words available to express the utter shock I have. My legs are milliseconds away from giving out from under me. This. Is. Far. From. Okay!

"I'm liking the new hair on my muse," Harlan comments on my short afro. "Can't help but miss it longer, though. Easier to play with... maybe grab on to when the occasion calls for it, you know?"

I keep pinching myself, but I'm not dreaming, and from the looks of my front door, it couldn't hold its own against him.

"Harlan, why are you in my apartment?"

At a leisurely pace, he walks toward me—eyes locked and loaded on mine—then rests his elbows on the breakfast bar. He snarls as he twirls an eight-inch slicing knife between his thumb and index finger. There's a cutting board beside him with a hunk of lettuce he chopped, but I have a hunch that's only for show.

"I asked you a question," he says.

"I don't give a shit about your question."

"You grew a backbone. Congrats."

"Get out of here. I didn't invite you in."

"So, invite me in. Make it official; it's not too late." Harlan touches things in my kitchen. Like napkins, paper towels, and plates.

Get help. Send an S.O.S. Something!

I waveringly go for my phone in my back pocket during Harlan's search for utensils. I get closer and closer to reach for it when—

"I wouldn't," Harlan says in a voice that seems deadlier than the knife in his hands. His sectoral heterochromia appears indistinct and glares me up and down. "You won't make it past the home screen before things go south. So, you might as well come closer."

"Put the knife away first," I barter with him as I try to minimize the timorous nature in my pitch. "Now."

Those are words I never thought I would have to tell my former lover.

"The rules should apply to both of us." Harlan points at my pocket. "No shiny objects in either of our hands, and it's a deal."

I step closer to the kitchen while I try to be mindful of not setting him off. "What are you doing?" I ask.

Harlan looks at me incredulously and flashes his vampire grin again. When I finally make my way into the kitchen, I find a full sandwich plated in front of him. "You want one? I don't mind whipping up another, honest."

Nothing about what he's doing is honest.

"No, look, what is this? What are you trying to do here? I mean, is there a plan for where it's going?"

Stay strong. And stay consistent.

Harlan takes his plate, and instead of responding, he heads over to the kitchen table and makes himself comfortable. No. No. No! He can't pull anything crazy right now. I have somewhere to be.

I have somewhere to be and fast.

"I'm heading to a rehearsal. I can't be here with you." My voice is a quivery jello that spills out each word as I try to take his plate. "Harlan, seriously, no more games. Get your shit and—"

THUNK!

He pounds the table with a mighty fist and shuts my mouth up on the double. "Don't test me, Patience. I came all this way, and you're going to let me take a load off."

"I need to go."

Harlan gestures to a neighboring seat. "We both know you're not heading anywhere. Be a good girl and sit. Now."

I shouldn't push my luck. I might not have much of it left.

After I'm seated, Harlan scarfs down the sandwich noisily in four bites. He sees his presence bothers me, and he revels in it. My heart races, and my palms clam up; I'm wishing I were anywhere but here.

"You never answered my question, by the way."

"Wh-what?"

Harlan postures up and points at me. "How's Marsha?"

"Living her best life without you," I say tartly.

"That makes one of you, at least."

A stream runs up my throat, and I projectile vomit in front of Harlan—who is now in fresh disgust.

"Holy—are you okay?" He finally breaks the act and frets over me.

I run to spew the rest of it in the trash can, or where the rest of my night is going. Harlan's hands rub my back in broad circles. I can't move. His touch makes my blood run cold.

"Come on, let it out and don't force it. It's easier that way."

"Don't touch... How many times do I have to tell you to

never touch me again?!" I've had it, and claw at him to get off of me.

A bewildered Harlan backs off and moves to the side. He then paces counter-clockwise strategically by the front door. I use my peripheral vision to make sure I keep him at bay.

"So, how far along are you?"

There's no way... no fucking way that's going to be my story.

"I'm not pregnant, so shut up!"

"You sure?" Harlan's voice reaches an octave that spooks me. "Let's consider how long it's been. There's a possibility."

This can't be happening. This can't be happening!

"*Stop!* Harlan, please—" I'm on my kitchen floor, kneeled over, eyes squeezed tight. "You made your point. It's done."

"That's yet to be determined, beautiful." He goes to the living room and sits on my olive-colored loveseat, then stretches lazily. "I wasn't crazy about it at first, that's true. But I'm warming up to the idea of parenthood now. So, granted, if I'm the father of the kid, it's nowhere near close to being done."

"Why did you have to come back?!" I scream. "I made it known that I hate you and want to be left alone!"

"Watch your tone with me," Harlan orders menacingly. "Or certain measures will have to be taken."

I'm in serious trouble for several reasons. My apartment isn't a traditional apartment, more of a duplex. As for trying to sneak out of my windows—unfortunately, my complex chose a fine time to get burglar bars installed. There's no one who lives below or above me that would hear if I called out for help. I live at the very end of my unit with my only neighbor being Mrs. Johnston—a retiree in her sixties who asked me to water her plants because she went on a cruise this week.

And Harlan can't know any of that.

Or what's worse, is he could've been plotting and casing my place the whole time, fully aware.

I have a choice to make—which is abundantly clear—comply or raise hell. I choose hell. He won't hurt me if he thinks I'm pregnant with his child, so I'll call his bluff.

"There's only two ways we can go about this," Harlan instructs. He walks closer, cracking his knuckles and disrupting the quiet. "As long as your phone stays outta sight, it'll be an okay night. Now if we try and get cute—"

Rather than reach for my phone, I glance at the shadow of kids walking past my window, laughing.

"Patience. Don't."

But I will.

"*Somebody help—*"

A rush of force knocks me to the ground, and my head is reeling. Damn.

"You'd better stay sweet for me, girl. Right now."

All I've managed to do is poke the bear, and now he's baring his teeth.

"Aye, Milo, you hear that?"

"Man, hear what?"

The sound of children talking outside drifts through the barred windows as Harlan clamps his hand over my mouth and holds me still on the floor. My arms are useless at my sides because I'm too afraid to move, too afraid of what it would mean if I fought to pull away.

"I thought I've seen just about all your selfish choices, but this wins the gold medal, babe. If those little shits show up knocking at your door..." Harlan whispers, piercingly, "I can't be held responsible for what happens to them—and that's on you.”

I don't think I've ever prayed harder for someone else's safety over my own.

"Guys, hurry up, or we'll be picked last again!"

"Bet! Let's go grab my ball from Aaron's house."

The shuffle of their footsteps fades, taking my last chance of escape with them.

Harlan grabs my collar so tightly that I'm breathless. "What the fuck did I tell you?!" he seethes, sending spittle on my face. "Do you think fucking with my life is a game?!"

Everything is going dark. Lines blur and angles grow fuzzy. I wish I could let Mom know I tried to make it to rehearsal.

He finally lets go. "Wake up."

I gasp and gather all the air in my lungs as much as possible before he changes his mind.

"Are you going to be good? Or am I gonna have to snag some tape and a sock? I have no issue with grabbing the dirtiest one I can find, either. Please, don't make me have to. I'd appreciate it if we could be civilized while I'm here."

The word *good* enrages me. I want to rip him limb from limb and set him on fire as I recall the brutality of Marsha's childhood pain.

"Listen, because I will only say it once. I will never be your muse, good girl, or anything else for you again. Ever. You rapist."

Harlan twitches. "I never raped you, you lying—"

"Marsha says differently."

"You have five seconds to change the subject."

"How does it work, Harlan? Being able to establish the persona of an accredited professor while you abuse and assault us?"

"You know what? I'll answer that. It went well until about three weeks ago. I got fired because of the shit with Kelsey you reported. Anonymous, my ass. Thanks for that, by the way. It's going to be kind of difficult to pay for child support if I'm unemployed." He sounds like a broken record.

"I will never be pregnant with your baby!"

"That might not be up to you."

My stomach twists and turns at the thought... Harlan might be right. With my endometriosis, it never occurred to me conceiving naturally was possible. Only through IVF with Obinna. So, I was never consistent using protection with Harlan. Ugh—so irresponsible—especially when diseases could be the case, too. But in the heat of it, all it takes is saying the right words to make you oblivious to the rest. How could I have overlooked the timeline? Pregnant by miracle through my abuser?

Hell no.

So, no time to beat myself up about it.

I made my poor choices when I made them. Now, I have to fight through each one. Regardless if a pregnancy test appears positive or not, one fact remains.

"Again... Harlan... I will never be pregnant with *your* baby."

"Hand over your phone, Patience," he orders.

Harlan's jaw clenches in a way that disfigures him. It's night now, so he switches on the lamp on my end table by the TV. My table clock reads seven forty-five, meaning the rehearsal is fifteen minutes in. Maybe if I'm unresponsive long enough, Mom might swing by to check up on me.

I stay on the floor as I sit in a huddle with my knees pulled up to my chest. Gotta think, think!

"Did you hear me?"

"Obviously."

"So then, give it up. Or I'll come over there and take it."

"I thought you said that you would never hurt me again," I say with my actress tears forming. "Now it's all you ever do."

Harlan crosses his legs and gestures with empty hands. "People have to be held accountable. Including you."

"Accountable. How rich."

"Is it?"

"Kinda. I have a theory." I speak fastidiously, making sure this prick takes in every word. "It wasn't drugs that made you go after Tori last year. It was all you. And maybe what saved her was you going apeshit in front of other people, almost exposing all your craziness. You probably tried to play it off as best as you could. Like blaming it on whatever substances you took. But when it came down to it, you couldn't keep your hooks stuck into Tori anymore. Am I close?"

Harlan bites his nails in a brusque manner. "Which answer will make you sleep soundly at night the easiest?"

Oh, how it pays to listen. I wish I knew then what I know now. It could have changed everything.

"I'm not giving you my phone."

"That's what you think, sweetness."

Mabel comes to mind now. She's lucky. Not only with finding Carl, but by sharing this warped maternal bond with Harlan after they slept together. I have a feeling... he came too close before with Mabel, popping out those fangs of his in front of her. Harlan never wanted to risk losing his chosen mom or disappointing her, which kept her safe.

"You're getting sloppy. A wolf in sheep's clothing sticks out like a sore thumb when their wool finally snags on a tree branch. Once it does, Harlan McCandles won't be able to hide in plain sight anymore. We—me and Tori—see you. And Kenji... Soon, even he won't be able to make excuses for you. You've given him a few sneak peeks of your true nature already."

Harlan ties his hair up and takes an exhausted breath.

"Who gives a shit? We won't be seeing them anymore after tonight," he says. His fingers lightly brush over the pillow tassels from the couch, as if it's a precious keepsake. "You're the perfect contradiction. You wanted out of your boring little life, and now you're nestled in my lurid one, like a venus fly trap. It's somewhat meta, isn't it? The escapee who tries to escape the escape."

"Harlan—people who do what you're doing—police will need to address what's happening soon."

"Christ, Patience. Think that's going to help your case to make me let you go?"

"I don't know. I don't know anything anymore."

"I know plenty." Harlan gets up and immediately strong-arms me to the floor.

I kick and swing, but he sucks in each striking hit. After yanking my phone from my back pocket, he pulls up my shirt halfway to expose my prism tattoo. Then he lustfully flicks the outline with his tongue.

"Get off of me, you freak!"

"That was a quality in me you liked in the beginning, no?" he taunts.

"Stop it, this isn't right!"

"Now... I think it's high time to cut the cord with these bracelets, don't you?"

"Noooo!"

Harlan yanks my bangles off and gold hoops fly everywhere,

bringing sparkle to a dreary situation.

And he finally sees it—forcing his lips into the thinnest grimace. "Hmm. I thought as much. Why didn't you say anything?" He lets go of my mouth to speak.

I keep sniveling and witness being violated, yet having no choice but to cooperate for my safety. "It wasn't yours to know or experience. It was mine, and like everything else, you stole that from me, too."

"But you don't need to hide from me," Harlan lessens his coldness. "Not anymore."

"Just leave, and we can pretend this never happened."
"You thought you could write me off after everything I've done for—"

"I felt scared!"
"Of what?"
"You!"
I might have shared that too soon.

"Thanks for the honesty. Only wish I didn't have to drag it out of you," Harlan says, snatching more gold hoops from me and tossing them across the room, one by one. "You gave me the impression you could take on my ferocity. My baggage. Or was that a lie, too?"

"Hey... don't—I can't—can't breathe!" My panic attack rears its ugly head.

"Patience..."
"Whatever y-you're... thinking of doing, don't—don't do it!"

"Hey, right over here," Harlan commands, but there's a gentleness in it.

I force my eyes open and see him. His smell gags me. It must have been days since he last took a shower.
"Breathe in with me. Slowly. We've done this before, kid." I want to live, but not on his terms.

Harlan inhales deeply, and I try to follow as his weight bears onto me even more. The air scrapes painfully through my throat. I face the truth of what we are and hate myself for relying on him to get me through this part.

"There you go," he says—a heroic feat accomplished in his head. He sits back on his heels and watches me—proud of himself, as if I should be grateful. "It's not like I've done anything to you yet."

Yet?! "You broke in."

"I had to see you."

"Please let me go! Forget what I said before. I won't tell anybody!"

"You sure you won't tell?"

"I won't! I won't!"

"Shh, shh... when you're this pathetic, how could I say no to you?" Harlan kisses my naked wrist genially, with me still on the ground, unable to move. "But you're mine, Patience. Indisputably, irrevocably, mine."

I try to peel him off, but his muscularity is unmatched. "Why are you doing this to me?!"

"You said I could keep you. Words straight from your luscious lips, remember?" he enunciates distinctly, savoring the words.

"You're crazy! If that's true, I didn't mean it. I was blazed out of my mind or in the middle of... whatever! And you knew that!"

A joke. A throwaway line, barely a thought, lost in the night's high. But for Harlan, apparently, an eternal vow.

"What's with that face you're making? That lost-deer-in-the-headlights look? Just stop it. Stop waiting for someone to come and save you. You don't know what real pain is—or what

it can make you do just to keep going. Dammit, Patience—
you're not even innocent in all this! Nothing is ever your fault, is
it?" he says nastily. "Is it?! Not your shitty marriage or your
pity party of a miscarriage—"

"*Fuck you!*"

"In due time. Be woman enough to admit you had a role in
making me this way. You're my creator, baby. Own it. I have
nothing else to lose."

Me—the wife, then the Jezebel, now the captive. I'm
believing maybe I *am* the architect of my imprisonment. "It
doesn't have... have to go this far."

"Oh no, it's not that simple. You're in me, everywhere.
Don't you think I tried getting you out? It fucking hurts! Get it?!
Like battery acid on my skin—it hurts me... to love you. To love
someone so goddamn selfish. You're a curse. No one else stood
a chance before. But... I do. And I will break you before I let you
break me."

"Harlan, no."

"*Yes!*" A line of drool escapes from him and attaches to my
cheek. "Since you left, my work has been nothing but shit. How
can I create my abstracts if I'm infested with thoughts of
Patience—in my bed and in my monochrome world? We're
inextricably linked to each other because of our child. And—
Look at me! Didn't I take good care of you when you had
nothing? Huh?! Here I am, making the best of it, and you
choose to pull the plug on us? Think again. Call it facing the
consequences and paying your dues. I don't want to let you go,
and I shouldn't have to."

Harlan sobs heavily into my chest and presses against my
ribs as though trying to crawl inside me. His hands clutch at my
back, with fingers digging in hard enough to bruise.

"But I don't want to be with you anymore!"

"For Christ's sake... I'm not Harlan without you."

He kisses me with my lips held in his manic capture. Then he parts away for a bit, with his fingers brushing the zipper on my jeans. "Want and crave with me, like before. Remember how good I used to make you feel, Patience? I can do it again, I promise—nothing's changed. You're trembling now, but wait till—"

"I told you—I don't like it when you touch me!"

"You'll learn to."

Another act that will never be my story.

It'll always end the same, with me being destroyed and wondering how I got here to begin with. The taboo nature of Harlan's hold against my will brings the focal point home.

Scheme by any means necessary.

"Ow! Biting? Are you kidding?!" Harlan roars, holding me down firmly. My teeth managed to nick his top lip. "Are you trying to make it turn unpleasant?"

"Nobody talks like this to people!" I wriggle under his weight.

"And nobody tastes like saffron but you."

I spit in Harlan's face, scratch his cheek, and go for it. Quick, yes! Now!

I make it to about three steps to the door before he seizes me by the leg, and I come crashing to the floor.

"Yeah, I get it—you had to try it once, right?" Harlan puts me in a chokehold and squeezes away. My five-foot frame immediately crumbles underneath him. "Get it out of your system, yet?! Huh?!"

"Please—please... don't kill me." The more I thrash, the louder he grunts.

"What great big manners she has."

"You—won't—do—it..."

"Your voice cutting out says otherwise, Patience."

I should save my strength, but this might resonate with him in order to survive. "But you need me... and you need to be needed."

All around me turns into black static. Harlan's grunting slowly abates. "You'll realize... everything I did... I did it for my shining sun."

"I'm dying... God... help."

"God? Oh, God?! Hmm. Nope. God isn't here."

My legs grow weak as Harlan bullies me some more.

"But soon... soon I'll teach you to worship me like one. You'll see."

* * *

"Mom....?" I call out, still static-brained.

The TV is on. I hear rummaging in my bedroom closet, and soon after, Harlan steps out with a suitcase. "Good, you're up," he says without looking at me. "We'll leave in a few minutes."

"Leave?" I exclaim. "Leave for where?"

"New Mexico. Already applied for and accepted a job to teach... meh, high school art. I know, I know, but hear me out... Beggars can't be choosers. Your teaching career is on a definite hiatus, though, so settling on becoming a mom should come first."

I wonder if Harlan hears himself when he speaks. Like, really listens. Does he truly believe the delusions that flow from him so easily? Or does he only do it to push his victims to their limit?

It's only when I try to get up from the living room floor that

I realize I'm tied up, bound wrist to ankles.

Please let this be a regular nightmare. I would love to see an ink demon greeting me from my bedroom for once. That way, waking up from these horrors is achievable.

There's only so much victimhood I can handle. Not knowing what's around the corner for me with what Harlan has planned makes my flesh creep.

"It's only temporary," he comments on the rope. "Sorry, but you're going to have to earn privileges in order for this to work, Patience."

All right, the aim now is to distract him. Say anything that may stall his plans long enough to get help.

Or, it will go in a bleak direction entirely.

"What about my family, my friends? They'll worry about me if I'm not heard from."

He gives me a look that says I don't have the faintest clue. "Cute. Still, I wouldn't worry. I took care of texting folks who needed a time-sensitive update."

No more half-measures. Drive it home to where it'll really get to him. "Marsha will call if she doesn't hear that I've made it safely away from you. We don't talk through text."

Harlan stops mid packing and becomes peeved. He takes out my phone and shoves it in my face. "Then, if I were you, I'd better send her a DM saying you're perfectly fine and a picture showing your best fraudulent self. Don't you agree? Should be easy enough, since you idiot bitches like to gossip among yourselves."

"No, don't. You can't make me do this!"

His horns couldn't protrude any farther. "I'm not asking twice."

"I'm allowed to no longer want you," I say, not backing

down. "That I know the full capacity of your monstrous ways. I'm allowed to forgive myself for letting your hooks stay fixed. Because, thanks to my new support system... your existence means less than nothing to me!"

Harlan backhands me across the face, and I see stars. The hit leaves a searing welt on my nose.

"You slapping me... is just proving my point."

"So what? It's not like your face is pregnant. It's your own damn fault. You got me out of character!"

He doesn't even try to hide his reprehensible behavior anymore. Still—even after today—I've faced worse.

"You've always been that character, Harlan."

His energy changes, and it seems I've found his weakness. He no longer looks like Prince Charming in his crafted scenario.

"Shit... hang on." Harlan stomps to the kitchen, wets a napkin under the sink, and comes forward. I prepare myself, hearing each step and squeak.

"Shush, hush now. It's okay..." He wipes the blood off my nose with such care, then kisses the welt. "Just like that, you're beautiful again. But see what you do to me? You're worse than kryptonite, yet I can't stay away."

My Jekyll and Hyde, he flips. Accusations turn to kind words, a bruising hit to a gentle touch.

Harlan stares but doesn't see who I am, not really. I'm just a pawn in the hollow fantasy he's constructed in his head. "There she is. Better?"

I'm stiff as a post but nod.

"Now, can you call her for me?"

"You asked twice. So, no."

"I said call her!" he yells again. "Stop being reckless with your life for once."

And he's back.

I thought he would forget about me completely, letting me fade away with the parade of muses he chased in the past. Wrong, deadass wrong. So, Patience, stick to the goal. Delay the drive to New Mexico as much as possible. Once an abductor takes their victim to the next location, it's all over. "You're worse than a psychopath and a sociopath. You're a quenchless void that takes and takes."

Harlan turns off the TV and examines my rope knots. "I'm not a fan of this slack here. Simple fix. Don't think you're getting out of it. Once I finish this and wrap up packing, you're calling her on the road." He squats and tightens my ropes.

"Harlan—it's not a good look for you. Think about it. You're a white guy."

"Thanks. You saved me a bill from ancestry.com."

"Who's obsessed with me! Who, instead of making honest efforts to get to know about my background, cultural ties, and who I am as a person, you get your jollies by isolating me from my friends and family, and you order me around and keep me all to yourself. All for the sake of seeing how it serves you. And when you don't get your way, you throw a tantrum and try to punish me. In America's history of events, does any of that seem familiar to you?"

I see a new expression on his face I've never encountered before, and it's intriguing. "It's admirable you're trying this hard and stuff. But you're still grasping at straws here."

But distracting you works for me, dumbass.

"Okay. Then grasp you're still that insecure, fifteen-year-old boy who couldn't get over a crush on his stepsister. Who uses the same demented *muse* and *good girl* tagline over and over with others... with me... It's sad. Certifiable, hands down. Sheila must be proud."

"What the hell did you say?"

Too far. Too far. Pull it back some.

"No—no, spit it out, it's fine. I want to make sure my ears aren't playing tricks on me," he says. Harlan's new tranquil turn is a whole other level. He pulls my legs under his and cups his hands to my face tightly, to an intolerable degree.

"Were you just referencing my deceased mother? Because if so—you know you're coming to blows with a certifiable person such as myself, correct? Don't think any bullshit self-defense class on every other Tuesday will cut it. Make no mistake, I'm a man. I will overpower you and gladly come after your family, Obinna, Neisa, or anyone else you ever loved. Remember—don't present a challenge for me, because it's an invitation to try."

Harlan shoves me off of him, looking up at my art piece above my television. It's a vibrant acrylic, messy and striking. Also a product of those glorious, free months after I left Harlan for good. "You must've had quite the girl power moment, painting this one, huh?" he says with an impish smile.

To my horror, he pulls out a box cutter, approaching the abstract. "If you were to ask me, I think being humble suits you much better."

"Don't you dare, you son of a bitch. Don't!" My abstract dedicated to the child that never was—called *Miracle Okoye*—is near his constant state of flux.

"That mouth of yours—as satisfying as it is from time to time—will get you in hot water one day. My handy tool here ain't just for cuttin' boxes. Keep it up, and your wrists may need extra bangles."

Harlan yanks the painting off the wall, and the canvas rips with a sickening screech. I flinch, the sound echoing the wrath I wish to release onto him. His ongoing need to exert power means the work I hold near to my heart has to suffer.

"Remember, I gave you the ability to think you could create. And I can take it away just as easily."

RIP!

Before I can react, he slashes the canvas, and a shower of many-hued flakes rains down on the carpet.

She's being taken from me—from a senseless reaction all over again.

I watch on, eclipsing Harlan's hatred of the thought of me thriving without him.

"Don't you sit there crying, now," he says, throwing the fresh canvas confetti in my hair. "There's more where that came from, or have you forgotten how prolific you were while I was gone?"

"I didn't expect to feel this way."

"Elaborate."

Ugh. I have no other choice. "Embarrassed. I can't hide the fact that I actually love you, too, anymore."

Harlan is visibly dumbstruck by my confession, tossing the box cutter aside on my coffee table. "Don't play with me."

"I said I love you. You. I love... you, Harlan. Our history is unmatched." I straighten up as much as I can, even while bound, so he can read me fully. "It's what you've always wanted, right? Me? None of this is necessary. I'm here and not going anywhere."

I didn't think it would be that easy; with Harlan, you never know. But he crawls to me—the same way he did when I was in the tub with a wounded back—and tugs on my ropes. "Say it again. You look so good tied up when you do."

Bastard. Hurt him where he lives, and most importantly, nab the box cutter. "See I could, ever so perfectly... but... just because someone says something over and over... like me going to New Mexico with you... *Doesn't make it true, asshole!*"

"What?!"

Say it with your whole chest, Patience.

"I don't love you, and I never will. You were... cheap, drug-fueled excitement, expected to expire at any minute. I used you to try to get over someone who... Well, someone who *you* could never touch. The more drugs that were funneled down my throat, the more control you had over me—it's a brilliant concept when you think about it. I couldn't leave until hitting an all-time low. After peeling back the layers, you reek of being an unfulfilled man child. Yeah. That's why they always leave. So, tell me, who's the idiot bitch now?"

THUNK!

"Argh!"

I headbutt him and leap for the box cutter—but I'm off by a few seconds.

THWACK!

...and end up with an agonizing punch to the cheekbone.

"Fucking slut!" Harlan grabs me by the neck and forces me onto the loveseat. "I see we're still whoring ourselves out like nothing's changed. You have a lot of nerve. You think you're better than me?! Better than this?!"

"I know I am. And make up your mind already. Am I beautiful and the love of your life? Or am I a bitch, a whore, or a slut? I never know with you. Hell. Pick. One."

Harlan lets go and straightens up. His once full, light blond hair is now greasy from tonight's events. "You always seem to get the rise out of me you're looking for, to where... Damn, maybe it's really *you* who owns *me*. But with that said... I'm over the interruptions. I tried to be civil about this, but you've just earned yourself some tape and a sock for your troubles."

I land on my bottom after Harlan throws me off the couch like a ragdoll. He runs in my room to find supplies to gag me with, not without angrily knocking over my cleaning caddy by the kitchen wastebasket. With a big clatter, a can of Raid roach spray rolls all the way to my feet. Wait, yes! Another plan! I grab it, then use the mildly sharp spray tab to cut at and loosen one of my bound wrists.

I shift the can up my shirt and sit upright to face my room door. He's angry, but I need a reason for proximity to him. My insides churn at the thought of it... but it may be life or death for me—so tough.

"Harlan! If—if we're gonna do this, let's do this right!"

I peek at him from the corner, watching him yank extension cords with violent rips. "I'm in the middle of damage control, so..."

"Please—why can't anyone understand that I'm scared!?" I put on an act as if my life were literally depending on it. "I don't want to be a mom. It's going to be too hard!"

Got him. Harlan looks at me, bunches the cords in his hands, and comes over. But not touching—he keeps a distance of four feet.

"Do you ever know what you're doing with your life? Like ever?" he asks, somewhat sincerely. "It's tiring to watch you flounder, Patience."

"I'm sorry."

"For what?"

"All of it," I say, buttering him up. I continue to watch him lean closer to me to crouch down in a sitting position. "For not being grateful."

"How can I trust a single word you say after the shit you just pulled?"

"You got under my skin, so I got under yours. I broke the miniature statues Kelsey gave you, so you ripped up my abstract."

"Huh, what are you talking about—"

"Stop already, it's okay. You slept with Kelsey after my visit to Obinna's and submitting my art to Colby against your wishes. Getting even is what we do."

Impassivity strikes Harlan. "Gotta keep things spicy every once in a while, don't we?"

"Right. Living for the push and pull. But... if we can stop the bullshit and learn to lean on each other, you could be my fresh start. Let's branch out and be great artists—maybe even more. Together. I wasn't ready then, but I'm ready now. Only... don't get in the way of us again."

Harlan nods approvingly but still watches for any surprises. "Not an outlandish thought, Okoye. There's one thing you have to do for me first."

He scoots down to the floor, inches away from me. Perfect. His ego hasn't grown past my flattery yet. If I can hop onto his upper body and spray the Raid directly in his eyes, a head-start to make a run for it is in the works.

Speaking of eyes, Harlan's are night and day from when we first met. Red and splotchy veins scatter around his yellow-tinted pupils. The blue and green gems of his eyes are now dulled and lackluster. There's no telling when the last time he slept was.

"You said you never loved me, ever. But I have doubts. Is that true?"

I do not plan for the somatic revulsion I have for his request. But I'm so close.

"Um…"

"A good muse—a good girl—does as she's told. So, say it."

The can of Raid cools the temperature that rises within my body. I can no longer perform for him. There's no giving him another piece of me and still being able to raise my head high.

Harlan grows irate, clicks his tongue, and grabs at the cords.

"I thought you were smarter than this," he says, wrapping them around my neck. "Time to sleep. We'll be in New Mexico the minute you wake up."

With every bit of energy I can muster, I slip the Raid spray out of my shirt and into my free hand, then smash the base of the can into Harlan's left ear. And he is absolutely livid.

"I'll crack your skull, you cunt!"

"Good luck finding me."

I spray every poisonous drop into his field of vision. Harlan writhes in agony and tries to run but tumbles into the coffee table because of his hindered sight. The glass shatters beneath him, with shards flying everywhere. He flails blindly and knocks over the side table lamp—almost putting us in pitch black darkness. I untie myself as fast as I can and kick over the other lamp by the TV.

Good, disorient him.

"Patience! Where the fuck are you?!" Harlan bellows. He reaches out and grabs the closest thing he can—a large, jagged piece of glass. Just what I need. He's back to blocking the doorway. "Feeling like you're so goddamn clever, huh?!" Harlan swings the shard around like a wild animal—eyes inflamed and squeezed shut. Dammit. He's too far gone.

"Harlan, stop!"

"There you are, bitch."

There's another loud *whoosh* as he swings the glass in the air, narrowly missing my face.

Quit talking. He'll find you.

"Think I'll just let you walk out of here?" Harlan is moving in circles now, still trying to listen for my movements. He's a rabid dog with intent to kill, so I try my best not to tread on any glass and make a crunch. "I'll take you to New Mexico in pieces if I have to."

He leaves the doorway and makes quick stabs, ripping up the loveseat.

Try now.

I make a run toward my front door but accidentally step on hidden littered glass along the way. Shit! He's more agile than I thought. Harlan turns around, pounces, and senses his target on the move.

Get down!

His weapon of choice aims in my direction, and I suddenly see my whole life flash before my eyes.

Swoosh!

"Nuh—"

He got me.

I have a deep cut on my palm, but I stifle my cries and screams. My body rolls to the right corner of the kitchen, and I swallow the torment.

Harlan makes his second lap around the living room. His nostrils are flared wide, and he looks partially anemic.

Aim for his legs. Do what you have to do, but quickly.

"Come out!" he roars and spins toward where he thinks I

am. He's close, too close. The shard swipes around my living room in his death grip. "I swear to God, I will fuck you with this, then disembowel you with it!"

Crouching under him and holding my breath, I hit his shins with all my might, using the bug spray can.

"Argh!" Harlan's down on the ground with one strike. I kick the glass shard out of his threatening grasp.

Wham! Wham! Wham!

I'm smashing the back of his head with the base of the can over and over. Blood from my cut hand splats out with each attack, making the can slippery.

He's earned the right to receive eight months of what I've pent-up because of him.

Huh?

The can is bent.

Pssh, fuck the can.

Finishing what Marsha's dad started years ago, I stomp on his ribs, his stomach, and anywhere else I can think of that would leave a mark bigger than what Harlan sought for me.

"I... belong to no one—least of all you. Not now, not ever. Say it! Admit it!"

"Urgh..."

"Now!"

"Was talking... t-talking s-shit earlier... that's all..." He lets out sounds similar to a dying whale. "P-Patience... hold on— stop and let's—"

"Shut up!" my foot lands against his tailbone. "You were going to rape me in my apartment! Then hurt me and take me who knows where!"

"N-no, I just wanted... wanted to r-remind you... how great we had it, and the great shit... we created b-because of it.

Baby... things... just... just got outta hand... like before. T-Talk to me..."

"There's nothing to fucking talk about!"

CRACK!

My foot dashes across his mouth. His teeth—with a likeness to Dracula's—rain and spatter onto my carpet. Harlan spits, and I see more fragments of white bone fly out, becoming broken ivory. He spouts even more crimson, as if he were a rotary sprinkler, creating a new abstract I never intended to. I don't stop. I kick him again, this time square in the jaw. There's another crack that's louder, deeper. His jaw pops, almost echoing a cherry bomb, and he howls in agony while blood is bubbling between his fingers. Harlan moves but slothfully, and tries to block my blows with his arms—still helpless on the floor. His lips are split wide open, his nose crooked, and some remaining teeth dangle on fleshy strings from his bulging, bright-red gums. Those same gums share the appearance of lumpy, uncooked ground beef.

"C-Come on... I... I can't... see... it burns," he gurgles and blubbers. "I'm swallowing... my-my own teeth here... goddammit... c-can't take any-anymore..."

I grab him by his hair and yank him forward. "You'll learn to."

Then his groaning stops.

Now for the back of the head.

You're going too far.

No, I'm just getting started. Maybe I'll rip his face off like in my dreams.

You'll kill him.

For what he had in store for me? That would be a kindness.

Know your limit. Walk away before it changes you for good.

But hurting him—

Feels good, yes. But killing him? You might not think so now, but in that way—he'll own you forever. Now go.

I stop and leave him with this.

"I'm a complete person... by myself... outside of you... remember that, fucker."

Harlan isn't responding, but blood pools out of his ear. The hell am I waiting for—get out!

I run out of the apartment to locate help, police, and am thankful as hell for my mild roach infestation.

FULL CIRCLE

The relief I had when the sirens sounded poured over me and became a tidal wave.

At the station, the officers were kind, but the process felt like an eternity. I went over every creepy detail with my past screams still raw in my throat and went through it all over again. But as I walked out into the crisp night air with Mom, I realized I wasn't alone anymore.

It started as a trickle, then turned into a flood.

Other women came forward and reported Harlan for several offenses after I pressed charges.

However, the statute of limitations wiped most of them.

And seeing him on the news brought up another matter.

I watched my nightmare plastered across the screen, and it fueled me, a constant reminder of how lucky I was. The news report crackled on, detailing his actions at Colby with Kelsey and other students that were left unnamed. Harlan's eyes looked unnaturally red, and his mouth, swollen as a catcher's mitt, yet he appeared calm with where he would be going.

I returned to that night, the way his hands flew to his eyes, clawing at them as he screeched from the poisonous bug spray. Hmm. On TV, he seemed too accepting, as though I hadn't done enough to hurt him. I wanted to cause harm all over again. So, I pictured myself grabbing the box cutter. Sharp and lethal. I sliced through the air, right across those pupils of his. They had split open with the white part rupturing first, spilling a milky fluid. His eyeballs turned to lopsided slits in the sudden burst of pain. Blood followed—dark and fast—pooling in the creases of his skin. Harlan's eyelids— those fucking arrogant eyelids that once closed in mockery— shredded like thin fabric, exposing the mess underneath.

But being unconscious, with bug spray sitting in his sockets and eating away at his vision—slowly but surely—works, too.

I turned off the TV and wanted to remember him that way from now on.

Outsmarted.

My Snapchat work group blew up with heartfelt messages, checking up on me like a no nonsense nurse. Neisa gave birth to her daughter, Raelyn, and was a wailing emotional mess on the phone after she heard about the kidnap attempt. She demanded I stay with her in California permanently as a nanny for her kids. If I were still looking to run away from my problems, I might've taken her offer. But nope, I'm on to reaching more considerable heights in my journey to self-restoration.

On that journey, an unexpected connection had shined through, rooted in knowing McCandles. Kenji covered every one of my tattoo removal sessions at his shop and apologized during each visit. "My fault, Patience. Shit, if I knew you were on something, I never would've inked you," he said, shaking his head. "Yeah, you were quieter that night, but when he and Roxy kept saying you were fine—and you didn't push back—I figured it was cool."

I nodded and gritted my teeth through the cuttings zaps.

"Has he reached out to anybody? Has anyone visited like Jayson or...?"

Kenji looked at me as if I splashed garbage water on him. "Are you kidding me!? Not gonna happen. Just when you think you know someone, right? I'm done with that asshole."

When he finished, I pulled my shirt back down and shook his hand. "No hard feelings, Kenji. He lied to me plenty of times, too."

He gave a hearty fist pump. "So tell me."

"Tell you what?"

"How's it feel to be the girl on the news... who officially fucked up Harlan McCandles?"

I soothed my tingling, faded tattoo with my fingers. "Like I should have done it sooner."

"Look who's getting feisty," Kenji teased. "But seriously, you don't gotta treat this like it's your origin story. You're not a DC villain just because you fell for the wrong guy. Just do what I do and keep it moving."

"Keep it moving? Aww, I was thinking we could start a crime stopping podcast together," I kidded around. "You gonna bail on all the juicy details?"

"A douchebag getting his ass handed to him? Ha! I'll make an exception for sweet justice. Hell, yeah."

"Hell, yeah, is right."

Then we fist bumped.

He was finally free from being the annoying kid brother— no longer hiding in Harlan's shadow.

Kenji Sato for the win.

Not long after, Tori also reached out with condolences. Her Instagram message, of all things, left me pleasantly surprised.

...you're definitely a doer, not a watcher. Way to take him

down, babe. You're my shero, Patience.

I moved back home with Mom after Harlan took the plea deal. It bothered me to see her cry and blame herself for not coming over to check on me the minute I was late for rehearsal. What she doesn't get is that it was probably for the best. Who knows what he would have done if she had shown up in the middle of it?

Fortunately, I'll never know.

I didn't want to go a day without talking to Mom again. So, while living with her, we're making up for lost time.

"Man, out of amethyst."

June heat isn't kind to my acrylics, and I missed painting with watercolors. Lately, my theme has been nature, primarily flowers and river banks. It's fine to take a break from the abstracts every once in a while. Not everything needs to be a guessing game. Sometimes the straightforward stuff is just as delightful.

"Patience, try not to have my house smelling like a bloody nail salon when I get back," Mom says on her way out to evening service at New Haven. "This hobby of yours will have me using a respirator before my seventies. God forbid!"

"Love you too, Mom."

"Yes, well—with that said..." She lingers by the doorway and quells her boldness. "Your artwork does uplift my spirits, dear."

Woah, my mother's growth keeps evolving and knows no bounds. "Hope you have a great service, okay?"

"Thank you. Enjoy your time to yourself. There is no one more deserving of it than you."

The front door closes, and I'm back to it. I sit on the floor of the living room, legs crossed, with an oversized tie dye

T-shirt swallowing my arms. My colors are scattered across the coffee table in little plastic trays, as each hue is ready to leap onto the page. Getting used to stability takes effort, but I know it will come soon. The faded patch on my belly makes me ecstatic that I'm done with Kenji's painful tattoo removal sessions. Harlan's mark on me has finally lifted.

My phone lights up, and I receive a message from Marsha. Sure, I could use a break.

@MarshaJ: What the hell, he got 5 years?

@PatOkoye: that's what happens when you take a plea deal for attempted kidnapping in the state of Texas

@MarshaJ: How are you feeling?

@PatOkoye: You might want to clear your meetings before I answer that

@MarshaJ: Seriously

@PatOkoye: Fine. In one word, numb.

@MarshaJ: That's normal

@PatOkoye: Like it doesn't feel like he's gone. And that he can still get to me at any time.

@MarshaJ: He should have gotten the death penalty.

@PatOkoye: I should've called the cops a long time ago and left a paper trail

@MarshaJ: Don't do that. Don't hold yourself responsible for his actions. I've been there too. We've all felt the same way. Then we finally came together to stop him.

@PatOkoye: Guess he had a diagnosis after all

@MarshaJ: which they were lenient about to a fault

@PatOkoye: Being Bi-Polar and having Borderline Personality Disorder explains a lot

@MarshaJ: I knew something was up with him back then.

But being bipolar and having BPD is just the tip of the iceberg. There's much more abhorrent underneath with him.

@PatOkoye: agreed.

@MarshaJ: So enough about that guy. He's been camping out in your life for far too long and you need to start anew

@PatOkoye: Thank you. I will.

@MarshaJ: Everything will be okay

@PatOkoye: It is now

@MarshaJ: And do me a favor

@PatOkoye: Yeah?

@MarshaJ: Keep your friends and family posted, okay? I don't think they realize how close they came to losing you.

* * *

Hell finally froze over, and Obinna reached out through WhatsApp to check on me today. I can't stop pinching myself as I wait in line for my tea. The separation that was filed before made me believe that a day like this would never come. Yet here we are, soon to sip boba and try to navigate the wreckage of our marriage.

Ugh, he said six-thirty, and it's a minute till, so why am I close to shitting bricks?

"Order 1632! Green tea with boba and lychee?"

"Here, thanks."

I grab my tea and find an empty booth inside the boba shop, called Sweetie Pop. The sugary aroma of tapioca pearls and fruit teas hangs in my nose. As I wrap my bandaged hand around the cup, feeling the coldness prickling into my skin, I can't help but soothe the itchy stitches in my palm.

There are mostly couples here of various ages—old, young,

and in between. Either way, they send reminders of what I've lost, and how I fumbled the ball at legitimate love.

So, all I'm able to do is to stir the colorful beads in my drink absentmindedly.

As six-thirty-two hits the next minute mark, I rethink every juncture that led me here. But when Obinna walks through the door, those thoughts disappear.

"Obi, over here!" I wave him down.

Obi turns to me, and I'm unsure if he's walking on sunshine over today's visit.

He looks so damn good though, wearing a fitted black Draco Collection sweatsuit. His haircut stands out, too, as I see a clean fade with 360 waves.

"Hey, Pat." Obinna slides into the booth seat across from me. "How, uh—how are you holding up?"

"I'm okay," I say, sipping jelly chunks through my enlarged straw. "It's only... I just wasn't expecting to hear from you."

Obinna takes his phone from his back pocket and looks over at the menu. "If you would've said that a couple months ago, I would've thought the same thing." He then punches his order through the Sweetie Pop app.

"Oh." I slump into my seat, disconsolately.

"But you seem good. You look good, and so does your latest artwork."

"Oh, but how did you—"

"Neisa sent me some pics she got from your Pinterest. What you have going on with your paintings is outstanding. I only wish..."

"Go ahead."

"We could have discovered that talent together."

Oh, Obinna. Coming in heavy with the guilt trips already.

"Thanks. Me, too. Well, um, how's Pongers and Priya?"

"Priya's enjoying her engagement. Glad she could find someone to put up with her. But Darrian will need the jaws of life to unwrap her head around signing a prenup."

"Good for her!" And it feels even better to say it and actually mean it.

"Pongers is… okay. She's an old gal now, so she has mild glaucoma, but it's expected. Actually, I'm thinking of having more of a fixed specialty soon. Like only focusing on small animals en route to the clinic, instead of doing farm calls for large animals. And I know what you're thinking: why couldn't I have done that when we were still together?"

"Order 1737! Black milk tea with red bean sauce!"

"Hang on. That's me."

As Obi goes to grab his order, I think back to the moment it went left between us. The Obi I needed so much to mourn our loss left me with a vacant house instead. So, was there ever a way I could have predicted the last ten months to happen? No way. But Obinna, in spite of it all, didn't shake me off like expected.

"Back." He plops down again. "Brought napkins in case."

"Obi, I straight up have no right to be mad at you about work. I put you through so much."

He hangs his head low and doesn't speak immediately after.

"It was wrong." I keep going and want him to listen and not just hear me. "I completely see that, and I'm so sorry."

"I have a question," Obi resumes.

"What?"

"What made you run into his arms and let him take you from me?"

I cough loudly into my straw at the question. "Do you think

it's a good idea we're doing this?"

Obi sits back, with his hands in his pockets. "Wouldn't ask if that wasn't the case."

"You stopped calling me Nami. Ever noticed that?"

"Nope."

"Remember what you used to say sometimes after you did?"

Obi buries his face in his elbow, totally embarrassed. "Aww, no, please... please don't make me relive how unbelievably lame I was, I'm begging you."

"You said, '*Apparently, Luffy wasn't the only one chasing treasure the night we met.*'" I tease, reminding him anyway.

Obi snickers and scratches his neck. "Ha, *One Piece*. Corny ass shit." Then he winks. "But not too corny, I see. I still snagged you."

Time to get serious, Patience. "I needed tenderness. A lot. When I said that, you told me I wanted too much. I became a clinger or a bloodsucker, trying to attach to you. Here I was, going through one of the most awful times in my life, and wanted my soulmate to be there. The same soulmate who told me how I showed my love was all wrong."

"So, I was inattentive and insensitive."

"At times."

"That's all?"

"I feel like we lost our way to each other."

Obi pounds the table and clicks his tongue. "Who would have thought I turned out to be my dad, after all?"

He catches the lost look on my face. "Patience, did you know I can count the number of times I cried in my life on one hand?"

"No."

"Crying for the sake of simply being devastated is unheard

of in our families. Like, if no one died, save your tears and such. So, even when the miscarriage happened, my dad told me to nut up. Taking on extra work hours was my way of doing that. I thought I was being strong for the both of us, not neglecting you."

My heart swells from his point of view. I had no clue, and it explains so much. "You're not your dad. There's so much more to you than you think, which was why I married you and never thought I was good enough."

Obinna twirls his straw around in his busy tea. "You were more than good enough, Patience. But I guess I wasn't."

So not true.

"Does it hurt to love me? What I mean is... Do you regret our marriage, Obinna?"

"I think a question like that needs more time and thought before answering."

Don't even start. He has all the reason in the world to feel that way. "Okay."

Obinna looks me directly in the face, intending for his message to stick. "You shattered us."

"I hate myself every day because of it."

"That's the thing. Hearing that should make me feel better, right? But it doesn't."

The loud, draining slurp from my straw signals that my tea is gone. "Why not?"

"You know why. Like, why do you think I reached out?"

Still clueless over here. "I figured Neisa kept you in the loop."

Obinna sighs in disappointment and takes my hands from under the table. His are so flat and wide, like leather mittens. "No, because even though I wanted to hate you as much as I could, I couldn't do it. That's why I filed for a separation and not a divorce, hoping that maybe one day we would come out of it fine. With the loss of our baby, you weren't in your right mind. Neither of us were. But then I had days when I thought, so the fuck what? Why make it that easy for her to come back after what she did?"

"I'm sorry."

"Yeah, I know. You said that already."

Knock it off. Before the words themselves lose their meaning. "I used to visit you, or rather—visit the townhome in the middle of the night to see what you were up to."

Obinna squints as he listens. "Oh. Damn. Didn't expect that update, to say the least."

"Were you... ever seeing anybody, then? How about now?"

"Uh, that's kind of private, Patience."

"My bad."

"It's okay."

We're two people who have weathered hurricanes and celebrated sunshine... our story, still being written as we speak. I don't want any of it to end, but we're out of tea and chewy boba. Therefore, what's next?

"Can I visit Pongers? I miss her so much and wanna see her in person."

Obinna hesitates and shoves his hands in his pockets. "Probably not a good idea," he says, his voice husky.

"I'll be in and out. Promise. Scout's honor," I persist in a low purr.

"You ain't no Scout."

"Couldn't hurt to try, could it?"

Obinna chuckles and shakes his head. "You always had a way of getting what you wanted."

Maybe that was the problem.

"Just this once," he says, leaving the booth and searching for his keys. "Let's go."

* * *

Raindrops splatter against the windshield that blur the street-lights into jagged lines of yellow. The cool night air is a welcome change from the warmth of the boba shop. We pull up at the house and emerge from both of our cars.

The townhouse looks so different, the paint crisper and the grass greener, somehow.

"You cleaned out the gutters," I note aloud. "Nice."

"Yeah, well, I try to find time." Obinna opens the front gate. "Come on."

We make our way inside, and I'm back to my old life. The kitchen is where I feel the most at peace, where I used to cook, clean, and delve into homemaking.

"You've really been busy keeping up with appearances." I trace my hands over the new backsplash above the oven. "That's fantastic, Obi."

"You're easily impressed then, because there's not much to it," Obinna states. "Pongers! Girl, where are you?"

No fur-ball in our vicinity.

"Pat, let's go to the living room. She's most likely lounging around there."

"Let's, please."

We arrive inside and sit by the fireplace.

"Pongers! Here, girl!" I try. And sure enough, the furry little scamp trots over to us happily.

"Pongy! Hi, baby! Did you miss Mama? I bet you did! That's

a good girl!"

Then I pause and nearly make myself regurgitate. Never again will those words leave my lips.

"You okay?" Obi catches my drawback.

"Yeah, I'm fine." I pet and kiss my furry companion even longer. "But has she always had this lump at the back of her neck?"

After a few minutes of prancing around, Pongers—usually a ball of boundless energy—goes to lay listlessly on the couch with her head lolling to one side.

Obinna drags out a cautious breath, then kneels beside me. "It's a tumor."

"Is it—"

"Cancerous, yeah."

I rest with the news about our fur daughter. Pongers is more than just a pet—she's a furry, goofy constant in our relationship. We got her together from the shelter five years ago. At six years old, she was already an adult, and she became a representation of our love and commitment.

What a joke I made that out to be.

Without thinking, I lean into Obinna, and he doesn't shrink from my touch.

Rather, he wraps his arms around me, his hands sending jolts and fire crackers through my pores. It's been almost a year since we were this close.

"It's okay to cry," Obinna coaxes. "I've done my fair share of that already."

"No," I exclaim, squeezing my eyes shut like a mousetrap. "No more crying. I need happy memories to keep me afloat— please."

He laughs.

"Obi, what's so funny?"

"Sorry, just thinking about when I failed organic chemistry freshman year and instead of letting me sulk about it, we went to like five anime conventions that weekend."

The early days of us were so wholesome. There was no sign of our journey landing here in sight. "Anime Matsuri was the best."

"Afraid not. A-kon was, hands down."

"Cosplaying was our love language, huh?"

Obinna plucks at his eyelashes. "My Dutch cosplay from *Black Lagoon* was pretty sweet."

"Sure was. We were unstoppable."

"But, Pat, it had nothing on your *Michiko & Hatchin* cosplay."

I flex my pretend muscles and strike a heroic pose. "Michiko was my alter ego, so it's only fair."

"It's crazy how we lost sight of these pastimes. Now we're grownups. By the way, my mom forgot about the separation for a split second and asked about you out of habit."

I miss Aunty so much. "Would it be a good idea to reach out to her?"

Obinna cringes. "I wouldn't just yet."

"Yeah, I figured. She hates me."

"I wouldn't say she hates you. Disappointed in you is more suitable."

I pray he doesn't let go of me, now that Pongers left. The picture in the far left corner of her doggy bed puts a smile on my face. "You kept up the photo of me and my 2009 Rihanna bob?"

"Yeah. How else would she know Mommy would always be with her, no matter what?"

"I would sweat out my silk press every other morning to walk across Kerr Hall, get to your dorm, then help you study."

"I don't think I ever said thank you for that." Obi doesn't disturb our embrace. He turns on the electric fireplace. "There were a lot of moments when you were selfless just because. Who would've guessed the cute, quiet girl from Maple Hall would change my life—all because I finally grew a spine, struck up a convo, and wowed you somehow."

That's easy... because it was effortless with him. But to recreate that now—where would it take us?

Our blast from the past stops suddenly at the sound of Pongers whimpering in pain.

"Come here, girl. She does this from time to time." Obinna finally lets go of me, and I watch Pongers limp to her father. "I went in for second and third opinions from other vets. But we're not sure how much time she has left, even with surgery."

A world without Pongy? Never. She was our confidante through countless movie nights and lazy Sundays. The thought of losing her feels like losing a piece of our history.

"Yeah, I thought the tears would get to you soon enough," Obi says. He hands me tissues. "Letting them out is easier."

"He just had to take this from me, too," I say darkly.

"What?"

"Time with her."

His dark eyes meet mine as I search for more. Forgiveness, perhaps? Or maybe confirmation that the woman sitting across from him isn't the same one who pulverized his trust.

"I messed up badly with you and me, huh?"

Actions speak louder than words. They damn near shriek to the moon.

"Patience, when I found you in the bathroom that day, with blood everywhere... It was one of the worst days of my life."

"I know."

"No, you don't!" Obinna lashes out. "You don't, because I was the one who found you with your wrists slit open. And I had to watch my wife get a 5150 hold in a hospital for three days. You wanna talk about how we never address things? Why didn't you come to me when you felt it was all getting to be hopeless?"

I travel to the moment I made such a final decision. My rationale was—if I couldn't be with my daughter in this world, then I would be with her in the next one. The scars are smaller now, no longer as jarring with my bangles to cover the ugliness...

...the true intent of my reliance on them.

But the scars I've left on him forever remain. There's no way I can put him through anything else.

Obinna dusts off his knees. "That was the first time you ever tried to leave me. Can you believe that? The first time, of all things..."

My eyes divert to the fireplace. "You've treated me like fine China ever since."

"I almost lost you. What did you expect?"

"So, you were afraid of me?"

"I was afraid for you—another reason I worked more hours. The chance of reminding you of that day if I stayed home for too long worried me. Could've said or done something that would've made you spiral again. I know... It was stupid then, and it's stupid now."

A bit of anger rests within me when I remember more lonely nights than I care to count. "You made me think—

you working those long hours was normal for your practice and everything else was in my head."

"I'm not proud of my hand in this, too, all right? We owed our marriage so much more than what we gave it. I'm sorry, too. Still, I wouldn't have dreamed of looking for meaning elsewhere—outside of us. You did, though."

What have I done? "Maybe it's not the best time to say it, but—I'll always love you, Obinna."

"Me, too. But sometimes that isn't enough."

"Is it a mistake for me to be here?"

"Depends if I do something unwise I can't take back." Obi is sitting perpendicular to where I am and stares at me in a way he probably shouldn't. "I thought I could do it, Pat. Just... move on. But then, when you left, it was one thing after the other. The house felt way off without the smell of your home-cooking. I never realized how much your laugh was the pick-me-up I needed after a shitty day at the clinic. And at night? Forget about it. Sleep was impossible. Did you know you have a scent?"

"I... I didn't," I say, as I keep listening while he pours out his internal strife onto me.

"Toasted almonds—without it beside me in bed, getting a good night's rest went out the door with you. Also, this may go without saying, but you were never a chore to me. I wouldn't wish trying to forget you on anyone."

Yes. Make him remember the ballad of Pat and Obi.

I get up to lean over and kiss him directly on the mouth. God, I'm so overjoyed he doesn't push me away.

"I know it adds to the list of selfish things I've done. But I've wanted to do that for so long."

Obinna takes hold of my waist and hoists me on to him in

one lift. "This promises nothing, but old habits die hard."

"You sure?"

"Once you give certain thoughts legs, they're bound to take you all kinds of places."

I shouldn't, but he smells so good.

We're going at it with no stop in sight. I seek his touch, the familiar way his fingers interlace with mine. But this feels different. This feels like a line crossed, a new territory neither of us dared to explore before.

His fingers are past my pants and underwear. My hands work their magic onto his lower half, too, as he reacts favorably.

"Shit, you'll always have a hold over me," a fervid Obinna moans.

Then I come to a halt.

He has to know. If I care about him like I say I do, then it'll work out. But let's quit using dishonesty as a crutch.

"Obi, please get off."

"Everything okay?"

"I need to tell you something."

"Not again, Patience. What now?"

"It'll be worse if you make it difficult for me."

"Shoot." He lets go of my body and scoots back.

I crawl to him and taste his mouth again to seal the vow. "Here's the part where you gotta decide if you can love me richly—because it's a lot."

"Yeah... okay... sure..." Obinna says, as he stares steadfastly.

"So, no more lies. I want to name her Grace." I watch and wait for the moment Obi puts it all together. "Because it'll take a lot of it to raise her unconditionally, despite where she came from."

Obinna clamors to his feet, discombobulated. "How—how long have you known?"

"About eleven weeks." I hold my belly with fondness. "Lies ended us, and I don't want them to be the foundation of us. As for Grace, I kinda took it as some sort of mystic sign from all these years I tried to get pregnant—yet, here's what stands."

"So, you're having his kid and—"

"No," I say, gravely. "I'm having *my* kid. She will come from a place of nurture and love. That's the way it has to be. Grace will never be his. Never."

He merely stares at my belly.

"Obinna, I'll completely get it if you choose to walk away. Maybe it's best that you do."

It's a harsh realization, but perhaps I'm more like my father than I ever wanted to admit.

Obi sighs, and stress puckers his handsome face. "It would have been a clean cut if not for the fact. Now we can't even pick up where we left off..."

"It's not like I haven't thought about... making a clean slate if you asked me to," I say, with a lump in my throat. "Only with the possibility of us—"

"Could you even still love me after such a request?"

"I don't know."

"Patience, you could never survive an abortion."

"Maybe. I do my best to be strong most days. But... sometimes, I wonder if I could survive losing you."

There's no telling what Obi is going through. Therefore, whatever choice he makes, I'll accept.

"Shit." Obinna exhales, comes back to sit, and lowers me back down in his arms. "I looked up and read his charges on file. It took everything in me not to smash my laptop seeing what he did to you... and what he almost did to you."

I'm compelled to lean back and make it last for as long as I can. "I handled myself."

Obinna tips my face up to his, and we touch noses. "But that's not the point. He never should have had access to you."

"I'll go, Obinna, okay? Um, sort of... overstayed long enough." I adjust my clothes and fix my hair.

He says nothing and steps aside, allowing me to leave. The townhome permeates with the scent of coffee and old books, reminding me of undemanding times of plain sailing.

But those days are long gone.

The front door is in my grasp and also a life without being an Okoye.

"Not so fast," Obinna runs to meet me by the door. He places his masculine hands over the doorknob.

"Obi, but why—"

"Make it make sense."

"What?"

He smiles, a small, sad smile—while taking both of my hands, thoughtfully. "I was screwed up in the head for a while, you know."

"I wanna change that."

"Then... make it make sense. Do I really still want the woman who did what she did to me, or do I just not want Harlan to win? That's the real reason I can't promise any-thing... because I can't figure it out."

I've rehearsed what I'm going to say a thousand times, but as the seconds tick by, believing in myself wanes. "Obinna, I can't."

His brows are in danger of disappearing into his hairline. "Why not?"

"If I try to make sense of it, then you'll come to *your* senses and have nothing to do with me."

Obi's cheeks blanch. "You got me there."

"I don't know what else you want me to say." I step away and search his expression for his train of thought. God, I love this man so much. I love him enough—never to shadow his doorway again if he asked me to. "You could do better than this, you know."

"Are you deciding for me?"

"No."

"Then let me decide for myself."

"Meaning?"

He lays me down on the floor gently and suspends himself over my body. "I can't help it—Pat, nothing tops what we had. What we *have*. But... moving forward... it won't be anything like what it was and we'll always know that."

"I'll take any form of being a fixture in your life. Such as, a friend?"

"And how do I know... you're not just afraid of being alone?"

I wait for a bit and make sure I say exactly what I need to in one momentous breath. "Harlan was only a placeholder who caught me in the middle of mourning our old life when I was defenseless. It would never be him... because it's been you from the get go. The impact you had or... have on my life never left—even he saw that. We hit a rough patch, and I got impatient. So, I'll do whatever it takes to earn your trust again, and if it never happens, I'll have to respect that, too."

His fingers touch my cheek fondly. "If one were to sleep with someone they used to see as their soulmate for the last time, how do you think it would go?"

"Tragic."

"As long as tragic feels... as good as you do. I'll be okay."

Clothes fly off, tongues wander and explore our willing bodies. Obinna's teeth tease my earlobes—testing the waters. Then he bites my bottom lip possessively and holds my arms by my sides. "Do you have to be somewhere soon after this?"

"Not likely," I say.

Thrusts, scratches, and screams of pure elation sound off from the living room all the way to the bedroom.

"So stupid... why am I so fucking stupid... when it comes to you?"

"It isn't too late for me to leave, Obi."

"Don't remind me. Come here."

Faster and faster we go, soaking in sweat. I yell his name from under him. Obi tongues the tenderest parts of my flesh. Then he seeks for more, brushing his fingers against my soft lips. His bare body is slick against mine.

Whether it's right or wrong to say... "I missed this."

"What?"

"Being touched by you."

"Then prove it."

I climb on top of him and have the most cathartic ride of my life. Convulsions rip through us like never before, as an unseen force takes hold and wrings us out from the inside. Pulses leave us dizzy and depleted, yet somehow bracing for the next surge. I'm fighting a chaotic rebellion beneath my skin. The heat of it all rises until there's no space left between us but our bleary sensations.

"Patience... shit... let me hear what I'm doing to you..." Obinna demands, squeezing the life out of my waist while his face twists and turns. His growing ache rocks me from side to side—as I gladly do my best to keep up.

"I want to, Obi... but..." I worry. What if my want is too much and I scare him away like before?

"God, I need to hear it, please... the need that's hurting for me... inside of you..."

"Yeah?"

"I asked for it, didn't I? Give me everything you got."

I scream and become a banshee who hits the sweet spot of release.

At last.

"Are you sure we will be okay?"

"I never said I was sure, Pat."

"That's true."

We don't ask what it means. Rather, we accept that it's happening—to give in and take each other, despite our uncertainty.

Over and over again.

* * *

The waiting room is dank and rusty, with old three-pronged chairs from the 1990s. Stale coffee permeates the air as I re-evaluate if what I'm doing is a great idea. So many things could go wrong and have. But at thirty-two, I've faced more than what most people have in their lifetime. So in the end, it'll come full circle.

My eyes drift down to my hands resting in my lap, and I see my scar from the shard of glass attack. It's a jagged line in the middle of my palm and an uneven texture. Quite thick and raised at the center, tapering off into thinner, more delicate lines at the edges—a ripple frozen in time.

It's strange how skin can heal, but never forget.

A squatty Correctional Officer enters the room with a clipboard. "Inmate is ready for a... for a... Patience..." she sputters. "Uh, a Patience—"

"I'm here!" I interrupt before she butchers my last name. I'm on my feet.

I walk the towering walls of the prison halls as I wait for a sign to turn me in the other direction.

Two years have passed since that terrifying night when Harlan's obsession nearly took me. Now, as I prepare to face him once again, I can't help but feel a sense of revelations mingled with hesitancy.

The guard escorts me through the maze of corridors and the sound of metal bars clang, echoing in my ears. Finally, we reach the visitation room, and there he sits, handcuffed and chained to the table—a shadow of the man he once was.

Harlan has lost a tremendous amount of weight, which is very noticeable on someone of his height. Tattoos that were once bright and colorful are pale and hang on his loose, leathery skin. With his haggard face—the vibrant eyes he used to have—now resemble two bowls of spoiled milk, sitting behind coke-bottle, plastic-rimmed glasses. Harlan no longer has the piercing gaze that haunted my nightmares. They're clouded over with film, evidence of the damage I inflicted upon him in my desperate bid for freedom.

I see the lightning in his stare, followed by a tremble that sends blaring signals down my spine.

He's real again.

"Harlan. It's me, Patience," I say, unsure how much of me he can make out in his eyesight.

"I know," he replies. "I only have thirty-five percent of my vision, but I'll always know your velvety voice."

The fact he still has the stamina to flirt under these circumstances almost leaves me speechless.

"I'm surprised this visit was approved, to be honest with you..." Harlan pats down his greasy hair curled behind his reddened ears. "Since you're seen as my harrowing victim, I figured they would keep you protected from me."

I sit and do my best to not make a repulsed face. "I pulled a few strings, that's how. This meeting is important, and it outweighs the potential risk."

"But you're not a stranger to risks, are you? No point in pretending to be now, sweetness."

"Believe me, I'm more familiar with taking risks than I would like to be. Do you think I enjoy being here?" I leave a dire reminder. "You were so crazed the last time we spoke— you threatened to do unspeakable things to me with a piece of glass. When I escaped, this was the cost." I raise my scarred palm in front of Harlan to present him with a better view.

Harlan's vampire smile lacks its authentic luster. Several teeth are missing—and the ones that remain have yellow plaque pockets on each revealing tooth. "Wear it like a badge of honor, babe. You lived to tell the tale."

"And you look terrible."

"Yeah, well, whose fault is that? You dislocated my fucking jaw and then some."

"I'm out of comfort to give you. I'm out of anything to give you."

Because of his missing teeth, he makes a little whistle with each syllable spoken. I cough dryly in response.

"We had good times, didn't we?" Harlan reminisces. "They weren't all bad, like you tried to make it out to be."

"There were other women you had the same feelings for,

I'm sure."

"But they could never hold a McCandles to you. Clearly."

"As long as my flame didn't burn brighter than yours, right?" I coolly mention. "Because, God help me if it did..."

He used to damn Obinna for compartmentalizing me, acting like he was so different. But all the while... he strived to make me unmemorable.

Harlan attempts to hold my hand, but then sits up rigidly, maybe realizing where he is for the first time. "I missed you."

"Why me?" A question that bided its time for two years finally presents itself. "What is it about me, Harlan, that incapacitates you?"

McCandles puts a pondering finger to his mouth and doesn't seem sure himself. "At first I thought it was the chase, then I thought—I couldn't resist your pillowy tits in my mouth. But now I see... you're the only woman I've ever met who carries great affliction wherever she goes, like it's nothing. The artistic edge that comes from you—you can't teach it to just anyone. We're the same."

"The hell we are," I object.

"No? Don't we work people? Don't we bend each day to our liking?"

"And because you believed that... you felt the need to make me indebted to you?"

He squishes his gaunt cheeks between his cracked palms. "Patience, come on."

"Well, I had a debilitating addiction to you. It almost killed me."

Harlan rolls whatever eyes he has left. "I was a drug that gave you purpose—a drug that honed your sense of exploration and achieved multiple orgasms. An indescribable high that—frankly—you weren't very appreciative of."

He's not using me for this. I won't let him.

"Love isn't a drug, Harlan. It's not healthy to feel that way all the time. And it's not healthy to make someone your everything," I say with hands folded. "That's why we didn't work, and why you will never have a meaningful relationship. You're a leech."

Harlan doesn't speak for a bit, chewing on his bottom lip scab.

"I suppose you're wondering why I'm here," I go on.

"Suppose right."

"I need to know a couple of things, and you're gonna tell me."

"You always did like to call the shots."

"Right, then—so I'm calling them now." I sit straight and look directly at him, with his warbled eyes pronounced. "You found me that night. How?"

"I'm guessing your people already filled you in on everything from my plea deal, right?"

"That's not the point. I want to hear it straight from you."

Harlan jumps back in stupefaction. "Don't think that's relevant to say now, do you?"

"It is."

"Convince me on how, Patience."

"It just is, okay?"

"I can't survive on *it just is*. I can barely survive Mondays here."

"Ask me no questions and I'll tell you no lies," I bring up.

"The tale of us since way back when. How could I forget?"

"You said that, and it stuck with me—so here it is. I know what you had in your car, the one you were going to use to take me with you. They brought it up during the plea deal."

"And?" Harlan asks, uninterested.

"My lawyer was good, but your lawyer was better. Besides the box cutter, the rope, pliers, screwdriver, bolts, and axe should have been enough to nail your ass to the wall. Plea deal or no, you should be serving more years, but you're not. Harlan, if you ever loved me at all—in your fucked up form of whatever that even looks like—tell me. How did you find out where I lived? Will I have to keep looking over my shoulder once you get out?"

I can't let him know the night terrors are back. And that they'll stick around unless I know the answer for sure.

Harlan's glasses catch a glare, and I can no longer read his face. "Even after all this time—with asking these long awaited questions, you still need me."

"That's not what's happening."

"What else is new, then?"

"Closure, so I can be done with you."

"Then I won't give you that!" he snaps, pounding the table with both palms.

I'm so pissed. It all turned to shit. Why do I keep letting him do this to me?

"I put you in here, got it? I did! You're not in the place to have a leg to stand on." My follow-through is resounding.

Harlan raises his shoulders, pointedly. "Patience, you would've stood beautifully in the box I had in mind for you."

"A box?"

"To wrap you in, remember? I dabbled in a bit of carpentry if you can believe it. I had tempered glass. The only thing I didn't purchase yet was wood. It was a tough choice between oak and hickory. I'd let you out from time to time; I'm not completely unreasonable. You would still have to tend to domestic duties and such. And tend to me, of course. Then I'd put you back up and seal you in for the night. Well, it was the plan until I got my noggin screwed back on properly."

The talk in his bed after Taos years ago—how could I miss that? He showed his true intentions back then, and I laughed it off as a goof. All the while, he planned to make me his personal trinket. "You won't always be able to hide your evil behind being bipolar with BPD forever."

"You know, on really bad days, I used to process the fact that I haven't seen an abstract painting in almost three years. So, it would always be the same two comforting fantasies about you—hearing the soft crunch of your windpipe after strangling you or the cute gurgling noises you would make when I'd suffocate you with a chloroform pillow. Either way, your lovely chestnut skin would turn a sickly gray in the end. Of course, routine therapy and meds helped with those troubled thoughts, so I don't have them anymore. But, man— did they sure help the time go by."

"That's bold to admit openly in a prison facility," I remind him.

He spits on the floor, narrowly missing my red bottom shoes. "You're not the only one who can pull strings. Scored us some extra privacy—CO's can be bought here, too, just like us piece of shit criminals. Gainful—symbiotic relationships are great, aren't they? That way, neither of us feels the need to hold back."

"You're lying."

"If you don't believe me, go for the door buzzer and see who comes to your rescue."

"Why? So you can attack me from behind?"

"I would never do that… unprovoked. We're just talking, baby. In the end, I was no match for the breathtaking, wondrous, yet disingenuous woman with a tight body and with an even tighter—wait, nope. I made a promise I'd be a gentleman."

"That ship has sailed. Your late mother was a hot topic of discussion, too, during the plea deal talk," I say, shutting him down. "Mainly, they questioned how she raised you."

A muscle twitches in Harlan's cheek. "I don't talk about my mother."

"Well, make an exception for the woman you said you loved once. Respect her time while she's here." This might not go where I want it to. I shift restlessly in the plastic chair with the fabric sticking to my thighs and try to ignore the lack of surveillance. "I know about the abuse."

"Hey—"

"I'll respect your wishes. You don't have to say a word, and I'll do the talking. Come on, it was a major factor in your defense. When it's all said and done, it makes sense—you being the person you are today. The constant need to gain power when you had very little of it to begin with. When your dad died, no one was truly looking out for you, were they?"

Harlan clatters his chains to throw me off. "Don't you look down on me. I don't need your pity. You think you can waltz in here and psychoanalyze me?"

"I'm trying to extend sympathy to the child you once were, which is way more than what you deserve."

Reasoning with him might work. But with the thought of needing him for anything else again—Christ, help me through this.

Harlan scoffs. His laughter is quite bitter. "Give it a try."

His anger seems to deflate slightly, then he looks away and stares at the beige wall. I take it as silent permission to continue to dissect further. "Your first client was right after your thirteenth birthday, right? Then the next one—a year after? It slowly became a ritual. Sheila had weird connections, and she needed money, since your dad was no longer the breadwinner. Those clients had some... peculiar interests, and they involved you. But that's the thing, isn't it? They weren't clients—they were monsters. What they demanded from an unsuspecting preteen made them that way."

I've been talking for so long, I lose track of time and see that I'm not getting to the main reason I came to see him fast enough. Hurry. "Those trips to fancy hotels that your little mind tried to understand were—Jesus. There was a time... *you* were called someone's muse while they painted you. One client, a frequent one, had a strange request. Said '*He's much too beautiful to be a boy.*' So, he made a suggestion, and Sheila agreed."

"You don't know what the hell you're saying."

"I believe I do. When the painting stopped and it became something else, he called you his *good girl* that night and many other nights after, didn't he? He fastened his hooks tight, and his phrases stayed buried within you. Even today. Does that hurt, too? Not being able to get him out of your skin, either?"

"Thin ice you're skating on there." Harlan rocks back and forth like he has to go to the restroom. "For your safety... wrap it up. And quick."

"You got somewhere to be?" I make myself even more comfortable and cross my legs. He's so full of shit, otherwise he would've handled me the moment I brought it up. "When Sheila married Marsha's dad, you didn't need to provide for the family anymore. But why, Harlan? After being exposed to so much, why shed the same pain on Marsha and pass on the trauma? Your mother's death promised your future so many possibilities. Yet, you supported yourself by looking for those same monsters with those same particular interests."

"She was a realist, goddammit." Harlan comes back to life. "I'm not a victim. You can parade around with that label all you want. Not me."

I'm just a glutton for punishment. Conversing with Harlan is comparable to walking through Dante's Inferno. "Your mother pimped you out and sold your soul. What else would you call it? Even lying, which is what you compulsively do— Harlan, you couldn't even come up with a lie about how you grew up, since it was too horrendous to mask."

"No, I was a hot commodity even back then, and we took advantage of it. Old European bitches would cream their panties and fly me anywhere I wanted, just to—"

"You barely reached puberty! That's sick!"

"Blow me."

I guess he could never truly escape that all-encompassing darkness he hated so much. In the shadows, the most shameful practices were inflicted on his young, fragile body, hidden from the world, with the lights off.

"How old did you say you were when you met Mabel again? Twenty-three? I'm thinking it's a lot younger now, before Camp Arnica."

"Patience," Harlan drawls, dragging out the 's' like a serpent. He bows his head at my statement. "Shut the fuck up about her."

"Her hooks run deep for you, especially."

"I told you when we first met, sex sells."

"Those sick things done to you weren't casual sex. You were a child!" I say, trying to keep my shaking under control. "Those animals wanted a piece of you each time. Which made you hollow all these years... That's why you needed me to make you whole."

"How's our daughter, Grace? Gonna be two in January, isn't she? Yeah, that's right... your turn."

Not fair.

He takes it. He takes the only playing card I have left. "We don't have a daughter."

"I'm sure we do. I have the utmost faith in that."

Harlan resumes the typical role as the puppet master manipulator, and I'm the lowly ballerina mannequin he plays with. "People often underestimate the value of connections in prison. So, be careful. Can't trust your neighbors or even your fucking mailman because who knows if they have relatives or friends in the same clink with the man you purposely blinded?"

There's no way. "Harlan, who do you have watching me?"

"Man, you're taking the fun out of this."

"Tell me!" My chair scrapes loudly, along with my exclamation. I can't bring myself to meet his leer, so I focus on the table instead. It's cold under my fingertips, almost arctic. How many others have sat in this exact spot? How many of them came here looking for answers they'll most likely never get?

Harlan leans back in his chair with a low squeak. He has one arm draped over the back as if discussing a trivial topic. His jawline is sharp as ever, only now accompanied by a thinning, patchy beard. "I'm sorry. Does that news upset you? Not being able to see my little girl really upsets me. If it helps, my spies never attack unless they're told to."

I can only think of one person desperate enough to do Harlan's bidding—someone who would do anything for his validation and approval, such as an overeager student. "K-Kelsey."

"Hmm?"

"You... you made Kelsey find my address, didn't you? A lesser person would've shot her for trespassing on their property and be done with it. You had her stalk me so you could stay undetectable. I'm sure she reported to you every step of the way—maybe still does."

Harlan's smirk widens and shows a flash of more piss-colored teeth. "Some could argue you've ruined the element of surprise here by telling me."

"I'm not afraid of you anymore." I scoot back in my chair while it pokes me with static. "So sit with that in your rotting cell."

"Kelsey. Now there's an idea. If only you could prove it. Besides, what makes you think she's the only one if it were the case? Harley gets around."

"Happy to see you're finding love in prison, too."

"Damn!" He laughs with a dangerous yet playful cackle. "Why couldn't I have seen more of this Patience when we were together? The one who did nothing but snivel and hide from me when I wanted to see her insides isn't as memorable. And as always, feel free to take that however you want."

"Your face... as we're talking, McCandles... that isn't noth-ing."

Harlan leans forward and rests his forearms on the table. "Grace will learn to get used to it."

My Gracie, whose smile is the only thing that restores my

faith in humanity. She's so pure, so uniquely her, yet her features carry a soul-stirring truth—part me, part him. Those sandy-blond curls, button nose, and single dimple that lights up with her giggles are still innocent. She'll never know what it's like to be trapped in Harlan's grasp.

Closure isn't coming. So, let's go with Plan B.

I take a deep breath, steeling myself for what's coming and meet his gaze head-on. "Harlan," I say, my voice steady inside me. "It doesn't matter. Grace is not yours to claim, and she will never know you exist. That way, she can stand a chance. My daughter has a good father—Obinna Okoye."

"You're shitting me, right?" His lips twist into a cruel smile, but there's a glimmer of doubt that wasn't there before. "More power to him for taking you back."

"No power needed. He's just more of a man than you will ever be," I say. "Obinna didn't limit my worth to that one mistake, which was you. And now, Grace will have a sister in four months."

"Two kids with two different fathers. What a legacy to leave behind."

"It didn't happen overnight. I had to put in a major effort to earn his trust back for a long time. We tried to save what was salvageable from our marriage. There were days we weren't sure if we would make it. Or survive your undoings. But we did. And if people were to see us today... They wouldn't even think we went through the hell that was you."

"Quite the love story. You're welcome."

"What don't you get? Our story continuing wasn't up for you to decide, asshole."

Harlan appears discomfited and shows strong resentment. Yes. This is bothering him. Hooks no longer fastened.

"But come on, beautiful. As well as you know me, do you really think I'll sit back and let another dude raise my goddamn kid?"

I shake my head as my resolve hardens with each passing second. "You don't have a choice, do you?"

"Hmm. Five years isn't that much of a stretch, and I already stretched out two of them."

"We'll see. You have a hell of a track record."

"You'll never be completely rid of me, Okoye. Ever. Our offspring is living proof of this. Besides, deep down, I think you already know that as true."

"But I'm happy about one thing that came out of it all," I reveal.

"Our kid, I assume?"

"The fact you will never have the experience to paint or create any form of art again, and it's because I took your eyes from you. Because I felt like it. Now you're broken and no longer able to tap into your precious core colors like before."

"Corneal transplants work wonders these days," Harlan says, with a lax approach. "Who knows? Maybe I'll be able to teach Grace an abstract lesson or two when she's older."

My anxiety climbs Mount Everest at the sound of her name coming from his mouth.

"That won't happen. She can learn at the art center Obi and I purchased together."

"But hey, from what I'm told—cute white picket fence, by the way. It's a bold choice with the cul-de-sac in front and the lavender driveway."

I have never looked forward to envisioning another person's demise as much as I do Harlan McCandles'.

"I will kill you, do you understand?!" My temper speeds up

to a frightening notch. "If you come near me or my family, I will make it so you won't be able to hurt anybody else again. Keep it up—this jail will be your coffin soon."

He raises his head in absolute brazenness. "There she is. There's my girl."

Let it go, Patience.

This isn't working.

Do not fall for another power play from Harlan. You've come too far.

I know, but—

It ends with you walking away. Can't you see the pattern by now?

No.

Deny McCandles access to you. It's the first step.

He needs to know that he didn't break me!

Why? Don't dwell on what's not in your control, like closure from him. That's how he manifests his hooks back into you.

Harlan doesn't get to be triumphant here.

Then go home to your family. Remember? Something you thought you'd never have at one point. Do what he actually can't. Walk the hell out of this building and never look back. And know that he can never take away your peace of mind like Marsha mentioned, unless you keep giving him the green light.

You're right.

After you.

"Still with me?" Harlan questions, waving a hand in front of me. "You there, kid?"

"No," I say, then rise from my seat. "And I will never be again. You might've gotten your kicks from controlling me before, but that's over. These bars aren't just keeping you in... They're letting me out for good. Here's to a lengthy imprisonment, Harlan. I'm not *your* sun. I'm *the* sun. My dawn breaks as your goddamn sunset fades."

With a defiant flick of my hair, I'm on my heels.

"You think you're leaving on that note?" McCandles is wired, clinking his chains and sweating bullets.

Then I buzz for the guards, praying they're not too out of earshot—because of Harlan buying them off. "Hello?! I'm ready! Let me out and hurry up. Now!"

"Patience, wait."

I say nothing.

"Really talk with me here. I'll stop dicking around and listen. I swear."

I must be the only one who's visited him in two years. Why else would he be anxious about never seeing the woman who blinded him again?

Sucks to suck.

Fortunately, a heavyset guard wearing a turban answers the door. "Sorry, ma'am—not sure who's supposed to be on watch here... was headed to the mailroom. Lucky for you, I was going the same direction."

"Thank you," I say to him.

I look back at Harlan.

He responds to my outline and shakes his head, perspiring even more. "We're not done."

My attention resumes to the guard. "There's nothing relevant left for me here. Could you walk me to the front?"

BANG!

The metal table leg sports a brand-new dent.

"Not relevant?! I fucking made you! You think you're finished with me?! Huh?!"

Looks like the cool as a cucumber shtick wore off.

Three delayed correctional officers rush past me, taking care of the enraged convict and putting him in restraints on the double. "McCandles, cool it!"

Harlan charges, reminiscent of an afflicted bull as he is being cuffed. His glasses fly off as he spews his ongoing hate. "*Get the fuck off, pigs! Patience! I don't need eyes to see you for who you really are, bitch! All I wanted to do was love you! Then you go and do this to me?! You should've fucking killed me! Oh, no, you're not above this, you're not untouchable—*"

Clunk goes the metal door.

I've never met someone who claims to love me so emphatically... only to find out they're not even capable of it. He calls after me, his voice only a pin drop. I step back out into the sunlight, and new liberation comes over me, taking back my narrative.

No, I will not rise from his ashes.

But I will continue to burn brightly for the rest of my days, never dimming my inner flame for anyone else again.

My daughter flutters in my belly as I rush home to feed her sister.

And find much more meaningful things to do.

Ada Afam is a Nigerian-American author based in Denton, TX, where she lives with her husband and two spirited dogs. Known for her gripping narratives, Ada delves deeply into the complexities of psychological thrillers. Her work intricately weaves haunting backstories with explorations of identity, resilience, and the shadowed nuances of human desire.

www.ingramcontent.com/pod-product-compliance
Lightning Source LLC
Chambersburg PA
CBHW031436160726
47994CB00005B/1746